Almost Royalty

A Romantic Comedy...of Sorts

Courtney Hamilton

Forrest Thompson Publishers

Almost Royalty

A Romantic Comedy...of Sorts

Courtney Hamilton

This is a work of fiction. All of the characters, organizations, and events portrayed in this novel are either products of the author's imagination or are used fictitiously. Any resemblance to actual persons, living or dead, locales, or events is entirely coincidental.

No part of this book may be used in any manner whatsoever without written permission except in the case of brief quotations embodied in critical articles and reviews.

Please visit our website at www.ecochainofdating.com.
Comments and requests may also be left at www.ecochainLA.com (the blog of www.ecochainofdating.com).

Copyright © 2014 Courtney Hamilton
Cover Copyright © 2014 Buzz & Earl Enterprises, Inc.
All Rights Reserved.

Published by Forrest Thompson Publishers LLC
466 Foothill Boulevard, #170
Flintridge, California 91011

Library of Congress Control Number 2014938520

ISBN-10: 098372671X

ISBN-13: 978-0-9837267-1-5

Printed in the United States of America.

For THG,
forever

The L.A. Eco-Chain of Dating
(According to my friend Marcie)

A-Level

Celebrity Royalty or Civilian (Non-Celeb) Royalty

First Rung

Who: If Celeb Royalty/Multimillionaire, usually first generation wealth or success in sports or entertainment; if Civilian Royalty/Multimillionaire, Billionaire, second or third generation money from business or oil; if first generation, usually from high-tech.

Requirements: If Your Money – A good attorney (a great prenup is mandatory). If potential spouse is 20 years or more younger, a fantastic attorney, a fertility specialist(s), and a therapist. **If Not Your Money** – You will spend $$$$$$$ per month on "maintenance" and live on a diet.

The Good: Status, big homes, high life, loved at L.A.'s best private schools, but expected to give $1,000,000+ donations.

The Bad: Prenups, a very public short marriage. Spouse subject to drug abuse, sporadic violence, immaturity and plastic surgery (on you), cult religions, and bankruptcy.

Prologue

January 2008

Prologue

How to Be an Adult

When I first pulled up to the address, I thought that something was missing. I looked at the house to the left. I scanned the house to the right. I looked at the address. Of course—I knew what was missing. The house at the address of my destination had been built precisely to the property line: there was no front lawn.

It was unsettling to drive into this Los Angeles residential area, one block west of Bundy, one block north of Wilshire—technically still Brentwood, but just barely. Previously, it was a middle-class neighborhood of 3-bedroom, 1.5-bathroom, 1500-square-foot homes with nice lawns, two trees, decent back yards, and detached garages. Now I found myself parking in front of a single-family residence modeled on a Cold War Era Russian Embassy with a satellite dish so enormous, it must have been on loan from the Strategic Air Command.

I knew the families that once lived here. Dad was a fireman, an engineer, or a teacher—maybe a college professor. Mom, like all moms, stayed at home, led the Brownie Troop, and took care of the kids until the kids were well into middle school. At that point, mom picked up her teaching credential, her real estate license, or worked as a receptionist in a doctor's or dentist's office.

The kids all went to public schools—Brentwood or Kenter Canyon for elementary, Hamilton for middle school, and University High ("Uni") for high school. If the kids did reasonably well at Uni, they went to UCLA if they wanted to stay local, UC Berkeley if they were tired of Southern California, or UC Santa Cruz if they couldn't get into Berkeley. A few would apply for Stanford and get rejected unless they were world class athletes, legacies, or had perfect SATs. A handful would decide that they would try a private college back East—Vassar, Harvard, or maybe Yale—but after experiencing a winter that started in mid-October and extended to a surprise snowstorm in early May, they'd pack it in and transfer to Berkeley.

I don't know when my mind started playing tricks on me but I found myself nostalgic for things I once despised. I knew that those 1500-square-foot homes had been bought in the early and mid-'70s for no more than $25,000. They were now tear-downs that would sell for over $1,000,000 for a normal size lot on a nice street or much more if there was a view of anything, even the service entrance to the golf course.

I knew those dads—once engineers, teachers, or firemen—had been replaced by partners in mid to large law firms, TV writers/executive producers, or actors who managed to land and stick in a successful network prime-time television series.

The moms—former attorneys, agents, or actresses—still stayed at home, but now they didn't even bother to take care of the kids because each family had a nanny—or nannies—whom they paid under the table. The nannies took care of the kids, cleaned the house, and cooked. The moms went to Yoga classes, had personal trainers, and planned their strategies.

Which Mommy and Me (excuse me: Parent and Me) Class and which church or temple did you have to join when your baby was 18 months old to ensure that your child would get into the right preschool at age three? It was pretty much understood that it was harder to get your child into Little Dolphins by the Sea, Wilshire Boulevard's Mann Early Childhood Center, or Brentwood Presbyterian's Nursery School than Brown, UCLA, or UPenn.

Which preschools fed into The Center for Early Education, Carlthorp, or John Thomas Dye? If you went to a public elementary school—if you were fortunate enough to live in the right neighborhood and get a spot at Warner or Kenter Canyon—what about middle school? The public middle school was awful. Could you still get them into a private?

If you could even get into a private school, what would you do if your kid got into a school in the San Fernando Valley when you lived on the Westside? The Westside to the Valley was a 45-minute drive, if there was no traffic—which was never. The only way this could work was if you drove your kid to school at 5:30 a.m. or joined one of those car-pools where the weekly schedule was emailed back and forth every Sunday night. Everyone knew parents with the nightmare of kids in two or more different private schools who spent three to four hours per day driving their kids to and from school. Was it too much to hire a car service for your child when he was in kindergarten?

Then there was high school. What if you spent $31,000 per year for a private high school and your kid still couldn't get into a good college? Everybody knew that your kid could have a 4.5 GPA with perfect SATs and still not get into Berkeley or UCLA.

I parked my car. Two stories. Two 15-foot white columns, a 15-foot door, and a turret/tower. Tiny windows. 5 bedrooms and 4.5 bathrooms, with a whirlpool in the master bedroom. A gourmet kitchen with an island, a marble or Corian countertop, a Viking stove, and a sub-zero refrigerator that no one would ever use because absolutely no one cooked anymore except to warm up take-out that had gotten cold. A garage—the only remnant of the pre-existing structure—and an extra wing of the house built over it that had become an office, a guest wing, or if you really pushed it, the children's quarters where they would stay with their nanny.

5000 to 7000 square feet, the size a reflection of the fact that most wanted homes that were much more than places to eat and sleep. Along with the home office, it was likely that the home would now include a pool and spa, a home gym, a home theatre and possibly a tennis/basketball court or a garden entertainment area with an outdoor barbecue.

$2,800,000. Reduced, $2,790,000. In Escrow, $2,650,000. It was a good guess. No matter what price you thought those homes that once housed families with modest dreams should sell for, it was always something around $2,500,000.

Who could afford these homes? What deluded buyer actually believed that they could afford these enormous mortgage payments? A fountain with water coming out the mouth of a ceramic lion's head was attached to the stone wall that ran down the property line on its west side. With the exception of two sad, three-foot ficus plants and a few isolated patches of grass, there was absolutely no foliage on the property.

I saw my friends, Bettina and Marcie, approaching. I got out of my car.

"Hi you guys," I said.

"You aren't still driving *that*, are you?" said Marcie.

"What's wrong with it?"

"It's a Honda," said Marcie.

"It's ugly," said Bettina.

"It's paid for," I said.

"Sure, but is that the statement you want to make?" said Marcie.

"I'm not making any statement."

"Exactly," said Marcie, "so why don't you go move *that* around the block so no one sees you getting into it when we leave."

I ignored the remark.

We walked up to the house and stared at the fountain.

"Isn't it fabulous?" said Marcie.

"I'm surprised you actually know someone who lives in one of these," I said.

Marcie frowned and looked at me. "What do you mean?"

"Well, I've watched a million of these little houses get torn down and replaced with these 5000-square-foot Russian Embassies—or my other personal favorite—the 7000-square-foot antebellum mansion. The 'For Sale' signs go up, and after a while—six to eight weeks—they're taken down. But you never see people living in these houses, even if they try to personalize the place, maybe they put a swing set in—you just never see kids on the swing set. And then you see a really crummy car out front so you know it didn't sell and they've got one of those professional house sitters in there."

"Just be quiet, OK?" said Bettina. "Leslee invited us—it's her book group with some of those Ivy & Elite people. You know, the ones who married well."

Well, it wasn't really that Leslee had invited us. It was more that she demanded that I come for re-education. More like reorientation. Like the Maoists re-educating the Imperialist Chinese, but in reverse, on "How to Be an Imperialist Resident of the Westside of Los Angeles, CA."

Or more to the point: "How to Marry Up the L.A. Eco-Chain of Dating."

"It would be good for you to come," said Leslee. "You really need to see how you should be presenting yourself. These women are role models."

"Wouldn't that be fraudulent misrepresentation? To pretend to be something I'm not to a potential life partner?"

"Excuse me?" said Leslee.

I don't know if they were my role models, but they were definitely Leslee's. Leslee, my best friend Jennifer's friend, had recently moved to Los Angeles from San Francisco. Like most transplants from the Bay Area, she hated Los Angeles long before she landed here.

A few months ago Leslee had been asked to transfer to the Los Angeles office of Hobeck, Berman, her uber-elite San Francisco law firm. Like any dutiful associate, she couldn't refuse. Of course, there were those financial rumors about Hobeck circulating. And being in the L.A. office of a San Francisco law firm never made anyone happy.

However, to insulate herself from the coarseness of Los Angeles, Leslee had joined the "Ivy & Elite," a group composed of graduates from the Ivy League, Stanford, Duke, and other elite universities. The main purpose of the Ivy & Elite was, of course, to provide a dating pool for its single members. But it also provided socializing evenings, such as lectures and book groups for its "success stories," the Ivy & Elite members (women) who had married, become mommies (a minimum of two children was required), and clawed their way into the B-Level of Los Angeles "Civilian" Royalty (the Rising Achievers professional class).

In Los Angeles, a town with few traditions, an unspoken class system existed. There was the Celebrity Royalty—the multi-millionaire (and somewhat feral) first-generation successes of the entertainment industry who behaved as if Los Angeles existed for their benefit only. The rules, schedules, and boundaries of civilized life existed for the others—the "Civilians," those who were not the multi-millionaire successes of the entertainment industry.

The Civilians had their own Royalty: They came from business, oil, high tech, or real estate. Unless it was from high tech, the Civilian Royalty tended to be from second- or third-generation money, very involved (through donations, mostly) in Los Angeles and its cultural institutions, and blessed with excellent educations. The women in the Civilian Royalty had married well (a weak prenup was always hoped for), would never again have to work, and always, always, always could be found filling the volunteer committees or serving hot lunch at the most exclusive private schools in Los Angeles.

Well, that's if they were B-Level.

The A-Level Civilian Royalty mommies would never, ever be caught dead serving hot lunch. Apparently, it seemed that a million—or more—dollar donation, tendered years before their five-year-old's application ever arrived at that exclusive private school, exonerated them from the task of ever passing out barbeque chicken wraps.

"These are the Ivy & Elite women who *married well*?" I said. "The role models?"

"Yup," said Leslee, "I think you'll be impressed."

Bettina and Marcie, her new best friends, were dying to come.

"Do you think any of them have put their kids in private schools?" said Bettina.

Marcie looked at her and rolled her eyes. "Really, Bettina? Where else would they put them?"

I love books—and I love book groups. A book group can be like a great travel agent or an expert in the place you're visiting, a guide who points out a wonderful museum, restaurant, or hike that you might have missed. Even though I was more than a little skeptical about this first step in my re-education, I couldn't wait to hear the insights and thoughts of the highly educated Ivy & Elite role models.

We were told to read *A Mighty Heart*, featured on Oprah, because someone in the group claimed to have seen Angelina Jolie walking around Santa Monica and thought she looked fabulous.

We knock on the door and are let in by Leslee.

"Oh hi," said Leslee. "You guys have to see this place. It's so amazing, I can't even believe we're in L.A."

We walk through the marble foyer into a small room that has wood floors and half of a wall. It has no furniture in it and is shaped like a triangle. This is the builder's special, a leftover space forgotten by the contractor in his rush to put this embassy on the market.

Up two steps—the kitchen with the Viking stove and sub-zero freezer with that island in the middle and a pot rack overhead containing nothing. We walk down two steps into a room where the book group—our role models—are sitting around a garage-sale coffee table on two ancient dirty-white futons and a lumpy stained chair. There are four neon-orange beanbag chairs on the floor. I guess that's where we're sitting.

House Poor.

"Elizabeth," said Leslee, "this is…"

"Hi, make yourself at home," said Elizabeth. "So I told him, 'What do you mean you're not getting a bonus? What do you think is going to pay for the back yard?'"

Elizabeth has long, straight blond hair, parted in the middle, that falls to the center of her back. She's wearing beige-velour yoga pants and a little white T-shirt which covers all but six inches of her belly, a belly that is a little lumpy and is decorated with her war wound: a stretch mark.

Leslee sits on the neon orange beanbag chair next to me. She turns her head away from the group and toward me.

"So Elizabeth," whispers Leslee.

"Yeah," I whisper.

"She went to UPenn, then she went to Columbia Journalism School."

"Oh. Does she work?"

"Well, she edits the newsletter for her Parent and Me Group."

"A stay-at-home-mom?"

Leslee looks at me with a puzzled look on her face. "Absolutely not. She hires and supervises the nannies and the housekeeper."

"That's a job?"

"The housekeeper comes twice a week. And she's in charge of redoing the house—she just finished the garden."

Two other women are sitting on one of the dirty-white futons with her.

"The one with the wispy black hair is Renata—she went to Vassar," whispers Leslee. "She was an editor at HarperCollins."

"What does she do now?" I whisper.

"She's married. I think she has a kid."

"The one with the long brown hair is Laura," continues Leslee. "She went to Duke. She's got her PhD in psychology."

I look at Leslee.

"Laura's married and has a kid."

So are June—a Harvard grad, Harvard Law, ("Not just a graduate from your second-tier UC law school") who is married with a kid. And then there's Patty, a Stanford grad who is married and trying to have kids. They're sitting on the other dirty-white futon.

No one works. Except for Leslee and me.

And their nannies.

"What did he say?" said Renata.

"He said that maybe we need to cut back a little bit," said Elizabeth. "So I told him, we don't need to cut back. You need to make more money. Whatever you did wrong, you need to fix it and get that damn bonus."

"Ugh. Doesn't he understand that you have a lifestyle to maintain?" said Renata. "I mean, these guys—what do they think we do all day?"

That would be a good question.

"I told my husband that he doesn't pay enough attention to my projects," said Laura. "I mean, here I am organizing this huge fundraiser for Weston, my kid's private school. And he's barely involved—he barely knows what I'm doing."

"Aren't we going to discuss *A Mighty Heart*," I said, suddenly noticing that everyone except for Marcie, Bettina, and I had some strawberry daiquiri-type drink in her hand.

"Forget the book," said Elizabeth.

"I'll buy the DVD," said June.

"Who has time to read anyway?" said Patty.

"I heard Angelina Jolie was terrific in it," said Marcie. "Do you think she's had plastic surgery?"

"Aren't her kids going to Crossroads?" said Bettina.

Elizabeth, Laura, Renata, and June turn and eye Bettina—for just a moment.

"I don't think so…" said Renata.

"I just want to know how she stays so thin," said Elizabeth. "So what did your husband say, Laura?"

"He said that he's tired," said Laura. "He's in trial on some huge case. But I told him that's not an excuse. My therapist told me that he needs to be involved in my things. And Weston is going to want to see that he's committed too. So I'm making him paint some of the crafts for the fundraiser."

"What's he painting?" said Elizabeth.

"Some lawn trolls. We're painting and selling those Hummel figure lawn trolls. And then he's in charge of driving them to Pasadena, where we're having the fundraiser."

Pasadena. Forty-five minutes away if there's no traffic—which is never.

"It's important that your husband be respectful of your projects, Laura if he's going to be present within the relationship," said Elizabeth. "My therapist tells me that I give everything to my husband and my children—that I don't do anything for myself."

"Mine too," said June.

"So I've decided to hire a cook," said Elizabeth. "I've found someone who will do it for a reasonable price."

"Don't tell me you cook every meal," said Renata.

"Well no," said Elizabeth. "I'm in charge of dinner on Monday and Wednesday. My husband has Tuesday and Thursday. And the nannies—our weekday and weekend—handle all other meals."

As if she even knew where the kitchen was.

"You've got to be careful about those cooks," said Renata. "Some of them don't know how to, well, you follow *The Zone*, right?"

"Of course," said Elizabeth.

"Well, you have to be sure that they don't put sauce or cheese on everything...unless you're following Atkins."

"May I have some water?" I asked.

"In the back—at the breakfast nook," said Elizabeth pointing to the back of the house. "I don't know where my husband thinks we're going to get the money to decorate the house. The back yard was so expensive—he has to get that bonus. I mean, there's the mortgage, the nannies, the kids' tuition at Crossroads, and those endless donations which you *must* give..."

"Don't get me started on private schools," said Bettina. "I mean, how *do* you get a recommendation to Thorton Hall?"

Dead silence in the room.

For five seconds.

I walked to the back of the house—the breakfast nook—something that looked like a laundry room or other odd-shaped leftover space at the back of the house that the builders had no idea what to do with, where there was a table, a half pitcher of the strawberry daiquiri-type drink, some bottled water, crackers, cheeses, and cookies set up for the book group's break. I looked out the window at the back yard.

Elizabeth had taken the postage stamp of space between the back door and the property line and obviously hired professional landscapers to plant wild pink roses, lavender mums, a purple-blue azalea that had exploded throughout the greater Brentwood metropolis, and some three-foot-tall white flower thing that looked to be a cross between a weed and a hydrangea, something which had obviously been engineered to populate the gardens and fuel the resulting garden wars. Oh no. This was Elizabeth's faux English garden.

In the middle of it was something that looked like a horse trough.

"Isn't it amazing," said Leslee, who had wandered out to get some water.

"What on earth is that?" I said.

"What?"

"That white thing out there. Is that a horse trough?"

"You idiot," said Leslee. "That's a bathtub."

"A bathtub? Why does she need a bathtub in her back yard?"

"So she can take baths in the moonlight."

"What?"

"Don't be so common. Elizabeth likes to take nude moonlight baths in the back yard."

"Oh."

We looked out at the horse trough/bathtub.

"I think I'm going to go home now," I said.

I walked to the family room.

"With my free evenings, I think that I'll take a course or two at the Learning Annex or UCLA extension. I'd kind of like to be a therapist," said Elizabeth.

"You'd make a great therapist," said Renata.

"Thanks," said Elizabeth. "I think I could really help people—women—take charge of their lives. And you know the first thing I'd recommend? What I'm going to do. As soon as the cook is in place, I'm going to get an assistant."

"That is *such* a great idea," said June. "It's so hard to keep track of the nannies, the gardeners, the cook, and the kids."

"Yes," said Elizabeth, "you just need someone to make sure that everyone is on track, in case something—like a car pool—should fall through the cracks."

"Ah..." I said, "thanks for inviting me. It was really fun, but I have to go. It's a school night."

"You work?" said Elizabeth.

"She's not married," whispered Bettina, "she broke up with her fiancé six months ago—he wouldn't set a date."

"She's an attorney...but she doesn't work in a firm," said Leslee.

June frowned and slightly shook her head right-left, right-left, right-left. She turned her head away from me.

"She's a sole practitioner with her own practice?" Leslee whispered.

"Ohhhhh," said Elizabeth, Renata, Laura, June, and Patty.

"Bye," I said.

I slowly walked to my Honda, my paid-for Honda, and looked through the neighborhood. I passed another Russian Embassy, a house that looked like a three-story A-frame mountain cabin with two Japanese maples, a koi pond, and a Zen garden in front, and another place that aspired to be Frank Lloyd Wright's Hollyhock House on a lot that was meant for a 2-bedroom, 1500-square-foot home.

Since the day of my high school graduation to the present moment, an awareness of age-appropriate behavior and age-appropriate circumstances had evolved from some unknown source.

There was a time to be an undergraduate and there was a time to leave your childhood behind.

There was a time to have a year abroad—preferably in France or any other highly westernized country that was known for importable culture—and there was a time to come home.

There was a time to go to graduate school and a time to move on.

There was a time to work.

I knew that this was a pivotal moment. It knew that it was right in front of me. I knew if there was someone other than myself who was keeping score, that I had fallen behind.

I knew this because as I walked out of Elizabeth's family room, I'm almost sure that I heard someone say, "There's a cautionary tale."

Part 1

March 2007

(9 Months Earlier)

1

Ruined By Therapy

Dinner at The Copper Pan always found me maxing out a credit card to pay for a meal that my mother would have served on a Wednesday night. Was it really necessary to pay $34 for crab cakes and a side of fries? But there I was, waiting for meatloaf and mashed potatoes in the very same restaurant where I dumped my last fiancé not three years ago.

I was listening to my current fiancé, Frank, reveal his pain. He was nearly 35 years old and he was angry—still—so angry with his father for putting a second mortgage on the house 20 years ago so that he could send his son to Phillips-Andover—the best prep school in the country. After an hour of sharing, Frank synthesized his torment in a phrase that put his entire essence into perspective: "I could have gotten laid during high school." And then it hit me: My competence had come back to haunt me.

I knew that by agreeing to marry him, I was looking at a lifetime of supporting a guy whose social circle consisted of low-impact buddies who felt comfortable letting their girlfriends/wives support them while they trashed their professional careers as attorneys, investment bankers, or accountants to pursue never-gonna-happen careers as screenwriters, film directors, or sous-chefs. "We men are tired," he said. "It's your turn to take over."

And I had agreed to this because I thought that I could do everything. And so far, I always had. And he knew it.

"Why are you doing this?" said my best friend, Jennifer. "You're marrying a piece of furniture, a lump, an energy-draining parasite." She should talk. Her college boyfriend, Tom, was such a dolt that he made *her* fill out all of his applications to every business school in the country that he never, ever would have the grades or scores to get into. Harvard. Wharton. Stanford. Chicago. Yale. He started his quest for admittance to "the elite" the year we applied for law school. When Jennifer and I graduated from law school, I heard that Tom was still buying into that nonsense and still applying.

I thought about it. I would have to support both of us, and not just in any manner, but in a way which would ensure that we could maintain a fashionable Westside Los Angeles lifestyle, complete with acceptable cars—Range Rovers, Lexus Hybrids, and a Prius or two—and a home in the acceptable area—Brentwood, Santa Monica above Wilshire, make that Montana, and Pacific Palisades. Naturally, this would mean that I would have to continue in my practice as an attorney, a career which had much to say for itself: Bone-crushing. Always-Hit-the-Ground-Running. TMJ, "a grinder" at 28. Easily excitable, high-blood pressure at 33. Weight issues and fertility problems at 38. Divorce (if I could even find a committed relationship) and high cholesterol at 45. That, combined with the reality of having less than a 20 percent chance of ever becoming a partner, was a lot to look forward to.

This was not going to happen. I loved litigation, my chosen area of the law—on TV. In real life, I was usually buried under a tsunami of paper while stuck in a 100 degree document facility in an isolated industrial park. I wanted to punch most of my clients for even bothering to consult an attorney with their idiotic cases. The judges that I practiced before were so embittered that they dreamt of their golf games and didn't hear a word that you said. And I had a sneaking suspicion that the red-faced, screaming litigators with whom I practiced were the very same knuckleheads who attempted to appear cool during law school by attending endless raves, taking X, and selling drugs.

The support obligation was going to be one thing, I was also going to have to be the cook. Somewhere after Martha Stewart, celebrity chefs, and the Food Network, cooking had taken on an entirely new dimension. Start-from-scratch. Free range. Grow your own herbs. Wine knowledgeable. Gourmet coffee or coffees. Whole wheat pasta and bread—La Brea Bakery, a must. Shop only at Whole Foods, Trader Joe's, or—if you're really the bomb—the endless farmers' markets that surrounded L.A. Compost. And of course, recycle—mandatory.

What a laugh. To begin with, I liked Velveeta. No—I loved Velveeta. I demanded that my local upscale grocers carry it and campaigned for a display case to showcase my treasure. My secret ingredient: more mushroom soup, in everything. I regularly urged my hide-your-middle-class-background friends to drop the faux pretension of an "official-preppie-background" and RETURN TO THEIR ROOTS by making me a dish that included hamburger, Velveeta, mushroom soup, and taco shells, chased with a tri-colored Jell-O creation.

And then there were my interior decorator obligations. I would have to rid myself of the early '90s white-on-white Southwest environment and embrace the faux French Provincial grandma's over-stuffed sofa look. All wood would be oak or walnut. All sofas so soft that you could drown yourself in them. Dried flowers would cascade over the armoire, fresh flowers would adorn every room. Cold white walls would suddenly be painted Vanilla Bean, Champagne Gold or Sea Shell Green, with border prints at the crease where the wall met the ceiling. God, I could kill Martha Stewart and her later-day by-product—the fashionafia—those gay and female friends who felt it was their self-appointed duty to give you advice on how to dress, whom to date, and how to decorate.

My personal interior design philosophy was that of a tornado—me being it. When I went into a room, everything physically left its place of order and was strewn in a dozen little piles. I had chosen to help my box-challenged cat, Abyss, with not one but two litter boxes, approximately ten feet apart. And this was in a one-bedroom apartment. My furniture was best described as "post-graduate"—a combination of Mom's leftover Danish modern, IKEA, and the pieces that a boyfriend had made during some revolutionary make-your-own-furniture phase. And I had cottage cheese ceilings to boot.

I guess you could say that I was not anyone's version of a perfect wife. But I, Courtney Hamilton, a woman who was a genetic mutation of the blond Californian looks of my San Marino, California-born Episcopalian father, and the searing ambition and overwhelming assimilation desires of my Brookline, Massachusetts-born Jewish mother, reluctantly acknowledged that I knew what I was getting into.

There were also going to be social obligations, as in, I was going to have to be the bonder with his difficult family, especially his father's second wife, a woman with a taste for outfits that included studded blue jeans and white patent leather heels, worn together. She was not more than 30 years younger than his father, nor two years older than Frank. His father described her as "a leader among women" because she religiously followed the advice of the female anchor on *Good Morning America* and once a year organized the Upper Cape Cod Home Craft Fair. And Frank detested her, especially after she did the unpardonable: she had a baby, a step-brother who was 31 years younger than he was.

The food arrived, and Frank wheezed forth. "You know, if I had stayed at my public high school and wasn't up against everyone from Andover, I could have gotten into Harvard." It was maybe the sixty-eighth time that I had heard this.

And then I knew—this wasn't going anywhere.

We had been together for two years. At the time that we had gotten together, I had been dating an artist named George who drove a '70s model Porsche and lived in an area of town where the windows and doors were covered with bars. Every time we went out we each paid for ourselves, and if I happened to eat, say, a couple of his fries, he would average out the cost of the fry and make me pay for it. "If we both pay for ourselves, I can go out with you more," he said. I almost bought into it until he did this in front of Jennifer at Cantor's Deli. That's when I met Frank, and he invited me to be his date at the Emmys.

"Let me see," said Jennifer, "the way I see it, you can pay for yourself with George at Cantor's, or you can go with Frank to the Emmys." Best friends are good for this. They often have a miraculous ability to make you see the obvious. I stopped returning George's phone calls after he left a message in which he screamed that he "wasn't seeing enough of me." I considered his statement and then decided—unless I was looking for an ugly fight—that I really didn't want to call him back that evening. The next day he left five messages on my voice mail and three messages taped to my door. And then he started blasting me with emails.

100 REASONS THAT I LOVE YOU. Interesting. Wonderful though I may be I was pretty sure that there were not 100 reasons to love me, at least not 100 apparent reasons. It was difficult for me to believe that he had taken the time to write this down. JUST CALL ME, ALL I WANT TO DO IS TALK WITH YOU. Sure. This was a running narrative of how he had fallen asleep with the phone cradled in his arms after I didn't return his call. WE ARE CO-DEPENDENTS. How could this be? I was trying to get away from him. Maybe he depended on me to make him feel awful.

After one email in which George stated that he had joined some co-dependents group, he stopped calling and taping notes to my door. I figured that he had found someone in one of the co-dependent groups to go Dutch with him at Cantor's.

But then there was Frank. We had known each other during my college days when I attended an arts institution at which Frank's father, an accomplished painter, taught, or should I say, was the dean of the art school. Frank attended this school because he didn't know what to do with his life after graduating from Andover. After his father told him that he could get him a full scholarship because he was his son, it was a plan. There was just one catch: Frank had to get in.

On his first try Frank's application was rejected because his portfolio didn't compare with the other applicants' portfolios. In a rare turn of events, the school's admissions committee decided to reconsider Frank's portfolio. Frank was then granted admission to the school, with full scholarship, for entrance into the very same class to which he had previously been rejected. I later learned that it was Frank's father who had strongly suggested to the admissions committee that he would really appreciate it if they would reconsider his son's portfolio.

We didn't date during college because I was too busy chasing pretty boys with faces like Botticelli cherubs who took speed and smoked unfiltered Camels. According to my friend Marcie, Frank was nowhere near my level on the L.A. Eco-Chain of Dating. "Date him," she said, "and it's nothing but Relationship Terrorism."

Later, after I had denounced my artistic past and attempted to establish credentials as a corporate attorney, I met him in the most unlikely of places.

I hadn't seen him for ten years. When he walked in, I thought he was his father. But then I found out. It wasn't his dad. It was the adult Frank.

At a few months shy of 36, Frank looked like they had ridden him hard and put him away wet. He was long past relaxed-fit, and had gone from eat-drink-anything-anywhere-you-want to a high-blood-pressure-cholesterol-producing machine that was gaining somewhere on the average of 15 to 20 pounds per year. In short, his youthful athletic beauty was going to require planning and hard work to maintain and it was too late for him to develop the discipline to do it. Besides, due to the fact that he was sporadically employed as a sound editor, he thought that he didn't need to. He considered himself "a catch" for the ladies of Los Angeles.

He wasn't a catch even by L.A. standards, which allow that if you don't have any recent felonies, have kicked the addiction over three months ago, and can name your illegitimate children, you're dateable, as long as you're "cute." He was, however, the current standard of what my friends had come to expect in a boyfriend—someone who was going to be there. And that's it. When I met him again, Roberta, a woman who had the audacity to counsel single people with their dating/relationship problems in the new millennium, despite having married her high school sweetheart in the late '70s, had finally gotten me to join the ultimate self-improvement setting: Group Therapy.

The Group was composed of the usual West Los Angeles types: a former child actress who was between shows—trying to make the nearly impossible leap from a teenage star-kiddie actress on a family cable channel to a grown-up prime-time adult actress on a network show; a female wardrobe supervisor, who, having seen firsthand the absurdly favorable treatment which stars received, really wanted to be an actress; a divorced housewife, who had already redecorated the house (and of course the garden) for the fifth time and really wanted to be a therapist; and me, an attorney who really hated life. There were also a couple of guys who really didn't want to be there, and Frank, a sound editor, who like everyone in L.A., really wanted to direct.

Roberta would lead the group from a large overstuffed velvet-green chair, which she referred to as "her space." She supplied the group with a large wicker basket filled with tea selections such as

"Wild Blackberry," "Country Green Apple," and "Cape Cod Cranberry," which to my utter delight all tasted like liquid Jell-O. We positioned ourselves around the room amidst Roberta's last season's love seats, throw pillows, and Hockney collection, which she had recently removed from her Benedict Canyon home because it was being remodeled. Again.

It often struck me as strange that Roberta was the only person in the entire group who was ever able to have or sustain a serious relationship. Whenever anyone in Group would even approach the concept of marriage, the relationship would quickly implode with chastened self-recriminations along the lines of, "I take responsibility for it," "I still have so much work to do," or "It just isn't right,"—and a knowing but approving nod from Roberta. But then that person would go through another three-year cycle of therapy because they were completely depressed by their inability to have a serious relationship. It frightened me: There were people in their late 40s who had done Group for over 15 years and had never finished their "work." And Roberta got a new Bentley every two years.

They loved having me in Group because I would "engage"— I fought like crazy with everyone. I couldn't believe that I was forced to sit in a room and discuss my most intimate and personal feelings with six other persons whom I had no use for, and pay for it. And I didn't believe the façade of confidentiality, which allegedly was going to keep Group—six of the biggest blabbers I had ever met—from spreading my intimate secrets throughout Los Angeles, or the world, for that matter.

"I see you have a problem with trust," said Roberta after hearing my issue with confidentiality, something which I discovered was violated by every Group member on a daily basis through incessant emails to everyone they knew, specifically when there was a hot topic or a famous Group member.

"No, I have a problem with confidentiality," I said. "There is none."

Almost Royalty

I ran into trouble by interfering when the divorced housewife was trying to "engage" with one of the guys in the group by asking him a question to which I thought the answer was painfully obvious: Why wouldn't he "be present" with her? she asked. "Because he thinks you're repulsive," I blurted out. That, by itself, did not get me kicked out of Group. I got kicked out when I, as Roberta put it, violated the "Implied Therapist-Patient Agreement" by asking her why I felt just as depressed as I did the day that I had entered therapy 15 years ago and for ruining the working relationship of Group by sleeping with Frank.

As for sleeping with Frank, well, that was a mistake. Not because I did it, at least I didn't think so. Sometime before he met me—or maybe it was always like this—Frank had developed different desires. If it had come down to three Big Macs, two large packs of fries and a Big Gulp Coke Classic, or five hours of the wildest, hottest, wettest sex with, let's say, a bouncy Laker Girl, there would have been no contest: it was Big Mac Time all the way. To Frank, sex had become a relationship obligation, like doing the dishes, cleaning out your car, or paying your Visa bill.

But Roberta had different ideas.

"You see," Roberta explained when she called to announce that I could return to Group, "Group is like a laboratory where you get to work on relationships, not have them."

"Ok," I said.

"So I need to know..." said Roberta.

"I take responsibility for it," I said.

"For what?" said Roberta.

"For having truly mediocre sex with Frank?" I said.

"Sounds like we have something to discuss in a session," said Roberta.

On our first date, Frank took me to the Emmys. Ten minutes before he was supposed to pick me up, he called me from the car wash to announce that he was going to be late because he needed to clean the car—and go to Bloomingdale's to buy a tie, pick up his suit at the cleaners, and take a shower. Interesting. It was 6:50 p.m. and the show started at 7:30.

We made it to the Emmys by 8:45 p.m. in time for his category. He won. That was enough to make me decide, OK, there may be a future with this guy.

There are always signs along the way that will show you what direction your relationship is headed, even if your boyfriend is telling you something different. If you honestly look at them, and don't rationalize the obvious failings, you won't find yourself chucking away the logic born of a college education to "consult" with someone answering the phones for 1-800-PSYCHIC.

"The bad sex, the passive-aggressiveness, the verbal warfare—you deserve it," said Marcie. "It's all a by-product of violating the L.A. Eco-Chain of Dating. I told you, only date people on your level. Not above. Not below. It's not like you haven't done this before."

She had a point.

On our first major holiday together, Thanksgiving, I wanted to attend my traditional celebration, a production of taste and refinement equaling a dinner created by Alice Waters which my gay friends James and Stefan produced. "But Blanche, we need you to come," said Stefan who referred to me as Blanche since the day he had his first boyfriend when we were fourteen. "We were counting on you to be the token heteros of the table. Someone has to dress terribly and have genetically inbred bad taste."

But Frank insisted that we celebrate with his family because this was a really important day for them. He won. When we walked in the door at 5:45 p.m., Frank's sisters, Mary and Sari, suddenly remembered that they had to defrost the skirt steak which Mary was planning to serve for dinner at 6:00 p.m. His sisters had forgotten because they were in their eighth hour of watching the Twilight Zone Marathon. Frank took it in stride as we ate at 9:00 p.m.

Almost Royalty

At Christmas, I was overjoyed to find Frank running around like a madman to buy presents—until I found out that they were all for his sisters. I didn't receive anything until the last day of January when I called him and told him that I was going to buy the bookcase which he had promised me, and either he paid for it or I would. Frank explained that he just couldn't get it together, and had thought that I "would be cool about it."

On Valentine's Day, Frank told me that he had a big surprise planned. At 8:00 p.m., he walked in the door with Chicken Fajitas for two from El Pollo Loco and a juicer, which he told me that I could use whenever I wanted to. He later confessed that he had tried to get reservations all over town, but at 7:30 p.m. when he called, everything was all booked up.

My birthday, however, was remarkably different from the pattern set on other major days—he forgot it entirely. Or I should say, he forgot it until Jennifer called him from my birthday dinner and asked him when, or if, he was planning to arrive. As we were cutting the cake, he waltzed in the door with a dozen short stem red roses and a bag of oranges which I knew he had gotten from the guy who sold flowers and fruit off the back of a pick-up near the Wilshire Boulevard on-ramp to the 405 freeway.

At year one—the legal deadline for determining the direction of relationships—Frank asked me to marry him on a Saturday morning after I had just paid for breakfast. The moment struck me as strange because Frank had just pulled the "forgot my wallet again" routine and we were suddenly surrounded by a chorus of car alarms that had been set off by an earthquake measuring 3.2 on the Richter scale which had its epicenter in Barstow.

I should have known that he wasn't really serious about the engagement because I never got a ring. Over the following year he would tell me that he was going ring shopping, but always ended up at an all-night gambling club in Gardena located near an off-ramp of the 710 freeway.

Our relationship was OK as long as I bought into the cup-is-half-empty victim's posture of life. After a while, the posture of downward mobility seemed pretty ridiculous for two people whose parents had performed heroic feats to give them the best education money could buy. And then I made a fatal mistake: I accidentally found something I liked to do. And then I did it well.

While stumbling through my I-Hate-Litigation career, I discovered an area of the law which catered to my two strongest talents, talking on the phone and going to lunch. I gained a small reputation among clients who made staggering amounts of money for surprisingly little work as being "an attorney who didn't seem like an attorney," a talent not completely appreciated by my former colleagues.

And then the fun began. It wasn't just that Frank blew it on all of the major holidays and events. It was more that I was beginning to notice that he had a latent talent that I had not previously noticed: He had all the makings of a world-class whiner and he was beginning to epitomize the Angry White Guy.

He was angry with his dad for leaving his mom, yet he despised his mother so much that he couldn't be in a room with her for more than an hour, even at Christmas. He was angry at his mom for giving him a watch with a scratch in it, feeling sure that she had personally put the scratch in it to hurt him. He was angry at his father's second wife because she was going to inherit his father's work, and rob him of his inheritance. He was angry at his sister for deciding at age ten that she wanted to be an artist, a position he felt robbed him of his chance. And he was angry with me because I refused to live life stuck in neutral. And this was just personally.

Professionally, Frank honestly felt that the reason his directing career had not taken off was because his student film had not been awarded a Student Academy Award. This he attributed to the fact that someone on the Academy judging committee had wanted to sabotage his career in its early stages. Nearly ten years later, he was still furious about it, and he insisted on projecting his student film on the white walls of my dining room at every dinner party I had, figuring someone would see the brilliance of his vision and hand him a sixty- million-dollar studio film to direct.

"I just don't feel seen in this relationship," lamented Frank on a regular basis. It's the skill of those who have spent too much of their lives in therapy to use jargon which they don't understand to signify feelings that they don't have the courage to be honest about. Roughly translated, this meant that Frank wanted me to take the attention and energy that I had to invest in my own career to be remotely successful and put it into his and make him successful.

This was to be the Faustian bargain of our marriage—I was to do everything, including the Herculean feat of creating a directing career for him while supporting us, and in exchange I would get to be Mrs. Frank Jamieson.

Maybe it was all those years of drinking liquid Jell-O with Roberta that made me believe that marriage was supposed to be a "shared equal partnership of responsible individuals with/without children." This was quite far from what I was experiencing. In retrospect, I now know that my utopian concept of marriage was about as far from reality as the O.J. Simpson Defense Team's theory of the Brown-Goldman murders, but that didn't keep me from attempting to engage with Frank, using the skills that Roberta had taught me.

As I plowed through my meatloaf, I surveyed the scenery. I wasn't going to go through another year of this. One of us had to make up our mind.

I started in. "Listen Frank, it's time to stop screwing around."

"OK, OK..." he mumbled, "I'll leave your mashed potatoes alone."

Hmmmmm. This was *not* going to be easy. "No," I said, "cut it with the potatoes. Where is this relationship going?"

If there are five words which can stop a man's heart quicker than those, I don't know what they are. Frank looked like I had just sucked the life out of him.

"Well...you know," he said, "it's going."

I shook my head. "Not good enough," I said. "That's not an answer."

I'm sure that Roberta would have counseled me to create a safe place in the dialogue where Frank felt that he could "be present" with me. I wasn't having any part of it.

"Look," I said, "we've been engaged for over a year. I still don't have a ring. Every time I suggest a date, you make it six months away. When three months pass, you put the date out another six months. Enough already."

Although I really should have seen it coming, when I heard it I laughed so hard that I fell right out of my Copper Pan chair.

"I still have so much work to do," said Frank, with the chastened look which I had seen so many of Roberta's patients adopt.

"Oh my God!" I said as I spit out my mashed potatoes. "Frank honey, the only work you need to do is to figure out how you can get it constantly, instead of occasionally."

I attempted to address the issue.

"Look, time is moving on. And while I'm willing to be in this relationship with you, I'm not willing to do it as your girlfriend."

Frank looked around the room.

"Well," he said, "I need more time."

"Well, I'm going to give you more time—two months to be precise. Two months to make 50 percent of the decisions in this relationship, two months to take 50 percent of all of the responsibilities, two months to pay 50 percent of all of our bills. And, two months to pick a wedding date, which must be executed by the end of this year, not the decade." I paused for a moment to get him some water because he appeared to be choking on his burger.

"Also, I want an engagement ring. So, I'll give you two months to find one. And I want at least a one carat ring, *with no inclusions in it.*"

I knew perfectly well that there was no chance on God's green earth that any of this was going to happen. Frank had been ruined by therapy. His ability to make any decision, from what color car to buy, to whether he should still be mad at his dad, had been handed over to Roberta. And unless Roberta gave him the "thumbs up," he wouldn't marry me. And I knew Roberta wouldn't.

But it was time to move on and this was another decision that he would not openly make. So I gave him his out. By doing what he always did—nothing—he would end the relationship.

As a matter of fact, he never did say or do anything. He just stopped coming over. Then he stopped calling. One morning when I went to make orange juice, I realized that his juicer was gone. And then his keys arrived in the mail.

About the time that the juicer disappeared, my friend Stefan met Frank at a gallery opening. Frank never did tell him that we had broken up. He just said, "Courtney was great to me. But it just wasn't right. And I have so much work to do."

2

Almost Single

"So?" asked my therapist, Roberta.

"Can we wait until my Blueberry Tea seeps?" I said.

Like into a Slurpee or Jell-O.

"Tick-Tock," said Roberta.

"More like cha-ching," I said.

"I don't like that."

"Sorry. Frank's juicer is gone. I'm pretty sure that this means he is gone."

"Yes. He told me."

"Told you? I thought you ordered it."

"Courtney."

"Get real," I said while rolling my eyes.

"Frank and I were working on—well—you know his issues regarding commitment."

"What did he say?" As if I didn't know.

Almost Royalty

"Courtney, you know I can't talk about this," said Roberta while giving me a disapproving look.

"Oh. Of course. Confidentiality," I said, hoping not to sound sarcastic.

"But *you* gave him the ultimatum," said Roberta, hoping to make me uncomfortable.

I took a sip of my blueberry tea. "Decaf or regular is an ultimatum to Frank."

"Well yes, he does have a lot of work to do."

I sensed that I was getting into dangerous territory, but decided to push it.

"You think?" I said with a big smile.

"I don't like cynicism. It makes our work so difficult."

I looked at Roberta and gave her my most serious look. "I take responsibility for it."

Roberta looked pissed. "Well, why the sudden ultimatum?" she asked. "You might have worked things out."

"Yes, after the next Ice Age. Look, I didn't see kids, a house, and a golden lab named 'Thor' in our future."

"No one does," said Roberta. "It's not 1975."

"Yeah. Well, our marriage would have been a horrible, horrible mess."

"Welcome to life," said Roberta.

Maybe I'd made a mistake. I know that Frank was never going to marry me. But he wasn't really awful. He didn't beat me or anything.

I was on a blind date with Josh, "a hot item," because my actress/Chinese herbalist friend, Halley, had set us up. I was a little unsettled about the whole thing, especially when Josh didn't pass my first requirement.

"He's single, right?" I asked her.

"Almost."

"Almost single?" I said.

"He's separated—they're planning to divorce," said Halley.

"That's a hot item?"

"Courtney, he's employed, tall, thin, under 40, and has hair. I'm giving you a crack at him," said Halley, with the same enthusiasm I had heard people use to describe their rent-controlled ocean view apartments in Santa Monica.

He sounded suspicious to me.

"Yeah. Why don't you date him?" I asked.

"I did. We're just friends now," she said.

"Uh huh. Why just friends?" I said.

"Because he can't help my career and he's not rich...enough."

Josh and I were at the hipster Berliner Café, my current Come-To-Jesus spot. When my clients had screwed up so enormously that even Olympic backpedaling wouldn't save them, I'd take them to Berliner Café to fire them, or force them into an act of contrition.

Today there was a table of three women—so thin—around 6 feet tall and 110 pounds, all angles, collarbones, hip bones and cheekbones. They were clearly addicted to dieting. Or something.

In the northeast corner table was a tiny Asian woman with 24-inch, platinum blond extensions who occasionally pecked at her laptop, but mostly chatted on her cell phone. Her conversations were loud and migraine-inducing annoying.

And of course, there *he* was. The short greasy guy with a three-day stubble and dirty blond hair: The Star—of course the male action star, the feral Celebrity Royalty of the moment—with about 20 extra pounds on his famous butt.

The Star was sitting with an even shorter nervous guy who looked like he had just graduated from the Ray Stark Producer's Program at USC. I guessed the shorter guy to be an agent's assistant who was assigned to run errands or babysit The Star. The assistant had styled himself in the agent-fashion of the moment: Lew Wasserman glasses—horn-rimmed, big and black—a shaved, bald white head and a $200 Macy's suit.

Almost Royalty

I wondered—why was it that the male action star of the moment was never a millimeter over five feet six inches tall? The Star got nervous when he thought that I was looking at him. Please. Did he really think I was going to call the paparazzi when he inhaled a piece of German chocolate cake?

Actually, I was almost positive that one of the waiters already had. Like I cared about the Star. The cake, however, had endless possibilities. I would have asked The Star his opinion of the cake, but I knew the L.A. Etiquette for Interacting with Star/Celebrity Royalty in Public Places:

(1) No eye contact and absolutely no gawking.

(2) No verbal interaction unless The Star/Celebrity Royalty first speaks to you.

(3) If spoken to by the Star/Celebrity Royalty the only thing that you may say is: "I love your work."

(4) If there should be an Accidental Public Encounter with a Star/Celeb and his/her Entourage, the non-Royalty must wait to be granted an audience with the Star/Celeb before joining the Star/Celeb's Entourage.

(5) The Star/Celebrity Royalty always goes first and has priority in every situation, even if they have arrived three hours after their scheduled reservation/appointment—and you were 45 minutes early for yours.

Josh and I had been sitting there for about 15 minutes. I wasn't going to give it much effort. I didn't think that Josh—"the hot item"—was at my level on the L.A. Eco-Chain of Dating. And I had made that mistake before.

Josh gave me a funny look and almost scowled.

I had the strange sensation of being viewed as a consolation prize, like Halley had said, "No really, she's a great girl."

Josh wasn't buying any of it.

"Tell me, Courtney," said Josh, "how do you survive in L.A. as a single woman?"

Rude.

But intriguing.

That was the absolutely nastiest thing that you could say to any single woman above the age of 30.

"Well," I said, "should I pull my hair back so that you can see my horns?"

Perhaps I should have employed a more graceful approach.

But ten years of practicing law had taught me how to verbally smack someone in the face.

And who was he to say that.

But more to the point: How did I get here?

I mean, what frightening vision of a compromised future had conspired to land me on a blind date with an "almost single" guy?

My girlfriends were once people that I liked. They did interesting things. They were photographing sharks. They were traveling through India. They were opening their one woman shows in New York.

I'm not exactly sure when they changed. I knew something had changed when I realized my female friends—Stanford, Yale, and Harvard graduates—were taking courses at The Learning Annex on "Finding the Man and Getting To I Do." And that included the lesbians.

I realized my friends no longer used the f-word to describe themselves. In fact, it had become a rejected label, almost a point of contempt: Feminist.

At some point I realized that there was something more than just a change among my friends. It was something close to a cultural phenomenon. And then I recognized it: That Couple Thing.

That Couple Thing seemed to hit women at age 35 to 90. It had become a mega-industry that made billions in online dating services, self-help books, and seminars. And it had exploded more quickly than reality television, fad diets, and housing foreclosures.

It wasn't anything obvious. It was simply a gradual shift in the landscape. Friends discontinued their grand ambition, big multi-year tracks, and bad boyfriends/girlfriends. Others quietly joined singles groups like "Athletic Singles." A few began submitting online personal ads.

Those who would never commit to marriage because "they didn't need some piece of paper," (translated: partner wouldn't commit) settled into permanent, live-in relationships resembling marriage. Suddenly, they began "trying" for pregnancy—not preventing. And some even "tried" without telling their partners.

Even Stefan, empowered once the *New York Times* started carrying same-sex Marriages/Commitment Ceremony Announcements in the Style Section, began angling for an engagement ring from his partner, James. Given that Stefan had once had nothing but disdain for "the heterosexual trap of marriage," this was a strange thing.

"Oh, Blanche, I really want that double-banded Cartier ring, you know the one…"

"I've seen it," I said—on every gay man in the greater West Hollywood metropolis.

"But James said we don't need to because we're already committed."

"A pity," I said.

"Yeah," said Stefan, "especially since I was having so much fun planning our wedding."

Not two weeks after I broke up with Frank, Marcie came over for some coffee. After I made her some of my famous homebrew, she sat down.

"Uhh. Strong coffee. Can you put some more milk in?"

I gave her the milk. She put in half a cup.

"That's better," she said, "but your coffee cups don't match."
"I have matching ones."
"Then why aren't you using them? And that yellow sweater—why are you wearing yellow?"
"I like yellow."
"It doesn't like you. It makes you look...too yellow," said Marcie while looking over my sweater.
"What's up?" I said, hoping to change the subject. "How's the wedding going?"
"OK. Ahh, do you think that there's any chance that you and Frank will get back together?"
"I don't know. Probably not. I think we're almost definitely completely broken up."
"Because I've decided to have a joint bridal and bachelor party. And I'm going to do 'a couples only' party. But since you're almost definitely not in a relationship, you can't come. You get it, right?" said Marcie.
"Not really," I said while looking away and attempting to sound nonchalant.
"Look," said Marcie as she inspected the coffee cup in her hand. "I know you introduced me to my fiancé. But I want to have a couples' party. And you aren't a couple. So you can't come."
"Uh huh..." I said while looking out the window.
"But I am going to give you some advice," said Marcie. You should *never* wear yellow. So give me that sweater. I think it's right for me."
"I'm keeping it."
"I'm just trying to help you."
"Still keeping it," I said.
Marcie stood up and walked over to the door. "Well I have to go because I have a lot of planning to do. So—remember—I'm *not* going to invite you to my couples' party. But don't worry, I'll find some way for you to be part of my wedding," she said as she walked out the door.

I called Marcie's maid of honor, Bettina, for an explanation.

"What's to explain?" said Bettina. "You're not in a relationship, and you're kinda…stale."

"How can I be stale?" I said. "I just got out of a relationship that I ended."

"You aren't married…and you know…you're kinda running out of time."

"I'm in my 30s."

"For now…but you know, you didn't close the deal. Again," said Bettina with a slight under-tone of disgust.

"So let me get this right," I said. "Because I didn't get Frank to marry me…"

"You have to wonder…" said Bettina. "Why is that? I mean, is there something wrong with you…like you're weird or going into the pile of the unwanted. What do they call that?"

I knew what they called that: an outcast.

"Oh really," I said. "You know, I'll find someone, I always do."

"I don't know, Courtney. I'm beginning to think that you might need some retooling…maybe a little help."

"And you, Bettina—a lesbian—are going to give it to me?"

"At least I got married," said Bettina.

"Yes you did," I said, "to a gay man. How's that working out for you?"

"You haven't told Marcie, have you?" asked Bettina. Before I could respond, I heard a crash, a screaming child, and Bettina say "kid emergency" as she hung up her cell.

Interesting.

Or not.

More like typical female Schadenfreude—joy at someone else's misery. It was part of the drill, part of the unsaid Female Scorecard that we kept with our female friends since age 12 or 13, the moment we understood that we were in competition for something we didn't even understand—the attraction of other people. The Female Scorecard was pretty simple: If one of your friends should suddenly be alone—not in a relationship—it gave *you* a point on your mental Scorecard if you happened to be in a relationship at that time. Likewise, if *you* fell out of a relationship, it gave your girlfriends a point on their scorecard if they were in a relationship—because they were in a relationship and you weren't. Yes, it was petty and ridiculous, because even your friends who were in stupid relationships with abusive idiots thought they were better than you, because you were alone and they were in a relationship.

Why? Because after ending a relationship the hard part came. No, not being alone.

The hard part was getting back into a relationship, because getting back into a relationship meant that you were going to cycle through those humiliating L.A. Singles Activities such as:

#1. Wine for Social Climbers—Along with pretending that you give a damn about cigars, wine courses at any of the restaurants or wine shops, a single's playground, the first baby step in distancing yourself from your ancestry in Butte, Montana—necessary for those who have decided that it raises one's social profile to B-Level Civilian Royalty—to know the difference between a Chardonnay, a Viognier, and a Sauvignon Blanc, and a good combination with:

#2. Restaurant of the Moment Finders—Generally, the activity of the sedentary, overweight, male crowd, a group more familiar with the Food Network than anything on ESPN, who are characterized by the elaborate game of food expert that they play with thinly-veiled condescension. The ones with ambition pretend to be a partner in the Celebrity or Civilian Royalty LLP which has just opened the restaurant of the moment. The more arrogant ones pretend to have discovered the obscure restaurant in L.A. County that served a delicacy—eel marinated in yogurt—which you never dreamt of eating.

Almost Royalty

#3. Museum Trustee Wannabes—Certified single jerks hoping to meet Civilian Royalty, who play an elaborate game of one-upmanship at art-related functions while knowing nothing about art and not having the cash to become a museum trustee.

#4. Political Activists—Young, youngish Westsiders usually involved in environmentally-related causes, who hope to possibly get an invitation to a Celebrity Political Royalty fundraiser or find a date at various political functions.

#5. Non-Practicing Catholics/Christians/Jews—Usually a gathering in the form of a non-religious fun service such as a "Shabbat for Singles," populated by those date-seeking individuals who were raised as Catholics, Christians, or Jews but who are now completely indifferent to the subject of organized religion.

#6. Elite College Alumni Singles—The absolute poser group of them all, frequented by those who haven't made good on their prestigious educations, but still are under the illusion that having an Ivy League education means something when you're 37 years old and still working as an assistant.

#7. Online Dating/Friend Set-ups—Everyone knows someone who claims to have made this work. However, the other 99.9999 percent have found this to be morbidly depressing.

But there sat Josh. Somehow, he had passed an unspoken L.A. category, that being: "Got the First One Out of the Way."

I don't know when it first struck me that people were looking at first marriages like affordable first homes, like an item to be acquired and discarded on your way to something better. For some reason, it was presumed that women would be lining up for him.

Josh seemed pretty pleased with himself. He was not the slightest bit embarrassed by his "almost single" status.

He seemed empowered. It was as if—for him—his failed first marriage had given him greatly enhanced desirability.

And I was alone and never married.

I wondered if I needed to do a quick reevaluation of our positions on the Eco-Chain.

I looked at the menu. Had I made some enormous mistake by booting Frank? Frank and I would have had a horrible, horrible marriage—I wanted kids, a house, and recipes involving Velveeta cheese. He wanted In-N-Out burgers and all-night gambling at that place off the 710 Freeway. We would've slogged through a couple years, wasted a lot of time, and then divorced.

I'm pretty sure that was the scenario.

It would have been awful.

But maybe I, too, could've felt greatly enhanced desirability and perhaps even elevated my status on the Eco-Chain.

I sipped my non-fat cappuccino and looked at Josh.

He didn't want me.

He was going to date the circuit—actresses, models, sexy/dangerous/industry types—before he would date a human. And I was very human.

I knew I would never hear from him again.

"Don't you want to ask me *the questions*?" said Josh.

"What *questions*?" I said.

Josh eyed me.

"Don't you want to know what I do?"

"No. OK. Whatever. What do *you* do?"

"I'm a *manager*..."

"Do you like German chocolate cake?" I said. I flagged the waiter over.

"What?" said Josh.

"Because it looks like they make a really good German chocolate cake here. And I was wondering if you'd like to split a piece?"

Josh looked puzzled.

"I'll have a small Cobb salad with no dressing, egg, Roquefort or bacon. And water. No bubbles," he said.

Of course, the West L.A. meal. Some flavor, few calories and almost no fat.

"And could you show me where the bathroom is?"

The waiter pointed to the back and Josh stood up and walked away. I didn't know if he would come back.

I gave the waiter my order.

While Josh was in the bathroom, our order arrived: A small Cobb salad and water for Josh. Baby back ribs, mashed Yukon potatoes, and that German chocolate cake for me.

It was a date-killing, relationship-squelching meal for any woman on the fat-obsessed Westside, a perfect mixture of moxie and self-loathing. I didn't care. I was hungry.

I dug into the mashed Yukon potatoes.

Across the room, the table of skinny-addicted girls were staring intently at me. They looked visibly alarmed and were just barely shaking their heads left-right, left-right, left-right.

Before I could get the fork in my mouth, Josh sat down.

"Oh. You got the German chocolate cake. I thought you were kidding."

"Want some?"

I pushed the cake toward him.

"Real food. I forgot what it tastes like," he said.

He ate half of my mashed Yukon potatoes and five out of eight of my baby back ribs. I think I got a bit of the cake. No one touched the Cobb salad. In between bites, we had a decent discussion about music. I was pleased to learn that he had traveled past the outer-border of civilization for most Westsiders, La Brea Boulevard. And I was shocked to discover that he was familiar with the major business and cultural center near the intersection of the 101 and 10 freeways: Downtown Los Angeles.

One hour later Josh walked me to my car.

"Well, thanks. It was nice of you to do this and stick it out," I said.

"It's not often that you get to have a real conversation," said Josh. "You're not like anyone I know."

"Since when is that good?" I said.

Josh kissed me on the cheek and made sure that I got into my car safely.

I told Bettina and Marcie about the date the next morning as we trained for what looked to be our third failed attempt at the L.A. Marathon. We usually met at one of the four unavoidable coffee franchises on San Vicente Boulevard, and then ran down San Vicente between Bundy and 26th Street and around the perimeter of the Brentwood Country Club. Our goal was to eventually run to the Santa Monica Pier and back.

"What kind of car does he drive?" said Marcie.

"You know I don't care about that. I didn't ask."

"No, well what does he do?" said Marcie.

"He's the manager of something."

"Like what? A Walmart, a car dealership?" said Marcie. "How do you know where he is on the Eco-Chain?"

"I don't know."

"You don't know anything about him," said Bettina.

"I know that he likes German chocolate cake."

"You each paid for yourself, right?" said Marcie.

"Sort of."

"Oh no. Did you pay for him?" said Marcie.

"Marcie, that *Rules* junk is pretty tired. Remember? The authors of that crap are both divorced."

"But you fought with him and then you paid for dinner?"

"I did. He seemed surprised."

"Surprised? I bet he wondered when you would beam back to Pluto," said Bettina.

"So what. He liked the German chocolate cake."

"You don't get what this is all about yet, do you? He'll never call you," said Marcie.

Almost Royalty

"I know that and he knows that. But he's not even single."
"Oh, he will be. But not for long," said Marcie.

At Group that week everyone contributed endless snotty remarks on my date-failure.

I mean they were very supportive.

Roberta seemed to be paying very careful attention.

Was she taking notes?

"No woman in L.A. eats on a date. Not like that," said the wardrobe supervisor during Group.

"I don't see how it would have turned out any differently. I was hungry," I said.

"Did you have to fight with him?" said the former kiddie-actress.

"You've got some work to do. You seem to create situations where you'll end up alone," said one of the guys.

"I'm not even sure what that therapy-babble means."

"That's very insulting, Courtney," said Roberta.

I tried to look very concerned. "Oh, OK. I take responsibility for it."

I looked at Roberta. She seemed pissed.

I didn't say anything else and went home depressed after that mandatory fake hug thing that Roberta made us do at the end of Group.

Oh God do I *hate* that fake hug thing.

3

Sibling Rivalry

"I love what you've done with your apartment," said my mother, Julia, who had appeared at my door on a Tuesday night without advance warning.

"Uh huh," I said. "Which part?"

"The little French doors on the bathroom," she said.

"That was there when I got the place."

"The sunken living room."

"Also there."

"The automatic faux fireplace."

"There."

"The three-tier halogen chandelier?"

"There."

"The plush gray shag carpeting?"

I turned away while I put my Velveeta mushroom soup—with little canned onions—and chicken in the oven. Of course, the gray shag carpeting, a choice only an artistically suicidal individual would make, was there also.

"Why don't you sit down and read the paper while I make dinner, Julia."

She didn't respond. It appeared that my mother had gotten lost in my 750-square-foot apartment.

"Ju-li-a?" I called.

On the morning of my twelfth birthday, my mother had told me that she had an unusual gift. "Now that you're almost an adult, I'm going to allow you, no, in fact, I think I'm going to insist that you call me 'Julia' instead of 'Mom.'"

"How will people know that you're my mother?" I said.

"Do they need to know that?" she said.

"Ju-li-a?"

"I'm in here." Here, was my rhombus shaped walk-in closet, obviously created when the genius developers who built my apartment realized that they had a leftover space between the bedroom and the living room that was too oddly shaped and too small to be called a room. I walked in.

"What are you doing in here?" I said. She was going through my dresses.

"Where is it?" she said. "Oh good. Here it is."

She pulled out my cherry-red cocktail dress, the one with the neckline that plunged to my navel.

I loved that dress. After finding the beautiful cherry-red material in a clothing store, I had found a Vogue pattern and had it made for me.

"I need to borrow this," she said.

"What for?"

"Your Aunt Katy's having an event."

"I know. I've been invited to it. It's Megan's baby shower."

My 42-year-old cousin, Megan, from my father's Episcopalian side of the family, had gotten pregnant by her boyfriend of eight weeks. There were rumors of a joint christening/wedding once Megan could fit into a wedding dress again. My Aunt Katy, delighted to finally have a grandchild, had chosen to forget that ten years ago she would have disowned her daughter on the spot after receiving news of her skanky behavior.

"Well, I want to make a statement," said Julia.

"What statement would that be? That you dress inappropriately for all occasions without discrimination?" I said.

"You're no fun."

"Look Julia, put the dress down and let's have dinner. I'll go shopping with you and help you find a great dress."

"I don't want dinner. If you're not going to let me have the dress, I'm leaving."

"Then it's time for you to go." I opened the door.

"Bye-bye," I said. "Drive safely."

She walked out the door without a word.

I knew my mother.

I made a mental note to keep the doors locked, round-the-clock, for the next month.

"Okay, Abyss, Velveeta mushroom soup and chicken?"

I gave up on the mushroom soup-chicken part of the equation and cut myself a big wedge of Velveeta.

"Put the Velveeta down," said Jennifer, whom I had speed-dialed.

"It's only a small piece," I said.

"I told you not to let her see the dress," said Jennifer.

"She showed up at New Year's just as I was getting ready for a party. I'm hoping it will be different this time," I said.

Jennifer sighed. "It won't be," she said. "What did she want for New Year's? To party with you?"

"A dress," I said.

"Did you let her in?"

"What could I do? She said she needed to go to the bathroom. Only she made a little detour into my closet and got something."

"What?"

I sighed. "My little black dress."

"Noooo!" said Jennifer. "Not the black dress. You searched for months for that."

"Yes," I said. "It's gone."

"And you let her have it?"

"What could I do?" I said. "Wrestle her for it?"

Not that I hadn't tried.

When she walked out of my closet with my little black dress, I walked over, grabbed it, and said, "No way."

"But I need to look special," said Julia.

"You look special every day of your life, just the way you are," I said.

"Don't try that psycho-babble nonsense on me," said Julia. "Remember, I'm the wife…"

"He's dead," I said. "He died 28 years ago." When I was seven.

"All right, I *was* the wife of a board-certified psychologist," said Julia. "I know all those stupid, self-esteem tricks."

"You're not getting the dress," I said. "Now leave. I need to finish getting ready for this New Year's party sometime before next year."

"Hmmm, nice dress," said Julia, looking a little too closely at the dress I was wearing.

"Don't even think about it," I said.

"Red is not my color."

"It's time for you to go." I opened the door. She gave me a dirty look.

"Bye-bye," I said. "Drive safely." I closed and locked the door and then went into my bathroom to blow-dry my hair. When I came out, the little black dress was gone. I forgot. She had used her emergency set of my keys to come back into my apartment and steal my dress.

A Post-it note was on the hanger.

"I took it. I'll have it cleaned."

On January 3, I had the locks on my doors changed.

After two weeks she called. "Ah c'mon, it's just a dress," was left on my voice mail.

After four weeks, she attempted to break into my apartment on a Sunday morning as I was having my morning coffee with Abyss and a copy of *The New York Times*. I heard her fumbling with the lock. Then she started pounding. "You had the locks changed? Open the door, right now." She gave up after five minutes.

On March 1, I received an email from her:

Dear Courtney:

I don't know why you're so mad. I'm your mother. Don't we share things? If you don't start talking to me I'm going to cut you out of my will.

Love,

Julia

Eventually, I got worn down and wanted the dress back. In June, I called her.

"Just give me the dress back, and I'll attempt to wipe the slate clean."

"Well," said Julia, "I had a little accident, so I had to change the dress. But you'll like what I did to it."

My little black dress, size 6, was strapless and a glove-tight fit on me—I had no idea how my mother, a size 12, well that's generous, a size 14-16, had thought she was going to squeeze into it. But somehow she packed herself in, and at her party the back seam burst open. She claimed she didn't hear anything, but her butt felt cold. The seam had burst from the middle of her back to below her knees.

"You weren't wearing underwear?" I said.

"I didn't want a visible panty line."

"No nylons with a control top?"

"Too confining."

"So the entire party saw your naked butt?"

"It wasn't all bad," said Julia. "I got a new boyfriend. Roy."
"Congratulations."

Roy lasted three weeks and then stole her George Forman Grill. The dress was irreparably ripped. So Julia, who for as long as I can remember had two seamstresses around to "take in things"—"I might as well show off my best assets"—took it to the German one, Greta, and asked her to repair it. She returned my little black dress with a 12-inch by 36-inch bright pink satin panel in the back where the back seam used to be and a big white ruffle over the butt.

"I see Greta has worked her magic," I said. "It's ruined."

"All the girls are wearing this," said Julia.

"Not the girls under 65," I said. "Take it. I won't wear it. It looks horrible."

"Why are you such a bitch?" she said. "Do you have your period?"

"Just like a sister, she's going to want what looks good on you," said Jennifer.

"Excuse me?" I said.

"Sorry," said Jennifer.

"I'm sure she'd be delighted." I said. "At 57, you'd think she'd stop wearing my clothes. Or at least know what's appropriate."

"Ha," said Jennifer. "Why stop now? Remember Graduation?"

I wish I could forget.

"Don't come. I'll be fine," I had said. "I'm sure that you're busy with other things—you don't even like ceremonies."

"No, I want to come," said Julia. "I've been planning for it."

This was surprising. Julia had been furious when I told her I was going to law school. She felt that I was throwing away the 18 years of expensive violin lessons for which she had paid.

"I won't pay for a damn thing," she said. And she didn't. As I backed out of the driveway to head to law school, car loaded up, she knocked on my window.

"You're making the biggest mistake of your life. You're going to be a terrible attorney—you don't have the brains. You'll end up in some place like Fresno doing tax law. And your thighs will get fat."

The day before graduation from law school, I went to the airport to pick her up. Someone who is almost Julia, only 45 pounds less, with a button for a nose, eyebrows where her forehead would be, kinky hair relaxed, with extensions, and lips—HUGE LIPS—arrived at San Francisco Airport.

Like she had told someone, "Make me into Naomi Judd."

And he did the best he could with her German-Hungarian parts.

And she looked like Naomi Judd—if Naomi Judd played the Borscht Belt and specialized in the beautiful music of Klezmer.

Ashkenazy Naomi Judd—with her 50,000 mile tune-up—waves at me.

She had never, ever had anything but little thin lips. *But she has huge lips.* And she had ponderous gravity defying breasts, which I can see because she's wearing a lime-green halter top and what I guess to be something close to Size 8 black jeans with three-inch mounds of flesh poking out between the top of her pants and the bottom of her halter top—and heels with four-inch spikes on them. Hair long, to the middle of her back, with a high-red gloss to it.

"Good bye, Fritz," she said to some guy who is carrying her bag for her. "Once I get settled, I'll give you a call."

"Hey. Who's this?" said Fritz, gesturing to me—rolling my eyes for the last three minutes.

"This is Courtney," said Julia.

"Cool," said Fritz. "You two gals come on over to my place in Marin. We can go hot tubbing together."

"Ohhh, that sounds like fun," said Julia. "Bye." Fritz walks away.

I'm staring at Julia, trying to decide if this woman really is my mother.

"I don't know what you've done to yourself," I said, "and I'm not going to ask."

Five years later I discovered that she had taken the contents of her IRA—$37,000—and spent it on a remodel of herself.

"But I beg of you, please, please, please, *Mom*, I'm graduating from law school. Please."

It was the first time in thirteen years that I had called her Mom.

"Ok," said Julia, "if little Miss Priss wants me to be good, I'll be good."

Good meant wearing the halter top (no bra) and Size 8 jeans to dinner with my boyfriend, Andre, his mother, Sylvia, and his father, Carl, and endlessly flirting with the militantly gay waiter—"this town has cute men." Good meant wearing my sheer blouse and no bra to graduation—after a 20-minute fight with me.

"Honey, I don't want to wear a jacket. Right at this University, at Sproul Plaza, the Free Speech Movement was invented."

"Julia," I said. "You're going to get arrested."

"Well," she said, "I'm exercising my First Amendment right."

"To do what?" I said. "Ruin everyone's graduation?"

We fought right up to the moment of graduation.

"God, you're a square," she screamed at me.

"You promised," I yelled at her.

"I already told you, I'll be good," she said.

We found a compromise—jacket for the ceremony, bra at the dinner, daisy-shaped nude pasties at the party. But to Julia, good meant, "Umm Courtney, Julia, is dancing in the living room and uh, well...everyone, I mean well, ahh those pasties have moved, and well, I can clearly see her breasts, and how old is she?" said Jennifer.

Age 7.

There is this guy hanging around the house who is not my dad. His name is Big Mike. I'm not sure, but I think that Big

Mike starts coming to our house when my daddy is still in the hospital. My mom tells me that Big Mike is a doctor. I think he is a doctor in the hospital where my dad was.

Big Mike doesn't like to wear a lot of clothes. He likes to walk around our house wearing a little swimsuit—he calls it "a Speedo"—and a knit fisherman's cap. Big Mike comes over a lot when I am asleep.

My mommy is laughing. She is writing down lots of things and making lots of phone calls. She has been like this for days. I ask her, "What are you doing, Mom?"

She giggles. "I'm sooo good at this," she says. She whispers, "I'm a divorce engineer. I engineer divorces."

"What's that?"

"Oh, I'm getting you a new daddy."

Not long after that, we have one of those "Jobs Our Daddies Do" assignments where we stand in front of class and tell a little story about what our daddy does. I tell my first grade teacher, Mrs. Emerson, that I don't have a daddy anymore. Mrs. Emerson tells me, "OK, Courtney, why don't you tell us what your mommy does?" She gives me a few minutes to think about it.

Five minutes later I raise my hand and tell Mrs. Emerson that I am ready.

"Go ahead, Courtney," said Mrs. Emerson.

"My mommy is a dee-vorce engineer."

"She's a divorce attorney?" said Mrs. Emerson.

"My mommy says that Big Mike, her boyfriend, is married. She says she's helping Big Mike get this dee-vorce. My mommy and Big Mike work on that dee-vorce all the time, so even though he's not my daddy, he sleeps at our house a lot. My mommy said that when the dee-vorce is over, Big Mike will be my new daddy."

There is complete silence in the room. I don't understand.

"Oh... The End," I said.

"Thank you, Courtney," said Mrs. Emerson. "Please be seated."

Almost Royalty

Big Julia is summoned to Mrs. Emerson's office, pronto.

Julia glosses over it by telling Mrs. Emerson that I have a good imagination.

One night, I hear Big Mike and Mommy talking when they think I'm asleep. Big Mike is talking very loudly.

It sounds like Mommy is crying.

Big Mike does not become my new daddy.

Big Mike stops coming over.

Age 10.

My mom is sad. She has a lot of boyfriends, but they don't stay around for long. I don't think that they like me. My mom starts going to church to meet people. I go to Sunday school. Sometimes, she goes away with a boyfriend from Friday evening to Sunday night. I ask my mom, "What about church?" My mom tells me to go to church on my own. On Sunday, I walk to Sunday school on my own.

On Easter, I put on my pink dress and walk to Sunday school. I hunt for Easter eggs at the church with the other kids and their parents. My mother is away with the new boyfriend. When she gets home that night, I tell her that I miss her. She is angry. She tells me, "Can't you leave me alone? I need my own social life."

The new boyfriend does not last long. She is sad again.

Age 12.

I am five foot four and weigh 89 pounds. My breasts appear and I try to pretend that nothing has changed by slouching.

One night after I'm in bed, I hear Julia talking on the phone. She's on the phone for a long time. I keep hearing her say, "I won't pressure you, I promise." The next day, Big Mike appears. Julia is happy.

He is older. He wears frayed jeans and T-shirts with holes in them. He sees me and says, "Jesus, look at you." He gives me a big hug, and moves his body around while hugging me, holding on way too long. He sticks his hands up my shirt and pretends to tickle me.

He does this a lot.

I don't like it.

I start to push him when he wants to "just give me a hug."

Julia catches me pushing him away.

She drags me into her bedroom. "If you push him away, he might go and leave us. If he leaves, I'm going to be sad again. You don't want that, do you? Good. Then don't push him away, damn it. He's just showing you that he likes you."

Julia and Big Mike decide to take a trip. Alone. For one week.

Age 15.

It's January. I've gone back East to look at colleges because I am graduating early from high school. My mom convinces me to visit her sister and brother-in-law, Ruth and Ben Stern, in Marblehead, a town outside of Boston. She gives me their phone number. I've never met my Aunt Ruth and Uncle Ben.

I have never met any member of my mother's family.

I call them. They're surprised to hear from me, but they invite me over. I take a bus from Boston to Marblehead.

"Oh my goodness, you look so much like Wendy," says my Aunt Ruth when she sees me. "But blonde."

Wendy, my mom's little sister.

"Your mom and Wendy didn't always get along," said Aunt Ruth.

"Why?" I ask.

Aunt Fran looks at me. "How old are you?"

"Fifteen."

"Well, Wendy was the baby of the family, closest to your mom in age. But she always stole your mom's boyfriends."

Aunt Ruth serves leftovers for dinner. After dinner, she asks me if I would like to see a picture of my grandfather.

She shows me a picture of an old man with a long beard, wearing a small cap over his head. I have seen this kind of cap before.

"Aunt Ruth," I ask, "why is my grandfather wearing a Yarmulke?"

"You don't know?"

I think for a moment. "Oh. My mom...you're not...the Fighting Irish Cohans of Boston?

"Cohen, not Cohan."

"What happened?"

"Your mom wanted to marry a Goy—your dad. She didn't want any problems."

Aunt Fran hands me the phone.

"Call your mother."

I call home. Julia picks up.

"Golda," I say, "when were you going to tell me?"

But now it's Megan's baby shower, which happens after the baby is born because Megan has an emergency C-section and the baby is born early. It's a boy. Aunt Katy has tried to put a good spin on things by inviting every member of the family.

Aunt Katy is the only member of my father's family who tries to include Julia in all family events. When I was a child, we were never invited to any Hamilton celebrations.

Three years ago, I was invited to Aunt Katy's annual Christmas party for the first time. There were a lot of whispers, sighs, and long looks from the Hamilton clan. While exchanging presents, I learned that my father was previously married.

I now have an uneasy feeling that Julia may have been a deevorce engineer for my father, and not just Big Mike.

"Your mother has always been so stylish," says my Uncle Jack.

Julia is wearing my cherry red cocktail dress with the cleavage that goes to her navel. About three weeks after our incident, I went looking for it. I couldn't find it, and tried to remember whether I had taken it to be cleaned. But when I went to deliver my rent check, the manager of my apartment house couldn't look me in the eye and seemed very sheepish.

"Rick," I said, "what's going on?"

She had told him that she had left her glasses in my apartment. He let her in. "I saw her stuff something into her bag," he said.

It's not too pretty; especially because she picks up the baby and holds him against her chest and he thinks it's time to nurse. So the baby tries to latch on to one of her breasts.

"Isn't that sweet," said Julia, as she hands the baby back to Megan as quickly as humanly possible without dropping him.

I sit down and eat some cake. Julia plops down at my table.

"You're looking well," Julia says, "but your hair doesn't have enough blond in it."

"It's my natural color," I say.

"Maybe you should change that," said Julia.

"So Julia," I said sipping punch, "now that you've been kinda a member of the Hamilton clan for over 30 years, do they know that you're Jewish yet?"

"Lower your voice, damn it," said Julia, "these people are highly anti-Semitic."

"Really...what are they, Bay Area Liberals?" I said.

"Very funny," said Julia. "Katy's husband—Charlie, your Uncle Jack, and Grandpa Hamilton—they're members of the Los Angeles Country Club. I'm pretty sure that they still don't let Jews into the Los Angeles Country Club."

"But do they—Aunt Katy, Uncle Charlie, Aunt Betsy, Uncle Jack, Grandma and Grandpa—know that you're Jewish, or are you still pushing that line of crap about your maiden name, Cohen— the fighting Irish Co-hans of Boston?"

"You don't know how hard it was to be accepted by this damn family," said Julia.

"It doesn't look like you're trying too hard to fit in," I said.

"It's been more than 30 years. They have to accept me."

"So why not tell them."

"Does it make any difference to anyone at this point?"

To have the long looks, the knowing silences, the frequent whispers, the turned away faces, the strange questions, the quick glances, the pauses in conversations, the big sighs and the mysterious innuendos explained.

"It would make a difference to me," I said.

And then Julia looked at me. Really looked at me.

"I'll think about it," she said.

"And the dress. Am I getting it back?"

Julia just looked at me. And smiled.

4

Therapy

"Just hold my hand. Tighter. There…doesn't that feel good?" said Roberta.

Roberta was holding my right hand and lightly massaging it. We were having a therapy session. Her face was two inches from mine and she was staring into my eyes.

I looked away so that I couldn't see the scars in her eyelids from her last eye-lift.

Were those new Sally Mann photographs on the walls?

Her hand was flabby, without texture or a discernible trace of a bone in it, greasy from fifteen years of moisturizing with Vaseline Intensive Care.

It felt like I was holding a banana slug.

"Tell me again why we're doing this?" I asked.

I wanted her to let go so that I could take a sip of my Washington Green Apple Tea, which had oozed to the consistency of a 7–Eleven Slurpee.

"You should know by now," said Roberta.

"Well," I said. "I guess I've forgotten."

"You know...well...explaining things...it's not the way I work," said Roberta for the millionth time.

I turned my head away so Roberta wouldn't see me roll my eyes.

I sighed. "Well, maybe today you should because I don't know what I'm doing here," I said.

Roberta gave me a look. I was pretty sure that I had just broken some unwritten rule of therapy such as the Implied Therapist-Patient agreement.

Somewhere during my fifteen years with Roberta, therapy had become a bad habit like Gap Khakis, Starbucks Coffee, and friends who always made you feel depressed. At some point I actually forgot why I was doing therapy.

I think I first entered therapy because I wanted to speak with a sober adult, someone who wasn't trying to rationalize a parenting style that equaled criminal negligence. What I got was Volvo-driving, pot-smoking, vegetarian women, the kind that lived in Santa Monica, Venice, Topanga, or Haight-Ashbury, went to Berkeley instead of Barnard and became Unitarian after being raised Jewish or Episcopalian. They could always be found supporting Save the Whales, Habitat for Humanity and Ralph Nader.

But more to the point, they were a stark contrast with my mother, Julia, something I craved.

In the fall my senior year of high school—actually September—I finished all of my applications for college. I sent out 17 applications, to every conservatory, school of fine arts, or university that I thought had promising violin teachers. I was hoping for at least one early admission.

In December, I got a call from one of the fine art schools. They had a shortage of violinists and "Did I want to come to college early?" They offered me a fairly substantial scholarship.

The school had been started with a radical faculty who thought that they would change the world with their artistic vision—30 years later all they wanted to do was make as much money as possible.

I started the arts school in the winter semester, three months before my seventeenth birthday. Due to all of the acceleration and extra credits from music summer schools, I was graduating early.

As I received my dorm room assignment, a hunk of metal which looked like a fatal car crash in red, yellow, and blue was wheeled to me on a dolly.

"What's this?" I asked.

"This is your furniture," said the dorm registrar.

The dorm registrar gave me a screwdriver, which was to be used to construct the hunk of metal into a bed, a desk, and a chair. I was also given two bright yellow trash baskets that looked like yellow traffic cones.

I wheeled the dolly with the red, yellow, and blue metal hunk and two yellow trash baskets down a long dark hallway and found my room. The metal was surprisingly heavy.

My room was made out of cinder blocks. It looked like an outdoor carport. The floor was covered with green indoor-outdoor carpeting that was mostly stained. There was one light switch for the panel of fluorescent lights that covered the ceiling. The lights hummed when turned on. The bathroom was shared and connected to another dorm room, the occupant of which was an albino lesbian dancer named Kimmy who was studying modern dance. My room overlooked the swimming pool.

No one—other than me—ever bothered to wear a bathing suit to that pool.

"The trash baskets are cute," said Julia, as she gazed out at the numerous naked 18-year-old bodies lounging around the pool.

"I guess," I said. "Do you think you could help me make some furniture out of this metal?"

"You know," Julia said, "I'm kinda hot. Mind if I go for a swim?"

"I'm not sure I have a bathing suit that'll fit you," I said.

"Don't worry about it," she said.

Not six minutes later, I watched as my naked mother did the breast stroke in the shallow end of the pool while simultaneously managing to engage two of the naked 18-year-old boys in conversation.

My roommate was a 25-year-old graduate student from New York. Her name was Bettina. She was in the art school and had recently created a group show in downtown L.A. at the Woman's Village with the Lesbian Women's Art Collective—a collective she had founded.

Bettina was the Queen of the Lesbian Collective. It was her subjective impulses that created the Collective's operating rules.

Admission to the Lesbian Collective was by application only, a review process for which Bettina had final approval. Only those who were militant lesbian-feminists—no guys (the oppressors), no flowery/romantic art (delusional), no make-up or girly clothing (slave garb) were admitted. If you were seen talking to a man for any reason other than necessary functions, wearing a tiny amount of make-up, or behaving in an "oppressed"—traditional female—manner, you were booted from the Collective without warning. For members of the Lesbian Collective, taking classes from male instructors was strictly forbidden.

Of course, Bettina objected to my being her roommate. She called me "a Breeder" because I wasn't a lesbian. But the registrar's office told her that she couldn't select her roommate by sexual orientation, and she either roomed with me or hit the street.

Bettina's show at the Lesbian Women's Art Collective was called "I Do...Not" and was performance art about destroying wedding images—literally. It featured Bettina and her Collective

Lesbians doing things like demolishing engagement rings with sledge hammers, ripping a bridal gown with shears, and smashing a wedding cake with their bare hands while chanting, "I Do… Not." Too bad about the cake—it was chocolate. I went to the show and waited to see if part of it was participatory, like everyone would get a piece of the cake. It wasn't.

But one night Bettina walked in the dorm with her girlfriend, Wanda, wearing the ripped wedding gown and said, "Have a piece of cake."

"Isn't she beautiful?" said Wanda, a welder in the art school. Evidently they all took turns playing the bride with the ripped wedding gown. Whoever played the bride got to take what was left of the cake home that night. Wanda and Bettina left me with the cake while they went for their honeymoon at Wanda's apartment in Van Nuys.

Except for Bettina and Wanda, no one spoke to me outside of class during the first month I was at the school, no one except for this nut on the Theater School Faculty—the dean—who chased me around the school screaming, "Hi Fake!" "Hey Fakie" or "Hello Ms. Fakie."

I couldn't find anything at the school because the administration had decided that signs ruined the visual "flow" of the building. The school itself was built on four straight levels with two central elevators connecting each floor, such that the building could be turned into a shopping center, insane asylum, or a rest home if the school failed.

At first I never saw anyone in the school. At most, I would walk down a hallway and see one person who would scurry down the hallway like a roach that had been exposed to light and would never acknowledge me.

A door would open, I'd wait for a person to appear, and the door would slam shut without anyone materializing. I would walk down empty concrete hallways seeing no one, hearing only the sound of my feet hitting the concrete or the hum of the fluorescent lights. And it was freezing. Although the temperature outside could often go above 105 degrees, the building seemed to have a thermostat that had been permanently stuck at 56.

After four weeks, I finally stumbled into the room where the mailboxes were located. Well, to be honest, it took me three weeks to realize that I had a mailbox, and one week to find it.

The mailboxes were situated in a large windowless room framed by three blank white walls and a solid black floor. The floor had been shined to such a gloss that it reflected the bank of fluorescent lights on the ceiling. No one was in the room when I found it. I found my mailbox, opened it, and sat on the floor to read the four weeks of mail that had accumulated for me.

After about eight minutes of reading I realized that someone was standing over me. I waited for the person to leave. After about two minutes I realized that the person was still in the room.

I looked up and saw a slightly overweight guy with short dark hair wearing a black leather motorcycle jacket, jeans that were ripped at the knee, and sunglasses with mirror lenses. An art school *geek*, trying to look tough.

Damn. Where were those cute gay guys from the theater school?

From the ground, I judged him to be around five foot five. He was leaning against the mailboxes, full of art school pretension. I knew he was going for a look like Erik Estrada in *CHIPS*, one of those retro '70s shows that sporadically appear on Nickelodeon. What he got was more like Barbra Streisand in *Yentl*.

He appeared to be staring at me.

I looked at him for ten seconds. He didn't say anything. I continued reading my mail. About five minutes later, I realized that he hadn't moved. I looked up.

"May I help you?" I said.

"Are *you* Courtney?" he said. I seriously wondered if I should answer this.

"I guess so," I said.

"Hmm. You're the new girl that everyone wants to screw," he said.

He walked out of the room.

Six years later, right after I managed to keep a straight face as his fiancée told me that she wanted "Memories" from the Broadway musical *Cats* and The Pachelbel Canon played at their wedding, Ronald Goldstein paid me $100 not to tell her how he first introduced himself to me.

"Look," he said, "this girl has big tits and likes me. And her dad is loaded. So I don't have to worry about selling my paintings, which even I think are crap, and I don't have to worry about finding booty."

"But Ronald," I said, "you made such an impression."

Right after my mail room introduction to Ronald, I walked back to my dorm room and decided to cook every Velveeta recipe that I had ever eaten. Unfortunately, the cooking equipment I had, a hot plate and toaster oven, was rather limited. However, my repertoire, which included Velveeta junior pizza, Velveeta broccoli-Cheese Nips-casserole, Velveeta enchiladas, Velveeta soup, Velveeta condensed-milk mushroom soup chicken, and Velveeta melt on salmon, was fairly extensive.

Bettina, after deciding that the Velveeta cook-off was not part of some feminist art performance piece about the capitalistic oppression of middle-class moms, was confused. She sat next as me as I thought about my next Velveeta concoction.

"I'm not sure whether I should be repulsed or worried," she said.

"Why? Want some Velveeta?" I said as I cut off a four-by-two-inch cube.

"Do you want to talk to someone?"

"I'm talking to you, aren't I?"

Somewhere in the middle of making Velveeta cheese bread, the dean of the music school knocked on my dorm door.

Almost Royalty

"Courtney," he said. "Are you in there?"

Apparently, my Velveeta bake-off had caused me to miss about ten days of classes. In a school with only nine violinists, this wasn't going unnoticed.

"Won't you open the door so that we can talk?"

"Listen, Dean Henderson," I said. "I'm busy right now."

"So I've heard," he said. "While we all love cheese creations..."

"Not cheese. Velveeta."

"Right," he said. "Velveeta. While we all love Velveeta, I was wondering if you were coming back to class any time soon."

"Well, Dean Henderson, I just need to make a few more things."

That seemed to satisfy him.

While waiting for my Velveeta cheese bread to rise, a towering six foot two Amazon-like woman with spiky magenta-red hair, closely resembling the crown of Woody Woodpecker, walked into my room from the bathroom. She had no boobs and small shoulders, but a thick waist which was balanced by size 18-plus hips and thighs. Her skin was alabaster white but her eyebrows were thick, long, and jet black. Her nose offered a landing spot for a flock of sparrows and her lips were circled with black lip-liner and painted blood-red. She looked like a cross between a middle-aged Elvis Presley with a spiky-punk hairdo and Marilyn Manson at age 48, but she appeared to have taken makeup lessons from Boy George.

She was wearing form-hugging black stretch pants, a scratchy Shetland wool blue and green sweater, black ballet slippers, and drop gold earrings that hung to her shoulder.

I thought that she must be the mom of my suite mate, Kimmy.

"Oh hi," I said. "Kimmy's not here right now."

She peered at me. "Who's Kimmy?"

"Who are you?"

"I'm Roberta. Are you Courtney?"

My recent experience in the mail room had taught me not to answer that question.

"Who wants to know?"

"I'll take that as a yes."

"What do you want?"

"Well, to begin with, this weather is making my hands so dry that I feel my skin is going to shed. Do you have any hand cream?"

I looked around.

"Take this."

I handed her my Vaseline Intensive Care.

"You can keep it. It creeps me out."

She squirted some on her hands and rubbed her hands together. I felt sick. "Hmmmm, Vaseline Intensive Care. I've never thought of that." she said.

"Well, uh Roberta, as you can see, I'm very busy right now. You'll have to excuse me if I don't show you out."

"Well, Courtney, I wasn't planning on leaving right now," she said. "You see, the dean of the music school, and well, your roommate, are worried about you. Would you like to talk to me?"

"Do you have any good Velveeta recipes?"

"I'm not here to talk about that."

"Then I need to get back to work. I have to knead my Velveeta cheese bread."

"Look, Courtney, I'm from the school counseling center. I really want, no, I need, to be present with you right now," said Roberta.

That was the first time I had ever heard that.

"Um Roberta, I have no idea what you just said."

She handed me her card.

"Why don't you come to the school counseling center? We might have some things to work on and we'll…talk."

"I don't think that I have anything to talk about."

She looked at my Velveeta creations.

"Well," she said, "we might. And if you come talk to me, I'll give you my recipe for broccoli and Velveeta soup."

"Really?"

Almost Royalty

"Really."

I still haven't gotten that recipe.

And after fifteen years, I was getting tired of never getting any explanations of "the work" that we were allegedly doing. And I hated that fake hug thing that I had to do when I finished a session or Group.

But the thing I hated most was holding Roberta's hand.

That repulsed me.

"I know you never explain things. I know that's not the way you work. But I've completely forgotten why I'm supposed to sit here and hold your hand for 45 minutes."

"Funny how you always forget when someone wants to show how much they appreciate you," said Roberta, without a hint of sarcasm in her voice.

"The part that doesn't work for me is where I hand you the check for $180 at the close of our time together, twice a week," I said.

Make that twice a week and throw in an extra $40 for Group.

"Why should that negate my feelings for you?" said Roberta.

"Because I feel like I'm paying you to like me," I said.

"I don't see how that makes my feelings any less real," said Roberta without a trace of irony.

"Isn't that another line of work?" I said. "Paying someone to imitate feelings for you?"

"When you say things like that, I feel so sad. I see that I still haven't penetrated your veil of cynicism," said Roberta.

"It's not that I'm cynical, it's just that I have questions," I said.

"That's just it. That's not what our work is about," said Roberta.

"What?" I said.

"Questions," said Roberta.

"Why not?" I said.

Roberta shot me an icy look.

Experience had shown me that Roberta felt I was just inches away from pushing some implied therapy boundary and receiving the resulting penalty.

So who were those mythical people who got to leave therapy with Roberta's blessing?

How does one become "whole" and what did that mean?

When was it that Roberta would tell you "you have no more 'work' to do?"

Was it like a ceremony, with robes, music and inspirational speeches where you were given a certificate that stated that you had now graduated to a perfect life?

Or was it like being before a parole board where someone carefully listened to you accept responsibility for your behavior and then decided whether you should be sprung from therapy-prison?

Fifteen years of therapy, on and off again with Roberta, had convinced me that the whole process was closer to a parole board review.

And like any smart prisoner who was desperate to be released, I knew what I had to do.

I had started lying to her.

Instead of telling her, "I was tooling around Culver City at around one a.m. and needed to score. So, I bought myself a pound of Velveeta at all night Vons," I invented a new scenario. My new scenario featured the person Roberta wanted to see.

I told her, "I was tooling around late, around nine p.m., and I suddenly felt an enormous craving. But like we discussed, I realized that cravings don't last very long. So I drove home, put on the *Lilith Fair: A Celebration of Women in Music* CD, and concentrated on my feelings. The cravings soon passed."

I couldn't look at her after I said these things because I was afraid I would start laughing, so I'd gaze off into space, sigh, and say, "Sometimes it's hard to know what to do."

I knew after I told her what I thought she wanted to hear that her eyes would be glowing. And then she'd say "Do you know how much I'm appreciating you right now?"

This was a problem. Her response completely repulsed me.

But she had a whole range of activities that completely repulsed me.

Tell her, "No, I'm repulsed and feel like bitch-slapping you when you do this," and it was three more years in therapy.

Respond with "I feel so warm when you do this," and you could see the parole board reconvening to consider your early release.

And along with the lying came the language.

There was a special therapy language which I began to understand through Group, a language mainly spoken by the inhabitants of Planet Therapy.

The key phrases were:

(1) **"I don't feel heard"** — "I don't feel heard" meant that the therapy veteran was not persuading anyone of her point or was losing an argument. A smart therapy vet would generally follow that line with a temper-tantrum or a crying jag mixed in with some unintelligible rumbling about "my mother," some mucus, and a nose blow. Endless boxes of Kleenex, the designer ones with little flowers on them, were strategically placed around Roberta's office.

(2) **"I don't feel seen"** — "I don't feel seen" was something Roberta would say right after she had said something so remarkably stupid that I had shot her a "You Moron" look. A therapy vet—such as Frank—would generally use this line during a time when their behavior was completely irresponsible, like during those 72-hour periods when Frank would lose himself—and his wages—in a 24-hour casino off the 710 Freeway or at the nearest Indian Res.

(3) **"Work"** as in, "This is our work" or "Look how much work she/he is doing." I realized that Roberta—or therapists in gen-

eral—referred to therapy sessions as "work" because they got paid very well for it. And maybe early on, I thought there was some connection between therapy "work" and becoming successful in "work." Work—something I got paid for—which was a result that I desired. But as I put in my time on Planet Therapy, a question about the kind of "work" we were doing began to evolve: For my "work" to be completed, was I expected to become a mini-version of Roberta and parrot Planet Therapy speak without thought?

(4) **"I take responsibility for it"** — "I take responsibility for it" was the one phrase that could be used to exonerate all behavior from bestiality to premeditated murder. It was a therapy incantation. Once said, it was as if the reprehensible behavior had magically disappeared or self-corrected.

Too many times in Group, I saw someone admit, "Yes, I got drunk and slept with my daughter's boyfriend. But I take responsibility for it." Unfortunately, it never quite worked for me because I never understood how that magic phrase was equivalent to correcting the horrific behavior, especially when the person who had just uttered their "responsibility" line didn't actually seem to feel guilty or even remorseful.

And that's when I would get in trouble. Because after the person would utter the hallowed, "I take responsibility for it," I would—according to Group—be judgmental. I would ask, "How? How do you take responsibility for it?"

Roberta didn't like that. She really didn't like that. She seemed to always add an additional six months to my Therapy Sentence by adding to the chorus of screaming Group members.

"Courtney," she'd say, "can't you see how much work she's doing? She just took responsibility for getting drunk and sleeping with her daughter's boyfriend."

"How? How is she taking responsibility for it," I'd ask. "Don't you think what she did is disgusting?"

Roberta would always give me an icy glance and say, "That's very judgmental."

"Ok..." I'd ask, "but has she apologized to her daughter?"

And Roberta, without missing a beat, would always respond, "That's irrelevant to our work here."

I knew which lie I was supposed to tell. I was expected to say "Yes" when asked, "Can't you see how much work she's doing?" But occasionally I would forget and be honest about my feelings. In those moments, I would reply, "No, I really don't see how much work she's doing." Then Roberta would reward my honesty by throwing me out of Group for an alleged violation of the Implied Therapist-Patient-Group Agreement.

Of course, there was also Roberta-Speak, a sub-dialect of therapy so obscure that the ancient language of the Incas would have seemed accessible by comparison.

"The Group is feeling a primitive pain."

"You've lost the way back to your emotional home."

"You've violated:

(1) the Implied Therapist-Patient Agreement;

(2) the Implied Group Agreement;

(3) the Implied Therapist-Patient-Group Agreement."

What did any of this mean?

Don't think that I didn't try to find out. During many sessions with Group, I would confess that I didn't understand what any of this jargon meant.

That was a mistake.

Group would respond with a series of snickers. Roberta would consider my confession an act of aggression, and always say, "It means whatever you want it to mean."

5

Testosterone Poisoning

"You're not the best-looking woman I've ever slept with," said Dr. Ted. "I know you think you are. But you're not."

Dr. Ted and I were having coffee at one the four unavoidable coffee franchises on San Vicente Blvd. This franchise actually knew that its coffee sucked and had just attempted to retrain its baristas. This was definitely an interesting choice for a conversation starter. But I had no idea what he was talking about.

"You know there are these actress-models, well, they're out here for a while, and maybe they're 27, 28…sick of waitressing and know they aren't gonna be a star… I'm beginning to look pretty good to them," said Dr. Ted, "because I'm a doctor."

"Yes you are, Ted," I said. "You're a doctor with a leased Mercedes. How's that working for you?"

Ted looked at me.

"I'll bet I'm even beginning to look pretty good to you," he said.

I was hoping we could have a friendship. Guess not.

It appeared that Dr. Ted had a bad case of T.P.—better known as Testosterone Poisoning—that lethal combination of money, career success, and newfound entitlement which transformed former male dorks into pure monsters.

Dr. Ted had classic Testosterone Poisoning. He had clearly been a kid who hadn't had a shot at the popular girls and burned with resentment thinking how "he'd show them."

In L.A., a town where being male and straight made him very eligible, he was having some success with women. What made him stand out from the rest was that he was: (1) educated and finished with his education (i.e. some poor woman/partner would NOT be required to put him through med school by waitressing at Norms; (2) currently employed with a visible means of support other than parental hand-outs; and, (3) unless he succumbed to professional burn-out or some latent desire to be an Olympic Curler, he had a definable career path that did not include the unlikely careers of rock star, movie/television star, or Calvin Klein underwear model. Of course, those *ER* and *Grey's Anatomy* writers who had first been M.D.s always made you wonder if there was a secret passion to be a screenwriter—currently in remission—that was hidden under that M.D. veneer.

But when I first met him I felt sorry for him. He had a really red face, like a newborn baby. He had acne scars, deep pits covering four inches on each side of his face, from jaw to cheekbone. His eyes were tiny, mud-brown, and hidden behind the thickest uni-brow west of Zagreb. He wore glasses, heavy glasses, with thick lenses. His hair was a coarse, unruly, dark brown/black that required a glob of styling gel and 30 minutes with a blow dryer to control. His clothes, striped colored pants and a bright colored T-shirt, were too tight, indicating a fight with his weight, a fight he had clearly won and lost, gaining and losing the same 35 pounds over and over.

He had a very low voice and mumbled when he spoke, never looking me in the eye, because one eye didn't seem to go straight.

"What?" I said.

He had come over one night when I was packing up to move out of my apartment. I was listening to music.

"I like this music," he said.

"You like Bartok's Concerto for Orchestra?" I said.

"Yeah. Can I come in and listen?"

"Sure."

We sat and listened for about two minutes.

"I really like this..." I said.

But before I could get to "part" he had grabbed my arms, pulled me toward him and lifted my shirt.

"You want this, don't you."

I jumped backwards.

"What are you doing?" I said.

"Stop playing games. You know you want it."

"I think you have me confused with someone you met...in your head."

"You can't deny that you sense the attraction. You send me these signals—you like me all right, I can see it in your eyes—and then you won't touch me."

"Those are generally the opening lines for a statutory rape conviction. Has this ever worked for you? Really?"

Ted let go of me and sat down.

"Sometimes. Girls still go for that 'gonna be a doctor' thing," he said.

In an alternate universe.

But then again...

"I might have some vile friends who would go for your 'doctor' thing," I said.

"Yeah?" said Ted.

One friend. The only friend who would think that dating a doctor would raise her position on her Eco-Chain.

Marcie.

"There's this weird guy, you know, Ted," I said.

"The med student," said Roberta during a session, "he really admires you—didn't he ask you to show him the CDs you liked?"

"Yeah," I said. "He's a resident now. But I don't know about the admiration."

Roberta looked at me. "Does it make you uncomfortable when someone expresses their admiration for you?" she said.

Ugh. I hated this particular line of Roberta's questioning, because I knew that Ted has no admiration for me. But if I told her that, this would start a year of "work" with Roberta on my low self-esteem. The easiest way out was to find a middle ground. "I don't know," I said. "Maybe."

"What's making this so difficult for you?" said Roberta. I wanted to tell her that what was making this so difficult was that she was completely wrong about Ted.

I looked Roberta in the eye and attempted to convince her that I was seriously considering her analysis of Ted. "Well," I said, "we were listening to the music. And then he put his hand down my shirt and pulled my breast out. And I shoved him away."

Roberta was silent.

"I think he's kind of an asshole," I said.

"You're awfully judgmental. He appreciates your ripe womanhood," said Roberta.

Ted calls.

"Here's something that may interest you, Miss Know-it-all," said Dr. Ted, the resident. "The administrator of my residency kinda likes me, so she started watching out for me. She told me who to suck up to, when I was getting into trouble, what jobs are opening up—that kind of stuff. So I pulled her into a closet and nailed her."

"Wrong," I said.

"What do you mean?" said Dr. Ted.

"I'm not interested. But for the sake of argument, was she into it?" I asked.

"It happened so quickly I don't think she knew what hit her. But she won't dare talk about it. She's married."

And later.

"Now that I'm a doctor, there's this nurse I work with who likes me," said Dr. Ted.

"Yeah..." I said.

"So I asked her if she wanted to go out with me."

"That's good. Is she nice?" I said.

"I dunno. So we went out to eat like it's a date, you know, nothing expensive, just pizza. And I had one of my friends, a buddy, meet us. So she's really excited because she thinks it's a date. Like, she's on a date with a doctor, and he invited his friend because she's special or something. And we all get really drunk. And then we went back to my place."

"We?" I said.

"My friend. The nurse. And me," smirked Dr. Ted.

"I don't think I want to know what happens next."

"Sure you do."

"No, I don't. You have a bad case of Testosterone Poisoning."

"What?"

"I'm going to hang up now. If you think that you need to talk with someone about this, find an online friend with a web-cam who'll be yours after your credit card clears PayPal."

As I hang up the phone, Dr. Ted barks out a term which I pray, for once, that my excellent long-term memory will allow me to forget.

6

The Zen of Fraud

I remember a time when the news was about distant people whom I would never know. I liked that time because I could pretend that those distant people had great lives and heroic qualities that made them seem so much better than me.

I remember one story I heard about the first family of American politics: They all spoke French at the dinner table. That seemed so incredible, so special, so amazing to me. Later, when they all grew up to bad marriages, tragic accidents, drug addiction, and squandered privilege, it made me sad. I missed the time when I thought that they would escape the disappointments which defined my life. I missed the time when I thought that they lived in a special world. I missed the time when I thought that they were better than me.

I missed my innocence.

So when I discovered that the dermatologist who had worked on my face with a laser was the star of an article entitled "Doctors and Demerol," it wasn't entirely surprising.

Who was real anymore?
Who actually was what they were hyped in the press to be?
Who delivered on those incredible publicist-planted stories?

The Zen of Fraud, a term uttered between my friends when the most highly publicized success story turned out to be the worst possible nightmare, was, once again, the most truthful description of my dermatologist.

I had come to the dermatologist, Dr. Laser, for a little problem which had bugged me forever. I had lived with this problem for my entire life, and since the age of eleven—for 24 years—had visited ten different doctors for ten different treatments. Each treatment had been a complete failure.

Due to the skill of her publicists, Dr. Laser's reputation was that of a modern-day Renoir. If anyone could get rid of it, smooth it out, or freshen it up, she could. Her specialty was the Laser, a recent technology in its most refined stage. Dr. Laser's trick was to blast the Laser on a tomato to demonstrate how proficient and skilled she was. Of course, that tomato always remained pristine and blemish-free.

I was different than most of Dr. Laser's patients. The majority of them came to her because they wanted to look like this year's version of beauty. They were there to eliminate hooked, big or wide noses, hooded eyes, receding chins or any genetic feature which was not currently popular. Unfortunately, most of the plastic surgeons, including Dr. Laser, were beginning to be a little too successful at their work. I knew that because the women on the Westside—especially the young actresses—had all begun to look very similar to each other.

At my first appointment, the waiting room was crammed full of patients, the phone was ringing off the hook, and six nurses worked like traffic cops to direct the flow of patients.

But the day I appeared for my procedure, there was nothing but silence in her office.

"Hello?"

I walked past the in-take desk.

I walked down the dark hallways of her medical suite.

I walked past the empty, dark, exam rooms.

I found a woman lifting weights in one of the supply rooms.

"Go into any room and sit down. Don't worry, the doctor will find you."

I turned the lights on in an exam room and read a book.

Forty-five minutes later Dr. Laser walked in wearing a T-shirt and stained sweat pants.

I thought it was strange.

Dr. Laser did a decent job on me. Her follow-up, a 15-second exam done by her assistant at a parking lot under the Century City Mall, was a bit dicey.

Then the article "Doctors and Demerol: The tragedy of Dr. Laser" came out. As I read the article, many of her other patients had not been as fortunate as I had: They were seared to a pulp and scarred.

Apparently, seven days before my appointment, she had purchased the equivalent of 822 individual doses of Demerol. Three days after my appointment, she purchased at least 950 more individual doses. During this same month, she had filed for bankruptcy. Investigators had gone to her office and found a soup pot of syringes and empty drug ampules covered with mold. In her home they found "insect infestation," numerous syringes and needle caps under cushions, on the floor, in a shopping bag, and behind a couch.

After I read the article, I called my friend Gabe. "I think we have a clear winner for this year's Zen of Fraud."

"No—someone who has so exceeded our extremely low standards that you would dare to select a winner in the second quarter of the year?"

"This is special."

The Zen of Fraud.

I think this category came about because Gabe and I worked in the same industry and were so amazed by the range of amoral scum we encountered.

Just when we thought that we had found the worst monster possible, someone more disgusting would appear. Thus the Zen of Fraud became a competition to see who had met the most arrogant wind-bag of hypocrisy, like the "genius" hedge fund manager who criticized your business practices and then stole the life savings of his retired clients, or the "hot" agent who blamed you for not doing more for a client and then destroyed the client's career because he couldn't control his own prescription drug addiction.

And I thought that Dr. Laser was my winner for the year.

That is until I saw Jon Gene Jenny, the former dean of the theater school where I did my undergraduate work, stride across the stage to accept his award at the Emmys.

In some bizarre turn of events, one of my clients had managed to get himself nominated for an Emmy. Even more unusual was the fact that my client felt some gratitude toward me for the three years of unpaid legal work. He asked me to accompany him to the awards ceremony. The ceremony was fatally boring.

However, when Jon Gene Jenny's name was called, I was suddenly thrown into an alternate universe where people I knew were accepting awards in nationally-televised ceremonies for things other than a stint in Celebrity Rehab.

Jon Gene Jenny, or "Genie," was more of a guru than a teacher. At age 49, he had taken over the theater school in a time of disarray and thus was given free rein to do whatever he wanted with it, as long as he fixed it. His theater school was the mirror image of his psyche: one-third cult, one-third Midwest theater philosophy, and one-third unresolved anger over every insult that he had ever suffered in high school and not yet worked out with his therapist.

Almost Royalty

Genie looked like a cross between a bantam rooster and Bette Davis in *Whatever Happened to Baby Jane*. He was five foot two of muscle with a 52-inch chest and a head cascading with graying blond ringlets that covered his electric-blue eyes. Given his looks and girth, he never wore conventional clothing. His typical outfit consisted of food-stained sweatpants coordinated with psychedelically colored suspenders covering a lavender or black T-shirt.

Clearly, Genie had been a dork in high school, someone who had suffered for his looks and devotion to theater. Now he had a virtual playground on which to torment whatever unsuspecting female student fell into his web.

It was frightening to watch Genie put those 18-year-olds through his sieve. He purposely kept the theater students isolated from the other students at the school. He told them that if they mixed with the other students, their work would be "diluted" and they would never have a life in the theater. Naturally, this had the effect of making them all sleep with each other and turning the atmosphere into a hotbed of gossip and intrigue.

Genie also kept his students ridiculously exhausted: No matter what the weather, they were outside doing Tai Chi at six a.m. At night, if they weren't rehearsing a production, those students, who were paying $38,000 per year in tuition alone, were ordered to do menial tasks like scrape gum off the floor of a 2000-seat theater until 10 p.m., Monday through Friday.

In Genie's program, women who were good-looking in a conventional sense were slightly tainted, or "bad," or automatically branded as "artificial." It was impossible to play a female lead in any of his productions unless you were extremely plain with six inches of cellulite hanging off your butt. He punished the good-looking ones by making them wear ridiculous costumes in minor roles that did nothing more than humiliate them. This, obviously, was nothing more than revenge for him.

I remember seeing a poor blonde girl who had the genetic misfortune, in Genie's world, to be strikingly beautiful. In typical

Genie fashion, he cast her as a spear carrier in his original interpretation of *Antigone*. Her costume consisted of a silver Harpo Marx wig, a tiny butt-slicing thong, and a tube top, which was purposely cut too small so that if she moved her right arm, her right boob would pop out.

Of course, he slept with all of the pretty ones. His line was that he was "going to show them what it was to be alive." And not just the ones in the theater school. He once tried to hook-up with me at a party with this "going to be alive" line. When I told him that I knew what it meant to "be alive" and that meant that I had to go do my laundry, he called me a "Fake," a plastic fake person who only wanted to be with non-real pretty boys. He called me that every time he saw me for the remaining three-plus years until I graduated, often yelling "Hey Fake!" across the cafeteria, or "Hi Fakie," if he found me in the library, "There's the Fake, hi Fakie!" if he saw me off campus.

But something about me must have resonated with him. Maybe it was my refusal to buy his lines. Maybe it was the fact that clearly I wasn't interested. Maybe it was that I was sixteen years old and I was challenging him, or simply, a challenge.

Genie managed to get one of his theater students with a work-study job in the registrar's office to give him my schedule and personal data, information which included my dorm room, car license-plate number, and phone number.

He appeared twice, sometimes three times a day outside my classes to tell me, "Tonight, you and me, Fakie." He knocked on my dorm room door at night whispering to my closed door, "C'mon Fakie—let's do it." He left notes for me on the windshield of my car which said, "Get Real Fakie—I'm Waiting for You."

Although obsessive, Genie's behavior was not unusual for some of the faculty members at the art school. Sleeping your way through the student body—or should I say, student bodies—was a rite of passage for some of the faculty, a passage which occasionally included dumping your current wife and marrying one of your students, who, on average, was 30 years younger than the faculty member.

Almost Royalty

Everyone knew about the music teacher who would sneak up on his students and fondle their breasts as they played. My own violin teacher had dumped three wives, one of them a previous student, during his ten-year teaching career. And the member of the administration who always managed to have the best-looking male students as his chauffeurs, a work/study job, was well known for his pretty-boy taste.

Personally, I was mostly annoyed, and occasionally terrified, by Genie's behavior. But I think even he knew his behavior had crossed the line on that Saturday night during March of my first year when he started banging on my door at 3:40 a.m. and began screaming, "Fakie—Open the Door." This went on for 23 minutes, and then he started throwing the furniture in the lounge near my room—a television, an ash-tray, a chair—against my door. When the off campus police responded to my call at 4:15 a.m. and took him away, it seemed to slow him down.

"Why did you call the police?" said the dean of the music school after I was summoned to his office. "You know, that's Genie. Boys will be boys."

"He's just having a little fun," said Roberta after I told her that Genie frightened me. "Don't be so judgmental."

Not long after that, he attached himself to some 19-year-old female directing student, a tiny girl with a head full of bright red ringlets who always wore jeans, white baker's smocks, and knee-high black leather boots with four-inch heels. She was a transfer from NYU who had crossed the country to work with Genie because she thought he was a genius.

The directing student kept him busy for a while. Between juvenile victims, Genie made hounding me a sport. Fortunately, there were enough innocents around to regularly supply him with fresh meat.

It was a lot of activity for a guy who was allegedly the Dean of the theater school, for whom 50 aspiring actors in their late teens and early twenties had entrusted their parents' life savings and their training in the dramatic arts. I remember wondering how any of them were going to make a living at this on a day when I watched Genie's students learn how to emote expression in an exercise in which they all played clams at the bottom of the ocean. And the answer, of course, was that none of them would. As I learned later, Genie's theater school philosophy was "we give you the desire, and you find the technique." And unfortunately, none of them found it.

In addition to the fact that few of them learned any technique, Genie actively discouraged his students from getting work in the entertainment industry by letting people know that they were "sellouts" for working in that materialistic world. The few students who did get work because they were too pretty not to be noticed by agents were punished by being thrown out of the program. In retrospect, these were the only students who ended up with careers in the industry. The rest became the word processors, waiters, and retail clerks of the world.

The irony of the situation was that while Genie actively discouraged his students from seeking work in the "plastic of tinsel town," he, and the rest of the faculty, were all over it. I remember watching TV and seeing a strange guy in a non-verbal role as a bailiff on some network Lawyer/Police show and thinking, "Hmmm, there must have been something to that clam training, because that was Genie." Or, while sitting in a bar, you'd catch a few seconds of some TV show and realize that the tubby waitress on the screen who just served coffee and maybe uttered the line "Non-fat latte, extra foam," was the world renowned expert on "Emotion through African Masks" who had been teaching at your school for 15 years. It was funny: the prestigious theater faculty of the school who had their books, theories, and New York or Chicago theater experience were the day players of the entertainment industry. And if you looked quickly and didn't turn your head, you could find them choking out lines like "Here's your drink," or "Your order's up."

Sometime after Genie's theater book, *I Experience It Therefore I Am It,* was published and the theater school went to some festival in New York where it proceeded to lose its accreditation, I heard that Genie had decided to "create productions" with the most Hollywood of all creatures. As it turned out, one of his former students from the ice age of his teaching days in the Midwest had become an enormous television star, creating such a hit that he would forever be remembered for this one particular character. After a lifetime of staging *Waiting for Godot* with 18-year-olds fresh off the bus from Wisconsin and at best, making a mid-five-figure income, it must have done something to him to see his former student with no possibility of an economic problem for the next three generations. That's when Genie decided that Hollywood, after everything was said and done, was not looking too bad after all. And so he hung up his suspenders and sweatpants.

It was around this time that our paths began to cross a little bit. I think that I began to catch glimmers of him running around in the trendy restaurants where I was forced to go to satisfy my clients after their first big deal came through. Later, I would see him at all of the premieres. Not long after that, I discovered that he and his production company were being represented by the most aggressive agency in town, an agency that had been thought to control the entertainment industry in the early '90s.

The most startling moment came when I started getting phone calls from the Stepford D- (D for Development) Girls at his production company. They wanted to go to lunch with me to find out more about my clients and how we could do business together.

"Do business together?" I asked one of them named "Autumn" who called to introduce herself. "You work for the Jon Gene Jenny who wrote *I Experience It Therefore I Am It*?"

"That was a previous lifetime. Jon Gene..."

"Genie..."

"Jon Gene just got a first look deal."

"Ugh..."

"What?"

"Oh."

Over the course of a decade Genie, alias "Jon Gene," had learned the ropes of the entertainment industry well enough that he had finally found a literary property concerning a historical tragedy that had taken place so long ago that it wasn't going to ruffle anyone's feathers and yet, the industry would congratulate itself for making it. Then he attached himself to it as a "producer." And somehow, despite all of the managers, agents, studios and other forces that had become involved in the project, he managed to stay involved enough in the project that he was the person who walked across the stage to pick up the award with the major star who also had produced it.

The world was not meant for people with excellent long-term memories. For those of us cursed with this particular genetic mutation, you can never see a person in the present moment without remembering your feelings about that person when you last saw them, as if it were yesterday, and not ten years ago, that you wanted to tell them that you would rather jump into a bucket of your own bile than speak to them again.

Even as I moved through my mid to late teens at a school which I knew would be the last outpost of my childhood, I somehow knew that Genie was squandering the precious years of his students' educations with his endless exercises and humiliations. Under the guise of "the training in theater," his program was nothing more than a sandbox for him to work out his inner demons in a human lab of 18–22-year-olds. In exchange, those students who had blindly followed him were guaranteed to graduate with no skills, some misguided theories, and debt that was so enormous that they would be servicing it well into middle age.

As I stood with my client at the reception after the awards ceremony and tried to avoid Genie, I didn't know how to react when I saw him striding toward me, a bantam rooster in an Armani Tux. But that didn't stop him.

I felt like throwing up.

"Well, if it isn't little Miss Fake. All grown-up and wearing black. Aren't we a little professional robot now," said Genie.

"I'm gonna go get a drink," said my client, who was beginning to have a relationship with alcohol that was more than social.

Just then, a waiter came by with a tray of hors d'oeuvre.

"Oh look," I said to Genie while gesturing to the waiter, "another successful graduate from your program."

"Well, well," he said, "tell me again what mindless occupation you've put yourself in? Oh, that's right—you've sold out and became an attorney. Such an appropriate profession for you."

"I'm sorry," I said. "My ambitions ran deeper than becoming an assistant with an MFA from your world-renowned theater arts program."

"Don't go away. I'm not done with you," he growled as he walked over to hug the female lead in his production.

As I watched him work the room, I looked for my escape. The bathroom looked likely. My client, who had discovered that he didn't have to pay for the drinks, was endlessly exploring the possibilities of an open bar.

I glanced back at Genie and saw that he was pressing the flesh with a group of baby-agents who had just made their highly publicized exit from their monolith parent agency and started their own boutique agency. Then I made a run for it.

"You can go to the bathroom later—now we're going to talk," Genie said as he pushed me into a corner. Funny how fast that little guy could move.

"Genie," I said, "what do we have to say to each other?"

"Well F...I mean Courtney...it is Courtney, isn't it?" he said as he smiled and revealed a set of choppers that had been permanently stained by over 40 years of daily hits on a bong. "I want to show you what it is to be alive."

Oh no. His lines hadn't even changed. And it still had the same result. I was suddenly seized with the knowledge that I had to go do my laundry.

"Genie," I said, "enough. You used that line on me over ten years ago. Did that ever work on anybody?"

"You bet," he said. "Why do you think I kept using it all these years?"

"Who would fall for that?" I said.

"What do you mean?" said Genie. "It was so easy. Maybe a girl say…was a little depressed, or missed mom and her boyfriend back home where she had been the star of her high school play… or maybe had just realized that she was young, fresh and pretty but so were the other 5,000 girls who got off the bus here every year… You don't think that some of them wouldn't jump at the chance to maybe help their career out a little bit by spending the night with a person who was powerful and connected?"

"Oh, I get it. It's a numbers game. But who was the powerful and connected person in this equation?"

"Bitch," he said.

"How many people have you used this line on tonight?" I asked.

"I didn't stop to count," he said.

"What a surprise."

"Damn. You still think too much," he said.

If that wasn't the classic line that every guy used when his attempts to hustle a girl were going south.

"Let me recount the obvious to you," he said raising his voice, and attracting a little more attention than I had hoped to get. "I just won an Emmy. And not just any Emmy, but one that counts. And I'm here alone. And by the looks of things, your escort, the one that's over there dismantling the celery sculpture, is more interested in eating for a week than anything that could happen with you tonight." I looked over to find my client eating the center of the vegetable display.

Almost Royalty

"And to be honest with you, Fakie, um, Courtney, I think you're special," he said.

"The bathroom," I said. "I really need to go to the bathroom." I struggled out of his grasp, spilled half my drink on him, and bolted into the bathroom.

Inside, it was impossible to see anything—it was packed, the lights were dim, and all of the approximately 50 women circling around the bathroom mirrors were wearing spaghetti-strap clingy little black dresses, push-up bras, beige lipstick, and four-inch stiletto heels—which brought them up to the imposing height of five foot four.

Oh No.

I was trapped in a bathroom with The Stepford D-Girls from Hell.

The Stepford D- (D for development) Girls from Hell were the mutant troops of women working in the entertainment industry who had the mind-numbing job of finding fresh new writers or hot new literary materials that could possibly be developed into a feature film or television series. They generally worked for abusively awful people who were nothing short of insane in a career which involved endless breakfasts, lunches and dinners with anyone who could help them keep their jobs. They always had two-syllable porn names like Amber or Kara, aspired to Armani but could only afford Forever 21, and seemed to be of the same uniform height and weight with the same long, straight hair which fell to the middle of their back and was parted in the middle. And as they all frequented the same plastic surgeons, they all had the same cheeks, noses, and ridiculously symmetrical facial structure which masked any individuality and made them—despite race or ethnicity, which ranged from Ireland to Sierra Leone—look the same.

But they were not depressed. They were suicidally cheerful. Of course, they all took Prozac.

I drank what was left of my drink, hoping to numb what might be coming next. It wasn't working. I thought about spending eternity in a bathroom stall, and then realized it was better to face Genie than die from overexposure to D-girls.

I walked out...and straight into Josh.

"Oh..." I said. "Hi."

"Courtney," Josh said. "Can I get you something to eat?" he said while holding up a plate of buffalo wings.

"Please," I said, "if you have a shred of humanity in you, help me. There's a bad memory walking around here, and I need an escape."

"Sorry. I'm here with somebody," he said, looking a little sheepish.

Just then, a woman wearing a spaghetti-strap clingy little black dress with pushed-up cleavage, beige lipstick, and four-inch stiletto heels which brought her up to the imposing height of five foot four came over and attached herself to Josh's arm. These D-Girls were everywhere.

"Hi," she said. "I'm Cody."

"Congratulations. I'm in hell," I said. Just then, Genie saw me and walked straight over.

"Here comes my bad memory," I said.

"Could I borrow your friend for a minute," Genie said as he yanked me aside.

"Help!" I mouthed to Josh and Cody.

"Let's go," said Genie as he shuttled me toward the door. Out of nowhere, my client appeared.

"I'm ready to go now," he said.

"Take a bus, junior. She's with me," Genie growled and dragged me toward an exit littered with extension cords.

I tripped over a cable and hit a tray of stuffed mushrooms, which drenched a group of Stepford D-Girls. Genie dragged me four feet before he released me.

Three hundred people turned and watched us, a silence punctuated only by the sound of a cocktail glass hitting the ground.

"Courtney, could we go home now?" said Josh and Cody, appearing at my side.
"What's this? A carpool to the Emmys?" said Genie.
"Kinda." I said.
Genie shook his head and let out a sound of disgust. "Nice try," he said.
Josh and Cody began herding me toward an exit. "I'm going," I said.
Genie shook his head right-left and frowned in disapproval, "Too bad. I could've given you the night of your life."
I sighed with relief. "That's what I'm afraid of," I said.
Genie grabbed my arm as I began walking away. "Remember," he said, "I know how to find you."

Josh and Cody were kind enough to escort me and my client to our car.
"I owe you."
"That's right," said Josh.
Genie must have struck gold with his "alive" line, because I saw him walk out with a girl wearing a spaghetti-strap clingy little black dress with pushed-up cleavage, bright lipstick, and four-inch stiletto heels which brought her up to the imposing height of five foot four, an inch shorter than Genie.
"I really had a good time tonight," said my client as I drove him home. "Would you like to do this again?" he asked.
"No, I wouldn't."
I left him off at his apartment in the Fairfax and waited until he safely got in the front door. He stumbled in. I'm sure he spent the next two hours barfing up the vegetable display.

7

The Eco-Chain of Dating

Most people love San Francisco. I think it's a retirement community for people in their early thirties. I don't know why, but once my friends move to San Francisco they end their careers as investment bankers, attorneys, and doctors and act like retired people: The men become samba dancers who compete internationally at the amateur level, BuJews (Jewish Buddhists) who study yoga and vegetable preparation, or acrobats who learn juggling and balloon-sculpturing before running away to join the circus. By contrast, my female friends have their own version of SF retirement: They become steroid-taking body-builders who pump iron and compete in the Ms. Universe Circuit or dance choreographers who recreate indigenous Native American dances and other lost sacred folk rituals, or ranchers, dairy farmers or organic produce growers in lesbian-only farm collectives that always fail after 18 months.

But one thing really bothers me about San Francisco. Every time I visit, some recent transplant who thinks that they're special just because they live there starts the same argument that I've heard over a thousand times: San Francisco vs. L.A.—Why San Francisco is better. And occasionally I run into someone so ridiculous that they actually want to fight with me just because I live in L.A. And when I tell them, "Look, we don't care. We like San Francisco. It's a *very* pretty food court," it just makes them crazy.

I had flown up to San Francisco to go to Jennifer's housewarming party which conveniently happened right after the Emmys, a moment when I desperately needed a retreat from my L.A. life. God knows why, but Jennifer had decided to move to San Francisco. Actually, I know why.

L.A. is the kind of town that people are always leaving, as if the ultimate act of maturity is to surrender the year-round beautiful weather for some destination that is more "real"—where you can experience the seasons—like Seattle, Boston, or Phoenix. However, once the ex-Angeleno discovers that "real" means 320 overcast–rainy days per year and bi-polar depression (Seattle), three months of bad weather and nine months of winter (Boston), or 150 days per year where you could fry an egg on your driveway (Phoenix), they tend to return. Quietly.

Although a native of L.A., Jennifer had issues with the national perception of Los Angeles. It bothered her that her home town was associated with the many exploding controversies of Rodney King, O. J. Simpson, Monica Lewinsky and the Menendez Brothers. It disturbed her that L.A., a city which thrived off an industry based upon illusion, had given Arnold Schwarzenegger a context in which to create his political viability as a candidate for public office—as a *Republican*. Finally, it just killed her when she realized that L.A. would never be considered cool (like Seattle), or important (like New York), or desirable (like Boulder): It would only be considered superficial.

Not long after that, she bought a two-story flat in San Francisco with Kevin, a classmate from law school. She lived in the upstairs, he lived downstairs.

Kevin was a partially domesticated animal in that he knew enough to buy a flat, but thought that he should furnish his little condo (currently worth $1,000,000) with his childhood bunkbed and an abandoned futon which he found on the street. He was also that unusual breed of San Francisco male who considered himself a member of the counter-culture while earning $675,000 per year working as a corporate transactions associate in the law firm which had produced most of Ronald Reagan's Kitchen Cabinet.

The worst day of Kevin's life was the day Jerry Garcia died. He insisted, despite all reports to the contrary, that Jerry died of "natural causes." Kevin never recovered, and soon, very soon, he too would retire: He wanted to quit practicing law to teach drumming classes in male-bonding groups.

I wasn't a big Kevin fan. To begin with, he had his own very specific criteria for dating women, which Jennifer and I referred to as "The List."

She couldn't live in Los Angeles.

She couldn't be taller than he was.

She couldn't drink—at all.

She couldn't make any decision, even a minor decision such as "turn left here" in the relationship.

She couldn't work in a job that he didn't like—or at all—if he didn't want her to work.

She couldn't eat meat, cheese or carbs—carbs were for losers.

She couldn't be a lawyer.

She couldn't make more money than he did.

She couldn't ever get to his money.

She couldn't be more than five years older/younger than his age.

She couldn't be religious, but had to be spiritual.

She couldn't be concerned about her physical appearance.

She couldn't wear makeup.

She couldn't just be pretty—she had to be *naturally* beautiful.

Of course he ended up alone. But there was one other reason I didn't like him. I didn't like his friend…make that closest friend. Because that best friend was my ex-fiancé, Andre.

Andre was the most ambitious person that I had ever met. He had to be. He had never quite gotten over how promising his future looked from high school. Boy most likely to succeed. Eagle Scout. Editor of the school paper. Captain of the swim team. Recruited by Stanford, Princeton, Yale, Dartmouth, and Harvard. By the time I met him at law school, Andre had gone through four careers.

Film Critic.

Art instructor.

Commodities Broker.

Steel Manufacturer.

He was 32. He knew more about French Burgundy than anyone I had ever met and endlessly lectured everyone on the proper techniques for tasting wine: "Pour, look, swirl, sniff, taste." He made the best veal meatloaf I had ever eaten. When I knocked on his door to get a class assignment, I noticed that his law school dormitory room was filled with the latest cookware from Williams-Sonoma. He was not gay. He was desperate.

Somewhere around 30, Andre discovered that the train to upper-middle-class heaven was pulling away and he was not on it. He was looking at a lifetime of creative odd jobs and a struggle just to pay the rent. All that high school promise and no pay off.

We were together for three years.

Six months before the wedding, Andre's mother announced that she had bought a full-length white ballroom gown to wear to the wedding, and "Was that all right?" I told her, "Sylvia, there's only one person at my wedding who's going to be wearing white. If you're not the bride, it's not you."

Four months before the wedding, Andre discovered my greatest flaws: I had said, "Congratulations" instead of "Best wishes" to the bride at a mutual friend's wedding, I didn't know how to screw bottle caps on correctly, and I couldn't turn out the lights the right way. He was relentless in his campaign to correct my poor breeding and insisted on choosing my wedding dress for me.

Two months before the wedding, Andre announced that he had just entered therapy and discovered that he had never loved anyone, including me.

When he left, he took all of the furniture, bedding, and cooking utensils. He also wanted back the ring, and his mother wanted back the diamond chip stud earrings which she had given me as an engagement present.

After a small skirmish, I gave him the ring and studs back because I had no use for a low-grade miner-cut diamond with too many inclusions and some cheap diamond studs that were obviously bought off the Home Shopping Network. I figured Sylvia needed those studs to go with her full length white ballroom gown.

I was left with one gray futon, an armless chair, and a cat named Abyss.

But here we were again, looking at the opportunity to see each other for the first time in six years. I had heard that he had married a woman who, for Andre, had it where it counted: in the bank account. It was a great match for a guy whose daily mantra was, "You can marry in a day what you'd take a lifetime to earn."

From the minute that I was picked up at the airport I was a kitchen slave.

"We need more music," yelled Jennifer while attempting to clean up her condo. "And can you make some brownies?" she begged.

Kevin, a guy who could write software code, claimed that he was completely incapable of reading the instructions on the brownie box and mixing together the contents of two separately packaged plastic pouches.

Six hours after I decided that no one would notice if I didn't make the brownies, the party started. It started raining and some buff-boys arrived: No chicken chests, no sagging butts, no sickly green-white complexions. I knew instantly. They weren't lawyers.

"Byron" could be described in two words: Mr. Yum. His light brown hair had blond streaks in it from his hours of windsurfing in Santa Cruz. He had no fat on his body, because he was training for the Boston Marathon. His cheekbones were perfectly placed on his face and appeared to reflect the light. He had no visible means of support. He and his friend "Jessie" were the eye-candy of the evening. What better way to enjoy the party.

While discussing the intricacies of windsurfing with "Byron," I saw Kevin standing with a small, dark-haired woman who was pointing at me. Who had the bad breeding to point and obviously speak about me? And then I found out. That wasn't just anyone with bad breeding: That was Andre's wife, Karen. He was here.

I went downstairs to Kevin's condo where a secretary from his firm was wearing gold lamé bicycle shorts and teaching everyone how to do a "Latin Love Dance."

Charming.

And there he was again. Andre had never been thin. In fact, he had the metabolism of a girl. If he even looked at food, his butt and thighs exploded. Lord, the years had not been kind.

He looked like he had gained ten pounds for every one of the six years we had been apart. His hairline had disappeared, recreating itself as the "Before" picture for a Rogaine advertisement.

And by the tone of his voice he sounded...well... bitter. Make that bitter and grumpy. Imagine. What happened to the boy most likely to succeed?

From the back of the room I could hear him lecturing to the same group of dope-dealing losers who had idolized him during law school, droning on about the Burgundy he had brought to the party as a present and the proper techniques for drinking it.

"Pour, look, swirl, smell, taste," he said. "That Cab—the one they're serving—is so...immature."

Nothing, except his waist, hairline, and bank account had changed.

Andre was the type of person who had to be the center of attention at all affairs. On one occasion, we all trooped out to the brown shag carpet track-condo that one of our law school buddies, Joe, had let his parents buy for him and his live-in girlfriend, Barb. Like many misguided people, Barb had made *the deal*: in exchange for financially and emotionally supporting Joe during law school, Joe was expected to marry her when he received his first tangible job offer.

On this particular occasion—which I later came to understand was really for the purpose of splitting up the hash which Joe had recently scored—Barb was attempting to make leg of lamb. Andre was beside himself, wondering if she was going to overcook the lamb. He left the hot tub—where he and the boys were sampling the hash—and took over the kitchen under the guise of "giving Barb a hand." When I walked into the kitchen I found him lecturing Barb on the correct technique for preparing lamb, making a gravy, whipping the potatoes, and writing down the wines he felt were appropriate to accompany the meal. He then sent Barb to the store to get the wines while he set out the place settings and served her dinner.

Then he taught her how to pour the wines. "Pour, look, swirl, smell, taste," he said in front of eight very high classmates.

Almost Royalty

During law school, I joined a gym to discourage the inevitable big-butt that would develop once I graduated. Andre stopped by my class one day and then began taking the class on a regular basis. Before the first week of sessions ended, I heard him lecturing our aerobics instructor with ways to improve the class.

Even on the evening that we were breaking up, Andre couldn't control his relentless need to be the center of everything. It so happened that my mother, Julia, had made arrangements for us to have dinner with her and some house guests at the Copper Pan on the very day that Andre had told me he didn't love me. Ever fearful of Julia, he insisted on coming to dinner with us, despite the fact that he had pronounced our engagement "over" two hours before the dinner. During dinner, he took it upon himself to instruct Julia's French house guests on the proper techniques of drinking wine.

"Pour, swirl, smell, taste," he said to Julia's shocked guests.

"Thank God. I always despised that pretentious ass," said Julia, when I told her that Andre and I had broken up. "And besides, I worried desperately about what your children would look like. How could you ever date him?"

That, of course, was the question of the decade.

Dating Andre had been the beginning of an experiment.

I called this experiment "Dating the Others."

It was an experiment based on dating people to whom you were not physically attracted.

The origin of the period came from dating the last musician whom I would ever date, a trumpet player from Alabama named Lucius. Lucius was so hot that Julia, a woman who was never at a loss for male companionship, actually started dating him behind my back.

Lucius was also so selfish that he never once paid for a meal, called gift-giving on holidays "bourgeois," and acknowledged giving me nothing on four consecutive birthdays with the comment, "Why should I spend my hard-earned money on you?" With any other guy with his looks, I probably would have rationalized his behavior by calling it "bohemian" and letting it go, even though I had basically supported him from the first night we were together and he moved in with me. But when he took my car to Canada for four months without telling me and then refused to return it, I grew weary. After months of negotiating, he returned my car with a flat, broke up with me, and then called me every night for 17 days to tell me, "I'm an artist and you're nothing."

I know that there is no guy on the planet who would ever intentionally date someone to whom they were not attracted, unless it's for money or a better place to live—it's simply impossible for them to even conceive of the idea. But after Lucius, I thought, well, if the good-looking ones treat you terribly, maybe the non-attractive ones will be nice to you.

"Of course Lucius treated you terribly," said Marcie after we broke up, "you violated the Eco-Chain of Dating."

"How so?" I asked.

"You know what I've always told you. Don't date above. Don't date below. Only date people at your level. Lucius was much higher than you on the Eco-Chain," said Marcie.

"Lucius was a raging alcoholic," I said.

"Then you two should have been on the same level," said Marcie.

The Eco-Chain of Dating was a system created by Marcie when we were twelve years old. Its purpose was to help us select our boyfriends. Back then, the criteria were whether our boyfriend was "cute" and popular. It was a mistake to follow her criteria; we missed out a lot of terrific, smart guys who would go on to have great lives.

But by the time we were in our twenties, Marcie had expanded the Eco-Chain to be the "L.A. Eco-Chain of Dating" to help us select our husbands such that we would, through appropriate self-selection, enhance our given gene pool and possibly become part of L.A.'s Royalty.

Marcie's L.A. Eco-Chain of Dating

Marci's "L.A. Eco-Chain of Dating" was defined such that potential dates could be designated to the following Eco-Chain Levels:

I. (1) A Level – Entertainment Royalty (Top of the Food Chain) First-generation money that had made it big in some aspect of the entertainment/sports industry. Very public. Very dangerous. If truth be told, this was always a recipe for a disaster and not marriage material unless you have an enormous trust fund and an army of lawyers at your disposal with which to prepare yourself for the most likely outcome: Divorce. Mercurial, flakey, philandering, subject to drugs, sporadic violence, immaturity, plastic surgery (on you), cult religions, bankruptcy, diets, therapies and always—the fad of the moment. This was a dangerous spouse to entertain for anything more than the 18 months necessary to obtain the material for a "tell all" book or a quick payout (especially if that prenup attempted to make you sign away child support, in addition to alimony and community property). **Physical Appearance Requirements:** The physical appearance of the entertainment royalty is not important as long as he/she is fantastically successful and wealthy and can find those individuals to whip him/her into shape if the need should arise. Many who marry these individuals find themselves publically making statements such as, "He/She is truly spiritual," or "He/She is really quite sensitive," or "He/She is so worldly," to explain how they could marry a very successful troll. However, if you're the person marrying the entertainment royalty, your physical appearance is very important and will continue to remain very, very important. But don't worry: after a few years as an A Level entertainment spouse, your basic genetic material will be so altered that you won't recognize yourself.

I. (2) A Level – Civilian Royalty (Top of the Food Chain) Unless it was from high-tech, the A Level Civilian Royalty was usually second or third generation non-entertainment money from business, oil, or land. Although quietly running the city and its cultural institutions, this group is generally well-educated, but also mercurial, flakey, philandering and has a tendency to treat marriage like a pro sport. Not necessarily marriage material, unless you yourself have the enormous trust fund and an army of lawyers at your disposal, 51 percent of the stock, or have managed to land and stick in marriage (with kids) for more than ten years without a prenup. **Physical Appearance Requirements:** For Civilian Royalty, not important, unless you are a younger member of the Civilian Royalty Family whom the family is attempting to use (a la Ivanka Trump/Aerin Lauder/Andrew Firestone) to restore the image of the family business or a younger image of the family business. Of course, if the Civilian Royalty is marrying someone 40 years younger there can be issues, especially if the chosen spouse is 20 years or more younger than their children by their first, second, or third wife. If you are marrying the Civilian Royalty, then you will probably spend $$$ per month on "maintenance" issues and be on a diet forever as your job will be to look good on all occasions.

II. B Level – Civilian Royalty Rising Achievers (Second Rung on the Food Chain) Filled with those who service the A Level Entertainment or Civilian Royalty of Los Angeles—the ambitious, reliable, and generally well-educated, lawyers, chefs, plastic surgeons, agents, business managers, dentists, stylists, makeup artists, investment bankers and trainers who can become A Level if very, very ambitious. The classic definition of "well-married" in Los Angeles and a good match for a highly-educated woman/man who never again wants to work, as the men at this level are generally too busy to wander. **General Requirements:** For spouses at this level, the general requirements include staying thin, fertile (the ability to bear at least two kids is mandatory), taking care of the house/staff/children, and the ability to stay sober and not embarrass their spouses at professional functions.

III. C Level – Workers (Third Rung of the Food Chain) In Los Angeles, the waiters, waitresses, temps, clerks, assistants, hostesses, and occasional nannies who generally are aspiring actors, screenwriters, directors, musicians, artists—if they have ambition. If not, they are the sporadically employed, not so ambitious, not particularly focused group who may have no other ambition than to work occasionally, or to get you to support them (which really isn't so different than the A or B Level Spouses, other than the less ambitious of this group tend to be men). A big gamble, and slightly dangerous, as you will most likely be the person providing all of the money. Generally a formula for a disaster, and not marriage material, unless you have enormous patience and are willing to participate in a thousand arguments where you are blamed for their inability to become a successful actor, screenwriter, director, musician or artist. **Physical Appearance Requirements:** If you have the money, none. But if your spouse/partner is the one with the looks and no ambition or career, hold on to your credit cards, don't have joint accounts, and for heaven's sake, *get* a prenup: This can be a positively lethal group if he/she has been blessed with good or extremely good looks.

"You see," said Marcie, "the Eco-Chain is the law of options. Those higher up on the food chain—because they have money or are better looking, have been given more options—that is, to find other mates—than those lower on the chain."

"Uh huh," I said.

"You have an every-girl look," said Marcie, "tall, thin, blonde. And you don't come from money, which really lowers your rank. Refinement in your gene pool is necessary for a higher position on the Eco-Chain, but that's going to be very difficult for you because you don't have a lot to offer. I'm sure you attract a lot of crap."

"I'm an attorney."

"But you're not that successful."

"Yet. I could be."

"But that takes *sooo* much work."

"And yourself?" I said.

"Too many options," said Marcie. "I have a classic look. And I'm very careful. I limit my potential gene pool dilution by only dating people on the upper level from the better areas like Brentwood, Pacific Palisades, Bel Air, Santa Monica above Wilshire, and where I was raised—South Pasadena. That's why Greg is perfect for me. He's from Bel Air and very handsome."

"Yeah, he's handsome in a Rowan Atkinson kind of way," I said.

"It's a simple equation," explained Marcie. "A couple at a similar attractiveness level and education on the Eco-Chain, like Greg and I, will have roughly the same options and therefore, a fairly good shot at a relationship, unless of course one mate has weighty baggage hanging over their head...like the Menendez Brothers..."

"They're serving life terms without any possibility of parole for killing their parents. That's pretty heavy baggage."

"But they were raised well," said Marcie, "in Bel Air. Isn't one of them still available?"

"I haven't checked."

"...or one mate has a truly disagreeable condition, like poverty."

According to Marcie, if two mates are not on the same Eco-Chain level and there is not a significant amount of money on the less attractive mate's side to balance out the looks scales, it's a recipe for hell. The less attractive mate will spend 75 percent of the relationship seeking revenge on the more attractive mate for pulling a winning ticket in the gene pool lottery.

Maybe she had a point.

When I first met Andre, I was five foot ten, 120 pounds, and had a body fat count of less than 16 percent. Andre was five foot six and weighed a shade over 190 pounds. He had a big bushy beard with food caught in it and a tiny button nose with a little bump in the middle. He wore sleeveless T-shirts, mid-thigh nylon shorts with elastic waistbands, and flip-flops to class even when it rained. He had buzzed his baby-fine blond hair to a quarter of an inch because he was losing it. That very same group of dope-dealing losers that now surrounded him in Kevin's living room took it upon themselves during our first year of law school to let me know that "he liked me." My response: not gonna happen.

Say what you want, but my first instinct was correct.

"Just remember, Andre," said Julia when she first met him, "plastic surgery is available for everyone."

There's no such thing as equal-opportunity dating: You're either attracted to someone, or you aren't. And I wasn't.

But he wasn't going to take "No" for an answer. Like any smart person who has ever experienced unrequited feelings, Andre knew how to wear down the object of his desire. He became my friend.

"I know that you have a thing for the pretty boys," he told me, "but isn't it time you were with someone who isn't fooled by your act and really sees who you are?"

I wish I had known then that Andre had a talent for creating phrases that sounded good and meant nothing.

Then he became my advisor.

"I hate to tell you this," he said, "but I think that you've seriously misinterpreted the fundamental elements of criminal law. Take my outline and see if my notes help you," was what he told me five days after my exam in criminal law.

Of course, he said nothing when I got an A, and he got a B–.

Then he lobbied my friends. They thought he was the king of arrogance. But he was persistent. He became their friend when he gave them access to an endless supply of speed during finals. But he became their hero when he cooked them a five-course meal with wine. I really couldn't blame them: For 17 weeks they had lived off nothing but coffee, diet Coke, and vending machine donuts, something they had in common with Andre.

Of course, he also showed them how to taste wine.

"Pour, look, swirl, smell, taste," he said to my exhausted, pre-finals classmates.

Although Andre pretended to be interested in nothing but gourmet delectables, his secret, nasty, pornographic obsession wasn't for coeds with EEE-sized breasts, boys who looked like Ashton Kutcher, or transsexuals who dressed like Marilyn Monroe. It was for donuts: glazed donuts, preferably freshly made, still hot, wet with sugar, in units of 12, generally two units of 12. He liked to have them alone, while watching *Letterman*, at 11:30 p.m.

Jennifer never liked Andre. During law school, she referred to him as "Walrus-Butt."

And then there was Marcie, or should I say Marcee'.

"You're diving into the wrong gene pool," said Marcie within 90 seconds of meeting Andre.

"Oh c'mon," I said.

Marcie looked at me and gave me a quick feet to head appraisal. "Although not the best gene pool, you have managed to breed out the short, fat, thin-hair gene. Andre will dilute that pool. You need to seriously consider what your offspring could look like."

"You sound like a dog breeder."

She sighed. "You've violated the Eco-Chain. Again. I assure you, Andre will give you nothing but classic Relationship Terrorism: bad sex, passive-aggressive behavior, and verbal warfare."

It was an interesting perspective.

But after putting up with the Bohemian antics of Lucius longer than was humanly possible, I thought, "Why not?"

The revenge techniques on an attractive mate differ between the sexes. From women, it's nothing but: "Do you think she's attractive?" "I bet you wish you were with her," and "You don't want to sleep with me because I'm fat."

In addition, the less attractive woman may increase the revenge principal by keeping the couple (if sharing expenses) consistently in debt by spending 110 percent more per year than the couple earns, sabotaging the occasional career plan or goal of the mate, or the ultimate: having an in-your-face affair or two with a complete loser, just to show him that someone finds her attractive.

However, Andre's revenge techniques were the classic male pattern. His intention was to make me believe that I was a mess. The dismantling took the route of a million small criticisms.

Did I know that I spoke too loudly? He began shushing me whenever he thought I was being too loud.

Then I walked too slowly. He started timing me—to the second—when we went grocery shopping to see how long it took me to get the milk and bring it to our cart.

Did I know that I would get a much better result if I wrote from my arm, and not from my hand? He tried to give me handwriting lessons.

And I never quite mastered his wine tasting techniques.

"Pour, look, swirl, smell, taste. Pour, look, swirl, smell, taste," he yelled at me. Unfortunately, my technique was pour, drink.

Of course the sex was a disaster. I was blamed for his sweaty anxiety and general inability to perform.

"You're just coarse and insensitive to my needs," said Andre.

"What would you like me do?" I asked. "Dress up like a glazed donut?"

Three months after we got together, he walked into the living room and threw a sponge at me as I was preparing for my Real Property final with my study group.

"Jesus," he said, "can't you see that this is dirty?"

Six weeks later, he dropped a box with four glasses in it on the bathroom floor as I was dashing to an interview.

"THESE HAVE SPOTS ON THEM!" he screamed.

I should've seen the signs. He started examining my nails in front of friends. "Look at these!" he'd say with disgust. I think I knew things had gone too far when he threw out half of my wardrobe one day while I was in class.

"It's time someone taught you how to dress," he said.

But here he was, at Jennifer's party. It was another chance to hear his opinion on everything.

I turned around, went back upstairs, and found Byron.

"You look stressed out," said Byron. "Why don't I give you a massage?"

"OK," I said.

We walked into Jennifer's freshly painted bedroom and closed the door. Fifteen minutes later the door flew open.

"Oh," said a familiar voice, "there she is."

Byron pulled himself off me. He was naked. My dress was wrapped around my neck.

Andre, Karen, and Susan stood there staring.

We attempted to take cover under a comforter. Just then, Jennifer walked by, did a double-take, and starting whooping with laughter.

"Let's go," said Andre. Karen and Susan walked out of the room. Andre started walking out of the room. He stopped at the door and turned around.

"You haven't changed. You still have a taste for that pretty boy crap," said Andre.

Byron put his clothes back on. I rearranged myself. He promised to take me windsurfing in Santa Cruz in the morning.

I went to get some water and found Jennifer shaking a martini.

She couldn't stop laughing.

"At least you didn't dilute your gene pool."

"I see you've been talking to Marcie."

Almost Royalty

"Well, you know Marcie," said Jennifer, "she may be insane, but she's not wrong."

"I think Andre got what he truly wanted: San Francisco Civilian Royalty. I hear that she's very nice," I said.

"Your marriage would have been horrible," said Jennifer.

My head hurt and I felt awful. "Does that even matter anymore?" I said.

Jennifer put her arm round me. "Don't do this," she said.

"Do what? All I know is that Andre is married and seems happy. And I'm still floating through the L.A. Eco-Chain, make that cesspool, of dating. And alone," I said, and then covered my eyes with my hands. "*Still alone.*"

From across the room, I could see Andre opening the wine he had brought to the party. He poured a third of a glass, looked at it, swirled it, smelled it, and then tasted it. He poured another third of a glass and gave it to Karen. Karen glanced around the room and…did she sigh? She then picked up the glass, looked at it, swirled, smelled it, and then tasted the wine as Andre nodded his head.

I'm sure it was an excellent French Burgundy.

8

Revisionist History

Marcie called me with an unusual request. She wanted to borrow my wedding dress, the one I had bought for my wedding to Andre.

Marcie was five foot one. I was five foot ten.

"Well, if we were closer in size, it might be OK. But if I give it to you, I'm never going to be able to wear it," I said.

"So what," said Marcie. "At least I'll put it to good use. No one thinks you're ever going to use it."

I thought about it.

"No," I said.

"But I really need it," she pleaded.

"I'll be honest with you. For whatever reason, your request really pisses me off."

I heard Marcie sigh. "Won't you consider it? I really need it."

"I did consider it, Marcie. And the answer is no."

"God, you're selfish," she said and hung up before I could answer.

Almost Royalty

One day later, I got a call from Bettina, Marcie's matron of honor.

"So the wedding dress..." said Bettina.

"Uh-huh," I said.

"You really should do more to help her," said Bettina. "It's not every day that your friend gets married."

"Uh huh."

"This is a good thing," said Bettina, "because at least someone will use that dress."

"Funny," I said. "Since I paid for it, I was planning on wearing it."

"You know, I think you're forgetting how much she needs this dress," said Bettina. "And you know how much this means to her."

How could I forget.

Unfortunately, this wasn't just about Marcie becoming a bride. That would have been fine and I could have played along, doing those fake bride-friend type things like telling her that her butt didn't look too big in the dress and pretending to like the groom. For Marcie, this was about her finally reaching her lifelong goal: Marrying into L.A.'s Civilian Class Royalty and becoming part of that unique group of L.A. women who: (1) married well, (2) never again had to work, and (3) staffed the volunteer committees of L.A.'s most exclusive private schools.

But there was a problem. Marcie, like every socially ambitious resident of Los Angeles, wanted to have "The L.A. Wedding." This meant: (1) a wedding at the Bel Air Hotel with those damn swans that always managed to swim in formation, on cue; (2) a designer dress, maybe a Vera Wang; (3) a sit-down dinner for more people than you could remember; (4) a string quartet to play at the wedding and the reception; (5) $100,000 for flowers (at least); (6) the $15,000 wedding cake; (7) hand-engraved invitations; and, (7) high-end photographers and videographers. The price tag for this event could get to the upper-six figures quite quickly. For a five-hour party.

Well, it wasn't just that Marcie wanted this. Marcie thought that if she was going to become part of L.A.'s Civilian Class Royalty she *needed* the L.A. Wedding. And Marcie and her parents couldn't afford it.

Not long after my conversation with Bettina came the call I had seen coming from the moment I heard she was engaged.

As it was, I had spent years trying to play down my first career, that of a classical violinist. The way I looked at it, my experience as a musician had been a long journey in the wrong direction for someone from my profoundly non-musical background.

It had started when I was in fourth grade, when my elementary school offered violin. I decided that this would be fun. I quickly discovered that practicing equaled improving. One day I was a kid who couldn't open her violin case. Not long after that, people were paying me to play at their weddings and parties. When I was twelve this was fun and I thought that I was special. When I was 22, after countless hours of practice, years of very expensive music lessons, and thousands spent for music programs in Aspen and Banff, I had a revelation: The thousands which my mother had paid for my musical education had trained me for a career in the serving class.

I had grown used to wearing a uniform that consisted of a black skirt with a white blouse. It no longer bothered me that I was to enter through the back door or that I was to be unseen, like the rest of the serving crew. But then some mother put her diapered two-year-old in front of us so that he would dance, and then clapped while we played a mid-Beethoven String Quartet while he jumped up and down. And then the bride asked us to play their special song and I suddenly realized that we, with our combined 80 years of musical training, were going to play The Pachelbel Canon for the 67th time that wedding season.

And then I knew: I couldn't do this anymore. I realized that I could slip into middle-age and despite years of training and effort I would merely be part of the background noise, something which you know is there but try to ignore, like the clean-up crew or housekeepers. And my 20 years of very expensive professional training had prepared me to be a member of the unseen serving class.

So when I took the Law School Entrance Exam and got a pretty decent score I thought it was better to become an attorney and join a profession where you're despised rather than pitied. I stopped playing at weddings, even when asked by friends, because I discovered that weddings were a lot more fun to attend than to work.

But that wasn't going to stop Marcie. As it was, Marcie's call came two weeks after I expected it.

"I was wondering if you had any other thoughts about your wedding dress," said Marcie.

"No, I haven't," I said.

"Well, it's really important to me that you're somehow represented in my wedding."

"That's so touching."

"Greg and I were wondering if maybe you would like to play at our wedding."

"I haven't played at a wedding in almost ten years."

"I'm sure if you practiced no one would notice."

"What makes you think your friends and family would know the difference?"

"They would notice. I'm sure you know that my family is very proper," she said.

Properly Nuevo Dinero.

"Absolutely," I said.

"Well, think about it, maybe you could start playing at weddings again," she said.

I sighed. "I'm an attorney, Marcie. Why would I want to play at weddings?"

"I'm getting another call so..."

My line went dead.

And five minutes later on my cell, "You won't even play at her wedding?" said Bettina. "What's wrong with you? You played at mine."

"I don't do that anymore. It's degrading."

"What are you talking about? No one would even notice you," said Bettina.

"That's right," I said. "They wouldn't notice me until I tried to walk in the front door and then the wedding coordinator would yell, 'The musicians come in the back door!' When I try to sit down with you, the caterer will grab me by the elbow and escort me to a table in the garage."

"Look," said Bettina, "I'll be honest with you. Marcie is way over-budget."

"Really," I said. "Why doesn't she just elope?"

"Why should Marcie have anything less than the wedding she's always dreamed of?"

"Because she can't afford it?"

"Why should that stop her?" said Bettina.

Why, indeed.

Marcie, Bettina, and I had a unique relationship which congealed the day that Marcie met Bettina in our dorm room at art school. I was making lunch for Marcie, who had come to visit, when Bettina walked into the room while I was cutting Velveeta to put into an omelet for our lunch. Bettina saw the Velveeta and then eyed Marcie.

"You're not going to give her that, are you?" said Bettina.

"Oh my God," said Marcie, "that's not even cheese."

"That's what I tell her all the time," said Bettina.

"Thank God you're here," said Marcie, "and what about her dishes? They don't even match!"

"I know," said Bettina, "the first thing I did when I got here was buy a matching set."

"For what," I said, "so you could smash them in some feminist performance piece?"

They both looked at me, then looked at each other.

"You just need to show her what to do," said Marcie.

"That's what I've been doing," said Bettina.

I rolled my eyes.

"Me too," said Marcie, "since we were in elementary school."

It was at that moment that I began to understand that Marcie was beginning her personal revisionist history, a transformation which would change her, Marcie (short for Marsha), a middle-class girl from Northridge who liked Shaun Cassidy, Hostess Ding-Dongs, and pink leggings, to Mar-cee (pronounced Mar-SEE), a preppie from South Pasadena who liked dressage, gin, and nothing but 100 percent cotton. She also became a self-appointed expert—on everything. There was nothing preppie, or to be honest, remotely upper class, about the Marcie I knew. I first met her at age 11 when her family moved to our extremely non-preppie neighborhood from Northridge, California. She, like me, went to public schools from kindergarten through high school and lived in a 3-bedroom, 1.5-bathroom, 1300-square-foot house, with a sister, a mother, and a father who worked as an accountant and drove a late model Ford.

But somewhere around the time that she graduated from high school a relative died and left her family some money. That's when her parents packed everything and moved to South Pasadena. Marcie, however, never actually lived in South Pasadena, but around the time she met Bettina, Marcie had decided that South Pasadena was much more impressive than Northridge or our town. Thus the transformation to a proper South Pasadena preppie had begun, and all mention of her previous middle-class life was expunged from her official bio.

I was a little surprised that Marcie and Bettina got along so well, as Marcie represented the antithesis of everything that Bettina's Lesbian Collective believed. But there was something about that meeting which was like watching two halves find a unified whole, as if Marcie had been separated at birth from her long lost twin, Bettina, and had finally found her.

They were both five foot one, brown-eyed, frizzy-haired, and about 35 pounds overweight. I was not part of that club.

"Small furry vicious things," said my friend, Stefan, after meeting Bettina and Marcie at a party, "yeeech."

"What are you talking about?" I said. "They're nice girls."

"Oh, Blanche," said Stefan, "you're not even from the same planet. In fact, I don't think you're from the same galaxy as those two."

"But they're nice girls—right?"

Stefan just looked at me, shook his head, and rolled his eyes.

Perhaps there was something comforting in seeing what was familiar to themselves. But I remembered that day as significant, as the moment when Marcie, self-appointed expert on everything, met Bettina, her long lost twin. Their bonding point: How they should reform their problem child—me.

From that day on and over the next decade they kept in constant touch through daily emails and phone calls. Marcie would give Bettina advice for me. Bettina would report my activities to Marcie. They visited each other, shopped together, and joined the same gym, which they both mutually failed to visit. Marcie would throw Bettina a yearly surprise birthday party. Bettina, who knew Marcie hated surprises, would consult with Marcie for six weeks regarding the proper arrangements prior to the yearly formal birthday dinner that Bettina held for Marcie.

Over time they began to look like each other. One day I returned to my room to find Bettina, who never wore a bra, in a push-up bra. Her face was covered in foundation, rouge, mascara, and bright red lipstick. Her hair had been rinsed with red and cut to her chin. Her oversized men's T-shirt and painter pants had been replaced with a tight red knit sweater and black Capri pants. Her hiking boots were gone. She was wearing heels.

This was an unusual look for a lesbian feminist who created performance art on the topic of oppressed women.

Clearly, Marcie had done one of her legendary makeovers.

"You look like Marcie," I said.

"Oh, thank you," said Bettina.

Almost Royalty

Both Marcie and Bettina shared the same tendency to gain weight. This caused them to vacation together, usually to the same spa boot camp—which they could not afford—where I saw the same seven pounds tortured off their bodies on a yearly basis during the last week of June. By July 15 they had usually gained back those seven pounds, as once they returned from their "vacation" half starved, a feeding frenzy of Mexican and Italian food would ensue.

By choosing to marry Greg, her boyfriend of five months, Marcie had put herself in a precarious position. She, herself, tried to pretend that she had the kind of upbringing which allowed her to think of money as an endless natural resource which she could dispose of like tap water. It was there for her to use, and such things as a credit limit—hers, her parents', her boyfriend's—never entered into her consciousness.

It was not that she was 18, idiotic, and just beginning to understand the world: She was 35, maxed to the limit on all fronts, and still wondering why the world treated her differently now than it did when she was ten.

But she had learned her urban survival skills a long time ago. She was an operator, someone who knew or had discovered how to use everyone who came into her universe. And like any operator she was a deflector, a girl who somehow pretended that negative things about herself did not exist. And that deflector trait gave her the confidence to be, or in fact, to insist on being the most popular girl in her school in every grade.

Marcie had best friends, and second best friends, and friends in waiting. Given the basic insecurity of all pre-teen girls it was easy for her to pretend to be an authority—none of her friends did anything without her approval. She told them what to wear, whom to date, and how to cut their hair, given their particular facial flaws.

I was told to cut my mid-back-length hair and dye it black.

"That Malibu blond hair makes you look so...so...common," she said.

She, of course, had no flaws.

"I have a classical look," she said.

I never knew what that meant.

Like any urban operator she wasn't good at anything, but invented arbitrary categories of importance. At ten, it was the proper music to be "cool." At twelve, it was the "must have" things—shoes, purses, hairstyles—for all occasions. At fourteen, it was the basics of finding your Proper Boyfriend on the School Eco-Chain of Dating and your correct level on it. At sixteen, it was the "must have" resume items to get into the college of your choice. At eighteen, it was absolute "must" colleges to apply to and receive acceptances. At twenty, it was the "must haves" for a complete and proper china collection.

Now, in our 30s, it was the basics of finding your Proper Mate (and correct gene pool) on the L.A. Eco-Chain of Dating. And as dating in L.A. was completely mystifying, some of us found ourselves listening to her, overlooking the fact that she was not exactly successful in finding boyfriends.

Like many of her friends, Marcie had become an attorney after graduating from a lower rated UC and stumbling through a law school of a Catholic persuasion. She thought "law" would be a cool thing to do after watching TV lawyers on popular dramas and seeing the neat suits that Ann Taylor was making for women. She even managed to get an offer from a medium-sized downtown firm, because one of her sorority sisters was the head of the recruiting committee.

But working came as a shock. She had assignments with deadlines. Many nights she was there beyond 7:00 p.m. Every other weekend she had to work. And her assistant laughed when she asked her to get her coffee or even pick up her calls.

Her first review at her law firm was not good: the partners thought she was a nice person but found her work to be sloppy. She was going to have to work much harder, just to make a passing grade. Unfortunately, her training as an urban operator and her skills of deflection did not work within the law firm environment. And it just killed her that Bettina had become a wife and SAHM, a Stay-At-Home Mom.

"If Bettina doesn't work, why should I?" she said.

"She has kids," I said.

"I'm preparing for that time," she said.

She decided to stop working until she determined her next step. However, most of her friends were still working—a fact which bored, then depressed her. She needed to go back to Europe, to collect herself.

After twelve months in Prague, drinking endless cups of coffee and having affairs with other American expatriates who, like herself, were doing their best to forget that they were in their thirties and at an age at which their parents had three kids, a mortgage, and a start on a summer house, she came back home, to nothing.

Nothing other than her $150,000+ in consumer debt.

She refused to work as an attorney. When I reminded her that she had an insanely expensive legal education, she shrugged her shoulders.

"So what. Practicing law is nothing like the cool stuff those lawyers on TV do—it sucks."

Her parents, house poor from the financial charade it took to both buy and live in South Pasadena, could not afford to bail her out.

Marcie realized that her urban survival skills had not prepared her to work. However, it had prepared her for the one job that eluded her: being a member of L.A.'s Civilian Class Royalty and one of the rare L.A. women who had married well. There was only one part missing: the groom.

When I saw her again she was dating—or should I say spending time with—an accountant for the adult movie industry named Russ.

Russ was bald except for the Ronald-McDonald red hair tufts that were two inches above each ear, weighed in at 260, and topped out at five foot seven. He never called her and refused to acknowledge that he was even dating her. He would only get together with her at her tiny apartment for sex and Chinese take-out (which he made her pay for) on his way home from work when he would drive by her apartment and remember that he had "a friend" living in the neighborhood.

Because of the amazing growth of his industry of expertise, Russ had money. But with money came the usual by-product: lots of women. Lots of women and an attitude.

"Aren't you going to tell Marcie to get rid of Russ?" I asked Bettina.

"Why?" said Bettina. "He's a good catch."

"He's in porn," I said.

"It's a growth industry. He'll make a good living," said Bettina.

"This is her proper mate on the Eco-Chain?" I asked.

"He has a huge house above Montana in Santa Monica," said Bettina.

Was it better to have your friend date someone you openly acknowledged as horrible or to help your friend get together with someone you knew was just terribly wrong?

I really didn't want to interfere in Marcie's life, but I thought that I might stage an intervention. I would find her someone who was so totally wrong that eventually they would both realize, *this will never work*. Hopefully, then she would find someone worthwhile.

I introduced her to the absolutely cheapest person I knew. I introduced her to Greg.

If Marcie was looking for a bucket of money to enable her to live out her preppie fantasies, Greg thought that every dollar that came across his hand was more precious than cheap real estate in San Francisco. As a partner in his father's real estate empire, Greg knew the location of every dollar in their empire, at all times.

Yes, his family lived in Bel Air, but they operated their real estate empire from that location so it was mostly a tax write-off.

He was a good businessman and as a partner in the business which had occasionally been on the verge of bankruptcy, he was very practical about money. Greg could, with ease, figure out everyone's collective contribution to a restaurant bill down to the penny, including the fact that although he had eaten as much as anyone, he never seemed to owe anything.

In the ten years that I had known Greg I rarely saw him pick up a check, bring a gift to a birthday party, or waste the gasoline in his car by picking up a stranded friend. That alone assured me that he and Marcie would not last. But the one thing that I knew would kill them instantly was his standard operating procedure with women: Greg insisted that all dates, no matter what their income, pay half of everything including those very expensive dinners to which he had invited them.

It would never go anywhere.

But Marcie didn't want to meet Greg, because she, like Bettina, thought Russ was great husband material and very close to giving her a ring. Although I explained to her that if she married Russ she was likely to have a best man at her wedding who was known for his ability to produce the money-shot, that still didn't stop her.

Fortunately, Russ proved himself true to form. He did something so despicable that she didn't need an intervention.

Marcie had invited me to Shutters on the Beach on the Santa Monica-Venice border for cocktail hour with Russ. We were to meet in the lounge, a room which reminded me of my grandmother's living room in San Marino because of the manner in which some interior designer had placed eight over-stuffed couches that were covered in a fuchsia floral print.

It was a big moment. Russ was finally going to be seen with her in public.

When I got there, Marcie was sitting on a fuchsia floral print couch by herself. Russ was sitting on another floral print couch, not ten feet from her. His hand was glued to the knee of some girl who looked like she was fourteen years old and his face was peering into the cleavage of the poor waitress who was serving him drinks. Although he was sitting so that he was staring right at Marcie, he pretended that he didn't know her. I sat down next to her.

"What's going on?" I said, trying to catch Russ's eye. She had tears in her eyes. She eyed me.

"Oh my God," she said. "I told you to throw that red sweater out. Blue is your color."

"I didn't."

I nodded at Russ.

"So what's he doing over there?"

"He told me that he can't be seen with me in public because it's bad for his professional profile."

"What?"

"He said that my breasts are too small and I'm too fat...and too old."

She started sobbing. "Don't tell Bettina."

"OK."

She blew her nose on a Shutters on the Beach cocktail napkin. The cocktail waitress came by and I ordered four martinis.

Marcie's mascara began to run down her face with her tears.

"I don't get it," she said.

I did.

After this, it was easy to dislodge Marcie from Russ. In fact, she called me the next day with her game plan. She would agree to meet Greg, as long as he met her very strict criteria.

"Does he make money?"

I decided to be honest.

"Yes..." I said, "but you'll have to pry it out of him."

I don't think that she ever heard the second part of my answer.

They met. They started dating. They hit it off. Greg called me and thanked me for the set-up of his life. Marcie seemed happy. Then they started complaining.

"She thinks I'm an ATM machine," he said.

"He's so tight," she said.

They broke up.

It was as it should be.

But then they got back together.

Not three days into reconciliation, they started fighting again.

"She actually expects me to pay for everything," he said.

"He actually expects me to pay for something," she said.

It seemed impossible.

I decided to help them end their pain once and for all by sending them to the Kevorkian of relationships.

I gave them Roberta's phone number. I was positive that she would tell them that they shouldn't be together because "they had so much work to do."

I was wrong.

Working with Roberta proved effective for them. They somehow came to some compromise with regard to their money problem.

They got engaged.

I thought the ring issue might prove to be another stumbling block. But Greg was able to get his family to cough up a stone which had belonged to his grandmother. He was thrilled. The total cost of the ring would be less than dinner for four at Melisse'. Then he insured the ring for a low five-figure amount and made it appear as if it were worth a respectable sum. It was a beautiful strategy. Marcie got a decent ring, and Greg had paid nothing.

About three weeks after my last conversation with Bettina, I ran into Marcie at the new face-lifted version of my local market. I was depressed. What formerly had been a slightly rundown grocery store where I could buy creamed corn, Velveeta, and Hostess Cupcakes—foods no one would admit eating—had been gutted.

My little market was now a glass and wood beam palace which contained trendy no-fat foods, 24 different versions of coffee, a holistic medicine section, free range ostrich meat, a wine store, organic fruits and vegetables, a flower market, and a pretty good take-out area where you could pick up everything. The heartbreaker was a cheese section labeled "Fromage."

"Is that a joke?" said the Cheese-Person Cyndee, when I asked her when the store would be getting its latest shipment of my beloved Velveeta.

Marcie told me that she missed me and asked if she could treat me to lunch. "But stop wearing that mauve lipstick," she said, "it's not your color."

She took me to lunch at a lovely little restaurant on the deceptively low-key Montana Avenue where you paid $50 for two heads of lettuce splashed with Ranch dressing while sitting on picnic benches with other people.

Not 30 seconds after I had parked myself on a bench, Marcie started in.

"Weddings are expensive," she said.

"Marcie," I said.

"Mar-cee," she corrected.

"That's what I said, Marcie."

"No, it's pronounced Mar-Cee," said Marcie, "like Mar-CEE."

"Whatever," I said. "Why don't you get a job in law again? Then you can pay for your wedding."

Marcie looked at me and rolled her eyes. "I *hate* being an attorney."

"Welcome to the party. Everybody hates it."

"But I wasn't having any fun whatsoever."

"You know," I said, "if it were fun, they'd call it *play*. Instead, they call it *work*."

"I don't see why I should have to do something that I don't want to do," said Marcie.

"Because that's what grown-ups do," I said.

"I've never had to do that and I never will," said Marcie.

I looked at her.

She looked at me.

Almost Royalty

"Hmmmm," she said, looking at my shirt, "you should never wear blue."

"Two months ago you told me that I should only wear blue."

"I can't believe I said that," she said.

"So help me out. You're not working. You're not independently wealthy. Your parents have cut you off. And you and Greg are planning The Dream Wedding, which in this town can easily come with a $500,000 to $1,000,000 price tag. How do you plan to pull this off?"

"Well, you see," she said as she pulled out a piece of paper, "we're planning on having our friends help us."

And then I saw it. Greg's itemized wedding budget. All of their close friends, including me, with their expected contribution to the blessed event next to their name.

This was the compromise they had come to in therapy. Marcie would have to be on Greg's budget for the rest of her life to make their relationship work. And that meant the urban operator was going to have the hand-me-down wedding of the century.

I found my name.

"$10,303?"

"Oh, don't get excited. It's not in money. It's in goods and services," said Marcie.

"Oh?"

"Greg and I figured that no matter what you said, you'd eventually let me have your dress because you're a practical person and now that you and Frank have split up, well, you wouldn't want that dress to go to waste."

"I thought you hated my dress...remember you told me 'the only proper dress is a Vera Wang. Everything else is trash'—after I bought my non-Vera Wang designer dress."

"Although you had a lapse in taste and it's not a Vera Wang, it is a designer dress. And I'll use your dress as my back-up—well, one of my back-up dresses, in case I don't get a Vera Wang from someone. So that dress has got to cost at least $5,000."

"$6,750 to be precise."

"Oh, great. Greg will be so happy to learn that we've saved another $1,750."

I took a deep breath and let it out slowly while the waiters came by and asked us if we wanted refills on ice tea, which they failed to tell us cost $2.50 apiece.

"And the other $5,303 that you had me down for?" I said.

"Oh, that should be obvious to you. We checked around, and found out that the going rate for a string quartet to entertain the guests for the time that we'll need one will be about $5,000."

"Uh-huh."

"Well, Greg and I realized that we wanted music for the hour before the wedding, to set the mood. And then we wanted music during the ceremony, so that we could be sure that everyone knew what our favorite song was."

"That wouldn't happen to be The Pachelbel Canon?" I said.

"Oh my God, how did you know?" she said with a thousand-watt smile.

"Of course, we have to have music to keep the guests entertained while we shoot our photographs and serve the hors d'oeuvre."

"Uh huh."

"You know as well as I do, dinner can't go without music. And we'll need some background music while the band sets up and maybe when it's on a break."

"God forbid that there should be a moment of silence."

"So, Greg calculated five hours of music at $1,000 per hour."

"Marcie…"

"So if you and your quartet…"

"Marcie, I don't play with a quartet anymore."

"Well, can't you find some people to play with you for our wedding?"

"If I *paid* them."

"That would be great! So if you and your quartet played for those five hours, it would save us another $5,000."

I stared at her for about five seconds in complete silence.

"You're not saying anything," she said.

I didn't know what to say. It was like inching by a six car pile-up on the San Diego Freeway during rush hour that was caused by a big-rig that jack-knifed across the center divider at the Sepulveda Pass. It was too awful to be believed, but you couldn't keep yourself from taking a long look at the whole thing.

"We're up to $10,000," I said. "Where does the other $303 come in?" I asked.

"Well, of course you're going to get us a present. And we registered at the Apple Store *and* Bloomingdales, so you can either get us something like a new IPhone. Or, if you want to be romantic, you can help me fill out my china pattern."

"I thought you filled out your proper formal china collection fifteen years ago."

"I need a few additional pieces."

"Like the whole set?" I said. "So $10,391?"

"Well, of course, Greg figured in the sales tax that you'd save us."

They had thought of everything.

"So, what do you think?"

"I think that you should get a job."

She looked at me with disgust.

"What is your problem? Are you that jealous of me?" She threw down her napkin and left the restaurant at the exact moment that the waiter was approaching us with the check, a trick I was sure that she picked up from Greg.

9

The Ivy & Elite

Aspire was a boutique Hollywood talent agency which started when five guys successfully stole most of the lucrative clients from the monolithic talent agency that had saved their careers after their last boutique agency had filed for bankruptcy. Despite being small creatures with odd shaped heads, munched hair, and pale, soft, expanding bodies which never saw a moment of exercise, they had perfected the mythology of their agency to such a pitch that they successfully concealed the fact that they never did an ounce of work for their clients—if the client was lucky. If cursed, an Aspire client could find themselves pitted against another Aspire client in the kind of agency self-dealing which always assured that Aspire would receive the maximum possible commission. By contrast, the cursed client would receive unreturned phone calls and a few sermons from a 22-year-old Aspire assistant on the glory of being part of the Aspire family and, most typically, a crushing career setback.

Currently, the Aspire agents were so removed from the reality of their own deceit that they honestly thought of their actions as pure, and considered themselves to be the kind of agents who would have killed (literally) for a client. However, they were an agency which was totally void of self-awareness because they were successful. At this point, they were the kind of agents who could lay a big pile of toxic waste on the table while smiling at a major client with a confident, toothy grin and say, "Look what we've done for you."

I suppose it shouldn't have surprised me when I finally ran into one of those munched-haired Aspire agents. Of course it happened at an event that I would have sneered at three years ago.

"Don't be so judgmental," said Jennifer. "You need to be open to new things."

"Boy, that makes me sad. That's the line you used to get me to spend a month with you on Mykonos, which was fabulous. Now you're using it to get me to go to an Ivy League '30s and Desperate' singles event."

"I'm doing this for your own good," said Jennifer.

"We'll see about that."

The Ivy & Elite, a group which held singles events exclusively for the discerning gold-digger graduates from the Ivy League who hadn't managed to hit pay-dirt while attending their respective schools, was clearly making a fortune off those profoundly deluded and thoroughly desperate graduates who still thought that attending the Ivy League made them better than everyone else, as if merely mumbling, "I went to Harvard," somehow entitled them to a successful career, a wonderful spouse, and an upper-six-figure income.

You couldn't go to an Ivy & Elite event unless you had matriculated through some program in the Ivy League, however, the word "program" was loosely applied: Summer Programs, total Ivy League shams like the cash grab "certificate" or "credential" programs, or executive tune-ups/vacations—"courses in professional studies"—counted.

I was there because Jennifer had begged me to help our law school classmate, Leslee, a recent transplant from the Bay Area, meet some people. Leslee, someone who never listened to anyone, thought that the best way to meet people—"her kind of people"—in L.A. was to attend a selective gathering.

She was sure to be unique among the participants. She was one of the few in the room who had actually attended an Ivy League school and had received a degree.

"But I don't like Leslee. She's mean. She's a self-appointed expert on what men want," I said. "And talking to her is like voluntarily attending a Bay Area Chamber of Commerce meeting. She's a one-person booster club for the City of San Francisco."

"Have a heart. She's lonely."

"What a surprise."

The last time I had seen Leslee had been at Jennifer and Kevin's housewarming party. Sometime after she realized that she wasn't going to land Kevin that evening—despite a near flawless performance by meeting his height requirement (under five foot six), not wearing a drop of makeup, slinging a thoroughly convincing but totally tired argument about the alleged Bay Area Superiority—she blew it. She tasted the wine in front of him. He turned cold. She wandered off and polished off the remaining two bottles by herself.

"You wear too much makeup, and your hair is too short," said someone from the darkened corner of Jennifer's hallway.

"Hello?" I walked over to where the voice came from. "Oh. Leslee. It's you. What are you doing here sitting by yourself?"

Then I saw the empty two bottles wine. "Oh, I see," I said.

"You know, you're never going to get married," she said.

I looked at her. "Uh huh..."

"Because I've done an empirical study. And my research has shown me that men don't like women who wear too much makeup," she said. "And they especially don't like short hair."

"Well, it's good to see that Harvard degree isn't going to waste."

"At least I'm not wasting it being a low-rent attorney with her own practice," she said.

Not 90 seconds later, Mr. Yum—Byron—walked me into a bedroom for a massage.

"I'm serious," Leslee yelled as we walked away.

"Of course you are," I said.

"Who's that?" said Byron.

"Oh, just a delegate from one of those Bay Area booster clubs."

"You're funny," he had said, as he massaged my shoulders.

"Sometimes," I said.

I think it was Latin Night at the Ivy & Elite because when I came in the door some Harvard grads were attempting to lead about twenty Ivy Elites in a group Samba. There were also four deserted pool tables that were covered with empty plastic cups from the crowd of Ivy Elites having animated conversation in their general area.

The general smell of a large fart permeated the room—cigars. Of course, about twenty Ivy Elites were on the balcony choking on inexpensive cigars.

"I see you didn't take my advice about the hair or makeup," said Leslee as she met me at the door.

We paid our $50 entrance fee, which gave us two drink tickets, one free cigar, and a chance to mingle with the "best and brightest" of Los Angeles.

We walked over to the bar.

"Ladies," said the bartender, "in keeping with this evening's theme, tonight our drink specials are Margaritas, Dos Equis, and shots of Tequila."

"Margarita, no salt," I said.

"Tequila," said Leslee.

"On second thought, make that a Shirley Temple with three, and I mean three, cherries," I said.

"What are you, six years old?" asked the bartender.

Well. His chance for a big tip had just been shot.

Leslee was in her element. She flirted with Bill, a trust and probate attorney (a certified specialist) from Boston. "Don't you just hate Los Angeles," she said. When Bill told her that he liked L.A. because he could ride his bicycle during the winter, her interest waned.

"You should see San Francisco," she said. "By the way, I work at Hobeck, Berman."

Bill gave her the strangest look when she mentioned Hobeck, Berman. Was that a look of sympathy? And then he told her that he had been to San Francisco and it reminded him too much of Boston. Leslee moved on.

Don was from the research and development division of a large tobacco conglomerate which was famous for its target market: children in third world countries. Mid-conversation, Leslee excused herself and motioned for me to join her.

"How much do you think he earns?" she whispered to me.

"Well, probably not enough to make you happy."

"You're right."

"No, I'm kidding," I said, "other than the fact that he may be creating lethal products, he seems fine."

"Nah," she said. "I'm going to get more tequila."

Hmmm. She was way past her two drink tickets.

"You know, you may want to slow down. I'm sure that free tequila they're serving is not exactly Don Julio. And nobody said you had to drink the worm tonight."

"I'm fine," she said.

I walked over to the pool tables and overheard a conversation between two women who were attempting to play pool.

"I took my entire salary in stock options," said a small, dark-haired woman as she laid down a fresh scratch.

"I just don't think you're Ivy Elite material," said Bettina, three days after Leslee had invited me to the Ivy Elite event. "I think you should pursue Dr. Ted. I mean, he's a doctor now. He could be making decent money."

Marcie was silent. I tried not to look at her.

"Don't you think so, Marcie?" said Bettina.

Marcie found out that Ted was a doctor around the time that Ted asked me why he never got to meet my friends.

"I have my needs, you know," said Dr. Ted.

"He's got a look," said Marcie, after I had him over with some of my friends.

"I don't know, Marcie, he's not what you're looking for," I said.

"You're just jealous that I could have something that you want, when you should be happy for me."

Dr. Ted would call me and tell me details.

"I had her come to my office and had a little fun with her while there was a patient behind the next screen."

Around the same time, Marcie would call me with her version of the encounter.

"He's really romantic," said Marcie.

"I hope this is what you want," I said.

"It's what you want, but I got it," said Marcie.

Ted began to complain.

"Her butt is too big. And she keeps asking me how much money I'm making," said Dr. Ted. "I'm sick of her."

Marcie began to get serious.

"I hope you don't mind, but I think Ted is going to propose to me," said Marcie. "He told me that he wanted a change in his life. I think he's truly ready to be serious with me."

"Mazel tov," I said.

Ted stopped calling her and never returned her calls. Marcie accused me of stealing him from her.

"I didn't know that you stopped dating him. I tried to warn you about him," I said.

She didn't say much, but soon after it was over, she left for Prague. When she came back, she was dating Russ, the accountant in the adult entertainment industry.

"Hey," said a small guy with an odd shaped head and a weird haircut. He was wearing a suit which was about two inches too short for him.

Since I had been virtually invisible to everyone all evening, I figured that he wasn't talking to me. I moved away.

The small guy appeared at my elbow again.

"Hey Katie," he said.

I turned around.

"You talking to me?" I said.

"Yeah, you."

"Well, to begin with, my name is Courtney."

"Right. Whatever. That's what your friend at the bar told me."

I looked over to the bar and saw Leslee, who appeared to be keeling over—with laughter.

"You know, my friend doesn't look well," I said. "I better go check up on her."

I looked over to the bar, silently mouthed a nasty word as I rolled my eyes.

"Relax," he said. "She's just stretching."

"More like retching," I said.

I looked over again. Leslee had stopped laughing and appeared to have attracted her own little nightmare—an Ivy Eliter who, even from ten yards, was clearly wearing a hairpiece.

"So," I said, "you are…"

"Richard. Your friend says you work in the entertainment industry."

"Well…"

"What do you do?" he said while looking around the room. I couldn't see it, but I could hear someone with a strong New Delhi accent belting out "Stand By Your Man."

"I do wardrobe for adult entertainment videos," I said.

"Oh, too bad. I was hoping that you were one of the writers from Wesleyan. I'm a lit agent. From Aspire. So where are they?"

"I have no idea. But..." I said as I started to walk away, "if I find them, I'll send them over to you."

He lurched forward and grabbed my arm. "I'm not done with you. Where're you going?"

"I'm going to get a drink," I said.

"Don't bother," he said. "You need to convince me that this evening hasn't been a total waste. How do I get invited to come to the set?"

"Of what?"

"Butt Detectives II."

"I'm an attorney. Entertainment. No porn."

"I knew that. Ivy League Law School?"

"No."

"Undergraduate?"

"No."

"Why'd they let you in?"

I stared at him.

"Represent anyone good enough for us?"

I yawned.

"OK," he said. "Give me a contact number. I'll take you to lunch. Then I'll find out."

"I can't wait," I said.

I gave him a contact number—a real one—which I quickly realized was a mistake. I mean, Richard was nowhere near my level on the L.A. Eco-Chain.

Richard wandered off. Before I lost sight of him, I saw him standing in a group of people. I think he found those Wesleyan writers.

I wandered through the room surveying the crowd. "Boots," a song close to my heart, was being mangled by someone in the Karaoke room. I walked in.

It was Leslee. She was tone deaf. She finished and walked over to me.

"You rebel, you," I said.

"I didn't know I had it in me," she said.

"You blew me away."

And everyone else. The room was totally empty.

"Where is everyone?" said Leslee.

"I think they're out on the balcony with their free cigars."

"Oh yeah. Let's go get our free cigars."

"Oh," I said. "I'm supposed to be training for a marathon."

"Oh—the marathon," said Leslee. "Jennifer told me about that. How many years have you been trying to do it?"

We got our cigars and found the door to the balcony. As we opened the door, a blast that made me think of 50 people farting as aggressively as possible hit us in the face. It was the desperate smell of a group cigar smoke.

Suddenly, Leslee ran into a dark corner of the balcony and started retching into a wayward trash can. Then she finished, walked toward me, started retching again and circled back toward the trash can while continuing to retch.

This was a surprise.

One usually didn't see a circle hurl unless it was New Year's. I went to Leslee and held her hair until she finished retching into the trash. When she was finished, I left her resting on a bench on the balcony and went to get her something that would calm her stomach.

I ordered a Shirley Temple, no grenadine, no cherries, with my second drink ticket.

"That's called a Seven-Up," said the bartender.

The bartender asked me if I wanted a little umbrella in it. I told him that I wanted the umbrella, but not to bother putting it in the drink. It was pink.

I took Leslee to a bathroom and helped her wash the puke out of her dress. We then attempted to leave the Ivy & Elite event without attracting too much attention. Nobody noticed us, because the Harvard grads had brought a large group to the dance floor to teach them a new dance.

Almost Royalty

I didn't recognize the dance, but it seemed that every five seconds they wiggled their hips back and forth and shouted out something that sounded a lot like "MAMBO!"

Leslee couldn't drive, so I stuffed her in my car. She fell asleep immediately. Before I got her home, she awakened from her stupor.

"Meet anybody cute tonight?"

"No," I replied, "but I got a pink umbrella." I twirled it for her. She rolled her eyes.

"Anybody ask for your phone number?" she said.

"Yes."

"Really? An Ivy Elite guy wanted your phone number? Before you blow it completely, let me give you some advice that I got from my research."

"Why am I so lucky?" I asked.

Leslee looked at me. "Because by the look of things, I think that you may be a little more clueless than everyone else."

"Mambo!" I said.

"This is a good place to start."

"Where?"

"Here," said Leslee. "You have a weird sense of humor."

"Since when is that a problem?"

"Since always, like every time I'm around you."

"And that's a problem?"

"Guys want to be the funny ones. I mean, think about it, do you think these guys really want a wife with a weird sense of humor?"

"I think it's important to have a good sense of humor, even if it's weird. What else?"

"You're cynical. And judgmental," said Leslee.

"You know what I do for a living."

"I know plenty of female attorneys who remain open-minded and fresh."

"They can't still be practicing," I said.

"Well, as a matter of fact," said Leslee, "they're not. They're married with children...you know, successful."

"What about you?" I said. "You're not married."

Leslee shook her head ever so slightly, right-left, right-left, right-left. "*I* work at Hobeck, so *I'm* part of something much bigger than your little practice. We've been here for over 100 years. That makes me highly desirable in the L.A. dating scene."

I looked at her. "So you want to keep practicing law?" I asked.

"Are you kidding me?" she said. "Only a masochist wants to keep practicing law. And you know about my research regarding your hair and makeup?"

"Yes. Your research has shown you that guys like less makeup and more hair."

"Right," said Leslee. "And you're too tall."

I looked at her and rolled my eyes.

"So start slouching," she said. "And you need to acquire the acquisition gene."

"What?" I said.

"You need to want things," she said. "Lots of things, like big houses, new cars, and new furniture. You need to be the person who consistently spends too much at Christmas every year."

"I don't celebrate Christmas."

"You know what I mean."

"But," I said. "I already have everything I need."

"That's pretty sad," said Leslee. "And by the way, I've seen your little post-graduate apartment. I sincerely hope that you want more than that."

"Well, what's the point?"

"The point is that you want and want and want. And you tell your husband that you want and want and want," she replied. "So you make your husband ambitious, because to shut you up, he has to work. So you become the backbone that makes your husband successful, because through your wanting, he works harder than he ever thought he would. That's how he becomes successful."

Almost Royalty

I shook my head. I was confused. "Sounds like you become the catalyst that gives your husband incurable debt."

"That's part of it," she said.

"Well, I'm ambitious. I can make the money."

"Are you crazy? Do you know how much work that'll take? Every woman I know, well, the *smart* ones, got rid of her ambition a long time ago. She gave it to her husband."

We pulled up at Leslee's apartment.

"Thanks for the info," I said.

"Think about what I told you. I mean, you're 35. It's almost too late for you."

I drove home and fed Abyss.

There was a message from Autumn, the Stepford D-girl at Genie's production company.

"Courtney, this is the third time I've called. Please call me. Jon Gene would like to have lunch with you."

More like have me for lunch.

I made myself one of my favorite Velveeta creations: toasted bread, mayonnaise, tomatoes, with Velveeta melted over it. A Velveeta junior pizza. It tasted great.

And then I thought about what Leslee had said.

Later that week, I brought it up in Group.

"I was one of those women once," said the nearly divorced housewife who really wanted to be a therapist.

"Which women?" I said.

"A woman who was truly successful. I had everything."

"What happened?"

"I got ambition."

"Isn't it better now," I said. "I mean, aren't you more realized as a person?"

"I went from having a 6-bedroom, 5-bathroom, 6,500-square-foot home on Mulholland Drive with a large Mercedes to having a 2-bedroom, 1-bathroom apartment off Ventura Boulevard and driving a Saturn. Yes, I'm more realized, but I also can't pay my bills."

Roberta broke in.

"I feel that the Group is a little off course tonight. Our purpose is to discuss what you feel, not what you think."

"Roberta, is it somehow not clear to you that we all feel horrible?" I said.

When I got home there were messages on my voice mail. Another couple messages from Autumn, Genie's Stepford-D girl, and six or seven empty messages which contained nothing but breathing.

Later that week Leslee called me.

"Oh hi, Leslee," I said. "Are you the Breather?"

"The what?" she said.

"The person who keeps calling and breathing on my voice mail and cell."

"Great. I see you've gotten yourself into another fine mess."

"I'm just asking."

"So Jennifer says I should keep helping you."

"I can see Jennifer is always thinking of me."

"She is. So is Bettina. Now there's a woman with her head on straight."

"Really?" I said. "That's not exactly what her girlfriends used to tell me."

"What?"

"Nothing. How'd you meet her?"

"Jennifer gave me her number. We went for coffee. It's nice to meet someone down here who isn't afraid of hugging and touching."

"And that's just the beginning."

"What?"

"Nothing. Did she invite you to train for the marathon with us?"

"She did. But like I told you, even she knows it's a joke."

"That's her opinion."

"It is. But it's also Bettina's, and your friend Marcie's."

"Marcie."

"She pronounces it Mar-cee."

"Whatever..."

"It's her opinion that I should keep helping you and maybe introduce you to some women who are successful role models. She calls the women the Civilian Royalty of L.A., like what I'll be once I get married. You know, married well, never have to work again."

"I might have heard something about this."

For the past ten years.

"And I might as well tell you...all of your friends think you're a mess."

"Really? Let me guess. No boyfriend, not married, close to 35, not in a big law firm—just me and my little practice."

"Exactly. So, there's this Ivy & Elite Book Group coming up and I might—if they're not too strict about you not really going to the right schools—you know those UCs—be able to bring you and your friends."

"Hmm. A book group. Oh boy."

"So I'll let you know if I can bring you."

"OK."

"If I can get them to let you in, you should really come. I think it would really help you to see the..."

"I get it. The role models, Marcie's..."

"Mar-cee's—"

"Marcie's L.A. Civilian Royalty."

"Yeah. I'm getting another call so..."

My cell went dead.

About two weeks later I got an email from Leslee. The Ivy & Elite book group would "make an exception" and allow me, Bettina, and Marcie to come. It was going to be in the home of an Ivy Elite member named Elizabeth, who lived in Brentwood.

"But," wrote Leslee, "please don't let them see the car—the Honda—you're driving. If you're going to come in that, could you please park around the block, or somewhere they won't see it?"

10

How Can I Be More Perfect For You?

Rabbi Francis O'Toole was the spiritual leader of a Westside synagogue that comprised born-again Jews, therapy-fried Episcopalians, guilt-fleeing Catholics, and pretty much everybody else who walked in the door. His Shul was a refuge for the disenfranchised—depressed from their recent job losses in the entertainment industry—who tended to be cautionary tales for the rage-of-the-moment drugs, cults, and sexual practices that had ravaged Los Angeles during the past 25 years.

Like many in his congregation, Rabbi O'Toole's acceptance of Judaism in his life was the result of a tortured spiritual and emotional odyssey. Never popular as a kid, he had formed several punk bands which had briefly flashed on the L.A. music scene in the early '80s, the most notorious being his last band, Dry-Gun-

Fly, a band known for creating mood by cranking up their smoke machine during their rock anthems.

When Dry-Gun-Fly exploded due to a lethal combination of drug-heightened ego and a general inability to determine who was rightfully sleeping with their Marilyn Monroe look-alike female lead singer, Francis smashed his guitar during their last concert at Madame Wong's and never came back. There would be no more 3:00 a.m. runs to Cantors Deli. It was over.

His next stop was a brief journey into EST. The "BIG MESSAGE" they were supposed to give him? Talk about stupid. It was nothing more than sadism with a therapy twist. And he resented being told when he could go to the bathroom.

He then became a disciple of the Guru Gorabi. After giving the kid-Guru all of his worldly possessions, he discovered The Universal Truth: The Guru was a fat, pimply-faced, dull 16-year-old who farted when he ate broccoli. Francis tried to retrieve his beloved 4-chamber bong, his Fender amps, and the mother of pearl roach clips which were given to him by some girl he had met at a Devo concert. But no such luck. The Guru knew when he had scored some good booty.

After spending some time on a kibbutz in Israel, he discovered two things: (1) this communal farming thing was for the birds, and (2) ab-busting physical labor was not what he wanted to do.

He also acquired a ferociously entrepreneurial wife named Sabre who pretty much figured that Francis was her ticket to the big time, that being American citizenship and the position of Rebbetzin in an affluent American congregation.

The citizenship she got hands down, but the Rebbetzin, the rabbi's wife? That meant Francis had to become a rabbi. How was that going to happen? He really liked Christmas and that big fat ol' smokey Easter ham he ate every spring. He was a Christian. But she pushed and campaigned and nagged.

Sometime after Sabre became profoundly unbearable, Francis had a vision. Sure, being an Herbalife distributor, his current gig, was OK, but wasn't he meant to do more than push biodegradable soap and overpriced vitamins?

Being a Rabbi actually give him everything he craved as a rock star. People would come to hear him. People would look to him for guidance. People might even revere him—all this, even without a current hit on the Billboard 100. He would never ever have to worry about fitting into tight clothes or being cute. He could eat. And besides, the Herbalife distributorship was not doing that well.

He converted to Judaism.

He slogged his way through rabbinical school and got a position as a junior rabbi in a large synagogue. Although given trivial duties, non-existent support, and thought generally to be an intellectual bantam-weight, he found a formula which made him a hit with the disappearing younger members: Rock-the-Shabbat. If his time as an Herbalife distributor had taught him anything, it had taught him this: to be successful, you must identify with the customer and find out what they want.

As Rabbi O'Toole was roughly the age of the quickly disappearing younger members of the synagogue, he knew what they wanted. Those assimilating sons and daughters of the affluent congregation, growing up in weather-wonderful Los Angeles County, wanted to be cool. They wanted to be in a band. They wanted to defy their parents—at least while they were in school. They wanted their religion made fun and easy, like everything else in their life. They wanted sex, drugs, and rock-n-roll.

The sex and drugs he couldn't deliver on, but the rock-n-roll... He put together a house band in the synagogue made up of various musician wannabes and installed himself on guitar. He called the band Mo-Zest-Flock.

Sabre was ecstatic. Not only did she get to be the wife of a rabbi, but after dogging Rabbi O'Toole every waking moment for three weeks she got to be the lead singer. Once again, Francis O'Toole was sleeping with the lead singer of his band.

Almost Royalty

Unlike most Los Angeles synagogues, Rabbi O'Toole had no problem attracting younger members. In fact, his congregation was exploding with them. His Rock-the-Shabbat was an enormous hit and heavily attended. But the more senior rabbis became jealous, and somewhat fearful for their jobs. A small internal campaign was waged, and Rabbi O'Toole was ejected on the basis that his Judaism was not philosophically compatible with the synagogue's existing philosophies, something to which the rabbinical staff had not given a second thought when Rabbi O'Toole was covering hospital visitations and funerals.

But Rabbi Francis O'Toole wasn't flustered. He had been anticipating this action for one year, and in fact, planning his departure.

Relying heavily on his experience as an Herbalife salesman, he and Sabre created a corporate structure for their synagogue which ensured that he and Sabre could never be fired. There would be no board of directors, no officers, no pesky president of the synagogue to appease over parking spaces or who got to carry the Torah this week. He and Sabre would have all of the power, and be accorded the title "Head Distributors." Everyone else would merely be their salesman.

But it wasn't just his Herbalife years he relied on. His rock-n-roll experience was put to good use. Instead of having a permanent location, Rabbi O'Toole used the model of the "disappearing nightclub which only the chosen can find" for his synagogue.

Sometimes they were in a vacated Koo Koo Roo, which still smelled of roast chicken. Sometimes they were in the bottom of an abandoned building. Sometimes they were in the abandoned offices of a bankrupt law firm.

What was left of that blond mane, bleached white by so many summers at the beach, was in a pony-tail that went down to the middle of his back. And of course, Mo-Zest-Flock, led by Sabre's original vocal stylings, rocked at every Shabbat, and his young congregation danced, pounded on the walls, and clapped themselves silly.

Whereas most synagogues followed a line of Judaism which generally fell into orthodox, conservative, or reform, Rabbi O'Toole's had an original vision of Judaism which he called, "progressive-eclectic." In truth, progressive-eclectic was a unique goulash of modern management orthodoxy, personal-empowerment psychology, and flagrant irresponsibility, for which he always attempted to find basis in the Torah through his original interpretations.

Short of singing "Jesus Loves Me" there was very little behavior which was unacceptable in Rabbi O'Toole's synagogue on Shabbat. In fact, it was unusual to go through a Rockin' Shabbat with Rabbi O'Toole and not see a minimum of twenty people talking on their cell phones while others checked email on their iPhones or ate Chinese food.

You wanted to read from Torah but weren't Jewish? Come on up and join the other Roman Catholics who preceded you. You were thinking of converting but thought it was too difficult. Don't worry. Come to synagogue for a while and when you're ready we'll have your conversion in someone's swimming pool during a barbecue.

Rabbi O'Toole was doing something that no other rabbi had done. He was making Judaism accessible and acceptable—to Catholics, Christians, Buddhists, and Mormons. And the crowds who stuffed into his "location of the week" showed that his take-what-you-want-and-leave-the-rest version of Judaism, his progressive-eclectic, was speaking to a large group of Southern Californians, few of whom ever actually bothered to convert.

By the time I actually walked in the door, I think that things had gone a little too far. Sure, who hadn't heard of Rabbi O'Toole's infamous "How to Survive the High Holidays" lecture, a speech which all but admitted, "The holidays are a drag, but what are you going to do?" When I finally stumbled on the secret location, he was on to something much bigger: Comparing the biblical prophets from the Torah to '60s, '70s and '80s television characters.

It was one thing when he compared Ruth, the Moabite who joined the tribe of Judah, to Alf, the alien, who joined the tribe of humans. I could almost understand his analogy of Jews, searching for a homeland, to the Tribbles on Star Trek, facing diaspora. But the day I got off Rabbi O'Toole's "Judaism made Accessible" train was the day he told the story of Rachel and Leah by comparing them to Marsha and Jan, from *The Brady Bunch*. Even for a religious lightweight like me this was too much.

"You see, although Marsha was older than Jan she was the babe whom everyone wanted to date, just like Rachel." I looked around the room and counted eight people who put their cell phones away as Rabbi O'Toole paused to see how his brilliance was affecting his congregation. "And Leah, like Jan, is the daughter that her dad needs to get connected, well in this case, he needs to marry her off...and we all remember how jealous Jan was of Marsha." OK. I was embarrassed to realize that I, like everyone else in the congregation, did remember this, having watched more than my share of Nick at Nite. More to the point, I had that stinging moment of self-recognition when I realized that I knew much more about *The Brady Bunch* than I ever would about the Torah.

"Thank God I live on the Westside," said some guy. Yes, I thought. Only on the Westside would you get challah with pesto in it. I was standing outside at Rabbi O'Toole's latest secret location, the Yoga studio of a gym in Brentwood which was rumored to have once had O.J. Simpson's football jersey hanging in it.

"Aren't you, uh...?" I turned around. Some guy wearing a Hawaiian shirt and jeans was talking into his cell phone which was plastered to the side of his head. "No, I can't go to the Laker's game with you tonight. My restaurant is opening."

He wasn't talking to me. I started to walk away.

"Hey, wait a minute," said Mr. Cell-Phone, who stopped me by grabbing my arm.

"Aren't you...Cathy?"

"No I'm not," I said as I walked away.

"Stop!" said Mr. Cell-Phone.

"Where did we meet, where did we meet?" said Mr. Cell-phone, eyeing me.

I knew where we had met.

Mr. Cell-Phone was that pompous guy Richard from the suicidally boring Ivy & Elite mixer.

"We met at an Ivy & Elite mixer. And your name is Richard."

"Right. And you're…Connie?"

"Courtney."

"Right. Didn't I get your phone number and everything?"

"I don't remember."

He had.

"Because if I did get your number, I was definitely going to call you. I mean, I never take someone's phone number unless I'm going to call them."

Silence from me.

"Well, how'd you convince them to let you in here…Connie?"

"Courtney."

"Right. I mean, this place is pretty exclusive."

"Richard, this isn't an Ivy & Elite mixer."

"I know. But…"

"And I think I have the credentials that this place might be looking for."

"What's that?"

"I'm Jewish."

"You are?"

"Yes."

"You don't look Jewish."

"Are you?" I asked.

"Am I what?"

"Are you Jewish?"

"Good Lord, no. I'm Episcopalian…Church of England."

"Then what are you doing here?"

"This place is hot. I mean everybody is trying to get in here, if they can find it."

"But you're Episcopalian?"

"So what."

"You follow 'The Father, the Son, and the Holy Ghost' party line?"

"Sure. Who doesn't?"

"Well, Rabbi O'Toole, for one. Unless his progressive-eclectic has gone very wide, I'm pretty sure that he doesn't follow your Holy Trinity line of reasoning."

"Oh, that's OK. To each his own. Besides, I'm not here for the religion. I'm here to pick up clients."

Richard proceeded to tell me that due to his extensive list of contacts, Rabbi O'Toole had made him the leader of his Young Professionals Group.

"If you give me your phone number and if you go out with me sometime, I'll bring you to the Young Pros Group," he said.

I think I was beginning to understand. Richard's interest in Rabbi O'Toole's congregation might have been about clients. He was an agent. But then again, it might have been about an available and rapidly expanding pool of eligible women.

Hmmm.

"Richard, I gave you my phone number at the Ivy & Elite mixer. And since you said that you never take anyone's phone number unless you're definitely going to call them, I'll definitely wait for you to call me."

A day and a half later, he called.

"Carrie, I'm at Bar Marmont right now. It's really hot. You should come down," said the message on my voice mail.

Was that an invitation?

"You've got to go out with him," said Bettina later that week while we were jogging.

"Yeah," said Marcie, who had joined us in a fit of inspiration.

We were attempting to run seven miles, and the going was slow.

"What are you, nuts?" I said. "This guy's a jerk."

"He sounds like great husband material," said Marcie.

"Would that be because you think he has money?" I said. "Why should I go out with someone who can't even get my name right?"

"That," said Bettina, "is the kind of detail that you need to overlook."

Later that week, I got another message on my voicemail. "Cory, it's Richard. Just checking in." That, and the other six hang-ups on my voicemail, were definitely worth ignoring.

"Connie?" said a voice on the phone.

"No," I said.

"I mean…Courtney?"

"Yeah…"

"Hey."

"What?"

"It's Richard."

"What can I do for you…Rick?"

"It's Richard, not Rick."

"Whatever."

"There's this restaurant that's opening."

"Yeah."

"And it's going to be really hot."

"OK."

"And I'm a limited partner in the restaurant."

"Uh-huh."

"And I was wondering if you'd like to go to it with me."

"I'm really busy right now, Rich."

"Richard."

"What?"

"It's Richard, not Rich."

"Whatever."

"But this is the type of thing that you need to be seen at."

"Excuse me?"

"You heard me. All the right people are going to be there."

"I was wondering where they were hiding."

"You really should take this more seriously," he said. "I'm sure you don't get invited to events like this too often."

"If you really think that's true, why would you want to be seen with me?"

"Because I think it will be...well...different. I've never dated a plus-size."

"I'm a size 6."

"That big? I thought you were a 4."

In a city which had seen the proliferation of actresses who had punished their bodies into semi-starvation, the average dress size for women living between La Brea Boulevard and the Pacific Ocean spanned between a size 0 and a size 2. What made this statistic all the more miraculous was that many of these size 0s had little boy hips and 36D-size breasts.

And I was a size 6 and nowhere near a 36D.

"Well, Rickie," I said.

"Richard."

"Uh huh. Let me check my schedule and get back to you."

It was a foregone conclusion that I was going to go out with him. I knew that Marcie and Bettina would nag me into it.

I wondered if I could find some place on the Westside that sold food with fat in it, so that maybe I could be really large—like a size 8—before we went out.

Richard took me to the restaurant of the moment, a Zagat-described "toughest ticket of the decade" on Melrose in West Hollywood.

"Did I tell you that I was a limited partner in this place?" he said, loudly enough to startle the non-English speaking valets.

"Every 15 minutes," I said.

We entered the restaurant.

"I'm sorry, we don't seem to have your reservation," said the maitre d'.

"But I'm…" Richard turned his body away from me and asked to see the manager.

After what appeared to be a heated discussion with the manager and maitre d' he came back.

"I set them straight. Let's go to the bar and wait while they set up my table."

The bar was, well, nice. I suppose the profit center of the restaurant has to be. I'm not sure what the normal mark-up is on wine, but Richard proceeded to order a Cab that even in the most marked up retail stores goes for $42.00. Only here, it's going for $90.00. And the two bottles of water he ordered (retail $2.00) are going for $18.00 a bottle.

We hadn't had a piece of bread before he downed the Cab like it was Gatorade. And then he ordered another bottle.

We've got $276 on the tab, he's a sloppy drunk, and we haven't eaten a thing.

We're finally seated at a table two inches from the swinging reach of the kitchen door, a table so small that it made the meal trays in an airline coach section look generous. It didn't really qualify as a table. It was more of a tablet, something that my mom would have put on my lap so that I could eat dinner while watching television and not spill anything on myself.

"I love being where the action is," said Richard.

"You know," he went on, "there are no smart people in Los Angeles."

Well, there were two things that I knew about Richard immediately.

Number 1.

"You went to SN-IVY," I said.

"How'd you know?" he replied while reaching for what would be his sixth glass of wine, which he proceeded to spill on our tablet.

It was easy.

You couldn't have a two-word conversation such as "excuse me" with a SN-IVY (my acronym for the School that was Not-Ivy League

Almost Royalty

but managed to produce the biggest jerks in the world) grad without receiving 20 minutes of pure disdain. Innocent remarks such as "That's interesting," "Turn left here," or "Can I help you?" could be counted on to produce a torrent of snotty remarks from a SN-IVY grad such as "Not really," "What do you know?" or "Why would you think that you could help me?"

It was as if they purposely asked you questions to set you up for their ludicrous reply, which was always delivered on autopilot as if it pulsed from a chip that had been implanted in their brain on the day they signed the SN-IVY acceptance letter and had Daddy send in the deposit.

I usually knew better than to engage with a SN-IVY person, but sometimes I slipped: A SN-IVY Grad once asked me the history of my violin and before I realized that it was a typical SN-IVY set-up, she cut me off after ten words with "Does anyone care?"

It was so easy. A SN-IVY alum would always start a conversation with an insult.

And Richard knew that I was born in Southern California.

I often pondered the genesis of this nastiness.

I occasionally encountered it from Harvard or Yale graduates, but after they dropped the word "Yale" for the 25th time in a three minute conversation, you knew that going to Yale was the most prestigious thing that had ever happened to them, that it had been a miserable mistake—given that they could have been in Palo Alto instead of New Haven—and that their Yale grades fell squarely at or below a 3.0 GPA.

But with the SN-IVY alumni, it was different.

I'm sure it killed them that in Los Angeles, SN-IVY meant about as much as any of the less competitive University of California schools.

But I think it was more that they never quite got over going to a school which was clearly not their first choice, a school which balanced on the very perimeter of the Ivy League, and that they were determined to spend the rest of their lives making up for it.

Number 2.

"And you grew up on the East Coast," I said, while waiting for the Chardonnay he spilled to dry from my clothes.

"I would never have taken you for such an observant person," said Richard, while trying to signal our waiter.

I might have been mistaken, but I thought I recognized our waiter as the lead from Genie's drama school production of a cross-dressing *Hamlet*, a play for which Genie was rumored to have been shortlisted for a MacArthur "Genius" Award.

Our waiter, true to his training, was pretending not to notice Richard while standing five feet from us and staring directly at him.

"How did you know that?" said Richard.

That was even easier.

Whereas someone who had lived in San Francisco would take a swipe at the physical characteristics of Los Angeles with a pathetic statement like, "L.A.'s so ugly," someone from the East Coast never dared do that.

I mean, what are they going to say? I hate living in a city that has consistently beautiful weather? But some of them did try out the idiotic "I miss the seasons" line. No, the disgruntled East Coast transplant usually came across with the hackneyed "This is definitely not New York."

But I had news for them.

We know that.

That's why we call it "Los Angeles."

Occasionally, you'd run across the very tired "There is/are no good...in L.A." a sentence which could be filled with nearly anything, but most often with: bagels, pizza, night-life, book-stores, bad weather, public transportation, or theater.

I never understood it.

You never found a person from L.A. going to Manhattan and complaining that there were no good beaches, the surfing was lousy, and there were no decent Mexican restaurants. I found

Richard's "There are no smart people in Los Angeles" statement so ridiculously stale.

And then I knew one more thing.

I truly didn't like him.

So it came as no surprise when he took it upon himself to correct my table manners.

"The way you hold your knife and fork, it's just…well…so common."

I looked around the room.

"I'm holding it like everyone else in the room."

"My point exactly. I prefer to hold my knife and fork as they do on the continent," he said.

"That's very interesting, Richard, but what continent would you be speaking of?"

"Why, Europe, of course."

"Really," I said looking at him, "that's very educational. Because I was unaware that in Europe, the main course was eaten with the salad fork."

Richard slumped in his chair like a balloon that had been popped by a machete. "Well," he said, "at least I wasn't born in Los Angeles."

"Really, Richard, really?" I said. "Because if you've been in L.A. longer than 24 hours, you'd know that almost no one is actually born in Los Angeles. That you've actually found a native, a true native, whose family has been in California over five generations, is highly unusual."

Richard looked away.

"And might I add," I said, "it's not…no, let me change that, it's *never* the natives who act like idiots, who drown in "The Grotto" at Hef's, who overdose on their toilets, who have seven wives and then get addicted to…whatever…in L.A. It's the people who come here."

Somewhere after Richard's lecture on the superiority of a private college (SN-IVY again) rather than a public university—

which I attended for law school—our bill arrived: $572.36, pre-tip.

I guess that's what four bottles of wine, five bottles of water, two appetizers, two main courses, two desserts, two coffees, and the sales tax costs. I quickly did the math. Ouch. With a 20 percent tip and sales tax, this was going to cost over $700. It was a good thing that he was a limited partner in this joint, or someone was going to see a small dent in their credit line.

"I'll take care of this," said Richard.

He picked up the check, and raced up to the front of the restaurant.

After what appeared to be another extremely animated discussion with the manager and the maitre d', Richard came back and sat down.

"It's all taken care of. I just had to remind them who I was."

Not two minutes later, our waiter appeared.

"I'm afraid your credit card has been denied, sir," said our waiter. "Would you care to try another card?"

Two credit card denials later, I found out Richard wasn't a limited partner in this place. His second cousin was. Although his cousin had let him eat for free a few times, Richard had been cut off.

Apparently, the third time he brought a party of ten at eight o'clock on a Saturday night and pulled the "limited partner routine" he had been shut down.

"I mean, she's my cousin and it's her restaurant, so what's the problem?" he said. "I don't get it."

I got it.

As it turned out, Mr. Ivy & Elite was maxed-out on all six cards, $40,000 on each, so that he's $160,000 in debt. He was waiting for his year-end bonus to pay it all off and it's only mid-August. He still had four and a half debt-filled months before bonus time and no credit left on his existing cards, which meant that the other person at the table who had decent credit was going to have to pay for dinner.

That would be me.

While processing my credit card, Richard table-hopped and decided to run out front to smoke a cigar with a guy from his health club.

I looked over at the bar and saw Josh, whom I hadn't seen since the Emmys. He was sitting alone. I walked over and sat down next to him.

"Hey. How's it going?"

"Well, well," said Josh. "If it isn't the little litigator. Come over here to start a fight?"

After my remarks on our first date, I guess that this was to be expected.

"Noooooo, I came over to say hello and see how you were," I said. "But I think I know the answer to that."

"Did the word drunk come to mind?"

"No. But the words extremely drunk did."

I motion to the bartender to cut him off, and he gets it.

"So what's going on?" I ask.

What's going on is that he's a mess. It turns out that Cody, the D-girl from the Emmys, has dumped him. After four months of dating, she told him that he wasn't powerful enough.

Then Richard reappears.

"What's this?" he said.

"This is my friend Josh," I say.

They look at each other.

"Hey," said Richard.

"Hey," said Josh.

I take Richard aside. "Look, my friend Josh just got dumped and is feeling pretty terrible. So I think I'm going to stay and make sure he gets home alive. OK?"

"But I thought you were with me tonight," said Richard.

"Look, my friend Josh is a mess. He needs some help."

"OK," said Richard. "But I'd like to do this again. I had a really good time tonight."

I just say "good night" and don't even go for the obligatory kiss.

I walk back over to Josh, order two coffees, tell the waiter to keep them coming and then wonder if I'm making a mistake. In this restaurant I could deplete my IRA trying to cover the cost of endless coffees. We stay until the restaurant closes. Then I take him to Canter's so he can talk himself out and I can stop paying for $6 cups of Maxwell House Blend.

Josh talks for four hours. Before I leave, I give him my cell phone number.

"Call me if you feel bad. Don't worry about the time. I'm a light sleeper," I tell Josh. This is a lie, but he looks awful.

When I get home, it's about 3 a.m.

My cell phone rings. I pick it up.

"Josh?" I say.

It's not. But there's breathing on the line.

"Whoever this is, this breather thing is so tired. Give it a rest."

"You're not the best-looking woman that I've ever slept with. I know you think you are. But you're not."

"Oh hi, Ted," I said. "Are you the Breather?"

"If you want, I'll come over," said Dr. Ted.

"Let it go, Ted. It's 3 a.m."

"You should feel lucky that I want you," said Dr. Ted.

"And why is that?"

"Because I'm a doctor."

"Really? Does the word HMO or...try this one, 'Managed Health Care' mean anything to you? Good night Ted. I'm going to lose you in a second."

"Bitch," barks Dr. Ted, just before my cell dies.

11

Did You Vest?

I'm not one of those people who like to stay in contact with a boyfriend after we break up. I think the act of breaking up demonstrates that on some level you hate each other. To stay in contact with each other on the basis of some ridiculous lie, like a pretense of friendship ("let's be friends"), only prolongs the inevitable. There isn't going to be any friendship. You're not going to get any closure. You repulse each other. So cut it off. When it comes to a former fiancé I take this theory to a higher level. Whereas with a boyfriend I'll acknowledge that I did date him, with a former fiancé I generally refuse to publicly acknowledge that he ever existed. This keeps me from inane thoughts about how our wedding would have been, what our children might have looked like, or what in God's name I'm going to do with the $6,500 raw silk wedding dress sitting in my closet. I find that this is the most effective method for enduring the naked humiliation of it all.

So when Frank disappeared from my life and never spoke to me again, I was actually quite relieved. It wasn't messy. It was just over, and he was gracious enough to remove his ancient gray spanky pants from my apartment before I actually gave him the boot.

What Frank did leave was an unreasonably permanent six-by-eight-inch carrot juice stain from all those sloppy mornings of running his juicer on my own primordial gray shag carpet. This confused my poor cat, Abyss, who wondered who had marked her domain. In an act of territorial rage, she began to pee on the carrot juice stain in a pattern which seemed to follow one spray every two weeks. To my horror, the fog of urine which sailed through my apartment on the 15th and 30th of every month became a never-ending reminder of Frank, the most recent disaster in my life.

So when I actually did hear from Frank again, I wasn't pleased. It wasn't much. It was a five-by-seven-inch cream- colored card, eleven lines long, written in black cursive handwriting.

It said the following:
Mr. and Mrs. Chad Bingham
request the honor of your presence
at the marriage of their daughter
Tracey Anne
to
Mr. Franklin Thomas Jamieson
Saturday, the Twentieth of October
at two o'clock in the afternoon
La Boca Inn
Palos Verdes, California

Well at least it wasn't going to be at the Bel Air.

I had played one too many weddings gigs at La Boca. It had a spectacular view, being located on one of those roads to nowhere on the bluffs of the Palos Verdes Peninsula. But the ballroom had a seedy, chipped paint, unglued wall paper, dusty chandelier look to it, like it was tired. I wondered if they were going to serve those little Swedish meatballs in that two-foot-deep serving vat.

Frank had attached a little handwritten note to the invitation. "I guess you're probably pretty surprised to receive this," he wrote. "Sorry we haven't spoken for a while, but I hope you're doing well. It would mean a lot to me if you would come. Call me if you get a chance."

No, I wasn't going to call him. This was my hard and fast rule, especially because in my world he no longer existed. But that rule was "never again publicly acknowledge," so technically, I could still call him and investigate who the intended was in this plane-crash of a marriage.

"Tracy Anne Bingham?"

"Uh-huh," said Frank.

"*You* are getting married?"

"Uh-huh."

"What happened to 'I just have so much work to do?'"

"Well, I have less with her."

"Because?"

"Because she's not as complex as you are."

I thought about it.

"But Frank, we've only been apart for six months. You met her and decided to marry her in six months?"

"I knew her from before."

"You did?"

"Uh-huh. And so did you."

"From where?"

"From Starbucks. Don't you remember, she was the one who always gave us extra foam on our lattes."

No.

"Tell me you don't mean that thirteen-year-old surfer-girl who always got our orders wrong."

"I take offense at that. First of all, she's nineteen, not thirteen."

"And you're 35."

"And she's not a surfer-girl. She's quite ambitious."

"Really?"

"Really."

"Do tell."

"She doesn't work at Starbucks anymore."

"Moved on to McDonalds?"

"She's a receptionist."

"Oh Frank..."

"A receptionist at a new internet company, E-Weddings. And they gave her stock options."

"Pre or post IPO?"

"Pre."

"An interesting choice for your soul mate. Will many of your Andover classmates be at the wedding?"

We were silent for about 15 seconds.

"OK. Just one more thing," I said.

"Yes?"

"Where *are* you two registered? Toys R Us?"

I hung up just as the word "ass..." came out of his mouth.

That conversation did not make me feel better. I moped around the two rooms of my apartment and wondered what to do. I needed something that would instantly take away the pain, but I struggled not to give in to temptation.

I resisted. I tried to distract myself by putting on my running clothes and stretching for a run.

But I knew myself. I was going to go for the hard stuff.

I decided to get it over with. I walked into my kitchen, cut myself a two-by-four-inch slab of Velveeta, and ate it like there was no tomorrow. It made me feel better, for a moment. I cut myself another Post-it size square of my beloved Velveeta brick.

Then I called Jennifer and I told her the Frank news.

"I hope you're not hitting the Velveeta," she said. "Your little addiction is nothing but an artery-clogging chunk of fat."

This from a woman who used to eat a quart of Ben N' Jerry's Chunky Monkey for dinner.

"It's very, very small," I said.

"I've seen your version of small, you could hurt someone with it."

"Well, I'm not too happy right now."

"Well, neither am I," said Jennifer. "Can you come up this weekend? I need your advice on a situation."

"You know how I feel about The City. Can't you just email me?"

"No," said Jennifer. "I need you to observe this situation."

"What's his name?"

"What do you mean?"

"Your situation. What is his name?"

"Funny."

"Uh huh."

"You'll hear all about it when you get up here."

During my flight to San Francisco, my seat companion, a thirtyish-looking six-foot guy with cropped hair, an earring, motorcycle boots, and a weathered black leather jacket continually eyed me. Finally I turned to him.

"What?" I said.

Just then, the flight waitress appeared with snacks. After I got my Snappy Tom and junior pack of pretzels, he turned to me. "I was wondering if you actually lived in Los Angeles?" he said.

"Yes, I actually live in Los Angeles. What's it to you?" He was going to tell me that although he was a 33-year-old Kinko's assistant manager living with eight other guys in a two-bedroom, one-bathroom flat in the Sunset, his achievements were far superior to mine because he lives in San Francisco.

I braced myself for the first punch.

"Because I've always heard that everyone in L.A. is really superficial."

"So you've met all eleven million of us."

"What?"

"Everyone in L.A. means that you've met all eleven million of us. And we're all superficial."

"Well, I mean…"

"I know exactly what you mean. You mean that there are no 'real' people in L.A. You mean that every woman has dyed blond hair, every body part is filled with silicone, and no one reads anything, unless it's script coverage or a menu, which damn well better not have anything on it but bottled flat water, poached salmon, sushi, or Chinese chicken salad. Right?"

He was silent.

"I…"

"Let it go," I said.

"I was going to tell you that I was surprised at how many creative people I met."

I looked at him.

"Yeah, it was really cool. I met writers."

"Screenwriters."

"Those too. I met musicians. I went to art shows. But the reason I came down is because I'm sick of The City."

What?

"San Francisco is the new Los Angeles. It's crowded. It's smoggy. And people are leaving because you have to make $350,000 to be able to live alone in a safe area. In L.A, I could afford my own apartment in Echo Park. Or Eagle Rock. Maybe even downtown. If I'm lucky, I might fall into a place in Venice with great light that's walking distance to the beach. In San Francisco, I can't even afford to live in the Mission, which—by the way—has become very, very hot."

"No way."

"You better believe it. There's nothing but bankers, lawyers, and technocrats in San Francisco now. They'll buy anything. In the Mission. In the Sunset. Alamo Square. They don't even care where it is or how much it costs."

All that to live in the world's only retirement community for people in their early 30s.

I had waited for an eternity to hear that someone else didn't think that San Francisco was The Lost Paradise. For years I had suffered in silence while my friends rhapsodized about The City.

The San Francisco I knew was a place where the fog rolled in from nowhere in the middle of July and chilled the city to 48 degrees in under 20 minutes and you were caught wearing a sleeveless T-shirt while waiting for the bus. Where you were much more likely to step in dog shit, get hassled by junkies looking for change, or accidentally see a prostitute doing business than to find an apartment with any kind of back yard. Where the most likely view you would ever get would not be one of the Golden Gate Bridge but that of the big hairy butt of the guy who lived in the building next to you.

Heresy—that's what it was to admit that you didn't like The City to any resident of San Francisco, especially if that resident wanted to hide the fact that they were originally from some uncool place like Long Beach or Glendale.

Before we landed, I apologized to my seat-mate.

"I'm sorry I was so rude," I said.

"It's OK," he said. "I used to give people from L.A. a hard time. And then I realized there's only one thing that San Francisco still has going for it."

"What's that?"

"Attitude. We still think that we're better than everyone else, like it's so great to live here. But it's not. You can get everything you can find here someplace else. And living here isn't great. It's just hard and expensive."

After the plane landed I went downstairs and waited for Jennifer on the Departures level at SFO. Thirty minutes later, a beach bunny with long, white-blond hair in a spanking new $85,000 black Range Rover pulled up at the curb and started honking her horn to attract the attention of some moron who had to be dead not to hear her. The bunny had clearly pulled every bit of equity out of her property to buy the Rover. Just then, two 23-year-old guys wearing Aqua Team Hunger Force jackets sitting not five feet from me decided that 10 a.m. on a Saturday morning, now, was the perfect time to start eating two huge orders of chili-cheese fries that smelled like 10,000 calories. I eyed the Hunger Force, glanced at Ms. Leveraged Equity and decided I would tell her that if she didn't cut it with the horn-honk symphony I'd key a scratch on her new purchase.

I walked over to Ms. Leveraged Equity and wondered if smearing my sticky bun on the passenger door of her new ride might accomplish the same effect. But just as I got to the new blonde and her Range Rover, I took a better look.

That beach girl drinking a pulverized grass concoction while applying hot pink lip-gloss to her mouth was Jennifer. I poked my head in the open window of the passenger side door.

"Don't I know you from somewhere?" I said.

"What's wrong with you?" she said. "I've been honking my horn for the last 15 minutes. Didn't you see me?"

"Oh, I saw you all right. I just didn't recognize you."

"What do you mean?"

"Since when did you enter the beach girl look-alike contest?"

"I decided to let my hair go back to its original color. You know I'm a natural blonde."

"Really. Because in the thirteen years I've known you, you've never had anything but dark brunette hair cut in a corporate attorney helmet. And right now you have a half-inch regrowth of your *natural* hair color. And it doesn't look blond."

"Well, Marshall really likes blond hair. He says that it reminds him of the innocence of children."

"Marshall?"

"My boyfriend. Kinda. This is his new car."

"Your friend Marshall just screams leveraged equity or vested options."

"Marshall is a wise soul searching for a resting place in the universe," said a voice from the back seat.

I turned to the back seat and saw a pumped-up guy with a pin head who looked like he had been existing on a 10-year diet of ground sirloin, raw eggs, and steroids. He had massive shoulders, a 50-inch chest, and the largest thighs I had ever seen.

He was a West Hollywood/Mr. Universe type somehow transplanted to the Bay Area.

"And you are?" I asked.

"Haggis. At your service."

The endless possibilities of that sentence entered my mind. It was more than I wanted to know. I rolled my eyes, hunched down in my seat and decided not to pursue it.

We left the airport circle and entered the 101 Freeway back to San Francisco. Then I saw something that I had never seen before in the Bay Area—a traffic jam running from the airport to the outskirts of San Francisco—at 10 a.m. on a Saturday morning. "Boy, I love coming to the Bay Area," I said. "It's just great to be able to get away from the stress and pressure of Los Angeles."

"At least we don't have the L.A. smog," said Jennifer.

My eye panned the horizon. I noticed a layer of brown haze that looked suspiciously familiar.

"Then what's that?"

"It's fog."

"It's 77 degrees outside. Sunshine burns off the fog."

"It's fog," she said.

"Uh-huh."

It was clear that we had entered some zone in which reality had become a missing ingredient in our conversation. Perhaps it had become a missing ingredient from our relationship. I took a hard look at Jennifer. Something else was missing.

"You're missing something."

"What?" she said.

I stared at her for about 30 seconds. I was puzzled.

"What?" she said. "Do we need to go back to the airport?"

"Only if that's where you left your butt."

"What …" she said with a laugh.

"Your butt."

Jennifer had once had a butt that would have courteously been considered ample. This was no surprise. Years of diligent studying, working 24-hour days as an associate in a big firm and a diet of take-out pizza eaten at 10 p.m. had created a body that reflected the toll extracted to stay partner-track in a first-tier legal practice. Now she had the butt of an eight-year-old boy.

I guess leaving the partner-track and becoming the in-house counsel at an internet company had given her new options.

"Jennifer and I have worked very diligently to create a new body and a new life," said Haggis.

"Did you also tell her that she needed to look like a 35-year-old beach bunny?"

"Courtney, cut it out. Haggis is my personal trainer."

"Personal trainer to the stars?" I said.

"Kinda," said Jennifer. "But more like personal trainer to the internet stars."

It turned out that Haggis was the personal trainer of Marshall, Jennifer's kinda new boyfriend. Marshall had told Jennifer that it would improve her "Chi" if she worked out with Haggis.

"How much are these butt-removal sessions costing?"

"Courtney, not in front of Haggis," said Jennifer.

"What do you mean? It's his business. He shouldn't be afraid to hear what his services cost."

"It costs $150 per session," said Jennifer.

"I guess I could live with shelling out $150 a week for a boy-butt."

"I've determined that my services aren't effective in a designated time span unless I work out with my clients at least three times per week," said Haggis.

"$450 per week. I hope Mr. Improve-Your-Chi is paying for this," I said.

Jennifer was silent for a moment.

"No," I said.

"Marshall and I decided that Jennifer wouldn't truly own her self-improvement, that it wouldn't be something she valued, unless she paid for it," said Haggis.

I turned to Jennifer.

"And you bought into this?" I said. "At $1,800 a month, you could *own* some pretty cool things."

We were silent for a few minutes.

"At least Marshall lets you drive his car," I said.

"Yeah, he's pretty cool about that. And to thank him, I drive Haggis home and get the car washed."

"Does he fine you if you're late?"

We dropped Haggis off at a Victorian house in the Castro which had a lavender exterior. The trim—the window frames, awnings, and door—had been painted a complementary eggshell blue. The bushes and hedges had been meticulously clipped into submission.

"Interesting. Haggis has matching trim on his house," I said.

"I know what you're thinking. But he's got an awful lot of female friends."

"I think the operative word would be 'friends.'"

We drove to her place in the outer Mission. When Jennifer and Kevin had first bought the place they had paid almost nothing: $200,000 for a two-story flat, a 3600-square-foot building.

They were considered urban pioneers for choosing to live in this slightly risky area of San Francisco, three blocks from the projects, which could only be described as massively overcrowded, covered in dog poop, and catering to the most aggressive street heroin trade in the Bay Area. Now, it was considered a desirable area. Each of them could have separately sold their flat for over $1,000,000.

When we got to her building, I noticed that something was different—her solid off-white building had been painted pale green. The trim—the window frames, awnings, and door—were now painted pine green.

"You repainted the building."

"Yeah, we just did it."

"And now you have matching pine green trim."

"That was Marshall's idea. He thought that the matching trim would give the building a balanced look, where I could do the necessary work to correct my Chi."

I took my things upstairs to Jennifer's guest room, a tiny room in the front of her flat which was always 15 degrees colder than the rest of her place. Despite the soft, lumpy bed which always gave me a crippling vertebra adjustment, I liked the room. It always gave me a bird's eye view of the local street life, which, of course, also involved male and female prostitutes giving blowjobs or dealers selling crack. Before I could get my fill of beautiful San Francisco, Jennifer walked in.

"I'm hungry. Let's go get something to eat," she said.

"What about the grass-goo you were drinking at the airport? Isn't that all that you're allowed to eat on your Chi-correction program?"

"That was just for Haggis. Now I want some real food."

We walked to a local cafe, carefully choosing our steps so as not to step on the items laid on the sidewalk by drug addicts who were selling their clothing so they could buy some more smack. Somewhere in the middle of her second cream-cheese-smeared bagel, I got the story.

"So Marshall," said Jennifer.

"Mr. Wise Soul, searching for a resting place in the infinity of the universe."

"Right.

"The architect of your new body, and your new life."

"Yeah."

"I get to meet him…"
"Tonight. So there's a little glitch in our relationship."
"Which is…"
"Well, you know I really like him."
"I didn't think you would transform yourself into Malibu Barbie unless you did."
"And I really appreciate all of his advice and guidance."
"Yes, Bo, tell us how your first met John Derek."
"But there's this little problem…"
"I feel myself aging just sitting here…"
"And I perfectly understand his position."
"More frightening words have never been uttered."
"Well, the truth is…"
"Yes…"
"He won't have a physical relationship with me."
"What?"
"You heard me. He won't…well, he won't touch me."
She let out a sigh.

I looked around the room for a few seconds and watched two lesbians split a cinnamon bun by biting the bun and transferring it to the other with a sloppy, moany kiss. In the corner, three guys who looked like they should have been the opening act for Mötley Crüe raged that "the American capitalist machine is killing music." Suddenly, the scream of hot milk being foamed by a Cappuccino machine blasted across the room. When was it that I came to hate the sound of bohemian pretension?

But I was in pain. I knew that Jennifer and I had arrived at some new place, some new reality, where nothing ever again would be easy. Where you would never again be electrified by the mere sight of a tall guy with green eyes, and some day, a week, a month, a semester later, find yourself sneaking a kiss that would cause a sigh 17 years later. Where we would never again greet each other on a Sunday morning with a hangover, a sly smile, and an ounce of regret. Where we would never again be breathless waiting for him to call, and think it was destiny when we realized that he too loved *The Adventures of Buckaroo Banzai*, French fries with mustard, or the orchestral recordings of Juan Garcia Esquivel.

"What's the deal?" I said.

"It's complicated."

"I'm listening."

"Well, Marshall works for Tibro Systems."

"Uh-huhhh."

"And I work for EBOL."

"Yes…"

"And you know…Tibro had its IPO early this year."

"Uh-huh…"

"And it actually makes a product."

"There is a point in here, isn't there?"

"Marshall got a lot of stock options, because he joined Tibro when it was just some guys working in their mom's basement. And EBOL hasn't had its IPO yet."

"OK. And with the Nasdaq struggling for support at 1750, things aren't looking good. Right?"

"Exactly. And of course, it's not the best time to have an IPO."

"A slight understatement."

"So Marshall's stock options have vested. And he's now a multi-millionaire, like about 35 of his co-workers."

"Cut to the chase."

"So he won't touch me because he's afraid I'll get pregnant and go after his money. And he doesn't want to complicate our relationship that way."

I had to look away.

My head began to throb and I felt dazed.

I didn't know what to think or what to say. All those hard-fought moral battles for sexual and personal freedom of the late '60s, fought in this very town, were suddenly thrown out the window for the San Francisco battle cry of the new millennium: Guard your stock options with your life.

Almost Royalty

"And you're OK with this?"

"Wait until you meet him. You'll see why."

That evening, Jennifer took me to a Labor Day/Non-Labor Day/Pink Slip party in a home of some internet czar in Palo Alto. The house was not one mile from the famed Sandhurst Road, the street where the entire high-tech explosion had started.

I had expected to descend into some glass and wood Frank Lloyd Wright extravaganza created from virgin pine with running brooks and pools of koi fish swimming through the center of 50,000 square feet.

What I saw was a 3-bedroom, 2.5-bathrooms, California ranch house, circa 1974–78, with a carport and no garage, that was covered with linoleum and shag carpeting in approximately 2,500 square feet.

It was identical to the millions of California starter houses that two-parent families with modest dreams had bought in the mid '70s.

"This is the home of an Internet czar?"

"This is Palo Alto. They paid two million and they were lucky—there were five other offers."

This was rich.

High-tech millionaires fighting to buy the very same style of home that middle-class families everywhere had bought in 1974.

There were about 100 people in their early 30s jammed into what my parents would have called the rumpus room, handing around their latest example of the market downturn: the pink slip. Snippets of conversations concerning touring Thailand, or the new home in Los Altos, or recent art purchases came my way, so it was hard to determine the crowd anxiety level regarding their collective unemployment as I ate everything in sight on the non-L.A. banquet spread (real food here), and everyone else proceeded to drink themselves silly.

As I stuffed my third helping of steamed fish with plum sauce into my mouth, I saw Jennifer coming toward me with her arm around a tall, almost good-looking guy who seemed to be examining his appearance in every reflective surface in the house. He seemed to be looking through me, and then I realized that he was, because he was looking at his reflection on the mirror behind the banquet table to which I was glued.

"Wow, Haggis has really done well with me," he said.

"Courtney, this is my Marshall," said Jennifer.

"What does that mean?" said Marshall while he picked Jennifer's arm off of his shoulder.

"Well…?" said Jennifer. "I'm, going to get a drink." She disappeared into the pink-slipped crowd.

"It means she's happy to know you," I said.

"Oh. I guess that's OK," said Marshall.

We sat in silence for what I counted to be 17 seconds on the digital wall clock.

"I'm going to get a drink," I said.

"No, wait. I wanted to ask you something."

"OK."

"Jen says that you work in the entertainment industry."

"Yeah."

"And I was wondering if you know anyone who represents actors."

"In film, television, theater or commercials?"

"Well, all of it. How about models?"

"Yes, to the first question, and yes to the second."

"How about spokespersons?"

"What, does your fresh-off-the-bus cousin from Tulsa want to be an actress-model-spokesperson?"

"No actually, it's me."

"You?"

"Well, now that I've vested, my therapist told me I should go for it and I've decided to pursue what I've always wanted to do."

"To become an actor-model-spokesperson? You graduated from Princeton."

"So did Dean Cain. And look, he got to play Superman in that TV show and then he got to do *Ripley's Believe It or Not*. But I have a plan."

"You do? What is it?"

"Well, Haggis and I have been working to prepare me for the *Faces of Tomorrow* competition."

"The *Faces of Tomorrow* competition? The model search?"

"Yes. I evaluated my chances, and I think that I have a good possibility of winning."

"Did Haggis tell you that? Is that why you have made him a rich man? Because except for the fact that you're probably 25 years older than every other contestant, that would be a realistic possibility."

"That's valuable information. Perhaps I should get some Botox injections."

"Sure. It'll take a good five years off your age."

"Does that mean you'll help me?"

"Excuse me. I need to find Jennifer."

I walked away without turning back.

I found Jennifer at the banquet table picking her way through the carcass of the steamed fish remains. I looked at the brown shag carpet and tried to collect myself, but instead of coherence I was struck by the need to eat a big piece of Velveeta.

"Uh oh," said Jennifer. "You've got that far away look in your eyes. Thinking about Velveeta?"

"At moments like this, I miss it so."

"If the need overwhelms you, try deep breathing."

"That was two minutes ago. And the desire hasn't left me. I think I'm getting the shakes."

"Hold on. I think I saw a cheese platter somewhere."

"Already found it. It's real cheese. Goat cheese is not going to work."

"Hold on. I think I saw something else."

Jennifer scurried away, and left me in the middle of a deep breath.

"Will this work?" said Jennifer.

"Cheese Nips? Are these being served?"

"Not exactly. I found them in the kitchen. They looked ignored."

"So you liberated them?"

"For you."

"Thanks," I said. I ate about ten and felt less anxious.

"So that guy you introduced me to?"

"Marshall."

"That couldn't be Marshall."

"Why not?"

"Because that was a gay man."

"I don't think so."

"I do. Let's think about it. Refusing to touch you added together with wanting to enter the *Faces of Tomorrow* competition at age 42 does not equal a straight man."

"There are good explanations for this."

"There always are. The most likely one being that Marshall is not as that pumped-up pin head described him."

"Haggis."

"Right. Marshall is not a wise soul searching for a resting place in the universe. He's a gay man who's desperate to burst out of the closet."

"I don't think you understand," said Jennifer.

I left the next day. Jennifer told me she couldn't drive me to the airport because she had to work out with Haggis.

As I sat on the plane, I read the online *New York Times*. While scanning the "most emailed" section, I noticed an interesting item: E-Weddings had held a moderately successful initial public offering. That meant that Frank's fiancée, Tracey, was most likely a millionaire. Maybe even a multi-millionaire.

I called him as soon as I got to Baggage Carousel 4 at LAX.

"So, how's America's newest millionaire."

"What're you talking about?"
"E-Weddings. Tracey. The IPO."
"That's her money, not mine."
"But you lucky boy, you're marrying a millionaire."
"Well, it's complicated."
"Since when?"
"Since the IPO happened six months before I thought it would."
"Yeah…"
"You know the drill. Those stock options are her separate property."

I did know the drill. Since E-Weddings had its IPO before Tracey and Frank were married, those stock options were Tracey's separate property. Frank would get no part of the options unless they appreciated.

"Frank, you know as well as I do that you'll get some money from those options."
"No. No. She took care of that. She downloaded a prenuptial agreement from the E-Weddings website."
"And…"
"She made me sign away any claim on those stock options forever."
"Even the interest?"
"All of it."

Well. I suddenly had a much higher opinion of Tracey Anne Bingham.

"You never made me do that," he said.
"No, I didn't."

I didn't know what to say.

"But Frank, your wedding is in six weeks," I said. "You're still going through with it, right?"

There was silence on the phone.

"Frank?"
"I think I need to speak to Roberta."

When I got home there were a couple of messages from the Breather. Autumn, the Stepford D-girl in Genie's company had left a message and Genie had grabbed the message mid-call and left his own remark, "Look Fake, you're being very unprofessional. I expect my calls returned…"

Then there was a message from Josh.

"Since you're a girl who likes to eat…" said his message.

Oh where was this going?

"I thought maybe I could take you to dinner to thank you for helping me out that night I wasn't doing very well."

Hmmmm.

"What do you think? Should we go to 'Berliner Café' again?"

Definitely not.

Josh's message ended with some nice words about me being a good person and some additional words of thanks. I took this to mean that he didn't have a shred of interest in me.

Two weeks later I received a card stating that Tracey and Frank's wedding had been cancelled. The card included a short message instructing that those guests who had sent presents would have them returned.

I never did get my lava lamp returned.

A few months later Bettina ran into Frank at a Westside Yoga studio. Frank told her that he was working the sound for a USC film student's short film. He didn't say much about Tracey. He just told her, "Tracey was great. And it was fun to be with someone so young. But it just wasn't right. And I have so much work to do."

12

Celebrity L.A.

"I've got a new nanny," said Bettina, biting into her cinnamon Bun. We were sitting in Brentwood in an unavoidable coffee house, the one that had a franchise on every corner in the known civilized world. It was Sunday morning at 7:00 a.m.

It was a hot day for October, a time of year in which the temperature usually dropped to a crisp 68 degrees and the leaves on the few deciduous trees turned a subtle orange-red. This year the temperature seemed stuck at 100, as if the seasons refused to change and September, usually our hottest month, was to continue for 61 days instead 30.

The heat, combined with the Santa Anas—dry, hot, and blustery winds that periodically unnerve the region—created a twinge of anxiety for anyone who had been in L.A. for over five years. It was fire and earthquake season.

Fires burned in the Simi Valley and Malibu, areas that were perpetually suffering some natural disaster. My gut told me that a little earthquake, probably a 4.2 on the Richter scale with its epicenter near Northridge, would follow in the next few days.

The usual crowd of vets from the local V.A. Hospital, the ones who were going through drug rehab, lined up for coffee. And the weekend bicycle guys in bicycle pants were there. When those guys in those tight black bicycle pants walked by, I was never sure where to look.

I think some of the guys in tight black bicycle pants wearing flashy form-fitting red-white racing shirts splashed with team names Like "Sponzi" or "Verti"—names that sounded like ice cream or opera composers—actually took a ride on those $5,000 Italian bikes. But I knew all of them were single. A $5,000 Italian bike was just like vintage Japanese movie posters or a faux wine collection: single guy gear, the kind of things a single guy bought to make himself seem interesting before every extra dollar went into private schools or mortgages.

When it wasn't too noisy with cell phones we went to the Coffee Joint Tehran, the Irano-chic coffee house across the street. It served this hairy cake, a white coconut cake with tiny lavender frosting flowers on it. The new coffee house, a San Francisco transplant located one block down in the location of the former Italian restaurant where Nicole Brown Simpson last lost her glasses, had not yet become a spot for us. It had tea but no sticky buns with icing.

"I didn't know you had a nanny," I said.

"Of course," said Marcie. "Everyone has a nanny."

"Why? You're not working, Bettina," I said. "Aren't they expensive?"

"Of course," said Marcie.

"I need time for myself," said Bettina.

"Don't you get about eight hours per day while your kids are in school?" I said. "How can you afford this? I thought the deal was that you quit being an artist so that you could stay at home and raise your kids."

"Everyone has a nanny," said Marcie.

"How much does this cost?" I said.

"The usual," said Bettina.

"What does it usually cost?"

"Don't worry about it," said Bettina.

"But your husband can't be making more than $55,000 per year. Who's paying for this?" I asked.

"That's not important," said Bettina.

"It's not," said Marcie.

"Not your in-laws."

"You're missing the point," said Bettina.

"As usual," said Marcie.

"They're already paying your mortgage."

"That's not the point," said Bettina.

"No, it's not," said Marcie.

"And they gave you the down on your house."

"You'll never guess who my nanny used to work for," said Bettina.

"Who?" said Marcie.

"It better be Angelina Jolie for this to be worthwhile," I said.

"Only the highest paid star in the known world—Tom Fricken West," said Bettina.

Marcie's mouth fell open.

"So? Is she any good?" I asked.

They both turned and looked at me.

"Did you hear what I said?" said Bettina.

"Yeah," said Marcie, "and why are you wearing blue? And so much makeup? We're going jogging."

"The color thing," I said. "C'mon. Every other week it's 'you should only wear blue,' 'you should never wear blue.' And you know about the makeup, so let's not pretend that you're bothered by it in year 20 of our friendship."

"But we're going jogging," said Marcie.

"No, I'm going jogging," I said. "You two are going to sit here and eat cinnamon rolls while you babble about how thrilled you are to get Tom Fricken West's former nanny."

I hate celebrities.

But I live in a town where I see them all the time.

I hate seeing them in my dentist's office but I especially hate that my dentist has their pictures plastered all over his office. Little Polaroids of himself with the stars—rock stars, movie stars, television stars, even sons and daughters of famous movie stars. I wonder if he's taken down any of those dead celeb pictures yet.

And it's not that being the dentist to the stars makes him a better dentist. It just means that you (not a star) are a second-class patient in his office, and even if you have an abscess the size of Jupiter in your mouth you will never, ever get an appointment with him and you *will* get bumped if any celebrity—ex-Baywatch babes, the son of the movie star legend from the '70s, or—Oh My Gosh—a remaining member of the Fab Four with his horrible English teeth, and especially Tom Fricking West or any of his wives or children—wants to come in. And then you can't even buy your way in, because even if you are paying 20,000 times the amount that the celeb patient is (since they never pay for anything, it's easy to do), your money counts for almost nothing.

I hate it that the Thai dental hygienist in my dentist's office feels compelled to tell me which friend of hers is trying to sleep with which barely-successful rock star who now has a T.V show.

"He has a thing for Asian women," she said.

"Is there any man alive who doesn't have a thing for Asian women?" I reply.

"You need to floss more."

"I floss like a demon."

"My friend wants to get pregnant with him," she said. "Maybe you want to show me how you floss?"

Almost Royalty

"Why does she want to get pregnant with him? Please, I stopped showing people how I floss around the time I lost my baby teeth."

"He has a TV show," she said. "If you don't floss right you'll get gingivitis. Look at this picture."

"His show is on basic cable, so he doesn't make squat. Tell your friend to go after a starter in the NBA. And I've seen that stupid picture on every visit to every dentist I have had since I was seven years old and I've still never gotten Gingivitis. If I floss any more, my gums will disappear into my brain. Stop trying to scare me."

I hate seeing them at my hairdresser's, but I especially hate that my hairdresser claims to be done with "the star thing" yet seems to have a client base made up exclusively of the actresses who played moms in '70s and '80s sitcoms. And none of these actresses have worked since 1987.

Somehow, being an ex-TV mom meant that I could sit for 90 minutes past my appointment time and if one of those *Family Ties*, *Family Affair*, *Facts of Life* TV moms were to walk in, wanting my appointment, my hairdresser would give it to them. It's sad. My hairdresser prattles on about the TV moms with words like "mystical," "magical" and "spiritual" when what they truly are is entitled, and he regularly confuses playing a good person on a TV show with being a good person in real life.

"See," I say to him, "on the TV show, they play a mom who shops, cooks, cleans, chauffeurs, visits their children's teachers, and knows how each of their three children is doing in each subject in school. *On the TV show.* In real life, their nannies shop, cook, clean, chauffeur, visit their children's teachers, and know how each of their three children is doing in each subject in school."

What makes me nauseous is when my hairdresser imbues his TV moms with the heroic characteristics of Greek gods or saints for the same behavior which we civilians follow to stay out of jail.

Star Philanthropy

"My God, she's generous," said my hairdresser.
"Oh," I said. "Did she give a $1,000,000 to charity?"
"She believes charity starts at home."
She's remodeling her house again.
"What did she do?" I said.
"She paid me," he said. "Today."
"Doesn't she usually pay when you do her hair?"
"It's not about the money."
"This is what you do for a living," I said.
He shrugs.
"Any tip?" I said.
"As a matter of fact, yes," he said. "She told me where she buys her green tea."

Star Wisdom

"I've learned so much from her," he'd say with a sigh.
"Really," I said.
"Today she told me how to make vegetarian chili," he whispered back.
"That's just chili where you don't put the ground chicken or beef in," I whispered.
"But it's her recipe, and she told me how to do it."
"Did she write it down?"
He looks at me for a moment.
"That's not what she does," he said.

Star Maturity

"I'm so proud of her," he said. "She's just celebrated her sixth month of sobriety."
"She just had a liver transplant. Isn't that part of the deal?"

"Yeah, but she really took the bull by the horns and turned her life around."

"Did she have a choice? She was almost dead."

And despite choosing a hairdresser with such a low profile that he works in a shop which is dominated by two gray parrots from Pluto who rap "Baby Got Back..." when approached by customers, I, despite being my hairdresser's "favorite person," will regularly be passed to his 19-year-old assistant at every conceivable opportunity, especially if he senses "TV Mom approaching" on his radar.

I hate going to parties that I think are going to be fun—non-celebrity—civilian events that evolve into faux celebrity events with people who have the attitude but not the status of a star. Events like a baby shower, where you think it's going to be relaxed and fun, and then you see the director of those absolutely horrible movies who married the rock star, the producer who just made the movie which nearly sank both a major actor's career and a studio, or the development exec of the low-budget studio unit which never produced a movie. Then the party becomes a delicate dance of "Forgive me for breathing the air that you breathe." I don't want to be there and don't want to talk to them, but they can't believe that. Maybe I just wanted some chips and a place to sit down. But that meant that you had to enter the room that they were in, and then they worried that you might want something from them—a job, to give them a script, a referral to an agent—when all you wanted was an extra chair and some blue corn tortilla chips.

I hate seeing them when I go jogging, but I especially hate that I invariably run into a former supermodel whose face was plastered on every magazine, monthly, for ten years, and that my brain involuntarily forms the syllables of her name—like it does right now because there she is, not 50 yards in front of me. And because I'm staring straight ahead and running forward, I see her, her personal trainer, someone I presume to be her muscle, her bodyguard, and a guy I recognize to be her new husband—

because I have read much too much about her, her fabulous modeling career, her fabulous new marriage, her fabulous Los Angeles home and the way that she miraculously managed to get back into a size 0 within four weeks of having her second baby.

I know that they assume that I will be excited, thrilled, or at a minimum interested by seeing them. But in reality, what I am is nauseated and bored, but mostly bothered, like the way you feel when you discover that you have acne on your butt and can't do anything about it except wait for it to go away.

They see me.

Go. Go away. Go back to your own planet.

It's like that moment in *The Matrix* where those alien-scanner things which have enslaved and deluded the human race have found the dump mother ship from which Keanu Reeves ("Neo" and more likely Very Luckio to have gotten that part), Carrie-Anne Moss, (Underpaidio, the chick who looks good and can move in tight black leather), and Lawrence Fishburn (Maxium Luckio or Oblio or whatever his name is) are attempting to save the free but boring realistic world.

Very Luckio, Underpaidio and Maxium Luckio can't move, breathe or have a heartbeat because if the alien-scanner things detect them, they will sense that dump mother ship's occupants are a threat to alien-scanner things' existence, meaning Very Luckio, Underpaidio, and Maxium Luckio will become enslaved and all hope for the free but boring realistic world will be lost.

About the alien-scanner things—the alien-scanner thing does not recognize the needs of other life forms. The alien-scanner thing does not want a connection with any other life force other than other alien-scanner things. The alien-scanner thing does not have a shred of humanity in it. The alien-scanner thing exists to use and destroy other life forms so that it may perpetuate the existence of itself and other alien-scanner things.

Alien-scanner thing fabulous ex-model has her alien-scanner thing Muscle move to the edge of the entourage to face me. He scans me to see if I am a threat to their existence. He puts his arms on his hips and slightly leans in. Oooo...big, bad boy. How menacing.

I stand very still and hope to blend into the neon blue-purple flowers which have erupted in this grossly over-built neighborhood—an area where the former one-story, 1600-square-foot, 2-bedroom, 1-bathroom homes with both a front and back yard have been leveled and replaced by three-story, 7000-square-foot behemoths—homes that look like a cross between a former Soviet bloc embassy and a Southern antebellum mansion.

It's not easy to blend into the neon blue-purple flowers because today I have chosen to jog dressed in a bright orange color which makes me look like a pumpkin, a pumpkin which would be visible at dusk to every motorist within 100 yards. If I were cool enough to be able to stop my heart, like Very Luckio, Underpaidio, and Maxium Luckio, I would. But I can't even hold my breath for very long.

And I'm bored.

Please Go. Go Away. Shoo.

I hate it when the Royalty of L.A.—celebrities—go to public places that are frequented by civilians, and bring their muscle. But I especially hate it when they—bless their little alien-scanner thing hearts—show up with their Muscle in Places Where They Are Not Supposed to Be.

They are not supposed to be at Best Buy, buying some electronic gizmo, using their 375-pound goon Muscle to create distance between themselves and the civilians who actually watch them portray a "teenager with unearthly powers" one night a week (5 nights on cable), when it is two days before Christmas.

And they're not supposed to be at a beauty supply store buying hair and skin care products when they have spent the last 12 years playing a tough-but-sexy cop/stud on a network primetime cop show.

A MEMO

TO: Stars, Celebs, and Anybody Else Who Goes to BEST BUY with a Bodyguard

I hate it that you've spent every day of the last 20 years trying to become a star and now that you're 23 and famous you seem to resent that fact that I, or anyone else in the civilized world, can recognize you in public. We wish that we couldn't.

But you do acne commercials. And you do hair color commercials. And you do lipstick commercials. And you star on a quirky television show that somehow got very popular—which we don't watch—usually.

The point being that unless I only watch C-Span (which I am considering), I'm going to encounter your image, which by the way, has become very annoying.

But because you're famous and people recognize you, you earn more money for one 20-week project than 1000 normal people will earn throughout their entire working lives.

So if you go to Best Buy to get a cell phone, don't have that 375-pound brute, your muscle, give me threatening looks if, when I turn around while getting my price check on my new not-so-smart phone, I see you.

I want the price check. I don't want to see you. In fact the words which form in my mind when I see you are, "Oh. No."

I don't want to talk to you.

I don't want to ask you why you're so short.

And I especially don't want to watch your show.

Anymore.

I wait two minutes for alien-scanner thing fabulous ex-model and the alien-scanner thing jogging entourage to go away so I can begin my run.

It takes me about 90 minutes to run two and a half times around the park, eight miles. It's about 8:30 a.m. when I finish.

Almost Royalty

I'm walking by the Starbucks on my way back and I look in. And then because of what I see, I go in again.

"You're still here," I said.

"You didn't run eight miles," said Bettina.

"You didn't collectively eat five cinnamon rolls and drink four cups of hot chocolate," I said. "You'll never guess who I saw running."

"Who?" said Marcie.

I tell them.

"Why didn't you come get us?" said Bettina.

"You wanted to discuss Tom Fricking West's nanny," I said.

"But this is bigger," said Bettina.

"Much bigger," said Marcie.

"Is she thin?" said Bettina.

"Her career is to be thin," I said. "Of course she is."

"After her second child?" said Bettina.

"Second child, fifth child, tenth child…" I said, throwing up my hands.

"Thin, huh," said Marcie.

"Did you ask her how she lost the weight?" said Bettina.

"You know better than that," I said.

She did.

You don't talk to L.A. Star/Celeb Royalty, especially if the Star/Celeb is an alien-scanner model thing with alien-scanner model thing's Muscle, because there are those unspoken but very well-known *Rules for Unexpected Encounters with L.A. Star/Celeb Royalty* in public places:

1. You never initiate conversation—Ever. If for some reason you're forced to speak with the star, because you are trapped in an elevator with them which is stuck between floors for more than three hours, there is only one thing you can say, which is of course, "I love your work." Then retreat as quickly as possible while breaking off eye contact.

2. If for some unknown reason the star/celeb should initiate conversation with you, look away, don't acknowledge who they are, and answer the question quickly. Don't pick up the conversation—they don't want to speak to you.

3. If a star should venture into public in the basic-star disguise—dark glasses, baseball cap, baggy clothes—and you don't recognize them and think that they are any other schlub—then it's OK. They didn't want to be recognized—and you didn't.

But there are gray areas. If a star/celeb, even an alien-scanner thing, should suddenly be outside your door because some unimaginable situation should transpire, e.g. he bought a condo in your building for his militant Goth daughter, and he knocks on your door and you open it:

"Can I help you?" You say to the top box office star of the '90s who—and you know this is not believable but it does happen—is standing there. Suddenly, you realize that your roots are showing and maybe these pants make your butt look like a lop-sided watermelon. But he doesn't look so good either.

"Boy he's short," you think, which shocks you because ever since his first movie, you've been stunned by his beauty. Was he always *this* short? (Which is six or so inches shorter than you.) What a nose.

And he wants to know where the circuit breaker is. Since you do know where the circuit breaker is and you do know where the key is, you can take him and go down the elevator with him and show him where the key is. "In the flower pot," you say, "clever huh?" "Thanks," he says, "ah…" and you can tell him any name you want because he will never remember yours, nor ever knock on your door again, so one day, a few months from now, you'll wonder if you dreamed this or if it actually happened.

And, if a star/celeb is the little sister of your best friend from high school and you can't believe that she's *this famous* because you were convinced no one from your high school would ever amount to a damn and as an *actor*? How likely is that? And you didn't exactly support her ambition because, well, you didn't think she had the looks to be an actor, which is stupid because who looks like an actor, but partially you think you might be right because it's absolutely amazing that she has been successful, but she has, and she actually gets to play a great *smart* lawyer—who is smarter on television than you actually are in your own legal practice and has much more interesting clients—which makes you kinda mad and somehow reminds you that if you are bothered by this you are watching too much television, and perhaps she is the one actress in America with a degree from Harvard who will not be forced to play an unimaginably stupid prostitute in the one role which will win her acclaim because, well, she's *fat* and has made a platform of it. And she looks fabulous.

Hey wait a minute, you were supposed to be successful, you were the big deal in high school and she was, well, kind of a mess. No one in your school thought anyone would be *this* successful. But there she is. What happened to me?

But your best friend from high school invites you to a brunch at her house and *she* is there. So you can say something other than "I love your work" because they don't expect that and you know her from *then*.

I leave Bettina and Marcie at the unavoidable coffee franchise with the resume of Tom Fricking West's nanny.

Ten days later.

"I just love my new nanny," is the message Bettina leaves on my cell. "She's fabulous."

A few days later.

"Bettina is a little concerned," said Marcie.

"What do you mean?" I said, placing my phone under my ear so I could hold my Velveeta.

"Her nanny showed up late three times the first week."

"True late or L.A. late," I said.

"True late. 60 minutes or more."

"Interesting. Did she ever check her references?"

"I don't think so," said Marcie.

"Hmmm."

"And then she arrived on Monday morning with $575 of purchases that she said Bettina's kids desperately needed."

"Like what?"

"A baby monitor. Those Einstein Baby tapes. Stuffed animals."

"Nice of her to give those things to Bettina's kids."

"She didn't give them. Bettina is expected to pay for them and reimburse her for overtime for buying those things."

"But her kids are in elementary school. They're too old for that stuff."

"I know," said Marcie. "What's that squishy sound?"

"What are you talking about?"

"Oh no, you don't still eat that awful Velveeta, do you?"

"No," I said as I spit it out, "of course not."

At Group that week everyone contributed endless snotty remarks about my alien-scanner theory.

I mean they were very supportive.

"This star/celeb thing really resonates with you," said the former kiddie-actress.

"I mean really...what does that mean? Can anyone help me?" I looked around the Group.

"Courtney..." said Roberta.

"What?" I said. "You said I could do whatever I wanted in here. Can't I ask for help?"

"Not if you're going to be provocative," said Roberta.

Oh here we go.

"OK," I said. "I'm sorry if I was provocative."

Not really.

"Does it bother you that you're not a celebrity?" said the former kiddie-actress, long between shows.

"Not exactly," I said. "Does it bother you that you're no longer a celebrity?"

"That's not very nice," said the divorced housewife.

"Since when was this about being nice," I said. "Look, this is Los Angeles. We don't have tradition. We don't have royalty. So we've invented our own royalty: stars and celebrities. An illusion of someone having a better life. But you stop being a celeb when no one other than your friends and family gives a damn about you anymore. Does that mean that you stop having a better life?"

Roberta was shaking her head left-right, left-right, left-right.

The former kiddie-actress started crying.

"Doesn't anyone want to say anything?" I said.

No one did.

And then there was the inevitable message in my voice mail.

"I think that you should stop coming to Group for a while," said Roberta. "You're very, very disrespectful. And you've become a lightning rod for the Group's anger."

Whatever.

13

A Dinner

Josh wants to take me to dinner.
"Why?" I said.
"It's a thank you. For being so nice to me when I was so sad."
"You already said thank you."
"But I want to say it in person."
"What if I eat?"
"I expect you to."
"Have you been dating?"
"Cody was it."
"D-girls don't eat."
"She ate."
"What?"
"Salad."
"Leafy salad or Cobb salad?"
"Leafy."

"With dressing?"
"Sometimes."
"I'll take that as no. Anything else?"
"Fish."
"Broiled with nothing on it?"
"There was something on it."
"Balsamic vinegar doesn't count."
"You're tough."
"I know how it goes. Why don't we go to IHOP?"
"Are you kidding?"
"I know this restaurant in Monterey Park."
"What?"

Monterey Park. No pressure. No pretense. No celebs.

"I was thinking of this new restaurant on Melrose that's gotten rave reviews..." said Josh.
"Hmmmmm..."
"Something wrong?"
"Well..."
"What?"
"It'll be celeb hell, which means that we don't have a chance of getting seated for two hours."
"I thought you liked celebs. You work in the industry."
"You're joking, right?
"Where's your sense of adventure?"
"I live in Brentwood. That's adventure enough."

The parking lot is full. People must leave the restaurant before there is room. And there is absolutely no street parking because this is a neighborhood where you must have that little sticker on your car to park or get towed. So the commercial area is jammed and the residential area is off-limits. Bad planning. Bad, bad planning. A seven-car line, extending one block down Melrose. Traffic has to come to a dead stop in front of the restaurant. All with reservations.

"Go in and tell them we're here," said Josh.

"It won't make any difference," I said. "Unless we're both there, it won't count."

We call and explain. The hostess tells me that unless we are in the restaurant in five minutes she will give our reservation away. We circle the block again. Finally a space in the lot clears. As we turn into the lot we have two minutes to go. But the valet fumbles and the machine which issues the parking tickets is out of paper.

"Just take our keys!" Josh says as he tosses his keys to the valet. We sprint into the restaurant with the valet chasing us, screaming, "I...can't...do...that."

"Ohhhh, I'm sorry," said the smiling hostess with the whitest white porcelains capping her teeth—and where did she get the money to pay for that? Josh, a panicked valet, and I are all standing with the hostess. A guy comes by and squeezes her butt and—oh yeah, that's the celebrity owner/chef—and I know where she got the money for those porcelains, and maybe her boobs.

"But we made it with 30 seconds to spare," I said.

"Not by my watch. I'm sorry. It's the policy of the restaurant. We gave your reservation away," said the hostess who is wearing what looks suspiciously like Gap khakis, a T-shirt with a *stain on it*, and flip-flops. Maybe they're fancy flip-flops.

"But go into the bar, and if you work with me I'll get you in," said the hostess.

"When did this become a group project?"

"Excuse me?" said the hostess.

"We'll be in the bar," said Josh.

"We should go."

"No. I want to try this restaurant," said Josh.

"We won't be seated for two hours."

"The hostess likes us. She'll fit us in," said Josh.

"I don't think so."

I'm right.

Seated at 10:00 p.m., after watching eight groups of celebs who maybe have reservations, but kiss the owner of the restau-

Almost Royalty

rant, "Congrats on opening this place," "No congrats on that big opening weekend…"

The food is good. And Josh and I are having a nice time eating forbidden foods: beef, mashed potatoes and creamed spinach.

"Man, who makes creamed spinach?" I said. "But it's great."

"I think after the cream, they topped the mashed potatoes with sour cream," said Josh.

"It's great," I say, with the biggest smile on my face. I love fat. I love fat food. I love to eat fat food.

And then I see him. Alien-scanner thing ex-TV star, who played a sensitive TV doctor who fought "the system" to save his patients, but truly is a major twit with an inflated sense of his own worth, bearing down on us at one o'clock.

"Don't breathe." I wonder if Josh can stop his heart.

"What?" said Josh.

"Stop talking. And hold your breath."

"Why?" said Josh. By then it's too late.

"It's over."

"What? Why?" said Josh.

Alien-scanner thing ex-TV star stops at our table. He's weaving and bumps into three tables on the way to ours.

"Beef," he said. "I haven't had beef in two years." Our waiter—not exactly present during dinner—appears at our table.

"We'd love you to sample all the beef you want, as a gift from us," said the waiter. "Go back to your table and we'll serve you."

Nice try. I suddenly see the owner/chef, someone who would normally stare through me, hovering.

"But I want this beef," said alien-scanner thing ex-TV star. He reaches down onto my plate and picks up my meat with his hands. He starts eating it.

"It's good," said the ex-TV star.

"Put her meat down," said Josh.

"OK," said alien-scanner ex-TV star as he spits out all of the meat, spraying both me and Josh.

"You shit," said Josh lurching out his chair, which makes it easier for alien-scanner ex-TV star to clock him in the face.

It goes without saying that dinner is "on the house." The battalion of waiters/starving actors who staff every restaurant in L.A. muscle alien scanner ex-TV star to an unseen part of the restaurant.

"I'm so, so, so, sorry," says the owner/chef. "Sometimes, I really hate these people,"

"Preaching to the choir."

"Are you OK?" I ask.

Josh has a little bump on his left temple. At least we get out of the parking lot in record time, what with the owner/chef personally overseeing the valet staff to ensure that we leave the restaurant premises safely.

"Really, I'll drive," I said.

"I see why these people irritate you," said Josh.

"That's not true."

"What? They don't irritate you."

"No. That they're people."

Part 2

January 2008

14

The Right Match

Headmistress Barbara Ellen ("Brell") Donovan stared at the color of the walls in her office. Something about it was just...well...a little off. Was it the shade of green she had chosen? She had always liked that forest green color and thought that it gave the room a formal, make that an imposing, look. But did that forest green really go well with that cream border print with the lavender pattern? Hmmmm. Perhaps the forest green didn't lift the mahogany furniture with the cream silk padding the way she wanted it to. Whatever it was about her forest green walls that didn't work, Brell was bothered. And when something in her domain bothered her it consumed her to an obsessive point to make it right again, which is why it was so important to Brell to only allow those individuals and their spawn who were right—who were a "a good match"—into Thorton, the one and only private academic (absolutely not-developmental) elementary school in Santa Monica, California.

As it was, the parents in front of her smelled of fear—no make that terror—and desperation. Sure they were blabbing their heads off, doing their best to entertain her, to connect with her on any level. Yes, they were high achievers—she an attorney, just like every working woman on the Westside (Where do they all come from?) and he some sort of producer of something with an impressive Ivy League education.

No doubt they had a fabulous application with lovely recommendations from highly impressive sources. And of course, their child was nothing short of a genius, a five-year-old who read at the fifth grade level, spoke three languages fluently, and played the violin like a young Jascha Heifetz. But maybe that was the problem: They were too good.

As it was, Brell didn't like to admit too many people who were accomplished. This would have destroyed the balance of her domain and perhaps not allowed her to meet her goals, well, the goals established by those ridiculously well-intentioned Thorton trustees, of a multi-cultural and diverse community. But more to the point, although these parents were accomplished, well-mannered, extraordinary, etc., she knew instantly that they were not going to significantly enable her to meet her number one goal: that of a new building and soccer field for the school, no easy feat in fantastically expensive Santa Monica, an area so valuable that it was more expensive than the fantastically expensive Beverly Hills area known as "the platinum triangle."

Sure these parents smelled of money—new money—and if they really pushed it and gave up some of their lifestyle, maybe the winter vacation in Vail, they probably could have given her a good $15,000–$20,000 per year "contribution" on top of the full $30,000 per year "comprehensive" tuition. But she needed more than that. Much more, and she wasn't going to waste a precious spot in that Kindergarten Class—one of the two to four spots open to non-diverse boy applicants—with good, but not great applicant parents. Brell had over 500 applications attempting to fill that spot and she was absolutely sure—because she had peeked—that the little darling of some software inventor, studio president, or high-tech venture capitalist, someone who could afford to give her the $500,000 she was seeking with ease, was in that pile.

Suddenly, Brell knew what was wrong with her room. It was the applicants. They just didn't look right in it. They just didn't fit. They were the worst thing that you could say about any applicant's parents at any private school anywhere: They were *not* a good match.

So Brell, expert verbal marksman that she was, decided to focus, aim, and kill the applicants' desire to be part of the Thorton community.

She scanned the application in front of her.

Ahh. Of course. This would be easy.

"Tell me, Wendy?" Brell said, looking the nervous motherparent of the prospective applicant in the face. "Where did you go to law school?"

Brell knew at that moment exactly what that mother wanted to say. She wanted to say, "I went to Harvard and clerked with the Fifth Circuit." She wanted to say, "I went to Yale and then did a Masters in public policy." She wanted to say, "I went to Stanford after working at McKinsey for two years."

But as Brell had that mother's application in front of her, she couldn't say that: she had to tell the truth.

The nervous mother swallowed and looked down. "I went to UC Davis," she said.

Brell pulled the trigger and let her bullet fly.

"Oh," Brell said with a big toothy smile, "I just *love* those public schools."

One shot, straight through the heart.

She was good.

It wasn't always like this. But certain events had conspired to make acceptance to an academic and selective private school in

Los Angeles much, much more difficult to obtain than membership to the most exclusive country club. And to be honest, acceptance in an exclusive private school was the new country club, where only the very, very select few were admitted. Frequently while she was out and about, getting her nails done, having a dinner, sitting in a waiting room, Brell heard parents boasting that their little angels just loved John Thomas Dye, Crossroads, or The Brentwood School as if admission to these schools by their child was some extraordinary accomplishment with which to trump their colleagues. Brell found this so amusing.

To begin with, the Los Angeles public schools were a mess. No, make that a disaster. Once upon a time, the California Public Schools were some of the best in the country. During that time, Brell practically had to beg applicants to come to Thorton.

At that time, attending a private school was almost considered quaint, something only the rich or troubled did to deal with their difficult offspring, a luxury few considered. Most who applied were accepted to Thorton and those who could pay the tuition had no problem gaining admission. But the problem was that this situation presented various conflicts as to who was in the power position in the school and Brell rarely won these power struggles with parents, especially when Brell's duties included driving the school bus—a little awkward when she was dressed in her classic Talbot's dress suit with matching Nordstrom's pumps—as well as being the headmistress of the school. This was something that Brell would most definitely like to forget. And anyone who ever spoke about *those days* would be frozen in place by one of Brell's infamous sideways glances, a look indicating that all hopes for that prospective Thorton application had been permanently and irrevocably dashed.

As it was, Brell took a little sadistic delight seeing the hoops, the exhaustion, the pure unadulterated humiliation—an exercise benignly known and outlined in the application as *The Steps to Thorton*—which she put those parents of prospective applicants through.

Step 1: The Application. Could they come by and simply pick one up? Absolutely not. You could not even physically get an application *unless* both parents—not just the mom or the dad—but both parents together (or both partners, or the sole legal guardian if that was the situation) submitted to a complete 90-minute tour of Thorton, a tour which was intentionally led by a well-intentioned but completely mono-toned and inarticulate eleven-year-old Thorton student. It always made life so spicy, so interesting for Brell to glance outside her window and see the parents, whom she knew to be divorced, attempting to create a façade of civility as they pretended to listen to a sixth-grade Thorton student lead a tour of something so very, very interesting, like that computer lab filled with 20 Apple computers which every private school in the city had.

But if they made it through the mind-numbing tour and got an application, then there was:

Step 2: Submitting the Application and $200 "Processing Fee." Could they just drive by and submit the application? Absolutely not. Thorton (and Brell) had created the most creative process for submitting applications for the incoming Kindergarten Class: (1) The applications could only be submitted during the second week of September, and not one day before; (2) The application must arrive by standard US mail (absolutely no overnight mail, messengers, faxes, pdf, or personal delivery was allowed); (3) The application *must* arrive before Thorton received 500 girl applications and 500 boy applications (which usually was more like September 10); (4) The application *must* arrive no later than September 14; and (5) The applicant (boy or girl) *must* have turned five years old by July 1 (a certified copy of the birth certificate had to be attached to the application).

Once the application was accepted there were the necessary events which both parents of the prospective applicant had to attend together:

Step 3: The Open House. Attendance mandatory. Watery coffee and broken Pepperidge Farm cookies to be served.

To Brell, Step 3 was truly the beginning of her "Kill the Enthusiasm" campaign. In Brell's design, the Open House was the day when she made her "very honest" speech, a speech which was intended to imply to prospective parents that, unless they were prepared to donate $500,000 or more, there was absolutely no chance that their little darlings would gain admission to Thorton.

The principal components of *the speech* were the infamous Three Statements, something Brell always referred to as the *ABC's of Thorton* to those grossly ambitious and highly educated parents:

A. The Numbers.

Brell's favorite way to begin her Open House Presentation was to present this bit of information and then see who actually sat through the next two and a half hours to sign their attendance slip (required to proceed to the next step).

"This year, we have 500 boy applicants competing for 40 spots (20 per Class) in the two Kindergarten Classes."

Brell would look around after this opening and usually hear nervous laughter.

"But to be fair, I need to clarify this issue. First of all we give preference to siblings, alumni children, the children of staff and faculty…"

(And of course what she didn't say but was clearly the subtext of her *"Goals of Thorton"* section of her speech was, preference was given to *anyone* who had ever contributed more than $500,000 for the greatly desired new building and new soccer field, which, of course, included the trustees' children, grandchildren and friends of the trustees' children and grandchildren.)

Brell loved to finish this beginning section of her Open House presentation by adding, "Unfortunately, we've just received 33 alumni/sibling applications for 40 spaces, and…" (to top it off by disclosing, shhh…like she was letting them in on a little secret which she really shouldn't tell anyone) "Three of those alumni/sibling boy applications were actually for three sets of twins."

To Brell, there was nothing like watching the faces of those mathematically inclined parents as the smart ones quickly computed that there were now 463 applications competing for four open spots. Brell loved to look around the room and guess by the horrified expression on their faces which parent was the first to realize that they had just spent $200 for a very, very nice two-line rejection letter. Because as smart parents, they had also clearly understood the subtext of her Open House presentation: Those four (or possibly fewer) remaining spots were clearly going to the highest bidder, and unless they were willing to donate their entire retirement account they could just forget about getting in.

B. Diversity

Most Westside parents pretended to love diversity but in reality, unless Grandpa Joe had given $50 million to Harvard, Yale, Princeton, Stanford or maybe even Pomona (in 1960, when that really meant something) and Dad had not embarrassed the family too badly when he attended, they pretty much knew that the odds were stacked against them once the well-intentioned "diversity" got into the picture. When you only had four openings in your Kindergarten class to begin with, and your well-meaning trustees (who, of course, had secured places at Thorton for their family for generations to come) began carping about "diversity," it was pretty much assured that you would be giving 20 percent of the openings in your class to someone who didn't necessarily know about Thorton, and someone who didn't necessarily care to attend.

Brell had heard the rumors about another Westside school which had such a commitment to diversity that it openly discouraged those in the wrong ethnic groups—white, Anglo-Saxon Protestant, Jewish—not to apply. So she thought that she would go with the current trend and give *her* diversity speech.

"Of course," Brell began, "Thorton has a deep commitment to diversity. We have 120 nationalities represented in the student body. We feel that this gives our students a more complete experience of the world."

Well, not really. Yes, there were many, many ethnicities represented at Thorton. But although there were many different nationalities, in Brell's mind the alleged 120 nationalities broke down into four prominent, four diverse, Thorton groups: Comfortable, Very Comfortable, Rich, and Fortune 500.

1. Comfortable was a description Brell used to describe those writer/TV producer types living on the Westside who had hit it big on some TV show that went to number one, or managed to continually produce hits and amassed a mid-eight-figure wealth (and a new young wife of child-bearing age). Average gross assets for these individuals tended to be in the $20,000,000 to $80,000,000 range. These parents tended to be nanny-centric because dad tended to work 48 hours per day, and mom was desperate to keep the goods—hair, body, wardrobe—together, so she really never saw the kids. As a rule, these families were easy to deal with, as long as the nanny could speak some English.

2. Very Comfortable tended to describe individuals who had gross assets in the $60,000,000 to $300,000,000 range. This description tended to go to those who had been the CEOs of major corporations, an occasional superstar athlete, or venture capitalists who had exercised their stock options sometime before April of 2000. These individuals tended to be very organized, generally provided excellent financial information regarding the assets to hold in the school's endowment and desperately wanted, and would pay for, the ego satisfaction of landing a place on the Thorton Board of Trustees.

3. Rich was a creative group if there ever was one, and fun to be with because these people usually had no ego. Typical to this group were the software-inventor types who drove 15-year-old Toyotas and found themselves in the ridiculous position of having

20,000,000 shares of a publicly traded company at its IPO. Average gross assets of this group tended to be in the 300 million to 10 billion dollar range (as it often happened, this group occasionally included people who actually had more money than those in #4, owing to the bull market and such). Lots of fun, hands on with the parenting, and generous with the donations owing to their usual middle-class background. Brell wondered how she could attract more of these people.

4. F5s (Fortune 500) Not as much fun as you would think, and generally stingy and eccentric. Most people didn't believe that there were F5s types floating around Los Angeles, but there were a few and they were a pain. These parents had always inherited their money and never, ever had any connection to reality because they had never worked. Ever. And unless there was some connection to some pet project that the parent was involved in—a Folk Art Collection of Tijuana Border Art, restoring the Great Barrier Reefs of Dubrovnik, or saving some strand of seaweed that existed only near Bikini Atoll—you could forget about a donation. Unless, of course, their kid was a total disaster. But then Brell had the job of explaining to the 38 other parents why it was so important that little Madison remained in that class because her frequent violent temper tantrums and biting represented an important real world experience for her 19 classmates.

C. A Good Match

Many private schools made the mistake of allowing average children to become members of the student body. That was never, ever going to happen at Thorton. The children admitted to Thorton would never be average (economically). Unless that horrible situation occurred where Brell recognized that the majority of sibling/legacies applicants, although passing the Thorton entrance exam, were actually slow or delayed. This presented a minor dilemma for Brell because she really needed to prop up the overall test scores of the Thorton students so that they didn't totally embarrass her on those public exams such as the ISEE or ERB over which she had no control.

For this, Brell had two strategies:
(1) Was the applicant *"ready?;"* and
(2) Was the applicant *"a good match?"*

"But of all of the things I have mentioned, we at Thorton know that despite everything, what we truly are looking for are those children who are (Brell loved to pause here for effect) *'ready.'*"

"Ready" was a term and factor which gave Brell all sorts of subjective room with which to play with admissions candidates. To be honest, *"ready"* was the only tool she had to ensure that her incoming kindergarten class was not composed of 40 legacy/sibling non-domesticated feral children.

It was one thing that the applicant had to be five years old by July 1, but what Brell and her admissions officers had been trained to look for were applicants who were not just five, but applicants who were *ready*—a word which had all sorts of unusual connotations on the Westside—to participate in a structured and highly academic kindergarten, but mostly to ensure that the little sibling/legacy was so overqualified for Thorton (or spread in small doses if truly "delayed") that they wouldn't dare lower Thorton's national ERB scores. However, should Brell suspect that the scores were going to be thrust down (because there was too much in-breeding between those legacies and absolutely no intelligence to balance it out), Brell would let in a few average (economically speaking) applicants who were exceptionally *"ready."*

The "readiness" of the child was to be judged in the famous Thorton "Readiness Exam," a little test given to the prospective students in January of the year the applicant expected to enter the kindergarten. The Thorton "Readiness Exam" was so basic that even the most *"delayed"* legacy/sibling usually could be expected to pass. Basically, it asked the admissions candidate: (1) to count to 20; (2) color a picture of a giraffe yellow, and (3) hold your hand up when the teacher called your name.

Almost Royalty

However, ever since it became accepted that boys developed slower than girls, many parents had decided that if their little Jonathan's birthday came close to the July 1 cut-off date they would simply hold him back for another year and give him "a gift year." The theory of "the gift year" was to give the socially immature child the ability to "mature" and thus be developmentally ready when the child entered kindergarten (and to ace the Thorton "Readiness Exam"). This made sense, somewhat, if the child's birthday fell in the spring, as a spring birthday translated into being one of the younger members of the class.

However, where it got interesting was when a the parent of a fall birthday decided to hold back their child for an additional year, a year beyond the year in which he was already being held back. This meant that little Jonathan would be seven when he started Kindergarten. But if those upper-middle class, highly educated parents were willing to put their little son into four to five years of pre-K, well, you had no idea how well they would perform on those national ERB's by third grade (much less the Thorton "Readiness Exam," especially when that six-year-six-month-old competed against the unsuspecting four-year-old boy). And this didn't even take into consideration those parents who would spring for the latest private school scam: Transitional Kindergarten.

Brell wasn't exactly sure, but it seemed that the Transitional Kindergarten for the offspring of highly-educated high achievers on the Westside first appeared in the Westside nursery schools when some ambitious Westside private school administrator realized that Westside parents would pay for, in fact were *desperate* for, anything which would give their little 5.6–6.1-year-old-child a leg up in the entrance exams for private schools.

Those Westside parents were so desperate to ingratiate themselves with their chosen private school that they were willing to pay for a *"gift year"* in the ridiculous $18,000 per year Transitional Kindergarten tuition at the private school at which they wished to send their children for two and a half hours of class per day ("circle time," singing, and macaroni crafts project included at no extra cost). Brell was surprised that those parents were willing to do this for their perfectly ready 5.6 year olds, especially since entrance to the Transitional Kindergarten program did not guarantee them entrance to the regular academic program at Thorton or any other private school. And even if they did the Transitional Kindergarten program, Brell (or any other Head Administrator) could—and usually did—decide that they, well the family, was *still* not *"a good match"* at Thorton. Yes, *"a good match"* was the last tool that Brell had to ensure that the students whom she admitted to Thorton were going to produce a diverse and balanced class. And to be sure, if the parents weren't at least "comfortable" and she didn't get the proper balance between "comfortable," "very comfortable," "rich," (the most desired group) and the very eccentric F5s, it just never ever seemed to work.

To be honest, it pained Brell to see a family who was not even "comfortable" attempt to compete with the other families during the thrice annual Thorton Foundation drives: the Fall Foundation Marathon, the Winter Silent Auction, and the Spring Golf/Tennis Classic. It just pained her to see a family who was not *a good match* pledge $50,000, 15 percent of their yearly income, by agreeing to pay $2,000 per mile run at the Fall Foundation Marathon (26.2 miles), to spend $15,000 to buy a fruit basket worth $25 at the silent auction, or to spend $25,000 to play tennis with a Rivera Pro who normally charged $100 per hour. That kind of donation, the expected donation, was truly going to play with their lifestyle. It was unfortunate, and exemplified the reason that Brell worked hard to find families who were *a good match*: those who could afford to donate not $50,000, but $500,000 without giving it a second thought.

"And because you will be in the Thorton community for the next seven years, what we are truly looking for is an experience which is *a good match*, for the entire family. It's just so important," said Brell at the very end of her presentation.

"Bullshit," thought Bettina as she listened to Headmistress Brell Donovan give her *"Steps to Thorton"* speech.

"Lies and bullshit," said Bettina in a stage whisper to the few startled and traumatized parents who could hear her.

Bettina was disgusted with herself. In fact, she didn't even recognize herself. Who was this person who wanted to send her child to this obviously life-sucking school where a child could not be more bored? That little robot who had taken her husband, Bernard Jean (aka "Bean"), and her on the school tour could not have been more depressed. Was that kid on tranquilizers? And Bean had gasped when, on the Thorton tour, they had wandered past a music class and heard 12–13-year-old boys who rode on skateboards, listened to rap, and probably hacked into pornography on their parents' computers singing "The Hills Are Alive With the Sound of Music."

"Oh. My. God," said Bean as he walked by, "$30,000 a year so that they can sing *that*?"

"You *love* that song," said Bettina.

"Sure," said Bean, "at a midnight *Sing along Sound of Music* when I'm high."

During the evening when we first came to Elizabeth's house and attended our first meeting of Leslee's Book Group, I noticed that the Book Group had seemed very uncomfortable when Bettina casually asked how one obtained a recommendation to Thorton Hall. But during our second meeting at Elizabeth's house, Bettina noticed that the room chatter came to a crashing halt when she told the Book Group that she wanted her daughter, little Sapphia, to attend Thorton, and had in fact applied.

They were attempting to discuss *The Lovely Bones*. It was Elizabeth's pick. Elizabeth thought it sounded like a good exercise and diet book.

The book group—Elizabeth, Renata, Laura, June and Patty—eyed each other with worried looks and put down their almost empty wine glasses. Leslee shook her head and rolled her eyes. In addition to Bettina's pronouncement, June had just told her that despite not having worked in twelve years, she was sending Leslee her resume. "Hobeck has a spot for a Harvard Law grad, right?" I couldn't tell if Leslee was more upset with June or Bettina.

I shrugged my shoulders. "What's the big deal about Thorton Hall? I pass it every day on the way to work and it looks like just another ordinary private school in a cramped space."

"Shhh...Courtney," whispered Marcie, rolling her eyes.

No one said a thing.

"Thorton...as in Thorton Hall?" said Renata.

"Yes," said Bettina.

"Interesting," said Elizabeth.

Again, dead silence in the room.

"Well," said Renata, "you'll be one of the many victims of the March Massacre."

"What's the March Massacre?" said Bettina.

"The last two weeks of March," said Elizabeth. "That's when all of the acceptance letters go out. But in your case, it'll be a rejection letter."

"How do you know I won't get in?" said Bettina.

"Oh, I know," said Elizabeth.

"We've all been there," said June.

"The most that you'll get will be wait-listed," said Renata.

"And then you'll have to start the campaign," said Elizabeth.

"What campaign?"

"The one where you spend every week from March until Labor Day sending emails asking for 'updates' and reassuring everyone that you remain 'committed,'" said Renata.

"Or making endless phone calls and desperately pleading with some alumnus of the school to write a good recommendation," said Laura.

"Basically, you spend March until Labor Day begging them to let your kid in," said Elizabeth.

"C'mon," said Bettina.

"No," said Renata, "it's real. We all know people who have spent two or three years begging or 'remaining committed' who were able to finally finagle their way into the school for their kids."

I looked at Bettina and rolled my eyes.

"Well, *everyone* knows how important the right private school education is," said Marcie.

"Yeech," said Bettina, "could it really be worth it? All that time wasted, begging, to get your kid into kindergarten? Do they all become incredible successes?"

Marcie flashed Bettina a quick, "You moron" look.

"No," said Elizabeth, "they become miserable entitled retards who can't do a thing unless we tell them every five minutes that they're wonderful and brilliant just for learning how to write their names."

"But they're safe," said June.

"Yes, that's true," said Elizabeth. "They're safe. Until middle school. Then there are those endless issues of drugs, sex, alcohol and driving."

"By the way, Elizabeth, did your husband ever get that bonus?" said Laura, attempting to change the subject.

Elizabeth bit her lip. "He better. Crossroads keeps bugging me about my planned donation. And we're a little extended with the garden and remodeling."

"Wait a minute. Are you sure there isn't any way I could get into Thorton?" said Bettina. Once again, the room chatter crashed to a halt. No one said a thing for a few seconds.

Elizabeth sighed. "Well," she said "if you get a good recommendation from the Governor, or maybe, I don't know, Bill Gates, you might get in."

"Oh," said Bettina "is that all?"

Miss Danko was the Admissions Director at Thorton Hall. She was very knowledgeable in the ways of Thorton Hall and its families. Five years ago she had been given a Senior Administration position at Thorton: Director of Admissions, a job which *finally* matched the Thorton uniform she was required to wear (a Classic Talbot's Suit and Nordstrom's Pumps) and for which she was qualified. Miss Danko's main job was pre-screening all parents of Thornton applicants who had made the first cut (not obvious admission rejections) and making an admissions recommendation (yes, no, or possible) to Brell Donovan, who made the final determination.

After 30 years at Thorton, Miss Danko knew exactly the types of families which Thorton hoped to attract and knew with little or no effort which applicant (and applicant family) would be *a good match*. And after interviewing 2500 or so families, Miss Danko and Brell had developed the Recommendation Code:

1. **NM:** An application marked No Match. Usually this family had no visible signs of money. This prospective family was an easy rejection, and absolutely NOT *a good match* for Thorton;

2. **SM:** An applicant marked SM meant Some Match. This prospective family usually had parents who were professionals and were an OK, but not ideal, match, and would most likely be wait-listed and have to decide whether they would participate in "the campaign" or move on to another school;

3. **GM:** An applicant marked GM, or Good Match, was the rarest of applicants, the kind of applicant that every one of the truly elite private schools in Los Angeles always found—no matter the merit of the child or the family—*"a good match"* and basically recruited through invitations to events, coffees, and fundraisers long before any application for a family member was ever submitted. These were the applications of the name families of Los Angeles...Chandler, Disney, Broad, Riordan, Wasserman, Spielberg, etc. and those who were known to have the right qualifications or friends who could vouch for the right qualifications: lots of money. Unfortunately, owing to the different educational theories in vogue, Thorton never received more than seven of these

applications per year, as every school in the city scrambled after these applicant families and their parents. Sometimes these individuals had a few known quirks that might make them interesting (disruptive) within the community, such as a known uncontrollable drug addiction, frequent and rotating sexual orientations, and a profound inability to adhere to schedules, appointments, deadlines, or basic hygiene.

But because these people were usually so *qualified*, Thorton (and Miss Danko) always attempted to make the application process as easy as possible for them by overlooking the various deadlines and *Steps to Thorton* which these people always missed, and no matter what, Thorton always, *always*, found them to be *a good match*. As it was, it was due to Miss Danko's tremendous understanding of the desired Thorton Hall family that she was completely puzzled by the two parents sitting in front of her: How had these two obvious admission rejects made the first cut? There was nothing, absolutely nothing, which suggested that this couple and their little girl would be a good match for Thorton.

The father was greasy, marginally employed, and somewhat ambiguous in his sexuality (if she could even comment on that) and he giggled so much that she was fairly sure that his sobriety could be in question. And he smelled like incense or something. The mother was so uncomfortable in her freshly purchased (so easy to spot) Talbot's classic navy blue suit and Nordstrom's pumps. In personality, she was the strangest combination of abrasive and obsequious, as if she was furious that she was actually taking part in this pre-screening interview and yet absolutely clear that she had no choice but to participate in it.

But just as Miss Danko was about to mark Bettina and Bean's application for little Sapphia the dreaded "NM" she looked at the recommendations.

And then she understood.

Bettina and Bean had somehow managed to obtain a terrific, make that a spectacular, recommendation from an alumnus named Robert Hutchinson. Young Robert, "Robbie," was universally remembered throughout Thorton as the fantastically talented theater student who had managed to step into the role of "Maria," the lead in Thorton's yearly production of *The Sound of Music*, at the very last moment. As it turned out, Thorton had been in a panic on opening night when the girl who had been cast as "Maria" came down with tonsillitis and had thoroughly lost her voice by curtain time. To this day, more than twenty years later, many remaining faculty and staff remembered how Robbie (who had been cast in a minor role as a German SS Officer) stepped into the role and performed brilliantly after convincing the theater faculty that he knew every line, every gesture, and every movement of Maria's and could perform in costumes which were much too big on him.

After graduation from Thorton, Robbie had pursued a theater education at a controversial college which was located not far from a major highway. After college, young Robbie had spent many, many years in off-off-off Broadway struggling and working in the same dimension where he had first shown his enormous talent at Thorton: as a female impersonator. Recently, he had landed a role in a Broadway production and appeared to be making quite a splash.

But more to the point, Robbie Hutchinson was the son of Alexander Hutchinson, a highly successful individual who had recently served two terms as the Secretary of State in a mostly Democratic cabinet for a US President.

And the Hutchinson's were so very, very, very *qualified*.

Brell Donovan stared at the color of the walls in her office. The instant that the receptionist from the front office led this couple up the staircase and into her office, she knew that something was off. It wasn't the shade of green she had chosen for her office walls, but the tangerine shirt of the father sitting before her didn't match, at all, the forest green walls of her domain. Brell was bothered by these applicants. It must have been some mistake, some oversight by Miss Danko, that they had even gotten far enough in the interview process to make it to an interview with her.

And, as it was, the parents in front of her didn't smell of the usual fear or even that usual combination of fear and desperation. These two smelled of something entirely different, and Brell was sure that what they smelled of was pot.

Sure they were blabbing their heads off, but not necessarily to her. They weren't even high achievers. She, the mother, led a Mommy (Parent) and Me class and had been an artist. And what did the father do? Did he have some sort of theater background?

Ick.

Not a good match.

Get them out of my office. Quickly.

She scanned the application in front of her.

Ahh. Of course. This would be easy.

"Tell me, Bettina?" Brell said, looking the mother-parent of the prospective applicant in the face, "What did you do at (with a visible sniff) ahhh...hmmm...Art School?"

Brell made sure that these prospective applicants saw her most bored look and an almost visible roll of her eyes. Brell knew at that moment exactly what that mother wanted to say. She wanted to say, "I went to the Tisch School and then started working at the Met."

She wanted to say, "I went to Yale and then got a position in the Contemporary Art Department at Sotheby's."

She wanted to say, "I went to Cooper Union and got gallery representation, then made it into the Whitney when I was thirty-one."

But as Brell had that mother's application in front of her, she couldn't say that. She had to tell the truth.

"Well, I did some paintings," said Bettina, feeling a little nervous.

"Paintings," said Brell, "how lovely. I love paintings. What did you paint?"

"Uhmmm...things," said Bettina.

This was harder than Bettina thought it was going to be, and it wasn't going well.

"Uh-huh," said Brell.

Time to take aim, focus, and kill these applicants as quickly as possible.

Brell gave Bettina a big, toothy smile, pulled the trigger and let her bullet fly.

"Did you ever get gallery representation or...say...work in your medium?"

Bettina swallowed and looked down.

But then she looked up, and did Brell hear her whisper the word "Bitch?"

"Oh *please*, as *if*," said Bettina. "I did Performance Art about the oppression of women in marriage and motherhood. And I was, and probably still am, a big ol' *lesbian*—and..."

Bettina looked at Bean.

"He's *gay*!"

Brell was silent and let Bettina's words reverberate off the walls. In all of the interviews which she had ever given at Thorton Hall, no one—*ever*—had uttered those words in an interview.

Brell cleared her throat.

"You know, when you choose a school for your child, it's so important that you choose a community in which you'll feel comfortable. Knowing what I do about the private schools in Los Angeles, well...I'm just wondering... Have you two considered... the public schools?"

"You know, I suffered through your *ABC's of Thorton* lecture," said Bettina.

"Yes, well, it's just so important that you choose a school which is right...well...for the entire family."

"And in addition to surviving your lecture and your hideously boring tour, I must tell you," said Bettina, "the coffee you serve *sucks*. You need to get a new coffee pot."

"But why would you choose Thorton?" said Brell, actually wondering.

"Robbie Hutchinson," said Bean, "one of my best friends. He told me that we would be a good match."

No.

Maybe she was tired from having done too many interviews in this application season. Brell silently cursed herself, reminding herself to always, always, *always*, review the entire application and recommendations before the interview, and suddenly noticed the bright-red warning sticker, too late, that Miss Danko had placed on the recommendations.

But maybe it would be OK.

"And Headmistress Donovan," said Bettina. "The Secretary, himself, called me yesterday and told me to call him right after our interview and let him know if you made me feel welcome at Thorton."

Bettina watched the color drain from Brell's face.

Bettina stood up.

"Let's go, Bean," said Bettina.

Bean stood up from his mahogany chair and walked toward the door. Even he knew that his tangerine-colored shirt didn't match Brell's forest-green domain.

Brell stood up and extended her hand.

"Well, thank you..."

"Skip it," said Bettina with a wave of her hand.

Bettina and Bean walked out of Brell's office and started down the staircase. Half-way down the stairs, they both burst out laughing, laughing so much that they began crying.

The receptionist at the front office became startled and looked up the staircase when their laughter turned to howls.

And Brell could hear them just as plainly as if they were standing next to her.

15

Roast Concrete

"You're not the best-looking woman I've ever slept with," said Dr. Ted. "I know you think you are. But you're not."

"Hmmmm," I said.

"What?" said Dr. Ted.

"I'm wondering why this coffee tastes like roast concrete," I said.

We were sitting in a retro coffeehouse located on Third Street that was a former pizza joint. It was decorated with free posters, thrift store couches, and drip-wax-wine-bottle candle holders. Miles Davis '60s jazz was playing in the background. One look said it all: It would go out of business 60 days after the landlord decided to raise the rent.

I watched a cockroach the size of a large paperclip march by my right foot. Our waitress, a volleyball Viking type with long, blondish brown hair in her early 20s, 5' 11"–135 pounds, wearing a UCLA wife-beater T-shirt and tight, tight, tight jeans came by. She gave us a menu.

Dr. Ted eyed her with interest.

I knew that sometime, maybe in front of me, when I went to the bathroom, or maybe if he could get me to leave early and pretend to have left something behind—keys, glasses, a cell phone—that he would try to get her cell number or email.

We were drinking coffee.

Well, I was.

He was drinking tea.

I love coffee. I love the smell of coffee, the taste of coffee, and the look of coffee. Nothing in the world smells better than opening a fresh bag of coffee beans. If I could bottle coffee perfume, I would, and I would wear it every single day. I'm so in love with coffee that I travel with a coffee grinder and my own coffee beans because I can't stand traveling to places where the coffee might not be good—and I am an expert at detecting old, weak, or watery coffee with one whiff. So when it comes to tea, I just don't get it. I've had delicious tea—Indian and Thai teas are my favorites—but as a rule, I don't understand teabags, tea balls, letting tea seep, and the fact that tea has no smell. Maybe it's because tea is the drink of therapy. Or because I'm addicted to coffee. Or because right now I really don't like Dr. Ted—and he's drinking tea.

It's a few days after our second book group meeting at Elizabeth's house (featuring our non-discussion of *The Lovely Bones*). My re-education with Leslee and the Ivy & Elite Book Group is depressing me.

And Dr. Ted isn't improving the situation much.

But I notice that Dr. Ted has changed physically.

It seems that he has that disease endemic to transplants, especially East Coast transplants, which causes them to think that being in L.A. made them have a skin peel, cheek implants, lasex, botox and porcelains put on their teeth. That if he had only stayed in Ohio, he would have been a brother to his five sisters, listening to their problems with boyfriends, helping them move out of their apartments, taking them to brunch.

He would have been a son, asking his father for advice, going to Sunday dinners, helping his parents with their house. He would have been a member of the community, volunteering in a free clinic, mentoring fatherless boys in the church, contributing to Doctors Without Borders.

As if living in Los Angeles, like claiming you're a victim of a dysfunctional family, is a justification for who you should have been and aren't.

"You should know I'm sleeping with six women. Six women. And they're all better looking than you are," said Dr. Ted.

My second cup of roast concrete was beginning to taste good.

"So like I said," he continued, "there's—hmmm—number one, a star of her high school play, out here with her headshots, from the Midwest, getting a little long in the tooth, she serves me breakfast. Number two, an Ivy League Grad actress who loves Chekhov, here for pilot season, usually serves me drinks—you know, the actress-waitresses types."

"I'm familiar with them."

"Uh-huh," said Ted. "Then number three, my personal trainer, loves to run, a college athlete who did the 100 meters. Umm, number four, a friend of my sister's, her first trip to Los Angeles. She was so excited. I'm supposed to show her around town."

"A friend of your sister's?"

"You're interrupting me," said Ted. "Number five, a nurse, a really good nurse, who works with newborns. And six, the receptionist who works in my office."

He looked at me.

"I told them, every single one of them, 'You're special.' And they ate it up."

He looked at me again.

"I guess I could still sleep with you too," said Dr. Ted. "If you want."

The roast concrete was going cold. I got a warm-up.

I think I could understand how it could happen. When you were almost ten years out of high school and no longer the star.

When the only opinion anyone wanted was when their order would be ready, not what you thought of *The Cherry Orchard*, or *Uncle Vanya*.

When the only guys who paid attention to you were guys who hung out in gyms, creeps who said they knew agents and agents who had no connections.

When you were in a new town and didn't know how to get anywhere.

When, "OK he's not good-looking, but at least he actually does something, I mean he's a professional—a doctor," sounded better than being alone.

When you really needed that job and the boss knew you came in late sometimes and didn't say anything, and he told you that you were special and wants to take you out for pizza and a beer.

And then I thought about these women, what they trained for, what they hoped for, and where they found themselves. And how they thought that this doctor, Dr. Ted, might help them, or even be the answer to their L.A. nightmare, or maybe just show them a little kindness.

"Well, that's very gracious of you, Ted. But here's the thing."

"What?" said Dr. Ted.

"We've never slept together."

"What? How's that possible? I've nailed everyone."

"I dunno. It just didn't happen. But here's what I want."

"You want to do it now?" said Dr. Ted.

"No. Whatever we have...and I'm not sure that I could call it a friendship...it's over. Don't call me, email me, instant message me. If you see me, pretend that you don't know me."

"Oh... You got it all figured out," said Dr. Ted, his voice a little too loud and a little too agitated. Our volleyball Viking waitress looked over at us.

"You know that's not true," I said.

Dr. Ted's face began to get red.

"You think you're too good for me," said Dr. Ted.

"You must be joking."

"Who are you to say this to me? I'm not even attracted to you. I get to say when it's over. Not you. Me. I do that."

"What's *it*, Ted? And what's over?"

I picked up my bag and walked toward the door.

"Take care of yourself, Ted."

"Where do you think you're going?" he yelled. "You don't get to walk out. I do."

The Viking volleyball-player waitress in the UCLA shirt looked at me with concern.

"You OK?" she said.

"Yeah, I'm OK."

I walked out the door and didn't look back.

16

Low Love

When I got home it was 8:30 p.m.

One email. It was from Leslee.

"You've probably heard about Hobeck. I'm attaching my resume as a PDF. Can you send it around? Thanks."

Leslee's law firm, Hobeck, Berman, had dissolved. The firm had been open for over 100 years. Leslee no longer had a job. Harvard Law grad June, from the Book Group, had already sent me her resume.

Five calls from the Breather on cell and voice mail.

Message six on my voice mail. "Group needs your fi…engaging spirt. We'd…all right, I'd…like you to come back next week," said Roberta. "Will you call me?"

I wondered if Roberta's checking account was running low.

The phone rings. I had given up answering my phone because of the Breather's calls. The caller I.D. was no good. No matter who called, it always said anonymous.

Oh, why not take a chance.

"Courtney."

"Yeah…"

"It's Aaron."

"Aaron?"

"Remember. We met at that speech you made for California Lawyers for the Arts."

Now I remember why I never pick up my calls.

"Did I give you my home phone number?"

"No. But I found it online."

"What can I do for you?"

"Well, if you ever have any free time, I'd love to meet for coffee and pick your brain. Career advice, you know?"

Aaron. I remembered Aaron. No sickly green skin, no chicken chest, no prematurely gray hair. He wasn't an attorney. Six foot one. 170 pounds. A college athlete. Cheekbones which reflected the light. Light brown hair, with golden streaks (natural) from his mornings surfing in Malibu. Crystal-blue eyes. Flirted with me after my speech, so I hoped. A beautiful smile, glistening white teeth. Placed one hand on my back. "Great Speech…" "Really?" Hand on my shoulder. "Well yeah, and you were so much fun." I did remember Aaron.

"What are you doing right now?" I said.

"Now?"

"C'mon over. Bring some wine and a bathing suit. I have a hot tub. I'll give you all the career advice you ever wanted. Where are you coming from, anyway?"

"Close to you."

"How do you know that?"

"I got your home address online too."

A tiny red flag.

I acknowledge that I knew this is the way you meet Ted Bundy.

Thirty minutes later with wine.

"You are close by."

"Hey." A hug. Lasting long enough so that I could smell his toothpaste.

"You look great," he said. Yes, I always had the shirt, the one shirt, which made me look like I had boobs, and one pair of jeans with strategically placed rips in it.

"Vino?" he said.

"Ab-so-lutely."

I had tidied up (I hid Abyss's second box). I managed to clean the water stains off two wine glasses. Fortunately, there were two matching wine glasses that were not broken. I had even located some cheese—*cheese*—not Velveeta (a little too early to spring this on him) to serve: brie. And I had opened my emergency can of smoked oysters to serve on the emergency box of fancy British too expensive pepper crackers which I had in reserve. I even sliced my reserve emergency pear, more like an apple, because pears were never ripe when I needed them to be.

Of course, I hid the Hostess Ding Dongs. The creamed corn. The Fritos. And the baloney, a little bit of a problem because if Mr. Yum stayed too long the baloney, hidden outside the refrigerator in a dish underneath my sink, might begin to sweat.

A girl never knew when she was going to need to be swanky.

I remembered the dates—especially Andre—the ones who had needed to search my refrigerator "just to see what kind of wine I was drinking." Where the cheap wine used for cooking, OK maybe for drinking, was always located. "You're drinking this? This?" Too loudly, in front of guests. The one who had found the Ritz Crackers—"Ohmygod, you *eat these*? Nobody eats these. *No-bo-dy*." Holding up the box like a dead rat. The one who had found the creamed corn. "How sweet, you're eating creamed corn? I didn't know that you could still buy creamed corn. Did you get it from your Grammy?"

As if buying food that was not stocked by Whole Foods Market instantly eliminated you from the eligible dating pool, this generation's declaration of a class stigma.

It just wouldn't do in West Los Angeles.

Of course I hid the Velveeta.

If it had been up to me I would have served a ground beef noodle casserole, broccoli with mayo topped with crunched Cheese Nips and Jell-O, tri-colored—with a pile of Cool Whip on top.

And I would have been nice. No attitude. Genuinely Interested. A Stimulating Conversationalist.

I placed the swanky food—smoked oysters, the brie, and the hard pear—on my recently (20 minutes ago) cleaned glass coffee table. Mr. Yum walked over to the couch with the wine. Pale Yellow. Interesting nose. Was that the wine, or had Abyss done her bimonthly spraying of the place before Mr. Yum, Aaron, had arrived?

"What are we drinking?" I said, sweetly, smiling. In the background I can hear Abyss scratching at her box, the beginning of a compulsive 20 minute process ensuring that she covers her recent deposit. And I smell...Abyss, or is that the baloney, getting ripe?

He can hear her, too.

"I have two cats," said Aaron, "The Captain...and Tenille."

"A little before your time," I said, "and even mine."

"My mom had some of their albums." Bringing the wine bottle over. A California Chardonnay from the Russian River area—that was nice. "The guy at the store told me this was good."

Sitting down next to me. "Prost," I said, taking a sip. "Not bad."

"So what can I do for you," I said. He moves in close to me and places his hand on the rip at my knee and slips his hand through the rip so that it is on the skin, his hand on my bare skin, just above my knee, sliding up my thigh, slightly bunching my jeans up.

"Uhhhhhhhhh..." I said.

Abyss is still attacking her plastic cat box and I'm beginning to wonder if I really didn't wish that I had a big ol' attack dog, maybe a German shepherd, named Peetee, or a Rottweiler named Bruiser.

"You know that I didn't come here, now, to get career advice," said Aaron.

"You could've. People always want career advice in this town." *Trying to convince myself.*

"Yeah, but you know when I met you at your speech, I could tell that we had a connection."

"We did?"

"Don't deny it, you felt it too and you want this..." *Leaning in for...his lips brushing my...*

"What is that smell?"

I jumped up, suddenly aware of ripe, ripe, baloney like—cat box—smells. "You know, I think it's time to move to the hot tub portion of tonight's program."

"OK," said Aaron, "that could be fun."

"Why don't you go into the bathroom and put on your bathing suit."

Bang. Bang. Bang. Bang. Oh no—I think the baloney was attempting to make a break from the cupboard beneath the sink or...

"What's that knocking sound?" said Aaron.

"I don't know."

I knew what it was—Abyss had discovered the baloney. Aaron—thank you Lord—graciously disappeared behind my swanky French doors and hopefully went into the bathroom.

Bang. Bang. Bang. Bang.

"There it is again," said Aaron.

"Thanks for telling me." Like thank you for telling me, "that skirt makes your hips look enormous."

Bang. Bang. Bang. Bang.

"Abyss...Abyss."

There she was, attempting to open the cabinet below the sink with her paw and letting the door bang shut.

"You silly fool, leave the baloney alone."

Abyss looked up from the cabinet and let it bang shut again. *Bang.* I went to the refrigerator and got her special treat.

"Here," I said, putting some in her dish and moving her away from the baloney-hiding cabinet. Honey-baked ham. The emergency stash. Six months ago, when Frank had left and Abyss had started her bi-monthly spraying of my apartment I had hired a behavior specialist for cats who thought Abyss had a bad relationship with her box. To turn this around and create a positive cat box experience he had me place bits of special food on the rim of her box. Turkey, she sniffed at and wouldn't touch. Roast beef, she knocked off and ran away. Honey-baked ham, she jumped in her box, ate every piece, and sat in her box, meowing, until I put more ham down. She was not Kosher.

"I'm ready," said Aaron. He was wrapped in a towel.

"I'm hoping that there's a bathing suit in there."

"Who needs a bathing suit."

"Me. I'm not ready for show-and-tell tonight."

"Sorry. Forgot to bring one."

"OK. Ready to go." I picked up some towels. "I put mine on under my clothes."

"Leave the baloney alone," I whispered to Abyss. We walked up the stairs to the roof, opened the door and walked to the hot tub. I prayed that the tub had been recently cleaned. Did the water temperature really kill all of those germs? I looked around. Not a lover of heights, it was slightly disorienting seeing L.A. from this angle, four stories up. We got in the tub.

"Why so far away," said Aaron.

"I'm fine over here."

I was sitting across from him next to a jet. I was beginning to feel a little nauseous. Cheap wine, height, heat, and oysters. Aaron moved next to me and started rubbing my back.

"You seem tense," said Aaron, "but I think I know how to make you feel better."

"You might be mistaken tonight. Aaron, I think I want to go..." He placed his tongue in my mouth and started kissing me. He pulled the straps down on my bathing suit and started feeling my breasts. I didn't feel well at all.

"I think that we could have a lot of fun together—exploring, experiencing, no rules, no promises," said Aaron. My stomach was cramping and I pulled my legs to my chest.

"How old are you?"

"24," he said.

24. 24. 24. I'm 35. No rules, no promises—no future. I'm pathetic. Someone who would sexually involve herself with a person—a person who probably was looking for career help—and was deluded into thinking this was how to play the game. This seemed very familiar. But now I was the older person.

I had become Gene Jenny. How had this happened?

"I think I'm going to..." I turned away and stood up, leaning over the side of the hot tub on the pavement as the vomit burst out of my mouth and on to the ground...cheap wine, height, heat, and oysters all combining to make swanky vomit, retching four times before I was done.

We walked downstairs without saying a thing. I opened the door to find a large swath of grease across my plush gray shag carpeting, littered with baloney trailing from the kitchen to the northeast corner of my sunken living room, where sat Abyss. She had dragged the entire package of baloney from the cabinet to the corner, in the process eating so much that she was covered in grease, fur slicked back, whiskers stuck to her face, fur matted to her head, face, and chest, only making it worse by trying to clean herself with tongue and paws that were also covered in baloney grease.

"Oh, Abyss."

Aaron had slipped away and returned with clothes on and a piece of paper with various numbers on it.

"Home, cell, work, email," he said, handing me a piece of paper with various numbers on them. "I meant what I said up there."

He walked toward the door, and stopped.

"Are you going to be OK?" said Aaron.

"No. Never."

"Call me tomorrow."

I didn't call. Three days later, he called me.

"You didn't call me. What's going on?"

"Nothing. You didn't really think I was going to call you, did you?"

"Well yeah. How often does a 24-year-old guy like me call you wanting you?"

As Roberta would have said, I was feeling an Ancient Pain.

"You know Aaron, attractive as your offer is, I just don't see what we have in common. I mean, you're 24. Go do your 24-year-old things."

"You're kidding me, right? Women like you don't turn me down."

"Women like me. You've done this before?"

"Sure. And it worked out really well. Sometimes they're married. Sometimes they're not. Always they're a little older. And alone."

"And what do you get out of this?"

"A car. An apartment. Help with my career," said Aaron.

"And they get?"

"Sensuality. Romance. All their desires met."

"I'm looking for something else."

"Don't tell me you think you need a boyfriend?"

"That's a start."

"A husband?"

I didn't say anything.

"Some of the women I've been with have been married, or even gotten married, and then returned to me. It's not like being married is going to solve any of your problems."

"It's not like being or having a sex toy with a pulse will either."

"God, you're puritanical. And you think too much."

"Do they recycle those lines every generation? What's next? *If it feels good, do it?*"

"Didn't you feel something when I was kissing you?"

"Aaron, I threw up."

"You're a mess. I'm going to give you a couple of days to think about it. Alone. You'll call me once you realize what we could have."

"Hmmm."

"No woman has ever turned me down."

I've often thought if I could just go back to age 15, read the classics and like them, study Latin, summer in Martha's Vineyard, apply to a school like…Vassar…Dartmouth…Princeton…or Stanford…it would've all been different.

Like I could have been reborn as the daughter of Todd, a Yale grad, a tax partner at a large law firm, and Carolyn, a stay-at-home mom who began chairing the fund-raising committees of local art museums when I entered Andover at 15, residents of some very leafy area of Connecticut, say New Canaan, where they owned a 10,000-, no, too big and not tasteful, 7500-square-foot two-story home on three acres of land, where they had a leafy fall during which they all wore beige and earth tones, and then celebrated a very white, and very Episcopalian Christmas with a big, *real*, not aluminum, Christmas tree, at which the women wore red and green plaid skirts, red sweaters and black tights, and served egg nog and sugar cookies with little sprinkles on them. And Todd and Carolyn stayed married, didn't die, and didn't divorce, so I never had to see them date someone else, and certainly didn't see them (mom or dad) date, or attempt to date, my boyfriends.

And after Andover, I, with Todd and Carolyn's help, visited all the Ivy-League schools (so in case everything failed, I could be a member of the Ivy & Elite) and decided that I would apply to the appropriate school in an appropriately leafy area, on the east coast, like Wellesley, which I got into, where, somewhere between my junior and senior year I met the big brother of one of my friends from school—John, who was in his third year at Yale Law—and we started dating. We dated until I graduated and started working in publicity or marketing for DKNY or Calvin Klein, and then after he finished his federal court clerkship and started working for Sullivan and Cromwell we got married in a 200-person wedding at my parents' place in The Hamptons during June when everyone looked very pretty, like tall, thin, high cheek-boned golden-haired models, like in the Ralph Lauren ads.

Or,

Wait a moment…

Was this entire fantasy an ad for Ralph Lauren? Yes, I already knew someone from Andover—Frank—and his prep school slacker life didn't at all resemble a Ralph Lauren ad, but I'm sure that mine would've turned out differently.

All right, so it was a few, make that many years later and I was starting to read the classics. I figured it was never too late to start down the right road.

First book up—Joyce's *Finnegan's Wake*.

First book down—Joyce's *Finnegan's Wake*.

One more try.

First book up—Edith Wharton's *Age of Innocence.*

No, seeing the movie, even the director's cut DVD, does not count as reading the book.

But I was hungry.

So I made my recipe for Velveeta junior pizza, slathering mayo and grated Velveeta on some La Brea Bakery rosemary and olive bread. Somewhere, I was sure that Nancy Silverton was going into anaphylactic shock.

I sat in bed with *House of Mirth*. Abyss hopped onto the bed, walked into my lap, and sniffed the junior pizza.

"Abyss, you don't like Velveeta junior pizza," I said.

Maybe not, but she seemed to go for the bread. She stuck her snout in the pizza and started to drag the entire thing off the bed, leaving a vertical trail of Velveeta grease three inches wide and three feet long down my ivory white comforter.

"All right, then, take it."

I walked into the kitchen to make another Velveeta junior pizza. La Brea Bakery rosemary and olive bread, mayo, tomatoes, grated Velveeta...

Bam bam. Pounding on my front door. *Bam bam bam bam.*

"Open the door, Courtney." A guy's voice. Not one that I recognized.

Had I forgotten to pay my cable bill again?

Bam bam bam. Louder now.

"Open the door, bitch."

If it was Time Warner cable I was definitely not going to contribute to their holiday toy campaign.

BAM BAM BAM.

"BITCH OPEN THE DOOR."

Not likely. A great way to get beaten to a pulp. I never understood why people opened the door and let go of the only protection between them and a crazed animal.

"Whoever it is, stop pounding on my door or I'll call the police."

"You don't know who it is?"

"Aaron?"

"Stupid bitch. Who's Aaron?"

"Dr. Ted?"

"You can't reject me. I do the rejecting."

"Frank?"

"You don't return my calls. Who do you think you are?"

"Genie?"

It occurred to me that I had a few too many possibilities in the angry guy category. Perhaps it was time to refine my list.

"Whore. You've got so many guys, don't you?"
"Andre?"
"You think you're better than me, but you're not as good."
"That's it. I'm calling the police."
"I'll get to you first."
Whack. Whack. Whack. Whack. It sounded like he was hitting my door with a hammer. I called 911.
"Are you in immediate danger?" said the 911 operator.
"The police won't touch me bitch."
Whack whack whack whack whack.
"What are you, O.J. Simpson? Pipe down, will you. I'm trying to talk to the 911 operator."
"Hello…" said the 911 operator.
"I don't think he has a gun," I said to the 911 operator, "but he's banging on my door with something and screaming."
"Don't open the door," said the 911 operator.
"Thanks for the advice," I said.
"I'll send someone around in a while to check up on you."
Crash—the sound of glass breaking.
"You idiot," I said. "Did you break my potted cactus?"
During my Southwest motif stage I had been gifted with a cactus in an Age-of-Aquarius turquoise blue pot. Through careful neglect, it grew about two feet. But Abyss spent endless hours using the cactus as a back scratcher, causing the cactus to be matted with her fur. I had put it out front at my door.
"If you knew anything, you'd know that Southwest is over."
"Oh." I knew who it was.
I thought about who lived close enough to get here quickly. I called Bettina.
"Can you come over, quickly, with Bean? Someone's trying to break my door down."
"We just sat down to dinner," said Bettina. "Call me back in 45 minutes, OK? I want to know who it is."
I called Marcie.

"Any possibility that you and Greg could pop over? Some guy's trying to break my door down."

Whack. Crash. The sound of the pot breaking into smaller pieces.

"I see that you've got yourself into another mess," said Marcie. "Where do you find these guys?"

"At the Ivy & Elite," I said. "I'm pretty sure that it's Richard from the Ivy & Elite."

"No way," said Marcie, "those people have good breeding. Nobody from that group would want you enough to break your door down."

"I'm guessing that you and Greg won't come over," I said. "I gotta go."

"Oh, the drama, Blanche. How exciting. Someone wants you," said Stefan. "Let him in. I'm sure you'd have fun."

"I don't think so, Stefan," I said. "I'm scared."

"Well, James and I are having drinks with friends."

"Gotta go," I said.

I didn't want to do it. But I did.

"So there's this guy hitting my door with a hammer," I said. *Crash crash crash whack.*

"I'll be right over," said Josh.

"Richard," I said, "it is you, isn't it? What are you doing?"

"YOU DIDN'T RETURN MY CALLS," said Richard

"It *was* you... You're the Breather, right?" I said.

"You didn't even go to an Ivy League School," said Richard, "but I did."

"So go find a little Ivy Eliter."

Whack Whack.

"You don't reject me. I reject you."

"So reject me, and go away."

BOOM. A thousand pieces hit the floor.

"Did you just throw my pot against the door?"

"I was going to show you how to be *one of us*."

"You and everyone else out there."

"Our children could have gone to the best schools and known the right people," said Richard.

"Look Richard, I'm sorry if I hurt your feelings. But you'd better go. I've called someone and they should be here soon."

"OK," said Richard. He sounded calm now. "I'm sorry about your pot. I'll buy you a new one—but Southwest is just so…"

"I got it Richard."

"Call me if you think you might want to go out. You've got so much potential. I really think I could do something with you."

It was suddenly quiet. I sat down on my gray futon, and greasy-Velveeta Abyss walked onto my lap, sat down and stuck her head into the crook of my elbow, something she had done every night since the day of her adoption. I knew that stroking her would feel like running your hands through a salad slathered in Ranch dressing. I did it anyway. She purred, and left an enormous grease spot on the inside left elbow of my favorite blue cashmere sweater, something no cleaner anywhere, not even the very exclusive Brown's, would ever be able to get rid of.

A few minutes later, someone knocked on my door.

"Go away Richard."

"It's me—Josh."

I unlocked the door and opened it. There were turquoise-blue shards everywhere. My little two-foot cactus sat in the corner, leaning against the wall, de-potted, looking as if it were being punished for bad behavior.

"Sorry," I said.

"Wow," said Josh, "are you OK?"

"Yeah, but I better get my cactus. Do you know anything about potting cactus?"

"Not a thing," said Josh.

"Hmm. I guess I'll put it in with the Ficus overnight." We walked into the apartment. Greasy-Velveeta-encrusted Abyss walked up to sniff Josh.

"What's that?" said Josh.

"Ah, that's my cat—Abyss. She took a liking to my sandwich. Normally, she resembles a fat Tabby."

"Did the guy go away?" said Josh.

"I think so."

"Want me to stick around for a while? To be sure? I'll make tea, or something—and you can tell me what happened."

Tea. I hate tea. Did I even have any?

"Sure. While I try to pot the cactus with the Ficus, you can make tea."

"Where do you keep your tea?"

"If I even have any, it would be in the cabinet above the microwave in the kitchen."

Josh walked into the kitchen and started scrounging through a cabinet. I dug a hole in the pot. Abyss trotted over, sniffed the cactus and started moving in.

"You listen here, young lady, you leave this cactus alone. OK Abyss?"

"What's this?" said Josh.

"Did you find some tea?"

"No. What's on your sandwich—with the tomatoes and mayo?" said Josh.

Oh. I forgot to hide the Velveeta.

I took a deep breath.

"It's Velveeta," I said.

Josh didn't say anything. He picked up the sandwich, put it in the microwave, and turned the microwave on.

"I love Velveeta," he said.

17

What Are You Hiding?

"OK—so who was it?" said Marcie.

"First say hello, and then let me get a cup of coffee," I said.

It was 6:30 a.m. on a 62-degree November morning. The sky was cornflower blue, not a cloud grazing past. The air was so clear that L.A. sparkled with sunlight, requiring me to wear my amber tinted, aviator sun glasses or risk a migraine from the bright sunlight.

From the Westside, you could see the snow caps on Mt. Baldy, 90 miles away. We had more days like this—sunny, clear, and smog-free, than the rest of the Los Angeles-hating US (especially our friends in "The City") would like to admit. But this was cool for Los Angeles. In Massachusetts, Indiana, and Wyoming, 62 degrees in November would have been a heat wave.

We were at one of the profoundly unavoidable coffee franchises on San Vicente Boulevard in Brentwood. Today our training program was to attempt 10 miles after fortifying ourselves with coffee.

Unfortunately, I could see that Marcie had already proceeded into the carb-loading period of this morning's agenda, two butter-drenched sticky buns and a hot chocolate Enormouso.

It appeared that our marathon training program was possibly having the opposite of the intended effect. I noticed that Marcie's wardrobe, instead of switching from summer to fall, had gone from wearing fun show yourself things—tight, form fitting, brightly colored—to cover and hide yourself things—black, oversized and baggy.

And yes, she was, as per her gain/lose cycle, growing her hair long and hiding.

Bettina stumbled in late. She was also a member of the opposite of the intended effect club. Her hair was long and her clothes were baggy.

Bettina headed straight to the butt-expanding counter. Her order: a glazed donut and a cinnamon twist with a vanilla latte Enormouso.

"Sorry, my nanny was late," said Bettina.

"Nanny?" I said. "I thought you fired her. You mean your mother-in-law?"

Bettina had reluctantly fired Tom-Fricken-West's nanny. It was one thing when her nanny had bought and then charged her for items which Bettina had neither asked for nor needed. Bettina had not been happy when she discovered that her nanny regularly talked on the phone, Bettina's phone, for two hours per day and ignored the children, even when they were crying.

But when Bettina began noticing that her clothes were missing because her nanny was "borrowing" them, she gave up. She fired her, and somehow didn't show up for our bi-weekly jogs for two weeks.

Bettina was pretty erratic with exercising, so it could have been a lot of things. When she finally showed again, I didn't press the case.

"Nanny. Mother-in-law. What's the difference?" said Bettina.

I looked at her.

"Well, to begin with, one is a member of your family...and I don't mean the one you pay. You know, the one who gave birth to your husband?"

Bettina yawned. "Look who's talking. How's your door?"

I ignored her. "So Miss Sticky Bun, what was your question?"

"Who was it?" yawned Marcie.

"Richard—the guy from the Ivy & Elite."

"What did he want?"

"After breaking my cactus pot..."

"Thank God..."

I rolled my eyes.

"...and pounding on my door for 20 minutes. He was mad at me for not returning his calls."

Marcie lurched forward at me. "You didn't return his calls! What's wrong with you?"

I looked at her.

"And he still wants to go out," I said.

"Yeech. Why?"

"He thinks I have potential to break into the L.A. Civilian Royalty...with the right coaching."

Marcie shook her head. "Give me his number. I'll straighten him out on that." She looked at me. "I think you should give him a second chance."

"Are you nuts? I had to call 911."

"Do you *really* think there are that many eligible guys in L.A.?" said Marcie.

Bettina looked up. "Did they come? The police?"

"Eventually. But first Josh came over."

Marcie looked surprised. "Josh?"

Bettina looked alarmed. "Josh? You didn't tell me that."

"You didn't ask."

"What did he want?" asked Marcie.

I looked at her.

"I don't know...to play with Abyss? He came over to help me."

"Why?" said Marcie

"Yeah, why?" said Bettina.

"I don't know...he's a nice guy."

"Do you think he likes you?" asked Marcie.

"I don't know."

"How long did he stay?"

"Overnight."

"Are you kidding?"

I was surprised by Bettina's interest.

"Did you sleep with him?"

"And improve on your record?"

"What?" asked Marcie.

Bettina started blushing. "She's kidding."

I smiled at her.

"He spent the night on the couch."

"Oh, he's just being nice."

"Maybe."

"What else would it be? Isn't he still dating that great girl... Carnie?" said Marcie.

"Cody. They broke up."

Marcie nodded her head. "Hmm."

"Why are you so interested?"

"He's a great guy," said Marcie, "but not right for you."

"Why not?"

Marcie shook her head. "He's just too classy and much higher than you on the Eco-Chain. He's not your type."

"Who is?"

Marcie raised her brows. "Hmmm, I need to think about that. But I know someone who might be a better match for him."

"Who's that?"

She smiled.

"You're engaged. Aren't you?"

I looked to Bettina, who turned her face away.

"Isn't she?"

Marcie arched her back and yawned. "Well, Greg and I couldn't agree on a budget for the wedding. My wedding should cost at least $250,000. He wants something different."

"When did this happen?"

"Early October," yawned Marcie. "I need more coffee."

"So for four weeks you didn't tell me that you broke up?"

"Not broke up. We're not broken up. We're just re-thinking things. Giving each other space."

"Over the wedding budget?"

"It's the most important day of my life and I deserve to have it the way I want it."

"I guess my wedding dress is safe again."

"It was always safe. But if I want it, I think you should let me have it. You know I should get what I want from my friends."

"It's a wedding, not a coronation."

"You wouldn't understand," said Bettina.

"You might be right."

Marcie smiled. "So Josh is available?"

I didn't like where this was going. "I guess so."

"What? Do you *like* him?" mumbled Marcie.

"Ye…ah."

"He's just not right for you. What does he think about all the makeup you wear?" sneered Marcie.

"He's a guy. He doesn't care."

Bettina looked at me. "I think I know someone to set you up with. He's more your style."

"I know," said Marcie. "Have you tried online dating?"

Bettina started laughing. "That's a great idea! But I'm still going to give this guy a call to find out if he's available."

"Speaking of available, could you let Josh know that I am?" said Marcie. "Work on your thing for those online personals. I'd love to see it."

"Hey, How about Richard? He's available," I suggested.

Marcie smiled contemptuously. "Nooo. He's definitely not right for me. If he's interested in you he wants a project not a princess."

"Are either of you planning on running today?" I asked.

They looked at me.

"I didn't think so." I stood up and put on my glasses.

"You aren't going to run in all that makeup?" Marcie said while rolling her eyes.

"Always have, always will. See ya."

I walked out of the coffee joint and began my run alone.

I started up San Vicente at my pace, which I had determined to be about 11 minutes per mile. By the time I crossed 26th and tripped over the pot holes bordering the Brentwood Country Club, I thought about bagging it all to order a mocha Grande Enormouso at another location of the coffee chain which was less than two miles from the other location that I had just left. And I thought about what, if any, personal ad I would place.

I was surprised and bothered that Marcie hid her "not a breakup..." from me. But I was also bothered that she continued to bug me about my makeup. Because she knew.

Marcie knows that for the last 18 years I have worn makeup to cover my birthmark. She knows that my recent trip to the Demorol-addicted Laser God was not just for a little scar. It was to attempt another treatment for my birthmark. Which didn't work. She knows that I've had many treatments that didn't work. But she doesn't know how many.

She doesn't know that I've had three operations to remove skin, which didn't work because it left scars. Five treatments with a laser which left a patch of my nose with the texture of cottage cheese, two operations to correct that, and two treatments with a new laser that doesn't leave a cottage cheese texture. I've had ten procedures.

She knows that in grade school I always got to play the lead in *Rudolph, the Red-Nosed Reindeer* without resorting to makeup or props.

She knows that the day that I discovered makeup I went from "The Girl with the Birthmark," "Oh my God, what happened to you?" and "Man, you're so ugly," to "Wow, who is that?" Like Julia, I'm not sure which one she is more comfortable with.

She knows that since that age of thirteen, I've worn makeup to run, swim, hike, scuba, study, and work.

When I get back to my apartment, Julia is sitting outside.
"Hello," I said.
"You've changed your locks," said Julia.
"I did that ages ago. Would you like to come in?"
"Thanks. Got any coffee?"
"I'm sure I could find some."
There are 15 bags of Whole Bean Guatemala Antigua in my freezer. I pulled one out, opened it, and began to grind. I know that the universal coffee to water ratio is one tablespoon coffee to one cup of water. Mine is closer to four to one.

In the background, I see a brown and white streak going through my French doors.
"Where's your cat?" asks Julia.
"I don't know," I lie.
Abyss hates Julia because Julia moves too quickly and has a habit of vacuuming my place when she's nervous. Abyss has hidden. I'm guessing she's under my bed.
"I need to borrow something from you," said Julia, "something to wear."
"Uh-huh."
"Christmas is coming. And I'm going to have the Hamiltons over for a tree-trimming party. I'd like you to co-host it with me."

"Julia."

"What?"

"We're Jewish. When are you going to tell them?'

"For a smart girl, you don't understand much," said Julia, "what was your IQ again?"

"148."

"No...no, that's not quite what I remember."

Age 9.

Something is wrong at school. I'm in the highest reading group, the highest math group, and get straight As. But the teacher hands out envelopes to all six of my friends in my reading and math group but not to me. I know something is different because my friends seem really happy and start to play with me less, but won't tell me what was in the envelope. They whisper, but when I ask them what they are talking about they won't tell me. Finally, my friend Frances breaks.

"You're smart, Courtney, but we're gifted and you're not."

I don't know what gifted is, but I know that it's something I need to be. I've figured out that it's my job to lead my mother and me out of the desperate mess of her husbandless and my fatherless life. I'm not sure how to do it, but I know that I better get into every good program and class that every kid with a father and mother and a big house gets into. So I shadow them and try to pick up the clues of what they, the kids whose parents are planning and paying attention, are doing. But now I know that I will not be in the gifted program. I've failed. I cry for weeks and make myself sick. The one thing I could always count on was my intelligence and I have failed. I'm not gifted.

"Go to the principal," I tell my mom.

"I'm busy," she says.

I am miserable for months and put myself on my first self-improvement program. I read two books per week and command myself to be the best in everything, from reading to kick-ball. I become the best violinist in the school because I start practicing three hours per day. I get the best grades and never make any mistakes. But I have failed. I will never be gifted. I will not be in the gifted program.

"I need you to go to the principal," I tell my mom.

"Stop bugging me," she says.

The principal calls me into her office because I'm crying in class.

"You're one of our finest students," she says.

"But I'm not gifted," I tell her.

The principal looks upset.

She tells me, "Have your mother call me."

I tell my mom.

"The principal wants you to call her."

My mom promises to call, but never quite gets around to it.

Four months later, the principal calls my mom. Even they know something is wrong: The recent state standardized test scores have been released and I have the highest score in the school in reading and rank in the 99-plus percentile in math. I have scored higher than all of the "gifted" kids in the school, but I am not "gifted" because I didn't show much imagination on the day that I was given my "gifted" test, which I come to learn, is called a Stanford–Binet: An IQ test.

"Bullshit," my mom tells the principal, "trust me, this kid has got more imagination than any person I've ever met."

I think I remember being tested. It was right after my dad died. I was hungry and cold and my shoes hurt. They put me in a room with a strange woman who asked me questions for three hours. She kept asking me, "What does it mean to 'plug in?'" I got exasperated and told her that her questions were stupid. There were square blocks that you had to fit into round holes. Then she showed me pictures and asked, "What's wrong with this?" I remember one picture that stumped me, the one with the cow and the sun. I couldn't get it.

My principal asks my mom, "What do you want us to do?"

"If you don't retest her, I'll make every day of the rest of your life a living hell," says my mom.

"140," my mom tells me. "You have to get a 140 this time. Remember, it's just you and the test giver. If they like you, they're probably going to give you the extra points. So be nice. Don't argue."

I know they are going to retest me, but I don't know when. I round up my "gifted" kids on the playground and ask them about the test.

"What about the picture with the cow and the sun? What's wrong with it?" I ask.

"The shadow," says Frances, "the shadow is going the wrong way."

The principal comes to my classroom one day at one o'clock and asks for me. She brings me to a small room. There's a woman sitting at a small desk. I recognize the square-block-round-hole set-up and see what looks to be the back of the "What's Wrong with This?" pictures. It's the test.

The principal tells me that the lady wants to ask me a few questions.

I know how this works. She starts with something innocent like, "What do you want to be when you grow up?" and slides into the, "What's wrong with this picture?" portion of the test.

And she does. But I'm ready.

When she asks me, "What do you want to be when you grow up?" I know that she's expecting "a mommy" or "a teacher." Instead, I tell her, "I'd like to enter the State Department. I'd love to study International Diplomacy at Georgetown, and hopefully, affect the foreign policy of the United States through postings in strategic areas of the world after placing well on my Foreign Service Exam," an answer one of my mom's brighter boyfriends has helped me work out.

When she slides into, "Gee, could you tell what's wrong with this picture?" I stare intently. It's the picture with the cow with the sun.

"Well," I say, "to begin with, the shadow, in relation to the setting of the sun, is, well, going the wrong way." And then, just to put some topping on it, I talk about the fact that the cow may be too big for the picture, something about proportion. I know it's not right, but think I might get extra points for imagination. Mucho, mucho imagination.

I love my embellishments. I'm flying along. I'm smiling. I'm soooo interested in what she has to say, and endlessly discuss the possibilities of each answer, looking her in the eye and working every moment for the most possible points.

And then we hit the vocabulary section.

"Tell me, Courtney, do you know what a HEE-o is?"

I'm stumped. Usually vocabulary is a breeze for me. I never have any problem with vocabulary, and frankly, am quite used to impressing with ease.

But I have no idea what a HEE-o is.

"No," I say in a small voice.

She has a gleam in her eye, like we're playing chess and she finally has me.

"Well, then you probably won't get this one. Do you know what HEEE-o-glyphics are?"

Checkmate.

I have just read *From the Mixed-Up Files of Mrs. Basil E. Frankweiler*. Claudia and Jamie, the kids in the story, spend a large portion of the book in the Ancient Egyptian section of Metropolitan Museum of Art attempting to decipher hieroglyphics.

I decide to take a stab.

"You don't by any chance mean *Hi-ro-glyphics*, do you?"

"Yes, that's one pronunciation."

It's the dumbest of dumb luck.

"Of course. Hi-ro-glyphics are the Egyptian scroll letters, the symbols, or um, sometimes pictures used primarily by the ancient Egyptians to mean a word, a sound or like a syllable, like our alphabet."

Almost Royalty

"Did I get it right?" I ask.

I think her lower jaw drops open half an inch. She is wondering how I knew the answer to that question.

"Yes," she says quietly.

"I read," I say.

And suddenly I get it. She's got a weird accent, and she's messing up the pronunciation of each word.

"Wait a minute, wait a minute," I say. That earlier question, HEE-o, wasn't *He-ro*, was it?

It was. "Of course I know what a *hero* is."

I babble endlessly. Now that I can understand her accent, I hit my stride, relentlessly pouncing on each vocabulary word as she mispronounces them.

I finish with a huge flourish, by endlessly discussing everything I read about HEE-o-glyphics—without revealing my source.

She begins tabulating my IQ as I sit at the table.

I, as a necessary survival skill, have long ago learned how to read upside-down.

148.

"Relax," I tell Julia when I get home, "we're in."

Of course, she knows already because she has been phoned and told of my "most impressive score" by not only my classroom teacher, but by the principal, before the bell rings to let me out for the day.

The next day I'm hurled into the "gifted program" in world record time. There's a little bit of grumbling on the playground about me getting two chances, "I got in the first time. She had to do it twice" type things, but after a few days, it dies down.

It takes me almost 20 years to discover that being "gifted," in the gifted program, or having an IQ of 148, means absolutely nothing.

But I still wonder about the first test.

"Try the green cashmere sweater. It'll look great with your hair."

"Oh now I remember," said Julia, "it was 148," as she walks into my closet.

"Aaaaahhh!" screams Julia. "There's an animal in your closet."

"Abyss..." I said.

Abyss has jumped onto my sweater shelf and burrowed into the white cashmere section, between the off-white and cream sweaters. Only her eyes are showing.

"Comfy?" I said.

Abyss purrs. I grabbed the green cashmere, which is cat-hair free.

"Here you go."

"This will go so nicely with my black pants," said Julia.

"Take it, and since I don't think I'm getting it back, Happy Hanukkah."

"You mean Merry Christmas," said Julia.

"Here's your coffee."

"Can I take it to go?" said Julia.

Julia leaves with my sweater. A pity. I really liked my green cashmere.

"It's interesting that you eat that toxin when you're upset or anxious," said Jennifer.

"For that kind of insight I should pay you $180."

"Is that what you pay Roberta?" said Jennifer. "$180 an hour?"

"No. For 45 minutes."

"Wow. And you're not even going to have a good butt when you're done with her. I think I'll tear up my State Bar Card right now and become a therapist."

"Very Funny."

"Have you noticed? You eat that crap in moments of distress."

"Really."

Later, I check my voice mail and find a message from Bettina.

"So I talked to my friend, and he's interested. He's going to give you a call."

Bettina's friend is named Marcus. He calls me and we talk.

Marcus is 39 years old.

Marcus went to Wharton Business School.

Marcus did his undergraduate at Amherst.

Marcus is a management consultant.

Marcus owns a condo in Santa Monica, three blocks from the beach.

Marcus had a Bar Mitzvah but is not observant. In fact he's a Unitarian.

Marcus is in a wine tasting group and writes their newsletter.

Marcus has a wine cellar (well, closet, because he doesn't have a cellar in his condo).

Marcus collects first edition books.

Marcus has an expensive Italian bike. It cost him $8,000.

Marcus tells me that three times. I mean four.

Marcus rides with a bike group on the weekends.

Marcus has an E-Series Mercedes.

Marcus has done everything right in his life.

Marcus is perfect.

We agree to go out.

"Choose some place you like," said Marcus.

I choose a place in West Hollywood that serves Italian. I think it will be fun to meet for drinks, appetizers, and desserts.

"OK..." said Marcus and then laughs. "How cute."

"What?" I ask.

"Nothin..."

We agree to meet the following Wednesday at 7:30.

7:25—I arrive at the restaurant and check in with the hostess. I am wearing a navy blue sleeveless dress with a little box jacket—it's a '60s Jackie-O retro look. Also, sling-back heels. Marcus has told me that his birthday is in a few days. I've bought him an inexpensive first edition of a book which is in decent condition and wrapped it. The hostess tells me—No Marcus. I look for a lone male. No one is there. The hostess tells me I can wait in the bar.

I go into the bar. The bar has a polished marble counter and 15 bar stools, a mirror and an enormous flower arrangement behind the counter. There is a couple on the other side of the bar. But no lone males, no Marcus there either. The bartender keeps bugging me. I order a glass of Chardonnay from a vintner on the Central Coast of California. The bartender gives me a basket of bread and a plate of butter. For $3.25 I can have a selection of olive oils. I decline.

At 7:40 I check in with the waitress again. She tells me that if my friend doesn't arrive within five minutes we'll lose our reservation. I go back to my seat at the bar which is filling up. The bartender is shooting me dirty looks.

7:50—No Marcus. We have lost our reservation. The hostess shrugs her shoulders. "Sorry—restaurant policy." I go back to my seat at the bar.

7:55—Still no Marcus. The bartender has come by twice. To keep my place at the bar, I order a refill of the Chardonnay. It sits there.

8:00—Still no Marcus. I should go. I sip my wine.

8:25—A lone man walks into the bar. He is about five foot five. He is wearing jeans with holes in them, running shoes, a cotton crew jacket with leather patches from the movie *Pulp Fiction* ("a great buy on eBay") and a baseball hat. He takes the hat and jacket off and looks around. He is wearing a white athletic shirt. He has short, blond, ultra-fine hair which he has combed in five different directions—back, forward, right, left, and up—because he's balding. I can see a bald spot near the front of his head and at the top of the back of his head. He looks to be in his mid to late 40s. He sees me, and walks over.

"Courtney?"

"Yeah."

"Hey, I'm Marcus. Sorry I'm late, but I got held up."

"I gave you my cell number. Why didn't you call?"

"Don't be such a bitch. I told you. I got held up."

"OK."

Marcus looks around. "What are you drinking?" he asks.

I take a sip of my wine. "A Chardonnay," I reply.

"Why?" said Marcus. He leans over and lurches for my glass, grabbing it by the stem and knocking some wine on me. As he brushes me, I smell alcohol.

"Whoops," said Marcus. He puts the glass to his lips, and drinks. "This isn't bad." He drinks my drink, the remainder of my glass which, but for my sip, is completely full.

"Let me look at the wine list," said Marcus. He motions to the bartender who brings him the list, a book, which is extensive. He searches the book and asks the bartender if the sommelier is available. The sommelier is summoned and he and Marcus enter into a ten-minute discussion. I sit at the bar.

"Well," said Marcus, "it looks like there is an extremely good and extremely rare Italian White available. It's kind of expensive."

"How expensive?" I ask.

"$300," said Marcus, "but if we both share the cost, it won't be too bad."

"I don't think so. That glass of Chard you drank was my second, so I'm pretty much done drinking for the evening—unless it's non-alcoholic."

"You're no fun," said Marcus. "Come on, Miss Perfect Makeup, live a little."

"I don't think so. But you get what you want."

The bartender returns.

"A coffee, regular," I say.

"And for you, sir?" said the bartender.

"I'll guess I'll have a glass of that lame Chard she's drinking," said Marcus.

"Shall I run a new tab?" said the bartender.

"No," said Marcus.

"Yes. That way you can get whatever you want," I say.

"A cheap one," says Marcus. "What do you have in your hand?"

"Oh. I got you a little birthday present."

"How sweet," sneers Marcus. "Are you going to let me admire it, or give it to me?"

"Here," I said. I give the gift to him. He opens it, and drops the wrapping on the floor.

"It's a first edition," I said.

"With no jacket," said Marcus. "This significantly lowers the value. Thanks."

"So Courtney, where are you from?" said Marcus. "Let me guess."

"South Pas?"

"No."

"San Marino?"

"No."

"Brentwood?"

"No."

"Where then?" I tell him.

"Ooh," said Marcus, "is there anything there but oil refineries and the Navy?"

"Lots."

"You should lie," said Marcus.

"Where are you from?"

"Let's just say, the Northeast," said Marcus. He chuckles, looks around the room, and laughs—loudly.

"Unbelievable," said Marcus.

"What?"

"Well…I've never been here on a Wednesday night."

"Oh."

"There are only two times anyone should come here," he said. "Thursday night—Sandwich Night—or for brunch on the weekends. Every other night is for the Bridge and Tunnel crowd."

"Oh." I think for a moment. "Will you excuse me?" I ask.

I walk out of the bar and speak to the hostess for a moment.

I cross through the restaurant. For Bridge and Tunnel Night, there's a lot of West Hollywood here, your basic smattering of TV stars, creative execs, and record industry types.

I find the bathroom and look in the mirror. "OK then," I say. I walk back through the restaurant and to the hostess.

"Done," said the hostess.

When I walk into the bar, Marcus is sharing a laugh with the bartender. It looks like he's ordered a second glass of the lame Chardonnay which I ordered. I sit down on the bar stool.

"Are you having a good time?" I said.

"Yeah," said Marcus.

"Good," I said, "because this is the last time you'll ever go out with me. I'm leaving."

I stand up and start to walk out.

"What?" said Marcus. "Wait."

I look at Marcus.

"Don't worry, I've paid for my tab."

I walk to my car, get in, and drive home.

It's 8:45.

"Did you talk to Josh for me?" asks Marcie.

"No."

Marcie looks at me. "Well, when are you going to?" she asks.

"I don't know," I reply.

"What's the problem?" asks Marcie.

Tuesday morning, 6:15 a.m. I am at one of the profoundly unavoidable coffee joints on San Vicente Boulevard. It's gray, drizzling and around 57 degrees. I think I just ordered a bottle of water and an Espresso Giganto. I need a wet drink and a dry drink.

Marcie orders a peppermint/vanilla cappuccino Bigio (the smallest size) with a bear claw.

It is six days after my encounter with Marcus. Marcus has left two voice mail messages since our date.

One day after our date:

"I'm impressed, a woman with moxie. Call me. We could have fun."

Three days after our date:

"C'mon, you got me to come on a Wednesday night with the Bridge and Tunnel crowd. I deserve a call back."

Bettina walks in at 6:30, orders, waits two minutes for her drink, and then sits down with her latte Enormouso and a cinnamon roll. I don't think she has bothered to wear running shoes.

Before her first sip of latte, Marcie gives me an annoyed look. "Marcus tells me you won't return his calls. If I go to the trouble to fix you up, you should at least return his calls."

"It wasn't a good match."

"What do you mean?" said Bettina.

"I mean I didn't like him."

"It's not about what you think, it's about what they think. You don't choose. They do," says Bettina quite harshly.

"Since when?"

"Since you started running out of time," said Bettina.

"Look, Marcus kinda hurt my feelings," I say.

"You're much too sensitive," said Marcie.

"Did you do the personal?" said Bettina.

"Yes," I said.

"Let me look at it," said Bettina.

I hand Bettina and Marcie a copy.

"When you're done, why don't you join me for a short 20-minute jog up San Vicente."

"I'll think about it," said Bettina.

"I don't know," said Marcie, "it's too cold."

"On the East Coast this would be a heat wave."

"Is this the East Coast?" said Marcie.

I looked out the window.

"I didn't think so," said Marcie.

"But we'll never be ready for the marathon."

"Who is going to run the marathon?" said Marcie.

"I thought we were," I said.

Marcie and Bettina look at me and laugh.

I look at both of them and say, "I am. I'm running the marathon."

"You've got much bigger things to worry about," said Marcie. She looked down at my personal. "Is this even how they're supposed to be written?"

"Yeah," said Bettina "I thought it was supposed to say like SWF, 31, Blond, ISO SM, non-smoker, for romantic candlelight dinners…" she laughed.

"This is for Match.com," I said. "You're supposed to describe yourself."

"Uh-huh," said Bettina, who with Marcie, began reading my personal.

Not What You Are Looking For in Los Angeles

I know that many of you are searching for a person—my mistake—the Right Person, to be your wife. Having graduated from college—UC Berkeley, U Penn, Brown—and possibly hidden out for a couple of extra years in graduate schools, or maybe padded your resume with various years abroad or fellowships that—really, if you were to be honest—did nothing more than make you want to come home, sit in your parents' back yard, and stick your face in a box of Oreos—you, like me, are anxious to hide your solidly middle-class background that your parents worked two jobs around the clock to achieve.

In addition to your education, most of you have worked very hard to transform yourself into your image of what you should be. You have your acceptable cars—your Range Rovers, your BMWs (5-series or above), your Mercedes. You live in an acceptable area—apartments/condos in Brentwood, Santa Monica (above Wilshire only), Beverly Hills, Pacific Palisades. You have taste—you're wine knowledgeable, have attended tastings and at some point, probably pretended to like cigars. You have things that make you interesting— first edition books, Japanese movie posters, Italian bicycles (a hobby/sport that hides the fact that you're profoundly uncoordinated and on the borderline of losing that battle with the 20 extra pounds) which you ride on Saturdays with your club. But you've never really done anything—other than law, business, or maybe, just maybe if you got decent grades in those science classes—med school—that required any real work.

So you've come to your 30s and you realize that the pool of available women is shrinking. Some of your friends, in fact more than a few of your friends, have gotten married and maybe a few of them are even starting on marriage #2. You know that it's time to get into the game, before it's too late.

I'm sure that you have your criteria. It might be looks— weight, height, hair color and acceptable age range. It might be inspirations—Schoenberg, loves David Hockney, collects daguerreotypes. It might be fundamental beliefs— Democrat, Moveon.org contributor, Save the Volvo.
But I'm going to guess that it's really something else.

I'm going to guess that you're embarrassed that your mom has a lot of recipes that involve mushroom soup, onion dip mix, and Velveeta—followed by a tri-colored Jell-O creation.
That your parents did and still do drive Fords and Chevys.

That your parents' house has one room—the fancy living room—which exists for show, that no one ever sits in, unless you have special guests.

Almost Royalty

That you weren't a debutante from Downey or a preppie from Peoria, because Downey had no debutantes, and Peoria no Prep Schools, and you never, ever knew what a debutante or preppie was until you landed in a college that was much better than your parents thought anyone in your family would ever achieve.
That you weren't Episcopalian, but Lutheran.

Your parents weren't the treasurers of your Reform synagogue; in fact, your parents didn't bother with temple membership at all.

But you—like most members of your generation—want to hide all of this.

So now you're looking for a girl who is slightly better than all that—Who Has the Right Stuff. Someone whose parents were professionals rather than laborers. Someone who lived in Beverly Hills, Brentwood, Bel Air, Holmby Hills, South Pasadena, San Marino, maybe Flintridge.

Someone who had a mom who didn't have to work, but maybe volunteered at The Museum of Modern Art, The Junior League or on the Music Center's Blue Ribbon Committee. Someone who had a dad who kept a job (in the case that he needed one), didn't run off, and wasn't a drunk, but instead had a yacht, played golf, and maybe even hunted.

Someone who has a family that has alumni ties to schools—Stanford, Harvard, or Yale—at the college level, and feeder private high schools, elementary schools and pre-schools. Someone who uses the word "summer" as a verb instead of a noun.
But that isn't me.

I will never have the goods—the money, the connections, the status—to get a child into the right pre-school, so that he can go to the right elementary school, so that he can go to the right middle school, so that he can go to the right high school, so that—of course—he can go to Harvard or Stanford.

And I went to public schools.

And I don't speak French.

And I believe in being nice because it is the right thing to do and not because you can get something from someone.

And I don't decorate or entertain like Martha Stewart.

And I am addicted to Velveeta.

And I refuse to hide any of this anymore.

Bettina finished reading, rolled her eyes, and sighed. Marcie shook her head.

"What is this?" said Bettina.

"The truth," I said, "something you have a distant relationship with, Bettina."

"What do you mean?" said Marcie.

"Marcie, how much do you think you know about Bettina?" I said.

"Don't," said Bettina. "Please."

"I don't want to hide anymore," I said. "I can't hide your past, my past, or my mother's."

Marcie looked at Bettina, "What about Bettina?" she asked.

"Bettina," I said, "why don't you and Marcie take this time to get acquainted. Start by telling her about your feminist performance art pieces. Remember, 'I Do—Not!' And what was the name of that truck-driving friend of yours—Luba? And what about Wanda?"

"I don't think I want to hear this," said Marcie.

"This is just diverting attention from your problem," said Bettina, "that you're running out of time. And alone."

"You do know of course that single woman-40-educated-no man thing has been revealed to be pure crap," I said.

"And the demographics have changed—there are slightly more men in my dating pool than women—something like a surplus of 80,000 guys for every million of us women in their 30s."

"We don't want you to be alone," Bettina said with a small smirk.

"I don't know what you want, but I don't think that you're thinking about me. And I won't be alone. Marcie will be fighting the good fight with me."

"What?" said Bettina.

"Tell her, Marcie," I said. "Tell Bettina the truth: that you and Greg—that it's completely over. That you've been hiding that from us."

"How did you find out?" said Marcie.

"On one of my jogs up San Vicente—the jogs neither of you ever do with me—I ran into him, with his new girlfriend—she's an accountant."

"We...I...was just trying to help you," said Marcie.

"Well, I don't want your help anymore if that's what it is. I don't want to be told I wear too much makeup, my hair is too long, too short, too blond, too common...blue is not my color, green is my color... I need these dishes, that car, this furniture...that Richard is right for me, Josh is wrong...and that I should ignore my feelings and hide my past."

"Josh is just soooo much higher than you on the Eco-Chain," said Marcie. "It would never work."

"*OH MY GOD*—the Eco-Chain...we're not eleven years old anymore."

"But the marathon?" said Bettina.

"We were just trying to help you make the right choices!" hissed Marcie.

"*When* did you decide that you knew what the right choices for me were?" I yelled.

Marcie looked down. Bettina sighed, and drank her latte.

"And *when* did you decide that your help included ignoring my feelings, pushing me to date stalkers, or celebrating my perceived inadequacies?

"Nothing to say, Marcie? No insight for me, Bettina?" I yelled, loud enough to get the attention of the assistant manager. "Then why don't you two take the next 30 minutes and get to know each other. And LEAVE ME OUT OF IT. That I confused this bitch-o-rama, this bi-weekly coven of witches, for a friendship—well, in the vernacular of my therapist—I take responsibility for it. But I'm done with it."

Then I stood up, threw out the last half of my Espresso Giganto, and walked out.

18

"In"

Jennifer called me while I was doing my laundry. I hate doing my laundry and I'm terrible at it.

"Marshall is coming down for the *Faces of Tomorrow Competition.*"

I started laughing. "He's a *Face of Tomorrow*? What, the face of Rogaine? Hey, do the reds go with the darks or do you do them alone?"

"Try a cold water wash, then you can put all the colors together. Seriously, he's coming down to be in the competition," said Jennifer. "And we need a place to stay."

"We?"

"Marshall and I. And Haggis."

"I thought Marshall had enough money to buy the Duchy of Luxemburg. Why don't you stay some place fun like The Standard."

"There's a problem."

"What? I know I have a problem. I don't have enough quarters to do my laundry."

"I'll tell you when I see you. But Marshall is tired of thinking for a living."

"He has a PhD in mathematics from Princeton."

"He wants a shot at exploiting his physical side."

"Who convinced him to do this?"

"His therapist. And of course, Haggis."

"I thought that was a joke. He can't be serious?"

"Oh yes. He's been doing a lot of work to get ready."

"Ready? For what?"

"The model/spokesperson category."

"No!" I laughed. "What preparation does he need? He's 42. It's 20 years too late for modelling."

"He's spent a lot of time working on his runway walk," said Jennifer. "He hired an expert, one of those guys who coaches regional beauty contestant winners on to national competitions. You know, the guys who coach Miss America contestants."

"What—did the coach teach him to apply hemorrhoid cream on his butt to reduce the jiggly factor during his stroll down the runway?"

"He didn't need to. Marshall had that taken care of."

"No."

"Yes. He had his eyelids redone, his forehead lifted, and his nose straightened."

"That's all?"

"That's all he'll admit. But I think he had some other things done too."

"Like what?"

"Well, he was working like a demon with Haggis to get ripped abs, you know, washboard abs."

"I guess. I've never seen them. I kinda thought that whole washboard ab thing was a Photoshop enhancement."

"Well, he couldn't seem to get rid of his little gut. Ever. And then overnight, it just disappeared."

"Did the gut's disappearance coincide with his visit to Dr. Fresh Face?"

"His gut and his jiggly butt. And then his hair, it's suddenly got all this sheen, this red in it."

"He had highlights put in?"

"He won't talk about it. Meanwhile he's working around the clock with Haggis. I almost never see him."

"Are you sure that's what he's doing with Haggis? Working?"

"You know, I told him what you said. He was really insulted."

"Oh yeah? Has your boyfriend touched you yet?"

"That's beside the point."

"It is?"

"He said he doesn't define himself by his sexuality," said Jennifer.

"Unlike most human adults. What is he…Pippi Longstocking?"

"That's not fair. Dating is different now."

"How so? Isn't a boyfriend still someone you're having a romantic relationship with, usually involving sex, on a regular basis?"

"It can be."

"Well if it isn't, isn't that a friendship?"

"It's not that."

"Then what?"

"The sexuality."

"What about it?"

"It's just not that clear anymore," said Jennifer.

"There are new categories?"

"There are no categories."

"Well, you guys will need to bring sleeping bags with you. If you're going to stay here, you'll be in the living room. With Abyss."

"Is she still up to her old tricks?"

"Which ones?"

"Barfing."

"Yes, she's barfing. And she's addicted to baloney. By the time you come down, I'll try to understand your confusion with Marshall."

"You mean my relationship?"

"Look, you know that someone's sexuality is about as interesting to me as the answer to the question 'de-caf' or 'regular?' But you know better than this. A guy who doesn't touch you within a month of dating you, unless there's a religious issue at hand…but that wouldn't be an issue because he wouldn't be around you for a month anyway…is gay. Or your brother."

"You're wrong if you think it's that simple anymore. You may be in for a surprise."

"You know what I think."

"I know, I know," said Jennifer. "There are no mysteries."

There was a time, well to be precise—right now—when I thought everyone was gay. It was almost a knee-jerk reaction, something that clearly came from a period of time when I viewed an enormous portion of the male population with a great deal of mystery.

Why did that guy who was so kind, so fun to be with, and such a wonderful cook never seem to have a girlfriend? Your terrifically witty classmate from your grad school who loved the theater just couldn't find a girl. What was the problem? And that friend of your roommate's boyfriend who was a male model—inhumanly gorgeous—who always seemed to be alone. Don't tell me they couldn't find a girlfriend.

At first it was all a mystery.

Then, I came to believe that there was no mystery.

"There's always an answer," I would say.

And the answer was that they were gay.

I would be told that a great potential date was "a terrific cook."

Almost Royalty

"Of course," I'd reply, "and he's also gay."

A description involving "male" and "loves the theater," would elicit a response of "And he's been with his boyfriend for how long?" And anyone who dared to tell me that some guy was "beautiful," without any further description, would receive a bored look, a roll of my eyes, and the word "gay" out of my mouth.

"But he's married," they would say.

"Still gay," I'd say.

"They have three children," they would say.

"Gay," I'd say, "his wife just doesn't know it."

"They've been together for 10 years."

"And he's still beautiful?" I'd say. "Absolutely gay."

I'm sure that this was cultivated by my high school education, an education in which my desperately experimental teachers—desperate because all the students had disappeared from the high school the year before I attended due to an untimely riot on the campus and the school needed some method to attract students back to the school—had followed a methodology now referred to as "experimental developmental."

"Developmental. Children know what they need to learn. Children learn at their own pace." It's all fine—if you're under five years old and potty training, the alphabet, and drinking from a sippy cup are relatively new skills.

At 14, "experimental developmental" means instead of reading Edith Wharton, Steinbeck, or Stendahl, you will pursue a course of study which will ensure that your SATs will be 60 to 200 points lower than what you would have scored had you received instruction for four years in a structured, academic English class.

You will keep a daily journal for three months, write what is important to you, and give a report at the end of the semester.

English Class. It's Report Day. I'm 14.

"Who would like to go first?" said my teacher, Mr. Levy.

"I would," said my friend, Steve Dutton. Steve walks to the front of the room.

"My report is titled, 'I Have a Boyfriend,'" said Steve. Laughter in the room.

Steve begins to read.

"I have always known that I was different," said Steve. "I wanted to do things different from other boys. I liked different things. I felt different things. I thought something might be wrong with me. I thought I might be sick. I thought that I was the only one like this and that I was alone. But now I know what I am: I'm gay."

For 10 minutes, Steve tells us the story—in details more graphic than anyone had ever wanted—of his sexual discovery.

"Thank you, Steve," said Mr. Levy, after he was finished. Mr. Levy seems disturbed and pale.

His boyfriend's name is Robert.

I have never heard the words "gay" or "out" before.

Steve changes his name to "Stefan."

I stretch to understand.

From Stefan and Robert I learn about gay clubs, gay drugs, and gay music. I see men who dance better than I ever will. I meet men who have a greater sense of hair, clothes and makeup than I do. I meet men who know how to cook and decorate a home with the flair and creativity that I will never have, men who spend hours obsessing over interior decor.

Jeans are replaced with tight, form-fitting clothes. Natural brown hair is highlighted with blond streaks. Then red. This year it's platinum blond and shoulder length, wavy: "My Marilyn Monroe look," said Stefan.

Then there are hair extensions—straight hair that falls to the center of his back, pulled back with a rubber band. Like the lead singer of Red Hot Chili Peppers.

Thin bodies become thinner. Then hard. Then buffed to an extreme, a scent of steroids in the atmosphere.

And then there are earrings.
I meet the Gay Fashionafia.
They called me "Blanche."
"Not that lipstick, Blanche," they tell me.
"Not those dishes, Blanche," they tell me.
"Not that boyfriend, Blanche," they tell me.
The gay-pretty-male version of Marcie.

In San Francisco, I am on the periphery of the community which is ravaged by Aids. Polk Street and The Castro are subdued. It's the Aids March, the Aids Walk, the Aids Run, the Aids Dance, the Aids Campaign. Everyone knows someone who is infected. The first sign: rapid weight loss. A persistent cough that won't go away. Then Sarcomas. Then gone.

At art school, it's Bettina and the lesbians. Bettina and her girlfriend, Luba, the truck driver. Bettina and her girlfriend, Wanda, the welder. Bettina and the Lesbian Art Collective. "If you loved yourself, you'd want to be with a woman," said Bettina.

"Then it's clear," I said, "I must hate myself."

For having a boyfriend, the lesbians call me "oppressed." For wanting to have children, the lesbians call me "a future breeder." For having gay male friends, the lesbians call me "confused."

So when Bettina starts hanging out with Marcie, and somewhat forgets her pronounced, political, and almost professional sexual orientation, I am confused. She never invites Marcie to her art performance, "I Do…Not," and pretends that the ripped wedding dress in her closet, rather than being a prop from her performance, is something on which she's hoping to model her future wedding dress.

"Uh," I say, "aren't you going to tell her that you're gay?"

"Why?" she answers.

"That's your thing. You've practically made a career out of being gay. That's who you are."

"Is it?" she says.

And I'm a little confused. Because two weeks earlier, when I had attended the Gay and Lesbian Film Festival premiere of Bettina's film about lesbian commitment ceremonies, *Wedding Belles*, I knew that she had begun to spend a lot of time with that guy, Bean. And he was there and winked at her when she went on stage to introduce her film. And then he gave me flowers to give to her. And sometime after the post-screening party, Bettina disappeared and didn't arrive at our dorm room until two days later, on Sunday afternoon.

"What about Luba?" I said. "I thought you were really involved with her." Bettina has practically moved into Luba's North Hollywood apartment after meeting her at The Woman's Village. Luba drives produce interstate for one of the large chain grocery stores.

"Luba," she said, "has parked her Big Rig at the door of another woman. I'm done with her."

I never "out" her to Marcie. But Bettina is mad at me now for bringing it all up.

On my voice mail: "I'm really mad at you. You just can't walk away from a friendship—just like that. I'm still your friend. But I'm mad at you for what you said...well almost said...about me to Marcie."

I'm not returning this call. Ever.

But Stefan has remained a constant in my life. "Not that skirt with that sweater," he would say. We have commiserated together about dating. Tearful late-night phone calls. "He said I wasn't buff enough," said Stefan.

Support dinners when relationships were going bad and after the inevitable break-up. Chocolates, "Because I Will Always Love You" on Valentine's Day. "I'm so proud of you." Always there when personal achievements are reached.

"I hate men," said Stefan, a constant topic for ten years. "I don't think that I'll ever find *the one*. My soul mate."

He invites me to dinner with his new friend, James. James is nice. Funny. Successful. He owns two homes. Athletic, working out every day with weights.

And 24 years older.

"I hear that you two go way back," says James.

"Way, way, back," I say.

"That would make you children when you met."

"We were."

I am there when Stefan moves in with him.

"I think he's the one," sighs Stefan, looking at me. "Those shoes, Blanche? ...hmmm."

I go to their housewarming party and bring a beautiful ripe brie.

"Where's my Velveeta?" said Stefan, he a secret indulger.

"Your boyfriend would kill me if I brought any onto your property."

"Not only the Velveeta," said Stefan, leading me to garage. He opens the garage door. In it, I see stacked furniture.

"He won't let me bring my furniture into the house," said Stefan. "He says it clashes with 'the décor.' Do you want any of my furniture Blanche?"

"Ohhhh," I say.

Stefan has spent the last seven years combing thrift shops and garage sales every weekend for forgotten Eames chairs, Le Corbusier lounges and Finn Juhl's classic Danish modern tables. He took pride in his design aesthetic.

"What I did for love," he said.

It's not just the furniture. James takes Stefan on a clothes shopping spree at Barney's. He makes Stefan throw out all of his old clothes.

I am invited to fabulous dinners. Parties. Thanksgivings. Fourth of July celebrations. But James travels, so Stefan travels. Hawaii. Martha's Vineyard. New York. Paris. Florence. San Francisco. Paris. Palm Springs. South Beach. Fire Island. The White Party Circuit.

Growing more distant in the last few years.

"I miss you," I say.

"James has so many friends," he says raising his left hand so that I notice the lapis and gold promise ring which he is wearing. "Is it so difficult out there in that straight world, Blanche? Can't you find yourself a husband?"

"Meow," I say, "et tu, Brutus?"

"Rethink your hair, Blanche," he says.

A near silence for two years.

Stefan calls.

"I sooo need to see you," he says.

"It's been a while," I say. "What's going on?"

"Can I take you out to dinner? Please?"

Dinner on Beverly Boulevard, the night before Jennifer, Marshall, and Haggis are arriving. Loud, small, but fun restaurant, known for cobbler and fried chicken.

I've been training for the marathon. I run by myself. 12 miles. The following week 6 miles. 14 miles. The following week 7 miles. 16 miles, the following week 8 miles. 18 miles then 9.

By the second week of January, I can do 20 miles. In the second week of February, I run 24 miles in just over 5 hours. So I am going to eat fried chicken. And maybe cobbler.

Stefan is waiting at the bar when I arrive. He is wearing a suit, blue shirt, and a tie. Not an Armani, or some hyper modern designer suit—just a suit, like Macy's Off-the-Rack. His hair is what I vaguely remember to be his natural hair color. No highlights, no platinum blond, no red. Just brown, clipped short. The earring is gone. The lapis and gold promise ring is missing. His body is thin.

He looks like a first year associate in the corporate practice group of a large Chicago law firm.

"Hello, stranger," I said.

"Hello, beautiful," said Stefan, "you look great."

"But the shoes..."

"Are great."

"And the skirt..."

"Is great."

"And the hair..."

"Looks great," said Stefan. "So stop picking on yourself. May I pour you some wine? I ordered a nice Pinot Grigio."

"Sure. It's nice to see you, Stefan."

"Steve."

"What?"

"Just Steve. Not Stefan. I dropped the 'efan' three months ago."

Our table is ready and the hostess seats us. I order the fried chicken and Steve orders crab cakes. I see the cobbler on the other tables and give it a look of desire, which Steve catches.

"And she's getting the cobbler, which I am going to split with her, to relieve her guilt," he says. "You know you want it."

"Once upon a time, that would have been the way to address a different topic."

"Yes. But my feelings are the same."

"You still have passionate feelings for cobbler?"

"Very funny. No, for you."

I'm a little confused.

"What?"

Steve looks me with a look I have never seen before. "You know that I love you."

"And I love you."

"No, I really love you...more like, I'm in love with you."

"What? Since when?" I see the hurt look on his face. "I'm sorry. I mean, great but..."

Steve is watching me very closely, and suddenly I'm a little nervous.

"Stop being so nice," said Steve. "Tell me what you really think."

"What about James?" I say.

"James doesn't want to have children. He thinks it would change his life too much."

"He's right about that," I said.

"And I'm sick of his lifestyle…the fabulous parties. The fabulous house, well, houses. The designer clothes, God…the designer clothes. Can't I just wear some jeans? Traveling. New York. Miami. Aspen. The Hamptons."

"Gee, it sounds pretty good to me."

"I'm sick of it," said Steve. "It's not real."

"But Steve, you're gay. I was there when you came out."

"So maybe I want to come back in," he said.

"What? All the way?"

"I think so. And I've been thinking about you quite a bit."

Just then, the waiter comes by with our food.

"Is there anything else I can get you?" asked the waiter.

"More alcohol?" I ask.

Steve looks upset.

"OK, maybe a diet coke."

The waiter leaves.

"Look, Courtney," says Steve.

He hasn't called me Courtney in 17 years.

"You're not getting any younger."

I sigh.

"Insulting your way into my heart no longer works."

"OK, but for some reason…completely mysterious to me…your soul mate doesn't seem to have appeared in your life," said Steve.

"I've been engaged twice," I say.

"Yes of course. Andre. And Frank. Did you ever really love either of them?"

"It's hard to say."

"Is it?" said Steve. "Because we get along very, very well. I know, and remember, everything. And I still love you. Not for what you could be. Not for what you will be. For what you are."

"But Steve, I really am female. Do you actually think that you could—or want—to do this?"

"Yes, I do," he says.

"Why?" I said. "You could have a great life—and kids—with someone that you're attracted to, which, much as I wish, is probably not me."

We sit in silence.

"Eat your chicken before it gets cold," said Steve. "You know that I'd give you the wedding you've always dreamed of. We could serve Velveeta appetizers."

"Are you asking me to marry you?" I said.

"Well, not on one knee. But will you at least think about it? Please?"

"This isn't just the I'm-scared-of-dying-alone-I'm-over-30-we've-always-gotten-along-thing, is it?" I said. "Are you serious?"

"Very," said Steve. "I've always been in love with you. And I'd like to make a commitment."

The waiter brought the cobbler straight from the oven. It was boysenberry with vanilla ice cream on it. The ice cream was melting and beginning to drip over the side of the dish.

"That looks amazing," I said.

"No cobbler for you, young lady," said Steve. "Not until you finish your chicken."

When the check came, I reached for it.

"No please, let me do this," he said. He put his credit card down.

When we left the restaurant, Steve walked me to the valet and then hugged me. He held me until my car arrived.

"No comments about the Honda?" I said.

"Stefan would have made a comment," he said, "but Steve thinks your Honda is a good, reliable car."

Jennifer, Marshall, and Haggis show up the next day at 7 p.m. just as I'm running out. I give Jennifer a quick hug. "Thanks for letting us stay with you," said Jennifer.

I look at her.

Jennifer has cut her hair to her shoulders. It's variations on the theme of blond—platinum, honey, and golden colors woven in—and ironed out straight—the straight perm look. Her body—Jeez she's tiny—like she's lost an additional 20 pounds, is stuffed into some little jade green top, sleeveless, breathtakingly tight and not covering her belly button, and some yoga pants. Not exactly the corporate counsel look. Whatever happened to khakis, cotton button-down shirts, and loafers?

"Wow," I said. "I guess those workouts are paying off."

"I should say so," said Marshall, whom I try not to stare at because Marshall... Marshall. His skin has been peeled to a soft, creamy-pink color, like a scoop of vanilla bean ice cream with the faintest hint of Pepto-Bismol. His eyes appear to be opened an extra half inch, giving him a perpetually alert, nearly surprised look. Where there was formerly a Roman nose which sloped to the left there is a straight, thin, little nose, like the muzzle of a greyhound. There are glints of gold, copper, and white in his previously dark brunette hair making him look like a surfer boy who rode the waves near the Huntington Beach Pier every morning at 6 a.m.

That is, a 42-year-old surfer boy with pronounced abdominal muscles, built-out shoulders, the butt of a slight 14-year-old boy, and dewy soft skin, like Remington's Blue Boy, like one of those boy-kid stars of a teen angst TV show on the WB, a former Abercrombie and Fitch model who you know is much prettier than the girls on the show.

It's hard to decide who is prettier: Jennifer or Marshall. But I begin to wonder if Marshall is prettier than most of my friends. Make that all of my friends. And me.

The pin head is there also.

"Hi, Haggis," I said. "There are fresh towels on the couch. The refrigerator is stocked with food that you probably won't eat. Here are two extra sets of keys. Abyss is running around somewhere—don't let her out. I'll be back at 10 p.m."

"Where are you going?" said Jennifer.

"I'll tell you later," I said.

Almost Royalty

Where I'm going is to therapy. Group therapy. After some incessant nagging from Roberta—"You know, I didn't end our therapeutic relationship, we just took a break"—I return. And it's like I've never been gone, but with a few twists. They're all there: the former kiddie-TV-actress who, beating all the odds, has done a Jason Bateman and managed to land on an adult primetime show; the nearly-divorced-housewife (who wants to be a therapist); the wardrobe-supervisor (who still wishes she were an actress) the guys who really don't want to be there (who still don't want to be there) and, "Frank? What are you doing here?"

"I thought it would be an interesting exercise for Group to observe Frank and Courtney interacting so we could all practice coping skills for dealing with an ex," said Roberta.

More like she wanted to throw a stick of dynamite into the room to wake things up a bit, and maybe, just maybe, try out a few of the Interaction Exercises she had created for her new book, entitled, surprisingly enough, *Coping Skills for Dealing with an Ex and Moving On.*

"So I asked Frank to transfer back from the Wednesday Night Group where I placed him after he and Courtney ended their relationship, to tonight's Group, the Tuesday Night Group. And Courtney was told that she could begin participating in Group again," said Roberta.

"You were in the Wednesday Night Group, Frank? Wow. How was it?"

The Wednesday Night Group was Roberta's triple Platinum Group, a By-Invitation-Only Group rumored to include an orchestral new music composer who had won a MacArthur (Genius) Award, a painter who was featured on the cover of *Art Forum* when he was 26, a chef who created the East Side renaissance by opening a restaurant in Silverlake *before* it was considered chic, a professional lesbian who produced highly successful award-winning gay and lesbian themed films, and the others: the usual smattering of actors, writers, and directors, but these entertainment types had the distinction of working regularly.

For many years, I had longed for an invitation to the Wednesday Night Group, thinking if I had to be in Group, why not let it be this one. I dropped hints. Well no, I directly told her.

"I'd prefer to be in the Wednesday Night Group," I'd say.

"But it wouldn't do," said Roberta, "because you're needed in Tuesday Night Group, because you're a Tuesday Night Person."

I wasn't really sure, but I thought that Roberta had a pecking order. I knew of the Wednesday Night Group and thought that there might be a Thursday night and maybe a Monday night group. If Wednesday Night was the Platinum Group, then we, the Tuesday Night Group, were either the Silver or Bronze Group.

"Courtney," said Roberta, "you know we're not supposed to discuss what goes on in Group."

"Oh right," I said, "I'm sorry. Confidentiality."

I did my best to muffle a snicker, but it was uncontainable and got the best of me. I exploded with laughter...with the rest of Group.

We all knew that obsessing about who was in Group, what topics were discussed, and ongoing fights was widely done through emails and phone calls during the 24 hours following a Tuesday night session. Unfortunately, spending so much time kicked out of group had left me no Group topics about which to obsess.

But then Roberta said, "The Group is being disrespectful to itself," which made me think of a bunch of sheep walking around in a circle kicking each other in the butt with a woolly, cloven hoof and since I already had the giggles, I started laughing again, starting another tidal wave of laughter.

Roberta looked at me and shook her head left-right, left-right, left-right.

"I'm disappointed with you," she said.

"Oh, me too," I said, desperately trying to sound sincere, but since I had tears running out of my eyes and was attempting to stifle more laughter, I sounded more like a helium-altered cartoon character, and then hiccupped very loudly, creating another tsunami of laughter and crying.

"I can see that we're not going to get any work done here tonight," said Roberta.

"No," I said, "let's do something."

"OK. So Courtney, how are you?" said Roberta.

"I'm fine," I said. "Fine. This guy asked me to marry him."

"What?" said the divorced housewife.

The laughter ended suddenly.

"What?" said Frank. "I didn't know you'd started seeing someone?"

"Frank," said Roberta, "how does that make you feel?"

"He's fine," I said. "Frank's already been around the block a couple of times since we broke up."

"Don't speak for him, Courtney," said Roberta.

"Look, it's over. Frank and I weren't right for each other. It would have been a horrible, horrible marriage. I told him very specifically what I wanted. Remember that night at the Copper Pan, Frank?"

"Yeah…" said Frank.

"…and he wasn't having any part of it," I said. "What more is there?"

"Is that the way you feel, Frank," said Roberta.

"Well…" said Frank.

"Wait a minute. Wait a minute," said the former kiddie-TV actress who now has a show. "I don't feel seen. I mean, she's back for ten minutes and how come it's suddenly all about her? I have needs too, you know."

"God forbid anyone should take the attention away from you," I said.

"Courtney," said Roberta. "The Group is a safe place for everyone, even if it has moments of disrespect,"—disrespect, a bad word to say, because again I think of the sheep walking around in a circle kicking each other in the butt with a woolly, cloven hoof, which makes me start giggling.

"God, you're a mess," said Roberta.

So I begin listening to the former kiddie-TV-actress-who-now-has-a-show, a real adult primetime network TV show, spend the next 30 minutes revealing her pain. She is angry, still, so angry at her mother who worked as a housekeeper so that she could help support her daughter's ambition to become a kiddie cable TV star with the pictures, the endless auditions, the agents, the managers. After that was over, and because some admissions officer thought that her daughter would make a very interesting addition to the class, her mother continued to work as a housekeeper so that she could send her to Yale, the best drama program in the country.

"She makes me feel so guilty," she said.

"She should," I blurted out, "your mother scrubbed floors on her hands and knees until she was 62 years old so that you could have a career shaking your hooters on a Tuesday night secret agent show."

The actress, forever playing some secret-undercover-super-CIA-FBI-KGB-female 007-type on her new network show, ensuring that she was always undercover as a prostitute, stripper, model, cocktail waitress, lap dancer, French maid, in some unknown Eastern European–Middle Eastern country sounding vaguely familiar, like Rekazistan or Biraq, ensuring that her Yale drama school degree could be used so that she could play out the primetime fantasies of the producers in some almost soft-porn kind of way, wearing short, short skirts, bustiers, push-up bras, wigs, leather, latex anything, tight, short with a lot of cleavage.

And suddenly I knew.

I hated this.

"You sound profoundly ridiculous to me," I said. "And I wish so much that I could call your mother and be appropriately grateful. For you. For our generation, who was given so much and has done so little."

Silence in the room.

"But maybe I should call my own mother," I said, "and see if I can find some way to thank her—despite being insane—and she is—for all those violin lessons, expensive instruments, and summer programs she sent me to when she didn't really have the money."

No one said a word.

"No one wants to engage—be present—with me?" I said. "Roberta?"

Nothing.

"I've been in therapy a long, long time. Too long. And you, Roberta, still think I'm...what did you just call me? A mess?"

"Well, I didn't mean..." said Roberta.

"Yes you did," I said. "I've spent so much more time in a therapist's office than I ever have in a church. Or maybe it should be a synagogue. I've spent so much time—in fact, over half my life—feeling. Being present. Wondering how to behave. And let's not forget, I've spent a lot of money, over $80,000, coming to you, my various therapists through the years, for the answers as to how I should live my life, as if you, or psychotherapy would give me answers, *the answers*, as to how I could have a successful and fulfilling life, like if I just stayed long enough, said the right thing, proved myself worthy, you would open the secret drawer and show me the little book which contained the answers to the meaning of life—you would show me how therapy was supposed to replace traditional morality. And you don't have any answers, do you, Roberta? It kills me to know that with the money I've spent, I could have owned something—a condo, maybe even a house—on the Westside!"

I looked around the room. All heads were down, not even giving me eye contact.

"But I think I have the answers...well, my answers," I said.

"What?" said the Group in almost unison, leaving me wondering who else in this room had never dared to say that they shared my confusion.

"Well, for one thing, it's time to leave," I said. "This. For good. But the other thing is that I think that I want to try to live as moral, humane people have for thousands of years. And there is a manual for that, and an endless interpretive commentary."

"Unfortunately, Courtney, our time is up," said Roberta. "It sounds like you have a lot of anger toward me which I think we need to address alone…in our next session."

"Forget it, Roberta," I said.

The Group gasped in unison.

"Feeling an Ancient Pain?" I said to the Group. "In the wallet?"

"We need a few sessions to say goodbye," said Roberta.

"Kids' tuition coming up, Roberta? Or is it time to trade in the Bentley for the new model? Sorry, Roberta, I'm not going to spend what's left in my IRA saying goodbye to you. Unless you want to give those sessions to me for free?"

Roberta sat in silence with her head down.

"Oh, nothing to say? I just want you to know, Roberta, that I've been lying to you for years. I've wanted out of therapy so much that I started telling you what I thought you wanted to hear, and you didn't even…"

"That's enough," said Roberta. "So is this it…you're not coming back—to Group or anything?"

"That's right," I said. I stood up and faced the Group, my Tuesday Night Group.

"I wish…all of you…the very best," I said. "You too, Frank."

I walked out the door and straight to my car.

When I got out of the elevator in my apartment building, I could hear a deep baritone voice singing what I thought was Papigano's Aria from Mozart's Opera, *The Magic Flute*.

"Pa-pa-geno, Pa-pa-geno, Pa-pa-geno," projected through the stucco walls of my apartment building, not deadened at all by the stained indoor-outdoor carpeting which graced every hallway. I didn't know we had an opera singer in the building, who was staying...in my apartment?

As I opened my door, Marshall, mid-aria, turned to greet me.

"PA-PA-GENO" roared out of his mouth.

"Don't tell me," I said, "there's a talent portion to the *Face of Tomorrow* competition?"

"Marshall sings opera in an amateur group," said Jennifer.

"Really. Where's Haggis?"

"Out buying us more grass goo," said Jennifer.

"SOME GUY NAMED JOSH CALLED, HE'D LIKE YOU TO CALL HIM," sang Marshall.

"Josh?" said Jennifer. "I thought..."

"Josh?" I said, pleased.

"YES, JOSH," sang Marshall, "CALL HIM. CALL HIM. CALLLLL HIMMMMMM."

And then I smelled something so familiar and so delicious. "What are you two eating?" I said.

Jennifer started laughing.

"You have to ask?" she said.

"Where is it?" I said.

"On the coffee table." And there it was in all of its gooey, sloppy splendor. Velveeta nachos.

"Good Lord, Marshall, are you sure you should eat this?" I said. "This is a butt builder if there ever was one. "What about all that work you had...did for the competition?"

"I'm planning on running with you tomorrow," he said. "I'll burn it off."

And he did want to run. They all did.

"Are you sure you want to do this?" I said. "I really am going to do about 10 miles."

"Sure," said Marshall.

"You bet," said Jennifer.

I didn't even know if I was going to do it. It was an overcast drizzly day that clearly could become a downpour. Seventy-two hours before the marathon. I wanted to take a little run to stay in shape, something short enough not to get hurt and long enough to keep my muscles warmed.

I also wanted a break from Jennifer, Marshall, and especially Haggis before I killed them.

When Haggis returned with his grass goo he immediately sniffed the air. He walked into my sunken living room and sniffed.

"Where is it?" he said. He opened the curtain on my faux fireplace and sniffed. He went into the kitchen and sniffed. He opened the French doors into my vanity/bathroom and sniffed. And then he opened the closet.

"Just what I expected. Aaaahhh!" he yelled. "What's that?" Abyss came trotting out with a Velveeta fondue mustache-goatee on her face and nuzzled my leg, leaving a greasy stain in the image of a hairy smiley face on my pants which I knew I would never get out. She had gotten into the nachos plate, which Jennifer and Marshall had hidden in my closet 15 seconds before Haggis opened the door.

Haggis walked out with his evidence, the remaining two soggy chips and the plate, licked free of Velveeta by Abyss.

He looked at me.

"You really are an unhealthy influence," he said. "After all the work I've done with these two."

I looked at Jennifer and Marshall. They turned their faces away.

"So leave," I said. "This is who I am. I'm addicted to Velveeta. A Velveetaholic. I own it. Wait. I take responsibility for it. This is the food I have. All of you know me and knew what to expect. So Leave."

"Look, I'm sorry, I just think that..." said Haggis.

"No, you don't," I said, "that's what you don't do...Think. Because if you did, you'd confront your clients, your two paying clients, who ate this stuff. It was their choice."

"But you need to know how bad..." said Haggis.

"No, I don't need to know anything out of your mouth. I just need to know that if you—someone who's not even a friend—ask for and accept my hospitality, you aren't going to insult me in my own home. And let me tell you, Haggis, it's only because I have the most marginal thread of tolerance left in my body that I don't say what I think of you and..."

"Courtney, don't!" said Jennifer.

I sighed.

And then I gave Haggis my nastiest possible look.

"That must be my marginal thread of tolerance talking to me," I said.

"Gee, I'm tired," said Marshall. "Why don't we all call it a night?"

"An excellent idea," said Haggis.

We started jogging at a fast walk pace, 13 minutes per mile. More like a fast crawl. I heard a few gasps, a few pants, but I pretended not to notice.

After about a half mile we came to the perimeter of the park just before we crossed the street.

And then I saw them.

"Oh no," I said.

I stopped abruptly, the way you do when you think you just ran into an ex-boyfriend who seems to be with someone who you quickly realize is much better looking than you are.

"What is it?" said Jennifer.

"Look," I said.

There she was. Alien-scanner model thing, alien-scanner model thing's fabulous husband, alien-scanner model thing's trainer.

Alien-scanner model thing's Muscle had already assumed the pose, standing on the edge of the group, sending us threatening looks.

Haggis took three steps in front of us, assumed the pose, and sent alien-scanner model's entourage threatening looks.

"Is that…?" said Marshall.

"It is," I said.

"Wait a minute. No…Reggie?" shouted Haggis. "Reggie McDougal, you little girl. Is that you?"

Alien-scanner's Muscle looked at us carefully.

"Haggis?" said alien-scanner model thing's Muscle. "Haggis, you fat head. Is that you?"

Haggis runs across the street and embraces Reggie. Reggie speaks to alien-scanner model thing, apparently introducing Haggis to her entourage. We wait on the curb, observing rule #4 of the *L.A. Etiquette for Interacting with Star/Celeb Royalty in Public Places*:

Rule #4

"During an accidental encounter with a star/celeb and his/her entourage, the non-royalty must wait to be granted an audience with the star/celeb before joining the star/celeb's entourage."

Haggis motions us to come over.

Before I can say anything, Marshall and Jennifer sprint across the street. I wait at the curb. Haggis turns toward me and motions me to come across the street. I start across.

Just as I reach the curb, I hear Marshall say to alien-scanner model thing, "It's impossible to believe, but you're more beautiful in person than the most beautiful picture which I have ever seen of you, and I think that you are the most beautiful woman in the world."

Always a good thing to say to an alien-scanner model thing, especially one who is a former model.

Alien-scanner model thing actually seems pleased. Marshall tells her he was here for the *Faces of Tomorrow* competition, the model/spokesperson category. Alien-scanner model thing didn't laugh. However, I think I saw alien-scanner model thing's husband turn away and roll his eyes.

I tell them that I need to keep running and excuse myself.

When I leave, alien-scanner model thing is giving Marshall pointers on working the runway for his walk in the model/spokesperson category during the competition.

When I get back to the apartment, Marshall, Jennifer, and Haggis were chatting about how nice alien-scanner model thing had been. She had promised to email over a list of her pointers for a successful walk down the runway.

"Great," I say, knowing she never will.

"Oh yeah," said Marshall, "some guy named Frank called. He'd really like you to call him."

19

Everything Old Is New Again

The Copper Pan had changed. A little.

The space next door once occupied by the ridiculously overpriced women's clothing store had been annexed by the Copper Pan once the clothing store patrons had grown weary of paying $375 for the same jeans you could buy at The Gap for $55.

Bigger, because of reasons having everything to do with population growth and nothing to do with itself, the Copper Pan was a success.

Those same young professionals who once lived in the apartments above San Vicente Boulevard, who came there nightly in their leased, 48-month payment plan, royal blue with cream interior BMW 325s on the way home—first, second, third year legal associates, junior agents, baby investment bankers—stopping by at 8:45 p.m. before the kitchen closed to pick up a salad to eat in their sweats while they watched 30 minutes of television before bedtime—had aged, gotten married, bought teardowns below San Vicente but above Wilshire, and had babies, that being the latest can't-do-without accessory on the Westside.

Those (now) married professionals, more than a few having become the infamous SAHMs (Stay-At-Home-Moms), wanted a restaurant where they could take their kids that cooked the same food that their mom (they and their spouses basically unwilling to cook, clean, or parent) had made on Tuesday, Wednesday, or Thursday night.

The cloth napkins, mysteriously gone for a few months, now brought back once those regular customers selected "going green" as their new cause du jour.

The frizzy red-haired five-foot-two hostess who came to L.A. to live with her boyfriend after graduating from Williams with a degree in applied mathematics, who ran the marathon in under four hours, who snickered and shook her head when she saw me, "Who you breaking up with now?"—gone, probably to marriage or a PhD program at Berkeley or Stanford.

She was replaced by a five-foot-eleven, 110-pound actor-model wannabe with long straight blond hair vaguely resembling alien-scanner model thing, a refugee from the actor-model immigrants who flood L.A. yearly, thinking that the hostess gig was a good place to be for a while.

"At least I'll be seen, I mean producers come here, right?" She was right about the producers and wrong about being seen.

The menu—gone, well not gone, but the things that I liked on it: pan fried chicken, pan fried whitefish, pan fried potatoes—gone, or only served as a special. The menus clearly "trimmed" (always a good word on the Westside) from four pages down to two, clearly reflecting the diets of the regulars, deleting anything with fat and carbs. A menu that also reflected the owner's calculations on how to maximize profits. I'm sure the owner was forever wondering, "How much can we charge for a salad?"

Something else that had changed. Frank was on time. Clean hair without that trademark baseball cap, pressed shirt (cotton, long-sleeved, not a faded T-shirt with holes from Senor Frog's Mazatlan or In-N-Out Burger, or the PoMo "Britney, I'm Not So Innocent" tour shirt), wearing a new leather jacket, clean jeans, and new Nikes, and looking about 20 pounds thinner. But nervous. When I returned his call, he asked if we could meet for lunch at the Copper Pan on Saturday.

"You sure you want to go there," I said. "I mean, Frank, that's our break-up spot. We already did that."

He wanted to go there.

It was important, he said.

"Thank you for coming," he said, "you look great."

"Thanks," I said. "What's up?"

"The guy who answered your phone. Is he the one who asked you to marry him?"

"No."

"Who was it?"

"Marshall. Jennifer's friend. They're here for the *Faces of Tomorrow* competition, which starts in 90 minutes, so we'd better hustle."

"I was hoping that we could talk for a while."

"I don't have much time," I said.

The waiter appeared. Too good-looking. An actor-wannabe, gay.

"I don't understand your menu anymore," I said. "So, just give me what everyone else orders."

"You mean solidified nothing?" said the waiter in rounded vowels, modulated, and perfectly spoken. Make that a Juilliard theater school-trained actor-wannabe, gay, with an attitude.

"OK, a Nicoise salad," I said.

"Bot-tled Wah-ter?" said the Waiter.

Almost Royalty

"Got any milkshakes?" I said.

The waiter gives me a sideways rolling eyes look.

"OK, lemonade," I said.

"Burger, well done. Fries. Root Beer," said Frank.

Frank looks around, jumpy. Appears to be catching his breath.

"Frank, what is it? Did you give me some disease?"

"No," he says. "OK, OK. When I saw you in Group recently, I realized something important. I…"

The waiter appeared with our drinks.

"The bartender told me to tell you that no one has ordered a milkshake in five years. But if you want it, he thinks he remembers how to make one."

"You're half way through your Improv class at The Groundlings, right?" I said. The waiter laughed and walked into the open kitchen.

Frank, taking a deep breath, pulls something out of his pocket.

"When I saw you in Group, I realized that I had made a big mistake," said Frank, "so I got this for you."

He pushes something across the table to me in a small, square, black box, which looks like something I once wanted so much.

It can't be.

It better not be.

I'm afraid to open it.

"Open it," said Frank, "it's for you, just like you wanted it."

"Frank…"

"Please open it," said Frank.

But I already know what it is.

I open it.

Ooof.

I suddenly feel like I'm in hour five of a *Twilight Zone* marathon showing on a major holiday, like Christmas Day, right after the Wim Wenders version of *Nosferatu* starring exceptionally weird Klaus Kinski, or something equally strange, like that fabulous version of *Dracula* starring Frank Langella.

"One carat, set in platinum, with as few inclusions as I could afford," said Frank, "and here's the report that they gave me."

He gives me the GSA report.

I look at it.

A VS1 rating.

Not bad.

"Oh Frank," I say. "Frank...it's...beautiful. But I can't take this." I push back the ring box.

"No. Take it. It's for you." He pushes the ring back.

"Look, when I saw you in Group, I realized something I'd been thinking for a long time: I really, really screwed up."

Something every girl dreams of hearing.

"You're a good person. A very good person. With some weird habits."

Not exactly what the girl dreams of hearing, the missing part being the garden variety-comment/lie—"You're so beautiful, I think of you night and day." But the girl is still listening.

"I love you and want to be with you. You were nice to me. At least you always tried to be."

Nice...nice. What? The girl dreams of hearing, "You complete me...You're my soul mate...You rock my world," not something you say about Becky, the girl who sat next to you in math class and loaned you an eraser when yours wore out.

"Yeah, but Frank, I doubt that Roberta is going to give you the thumbs up on this decision. I mean what about, "I have so much work to do?"

"Forget Roberta. It's my life, not hers."

"And there were those other problems..."

"I'm ready to make a commitment. So, also, I promise to do 50 percent of everything. And because you're an attorney, I wrote it down."

Frank hands me a piece of paper which he has written, "I promise to do 50 percent of everything. Agreed and Accepted, Frank Jamieson."

Almost Royalty

"Oh, Frank."

"Do you want me to have my signature notarized?" he says.

"Look, this is so sweet but..." I push the ring back.

Frank hands me a piece of paper with some dates on it.

"I've written the dates which I think would be good dates to get married on. I'm partial to June or October, but why don't you choose a date that you would like. And remember it has to be before the end of the year. And take the ring."

He pushes the ring box back.

It's 2:10. If I really hurry, I can make it by 2:30 to the Santa Monica Civic Auditorium where *The Faces of Tomorrow* competition is being held.

Of course, that presupposes that you believe the L.A. mythology that you can get anywhere in L.A. in 20 minutes.

"Just think about it," said Frank. "OK?"

"OK." I take the ring.

"I have to go," I say just as the waiter arrives. I fish out my credit card to give to the waiter.

"It's OK, Courtney," says Frank. "I remembered my wallet."

A change. Interesting.

I stand up to leave.

"But you haven't eaten a thing," said the waiter, sounding more like he was reading a line from a Eugene O'Neill/Chekhov drama, projecting to the back of the theater, rounded vowels, head up, chest thrust forward, but instead standing smack in the middle of the Westside of L.A., "just like every woman on the Westside."

"You're a bit over-trained and over-qualified for this line of work," I say to the waiter, gathering my things and jogging out that idiotic revolving Copper Pan front door, the one that never stops.

The *Faces of Tomorrow* competition was held in the Santa Monica Civic Auditorium. It was a place where Jefferson Starship, Cream, and possibly the Moody Blues had played in the early '70s, back when the clubs on Sunset—Doug Weston's The Troubadour, The Roxy, The Whisky, Gazzarri's on the Strip, and later Madame Wong's—were places that you could discover something from some homemade garage band: an intensity, a passion, a voice with something to say even if it was *"We don't want our parents' life."*

The kids in those homemade garage bands didn't know that coming out here from Kentucky, Indiana, Georgia to "make it" in the music industry was a crazy dream; that some might not, and 20 years later while still "chasing the dream" they'd manage a cheese shop as "their day gig" and have kids, a mortgage and a bad marriage with their former lead singer.

But now, the music industry had been flooded with useless Harvard/Wharton MBAs, who were ruining the music industry, turning it into publicly traded businesses with *shareholders* that needed profitable quarters. It was a time when the music industry demanded product: girls or boys with minimal talent, *absolutely nothing to say*, shells, lumps of clay, finding them after a run on *kiddie cable shows* and bringing them to the fashionafia who made their hair straighter, their noses smaller and did away with their flabby stomachs, fat thighs and big butts.

The Santa Monica Civic Auditorium. Rock Gods had once played in the Santa Monica Civic Auditorium during a time when they had advocated anarchy, ending the war, overthrowing the government, speaking the truth even if no one wants to hear it, thinking their children with their unconventional names and their *genius* fathers might be the force of the future, never thinking that sometime after they were gone their children might not embrace their revolution, might lose direction, and might find themselves on network talent shows not as the talent, but as judges. No one would ever say, "Why are they judges, they've never done anything but be the kids of Rock Gods?" But everyone would think it.

But this is barely a rock venue now—Santa Monica Civic. It doesn't hold enough people to turn the enormous kind of profit requiring 50,000 people for some corporate favorite like The

Stones, with their T-shirts and beer mugs. And now, because it's 40 years later and the guys are all looking at 65, they just plop out another version of "Brown Sugar," or "Satisfaction," right after that puff-piece/love-fest interview on *60 Minutes* runs.

Now there are foreign policy evenings with speeches by former presidents and secretaries of state, desperate to make some money after their years in government.

"How you doing?" I say, sliding into the seat next to Jennifer's.

"OK," she says.

I doubt it. Last night Marshall went to assemble his things for the competition. He couldn't find the T-shirt or jeans he planned to wear.

"Jennifer," he said, "where did you pack my things?"

I gave her a look. She ignored me.

"Just a minute," she said. She ran into the bedroom where he was.

"I know I packed them," she said.

"Where the hell are they?" said Marshall.

"I'll find them, really, I remember packing them."

"Damn it," said Marshall, "you forgot to pack it. You're just afraid to tell me."

"I swear I didn't," said Jennifer, "it's here somewhere."

"It's people like you—incompetents—who are holding me back. This is all that I needed you to do, and you can't even do this."

And that was my cue to walk into the room, where I found Jennifer crying.

"What's going on?" I said.

"It's a disaster," said Marshall. "I don't have clothes. I'll have to drop out of the competition."

"I have a friend around your size," I said. "I'll call him."

"I'll never win now. It's all her fault."

"Shut up, Marshall," I said. "Jennifer has done everything possible to help you. We'll get you a back-up T-shirt and shorts, and then we'll keep searching for your things."

"But now I'm too upset. I'm not in the right frame of mind to compete."

"Then don't," I said. "It's your choice. But next time take responsibility for your own things. She's not your servant."

And later, after Josh was on his way over with several T-shirts and jeans, Haggis came back from the store with "products" that Marshall needed for the competition: a laxative—"I mean, Marshall, I can see those Nachos sitting on your stomach" and a diuretic—"Too much water weight—you look like a girl who's getting her period."

"What's the point?" said Marshall. "Jennifer forgot to pack my clothes."

"Aah, Marshall," said Haggis.

"I mean, that's all I asked her to do and she couldn't even..."

Jennifer continuing to cry.

"Uhh Marshall," said Haggis, "remember? I..."

"...competently..."

"Marshall, we put your clothes in my car yesterday. So you wouldn't forget them at the last moment. Remember?"

He didn't even apologize. Not a look, a glance, or an "I'm sorry."

He didn't even apologize.

And Jennifer? She just sat there. Crying.

In the program that they gave out, it appeared that there were about 25 candidates in the male model/spokesperson category—the program listing height, weight, hair/eye color—and age. Twenty-five guys (their boyfriends—past, present, future, in the audience) all under the age of 22.

And Marshall.

Almost Royalty

Most of them skateboarding, snowboarding, rock climbing, bulked up natural athletes, young girlish baby faces, the flush beautiful face of someone still a child with the body of an adult, that first moment, the first face making the transition from child to adult still excited about the possibilities of what they hoped for but didn't know would never ever happen.

The M.C., a refugee from a successful TV moment of the late '80s hoping to be recognized as a star—like maybe Arsenio, Donny Osmond, or that guy who shaved his head and played that tough cop.

"Ethan is 18 years old, six foot two tall, a surfer..."

The boys in the audience whoop it up for Ethan as all the other young, innocent beauties parade their wares. Ethan gets a 9.7 for body, a 9.8 for face, and an 8.7 for presentation. Clearly, Ethan, who raced through the walk like someone trying to escape his own fart-trailer doesn't know a thing about working the ramp, but the judges—a former child star back from rehab who played the best kid in the family in a mid-80s family sitcom, a former model now divorced again making another tired run at "models who act," and a former athlete who won six Olympic gold medals at some point, but must have the same plastic surgeon as Joan Rivers because he now looks like a Mary Kay Cosmetics saleswoman from Indianapolis—they sense his potential.

I looked over at my friend Jennifer. A good person, a loyal friend, smart, reliable. A good attorney. Educated. Kind. Nice. And pretty. Wasn't that enough?

"Jeremy is 17 years old, six foot four tall, a starter on his high school varsity basketball team..."

A lot of love for Jeremy, some wise-cracking guy in the audience yelling, "Come to Mama, baby."

9.5 on body, 9.4 on face, 9.0 on presentation.

"You know, Jennifer," I said, "I want to support you in whatever you want to do. But Marshall? Is it his money?"

"Wouldn't that make me shallow?" said Jennifer. "To want him for his money?"

"You and every other woman in America," I said, "but at least I'd understand it. Kinda."

"Well, he doesn't have any money anymore," she said.

"Randy is 20 years old, six foot three, a nationally ranked snow-boarder…"

"Sold! I'll take ya, baby," yelled the wise-cracking guy, who was dominating the audience judging, a category not necessarily wanted by the promoters, the M.C. growing a little edgy.

9.3 on body, 9.2 on face, 9.0 on presentation.

"What do you mean? What about all those stock options?" I said.

"They're under water," she said. "Their exercise price is higher than their current price per share. So he'd lose money if he exercised the options now."

"Didn't he exercise any options when the market was roaring?"

"Nope," she said. "He was waiting for the NASDAQ to hit 4000. And then he was laid off. Like most of Silicon Valley."

The NASDAQ now being over-sold into submission, plummeting through every support level, finding no bottom.

"So what is it?" I said. "I mean, the sex can't be great because you two don't sleep together."

"Frederico is 21 years old, six foot four, a competitive ballroom dancer…"

"Baby, you already danced your way into my heart…" yelled the wise-cracking guy, the M.C. by now having given up.

9.8 on body, 9.9 on face, 9.9 on presentation. A contender.

"I don't see you doing so well," said Jennifer. "I mean, where's your fabulous husband?"

A good question. Of course, there was Stefan, I mean Steve. And Frank.

"I don't know how to answer that question," I said. "But maybe it's not about having a fabulous husband. I mean, if you have to change every fiber of who you are just to be with someone, how is that going to work?"

"I could do that."

I knew she could. She had worked two jobs through college and managed to graduate summa cum laude. She had gutted her way through being an associate in a notorious sweat shop of a New York-based law firm and managed to keep her focus and stay partner track in securities litigation. She and Kevin had not bought a condo, they had bought a building, in an area of San Francisco so dubious we once considered them urban pioneers. But they had refurbished the building and each had close to a million dollars in equity.

And then I knew: Jennifer's competence had come back to haunt her.

"Of course you could," I said. "But it's not whether you could. It's whether you should. Let me just make myself perfectly clear. Marshall is a pig and he treats you terribly."

"Not all the time," she said.

"Only all the times I've seen you with him."

"I don't want to be alone. I'm just sick and tired of being alone. I mean, do you enjoy being—what did you call it—in the reject pile?"

A term I had not thought about for some time.

"Well," I said, "there is that. But don't you think that no company is better than bad company?"

"Definitely," said a voice coming from the seat behind me. It was Josh.

"Hey," I said, "what are you doing here?"

"Are you kidding?" he said. "Did you think I was going to miss seeing my clothes appear in *The Faces of Tomorrow* competition?"

Last night, about 20 minutes after Marshall was done screaming at Jennifer, Josh appeared with several T-shirts and short selections. And pizza.

"Marshall, I will break your arm if you even attempt to sniff one slice of that pizza," Haggis had said.

"Don't worry," said Marshall. "I learned my lesson. Those Velveeta nachos are still riding on my stomach like a fanny pack. But I would like to examine the clothes."

How fortunate for us to receive our own private modeling session, highlighted by the exclusive, professional techniques that alien-scanner thing had revealed to Marshall. "OK, so pick one person in the audience, way in the back, and stare at them like your eyes are lasers which are going to burn a hole in them."

Marshall, desperate to find the best outfit to show off what he considered to be his prize assets (surgically enhanced washboard abs and chest), trying on all possible combinations of clothing, walked through my sunken living room with its gray shag carpeting like he was working the runway. For 50 minutes.

"Who is this guy again?" said Josh as he watched Marshall walk through my living room with his shorts on, "Jennifer's boyfriend?"

"Kinda," I said.

"Interesting," said Josh. "Does Marshall know that he looks like a middle-aged Liz Taylor around her *Cleopatra* period?"

Josh stayed about two hours. He, along with Haggis and Jennifer and me, voicing his opinion, helping Marshall select his first outfit for the competition. And then he took the empty pizza box to the dumpster downstairs.

"Nicholas is 18 years old, six foot two, nationally ranked in competitive surfing..."

The audience went wild for Nicholas, so I looked at him. The all-out fantasy of a Swedish beauty-Viking warrior. Blond on blond hair, the kind that had been lightened by many hours at the beach, the darkest color on his head being golden blond highlighted perfectly by his café latte tanned skin. Square jaw. Small nose. High cheekbones. Twinkly eyes, probably ice-blue or white-green. Perfectly

Almost Royalty

proportioned upper body in a V-shape, strong legs to support him, ripped torso, tiny butt. Nicholas, not putting any preparation into this, probably having a buddy drive him to the competition after he woke up late, making a sloppy turn in his walk which almost causes him to fall, not even knowing how to walk the ramp, and at 18, not needing to.

"You could run, but I'd catch you," yelled the wise-cracking guy, "and baby, I'd never let go."

9.9 on body, 9.9 for face, 8.5 for presentation, the judges knowing he deserved a 1.0 for presentation, but realizing that a score like that would knock Nicholas, the best hope for a true *Face of Tomorrow*, out of the competition.

"Has Marshall been up yet?" said Josh.

"He's coming up next," said Jennifer.

There he was. Poised. Regal. Taking it all seriously, thinking, "This could be my future, this is for real; I'm having my moment." All the work, those modeling techniques from alien-scanner thing actually working, doing the walk, making the turn, body erect, head high, feeling the music, working it like he was in Milan with the Versace collection instead of in Santa Monica in a pair of Hang Ten trunks, the effect a little weird, like getting a gift enclosed in a classic aqua-blue Tiffany's box with the white ribbon and black embossed lettering, and opening it, and finding a very, very, very nice Snickers bar.

"Marshall is 42 years old, six foot four, a PhD in mathematics from Princeton…"

The audience was dead silent for 10 seconds as Marshall walked—then a cough—maybe from the M.C. Restless, polite, scattered applause sprinkling through—some mumbling—a collective unease rippling through the audience.

"You a little old," yelled the wise-cracking guy, "but baby, I dig your spirit."

Marshall, hearing this, just finishing up the last 15 feet of his walk, throws in the tiniest butt wiggle, imperceptible to the judges from their position, the audience catching it and going wild.

"You show 'em, baby," screams the guy, the audience going crazy.

"There's your boyfriend," I said.

Jennifer doesn't say anything.

"That went well," said Josh.

8.7 on body, 9.3 on face, 10.00 on presentation, a high enough score to get him into the second round of the competition, which is starting in 30 minutes.

"I gotta go," I said.

"Where are you going?" said Josh.

"I'm running the L.A. Marathon tomorrow."

"Really?" said Josh. "You're actually going to do it?"

"I guess. Anyway, I've got to go get ready."

Josh walks me to my car after I say goodbye to Jennifer. I've made reservations at a downtown hotel near the start of the Marathon where I'm going to spend the night. Jennifer, Haggis, and Marshall have their key and are going to stay in my apartment overnight without me. I'm hoping, but not expecting, that they will remember to feed Abyss, but just in case everything goes just like I think it will I've left extra food and water for her.

"You know, people get hurt running these marathons," said Josh.

"Not at my speed."

"Well, if you're tired or in pain, you don't have to finish. You don't have to prove anything. Just attempting it is more than enough."

20

The Marathon

It's 7:58 a.m. and it looks like the Mayor is about to crank up the official tune of the L.A. Marathon, Randy Newman's "I Love L.A." And right about then it hits me that 26.2 miles is a long, long, distance, like to Long Beach, and I'm a little scared and have that twisty feeling in my stomach. What am I doing here? Who do I think I am? I could just go home and get back into bed and tell everyone that I ran it. Who would know?

Part of this fantasy about not being in downtown L.A. listening to—there it goes, "I love L.A."—and about to subject myself to a lot of pain is the hope that Haggis, that *Face of Tomorrow*—Marshall—and Jennifer, have done the right thing and left my apartment so that I can have a break. From them. Then I remember that I don't even need to go home. I could just go back upstairs to my hotel room and order room service.

But just as I'm about to try to find my escape route the race starts. And since the estimates are that 33,000 people are starting the race with me, I'm caught in a pack and pushed forward. I take it as a sign that someone, somewhere, wants me to run this marathon.

At some point, although I am jogging at my normal pace, I realize that I've been listening to "I Love L.A." for more than ten minutes, a fact which may indicate that I haven't even crossed the starting line, which, a few minutes later, when I go over the starting bump, proves to be correct. OK, not the best start. Allegedly the chip given to me with my registration pack, tied onto my shoelaces, will set off my personal electronic stop watch when I go over the starting line. But I make a note to myself: Subtract ten minutes from my personal time when I finish just in case the chip fails me. That somehow makes me happy, like getting to subtract a pound or two from your weight after weighing yourself because you forgot to take your shoes off. Of course, it struck me a few minutes later that I was forgetting the fact that I might not finish at all.

At mile five, I feel fine. We are down near USC running near Exposition Park. Maybe a little hungry—not a good sign, because this means all my carb loading—cookies, ding-dongs, pasta—has backfired.

At mile 10, I'm cold. We're running near Hancock Park, which gives me an opportunity to examine some of the more affordable real estate in Los Angeles that I may have overlooked. And then I realize that just the fact that I am thinking that Hancock Park represents affordable real estate means that my race-induced hallucinating, caused by a lack of food and water and physical exhaustion, has begun. At least I'm still coherent enough to know. But it's OK because the hallucination is only about real estate. When I start seeing six-foot chili dogs running toward me I know that I've veered into the danger zone.

At mile 15, we seem to be running through Korea Town. It seems like I'm running alone. Maybe everyone has finished the

Almost Royalty

race. So I check the official clock and realize that we're about two hours and 30 minutes into the race. OK, the elite runners—the Kenyans—God's gift to the world of running, and those Russian women who claim to never train and can run a marathon in two hours and 18 minutes on a bad day—should be done. Where is everyone? And then I look to the sidelines of the race. The medical stations are jammed. The sidewalks: jammed with runners who have given up.

The thinning out has begun. Those entering the Marathon "on a lark" with no training and not happening to be in particularly good shape are gone.

But I'm still good, except that I thought that I saw a three-foot chicken taco, with a crispy, not soft, taco shell wink at me at about mile 16 just when I rounded the corner of Figueroa and 11th.

And then I know I'm in trouble because I've hit mile 18, Heartbreak Hill, a three-mile hill angled up at a 45-degree grade. And I see another chicken taco, this one bigger, around five feet, winking at me through its crispy shell as I start the hill. In a brief moment of clarity I realize that seeing the chicken taco hallucinations isn't a good sign. In fact, it generally means that I'm beginning to hit my wall, my own point of complete physical and mental deterioration.

I keep going. It seems like that dream you have when you're running, but not moving forward. But I am moving forward. Slowly. And then walking. And then giving running a chance for a few more feet. And then walking.

I'm tired, hungry and cold.

For a few moments I think about my friends. Maybe we all have our own path, our own timetable. And this is mine.

At mile 21, I'm not really running anymore. It's more like a fast hop because there is no more bend in my legs. They've locked and I feel like I'm pogoing rather than running.

Someone holds up a sign.

"You're already a winner," it says.

Nice. A few scattered individuals still standing on the race course cheer for me. Or someone.

The six-foot chili dogs have joined the chicken tacos standing along the race course.

I get a little adrenaline and give it a push. Someone gives me a candy, hard, green, sugary, lime, to suck on. It takes my mind off the pain for a moment.

At mile 24 I'm freezing and shivering. I'm not sure how, but I slip and fall over the 10,000 paper cups left by the runners coming before me at one of the water stations.

I'm down and my right leg hurts. It's bleeding.

A medical volunteer runs over. "Are you OK?"

"I don't know," I said.

The volunteer lifts my right leg.

"There's a little swelling here at the knee cap," she says. "I think you're done."

Just then, I see two large rabbits on the side of the race course, standing with the chicken tacos and chili dogs. Only the rabbits seem to know my name.

"Courtney!" yells one of the rabbits. "Over here!" I look over at the rabbit.

It appears that the rabbits are holding a sign which says, "COURTNEY WE KNEW YOU'D MAKE IT!"

I decide not to pay attention.

"Friends of yours?" said the medical volunteer, who by now has applied a bandage to my knee.

"You see that too?" I say. Well, I can feel her, so the medical volunteer is real.

"Looks like you have a couple of fans," she says.

The medical volunteer is finished with me so I limp over to take a closer look at the sign-carrying rabbits.

Only it's not rabbits. It's Bettina and Marcie wearing plush Easter-bunny ears, pink velvet with white inlay on a headband, sold at the local drug stores for $3.99 at Easter. They have a black smudge on their noses, black whiskers painted on, and cotton tails pinned to their butts.

"Is it really you," I said.

"Why wouldn't it be?" said Bettina.

"Well, I'm in the hallucination portion of my run and I just saw a six-foot chicken taco wink at me. And I don't see a Starbucks within 200 yards."

"For your next marathon I think that you should re-think your outfit," said Marcie.

It's them.

"What are you doing here?" I said.

"We're here to be your rabbits," said Bettina.

"My what?"

"We're going to make sure you finish the race," said Bettina. "We're going to run the last two miles with you, like the rabbits do at dog races."

"I'm not sure I can do it," I said.

"We'll make sure you do," said Bettina.

"Even if we have to carry you," said Marcie.

"It's just like you to let me do all the work and then show up at mile 24," I said. I started shivering. "I really don't think I can do this."

"Sure you can," said Bettina. Bettina walks over and throws one of my arms over her shoulder on her five-foot-one body. Marcie walks over and places my other arm over her shoulder on her five-foot-one body.

"Sure you can," said Marcie. "You always could."

They drag me forward, staggering under my five-foot-ten body.

"Wait, wait..." I said. "If I agree to do this, you aren't going to run around telling people that you ran the entire race with me, are you?"

"Of course not," said Bettina.

"Never," said Marcie.

They jogged the last two miles with me as I finished the race in just under five hours.

"Not five hours," said Marcie recounting the story in years to come, "we finished the race together in 4 hours, 50 minutes, and 33 seconds."

"We?" I'd say.

"We finished with you," said Bettina, "Remember?"

In the months after the Marathon, the bubble—the real estate bubble—would officially burst, the stock market would have days where it plummeted 500 points, and most of the fuel which propelled the lifestyles of my friends would end, dramatically changing their lives.

Marcie realized that she might never get back together with Greg and decided to begin working again. Rather than attempting to find a job practicing law, she started a new business. She created a business as a pre-school application specialist, someone who helps parents create the right pre-school application such that they would appear to be "the right match" to the feeder pre-schools of Los Angeles' most exclusive private schools.

Greg, well-versed in the cycles of real estate, predicted that the real estate bubble was going to burst and sold the last holdings in his real estate portfolio in the spring of 2008. Currently, he is creating a portfolio filled with distressed or foreclosed properties. His new accountant girlfriend is helping him find great bargains.

Harvard Law Grad June (from the Ivy & Elite Book Group) attempted to get a job in a law firm. After sending her resume around for an extended time, the only legal job she could get was an unpaid internship as she had no experience and had been out of the working world for 10 years. June might be partnering with Marcie in her business.

Leslee is still not working. After Hobeck, Berman dissolved she sent her resume around and then decided to take some time off.

Elizabeth's husband never did get that bonus. I understand that her children now attend public schools.

Not 10 days after Bettina and Bean's interview at Thorton Hall, Headmistress Brell Dononvan received a persuasive recommendation letter from a Board of Trustee member who contributed close to 15 percent of Thorton's annual operating budget. The recommendation came from Secretary Hutchinson, the father of their good friend, Thorton Hall graduate Robbie Hutchinson. In his letter, Secretary Hutchinson stated that if Thorton Hall didn't show a true commitment to diversity including gay parents (and it did not admit the children of Bettina and Bean) he would not be able to make any additional financial commitment to the school. In an unusual move by Headmistress Donovan, Bettina and Bean received Sapphia's acceptance letter from Thorton Hall weeks ahead of any other acceptance letter. After receiving lunches, goodie baskets and tickets to special events from Headmistress Donovan, Bettina and Bean signed their acceptance letter. "Once you get to know her, she's really quite nice," said Bettina at one of our mornings in an unavoidable coffee shop. Marcie just rolled her eyes. Bettina's in-laws agreed to pay for the $30,000 per year tuition and to kick in the expected Thorton Hall "donations."

Marshall was the fourth runner-up in the *Faces of Tomorrow* competition. In the second round—the talent section—he sang the Papageno's aria from *The Magic Flute*. That he actually had a talent stunned the judges and kept him in the competition. After the initial shock about his age, the judges realized that Marshall represented a large market segment and that there was a need for models above the age of 40. Before the competition was over, Marshall got an agent, after promising the agent that he would move to Los Angeles. Marshall's agent thinks that he has a big future in reality TV.

Jennifer told Marshall to take a hike after the *Faces of Tomorrow* competition. I think it was too much for her when Marshall got an agent and promised to move to Los Angeles because his agent said he had a big future in reality TV. After eliminating Marshall from her life, Jennifer dyed her hair to a red-auburn with honey-blond highlights. It looks beautiful. She's seriously dating a guy who works at a non-profit in San Francisco. He seems nice.

About six weeks after my Copper Pan lunch with Frank, I treated Frank to breakfast at a tiny place on Montana Avenue that serves great blueberry pancakes. Frank loves blueberry pancakes. "Someday, soon, I'm sure, some woman is going to be so honored to wear this," I said as I gave him back the ring. "It should have been you," said Frank.

Steve/Stefan started working with a company that had created a micro blogging platform and social networking website and it was very popular with designers and the fashion industry. He has gotten involved with someone who has been at the company since its inception, a smart, kind, brilliant techie named John. We talk often, although he is crazy busy—but happy.

In November of 2008, those Hamiltons willing to let go of their long-standing or current grudges long enough to have a meal together got together at the rehearsal dinner on the night before my cousin Megan's wedding. Fortunately, Megan's boyfriend, the father of her baby, has asked her to marry him. Aunt Katy was so delighted (relieved) that she decided to have the dinner in a private room on the Queen Mary and have a five-course meal with champagne.

Somewhere between the salad and Uncle Joe's toast I took a small walk to get some air. Just after I walked back into the room I overheard a conversation between Julia and my Aunt Katy.

"Katy," said Julia, "I have something to tell you."

"What is it?" said Aunt Katy.

"I'm Jewish," said Julia.

Aunt Katy burst out laughing.

Almost Royalty

Julia looked crestfallen.

And then Aunt Katy grabbed Julia and hugged her.

"Julia," she said, "we've known that for 30 years. We were just waiting for you to be comfortable enough to tell us." I don't think my mother knew that I was standing three feet from her very exposed left shoulder (revealed by a strapless turquoise dress which I had worn on New Year's '04) when this exchange took place. But when I returned to my chair and sat down, Aunt Katy turned to me, and winked.

And then there was me. What happened during the 26.2 miles of that marathon, and what I never forgot, was that I had done something no one, not even I, thought I could do: I ran 26.2 miles. And while running those 26.2 miles I realized that every life has its own path and every person has their own timetable, and that all of the commentary from friends and acquaintances about me running out of time, getting old, getting stale and what I needed to do to attract the right person—even telling me who was the right person—was just commentary, or noise. I realized that it was my choice whether to accept those comments from people I knew, or to reject them because the ultimate truth was that they didn't define who I was, what I did, or how I chose to live. Unlike that comment when I left Elizabeth's Ivy & Elite Book group, I could never be a cautionary tale, unless I chose to be. Who I was, what I did, what values I embraced—this was all my choice. And after leaving therapy with Roberta, I had gotten a list of books from Rabbi O'Toole and started reading so that I could choose my own values. The thing is, you can change and you can pick and choose what values and what life you want—the Velveeta or the Brie—and leave the rest. But what I realized, and what surprised me the most was that someone had come to appreciate me for who I was and what I was attempting to do, even though I wasn't perfect, didn't come from the "right family," would never be part of the Ivy & Elite, sometimes made mistakes, occasionally said goofy things, have a weird sense of humor—and am tall. And that person wanted to be with me. Because that person was standing there with a space blanket, water and a big hug as I crossed over the finish line of that endless 26.2 mile marathon. And you already know who it was.

    It was Josh.

Acknowledgements

THG—None of this would have ever happened without you. I've never won a lottery, but the day I met you I knew that you were my big win in life—and I had won huge.

Jo Berryman—Thank you so much for always believing in my writing and for your wonderful friendship. You are the kindest and loveliest person I have ever met and the role model whom I attempt to emulate.

Tim Ingelson—Thank you for your tremendous marketing strategy.

Michael Alvear—Thank you for your excellent media strategy.

Forrest Thompson Publishers—Thank you for publishing this book and for your patient editorial support. Thank you, Amanda Larson, for all your wonderful assistance.

All Early Readers—Thank you so much for your kind reviews and valuable suggestions.

Made in the USA
Charleston, SC
12 October 2014